THE DARK SUNRISE

The Sheriff Aaron Mackey Westerns
by TERRENCE MCCAULEY

Where the Bullets Fly

Dark Territory

Get Out of Town

The Dark Sunrise

THE DARK SUNRISE

A Sheriff Aaron Mackey Western

TERRENCE McCAULEY

PINNACLE BOOKS
Kensington Publishing Corp.
www.kensingtonbooks.com

PINNACLE BOOKS are published by

Kensington Publishing Corp.
119 West 40th Street
New York, NY 10018

All Kensington titles, imprints, and distributed lines are available at special quantity discounts for bulk purchases for sales promotions, premiums, fund-raising, educational, or institutional use. Special book excerpts or customized printings can also be created to fit specific needs. For details, write or phone the office of the Kensington sales manager: Kensington Publishing Corp., 119 West 40th Street, New York, NY 10018, attn: Sales Department; phone 1-800-221-2647.

PINNACLE BOOKS and the Pinnacle logo are Reg. U.S. Pat. & TM Off.

ISBN-13: 978-0-7860-4654-6
ISBN-10: 0-7860-4654-6

First printing: December 2020

10 9 8 7 6 5 4 3 2 1

Printed in the United States of America

Electronic edition:

ISBN-13: 978-0-7860-4655-3 (e-book)
ISBN-10: 0-7860-4655-4 (e-book)

FOR ANNEMARIE

CHAPTER 1

Dover Station, Montana Territory, late summer 1889

"Looks like they're coming," Deputy Billy Sunday said from the jailhouse porch. "A whole lot of them, too."

But U.S. Marshal Aaron Mackey had already known that. Adair had begun to paw at the ground a few moments earlier, when the wind along Front Street had shifted and carried the smell of men and torch fires her way. He knew the Arabian was not fussing out of nervousness. The warhorse was fussing because she was anxious to ride into the fray, just like her rider.

Despite the approaching darkness, Mackey counted about forty torches among the men marching down Front Street toward the jailhouse. He pegged the actual size of the crowd to be more than sixty or so.

He and Billy had been expecting something like this since word spread that Dover Station Police Chief Walter Underhill had finally succumbed to the belly wound that had been plaguing him for weeks. Mackey knew the townspeople blamed James Grant and Al Brenner for Underhill's death. Mackey blamed them, too.

But unfortunately, Grant and Brenner were currently his

prisoners, awaiting extradition to Helena on the morning train. Underhill's death was only one more charge to be added to the numerous other charges they already faced in Judge Forester's courtroom.

But the big Texan had always been popular in Dover Station, and people did not want to wait for the scales of justice to tip in their favor. They wanted blood for blood, and they wanted it right now.

Aaron Mackey and Billy Sunday had never lost a prisoner to a mob before. They had no intention of starting now.

"I'll head out to meet them," Mackey said. "Turn them if I can."

"And if you can't?" Billy asked.

The marshal glanced down at the big Sharps rifle leaning against the porch post of the jailhouse. "Then you're going to have a busy start to your night."

Billy grinned as he picked up the fifty-caliber rifle. "Ride to your left so I can have my choice of targets. They'll start dropping on your right if it comes to that."

"Let's hope it doesn't." Mackey had barely lifted the reins before Adair began walking up Front Street on her own steam. She was moving at a quick pace, and Mackey saw no reason to make the mare move any faster.

Mackey could not swear to it, but the mob looked like it slowed down just a bit as the lone rider on the black horse moved toward them.

He reined Adair to a stop about thirty yards in front of where the mob had stopped. He angled her to the left, so the butt of the Peacemaker on his belly pointed right. He could draw, aim, and fire quicker that way if it came to that.

He looked over the crowd and saw few familiar faces among the torchlight. So many strangers had moved into his boyhood town so quickly that he hardly knew anyone anymore.

"Evening," he said to none of them in particular. "What are you boys up to tonight?"

"Justice," a tall thin man in a slouch hat and long face said. "Justice for our friend and yours, Walter Underhill."

"Me, too," Mackey said loud enough for the crowd to hear him. "That's why we are scheduled to take Grant and Brenner to Helena tomorrow. To stand before Judge Forester for what they've done and answer for it. That was before Underhill died, and I promise his death will be added to the charges read out to them."

"Charges," one man in the middle of the crowd said. "Courts. Judges. Juries. A lot of folderol and fuss over a couple of cold-blooded killers. We're here to string 'em up, Marshal. String 'em up right here and now and save you the trouble of a trip to Helena."

A murmur of assent went through the mob.

"On behalf of Billy Sunday and myself, I appreciate the sentiment, boys. But the judge would look poorly on us and this town if we were to hand them over to you like this. I think he's looking forward to hanging them himself. It's never a good idea to disappoint a federal judge, believe me."

"Judge Forester is way down in Helena," came another voice in the crowd. "And we're right here right now ready to dispense justice. We aim to do that this very night, Marshal."

Adair raised her head, sensing a change in the air.

A change that Mackey sensed, too. "No."

The gaunt man who had spoken first said, "We've got a lot of respect for you, Marshal, and we hate to go against you like this, but we're taking Grant and Brenner with us, and there ain't a whole lot you and your deputies can do to stop us."

"And don't go countin' on Chief Edison to back your play, either," said another voice from the crowd. "They was all mighty partial to Walter and are as anxious to see Grant swing as the rest of us."

He had not seen any of Edison's men coming to break up the mob, even though this was technically a town matter. He had not counted on their support, either. Grant and Brenner were his prisoners. His responsibility. His and Billy's. And they would defend them, just like they had defended all of the other prisoners they had held over the years.

"Doesn't matter what Edison and his men do," Mackey said. "Only matters what Billy and I do. And we say you can't have them. You boys best put out those torches and go home before someone gets hurt. We're burying Underhill at first light. No sense in having more men to bury tomorrow."

"Only one around here who'll get hurt is you, Marshal," said yet another voice from the crowd. "If you know what's good for you, you'll move out of the way."

Adair blew through her nose and raised her head higher. The men on the left side of the mob flinched.

Mackey felt Adair's muscles tense as she was getting ready to respond to his command.

Mackey's hand inched closer to the butt of the Peacemaker. "I'm not going anywhere, boys, and neither are my prisoners. I told you to go home. I won't tell you again."

Then Mackey heard the unmistakable sound of a hammer being cocked on his right side.

In one practiced motion, he drew, aimed, and fired, striking a man who had raised a pistol at him. Mackey's bullet struck him in the chest and put him down against the boardwalk.

Mackey shifted his aim to a man behind the fallen man, but Billy's big Sharps boomed as a fifty-caliber slug punched through the rifle stock and obliterated the neck of the man holding it. He was dead before he hit the boardwalk.

And despite the gunfire, Adair had not moved an inch.

Mackey brought the Peacemaker back and aimed it down at the gaunt man who had spoken for the mob. "Anyone else want to die?"

The gaunt man glowered up at Mackey. "Damn it, man. Underhill was your friend, too."

"He was," Mackey told him. "And he wouldn't want this. He'd want Grant and Brenner to stand trial, which they will. I promise you that. But if any of you take another step, you'll die. I promise you that, too."

The gaunt man and the rest of the mob did not move, though he could sense their resolve beginning to fade. Watching two of their men die had that effect.

Their resolve may have been fading, but Mackey wanted to wreck it altogether.

He kept the Colt aimed at the gaunt man and thumbed back the hammer. "I gave you an order. Move."

Another murmur went through the mob. Their torches sagged a bit. They were having second thoughts.

The gaunt man took a step back, but no further.

Mackey fired into the air, making the men jump. "I said move!"

He picked up the reins, and Adair shot to the left side of the mob. The men scrambled out of the way and moved backward. Mackey brought the black horse around and rode along the front of the crowd, pushing them back even farther. A few on the right side held their ground until he turned Adair sharply, and her flank knocked them back.

She snorted again as Mackey began riding back the other way, pushing them some more. The gaunt man broke first and the rest of the men followed. None of them wanted any part of the dark mare or the man who rode her.

The mob broke slowly and began to slip backward, back up Front Street.

Mackey brought Adair back to the center of the thoroughfare and stood in the spot where he had turned them, watching them go.

The gaunt man picked himself up off the ground and glowered at Mackey. His mob may have been broken, but his resolve had not. "You've made a whole lot of enemies for yourself here today, Marshal."

Mackey kept the Colt aimed at him. "They're in good company. Now get going while you still can."

The gaunt men looked at the two dead men on the boardwalk. "You just gonna let them stay like that in the street?"

"I'll stay with them while you fetch Cy Wallach to fetch them. The quicker you move, the quicker they'll be tended to."

The gaunt man pushed the mud of the thoroughfare off his clothes as he backed away. "You're a hard man, Aaron Mackey. And that ain't a compliment, neither."

Mackey had not taken it as one.

He holstered his Peacemaker when the man moved out of sight and stood watch over the men he and Billy had killed while he waited for the mortician to come.

He may have won the battle but knew he had lost the

town. But he did not bother about that. He had lost it long ago.

As soon as Cy Wallach brought his wagon to pick up the dead bodies, Mackey turned Adair and rode back to the jailhouse. He climbed down from the saddle and wrapped Adair's reins around the hitching post. He patted the horse on the neck. "Good girl."

The Arabian nudged him before lowering her head to drink water from the trough in front of the jailhouse.

Mackey climbed the front steps and found Billy waiting for him. "That went about as expected."

Mackey walked into the jailhouse. "Didn't count on having to kill anyone. There was a time when we wouldn't have had to."

Billy followed him into the jailhouse. "Time was they wouldn't have formed a mob. The town's changing, Aaron. We're smart for changing along with it."

Inside, young Joshua Sandborne locked the heavy jail-house door behind them and was eager to talk about what had just transpired. "You turned them, Aaron. Turned them all the way."

He knew the young deputy looked up to him and Billy. He did not want the young man to get the idea that gunplay was the first order of being a lawman. "Turned them after two of them got killed. That's nothing to be proud of, Josh. Things could've just as easily gone the other way. Let's just be glad it didn't."

He broke the cylinder on his Colt, pulled out the spent round, and replaced it with a fresh bullet from the rifle rack. He snapped the cylinder shut and placed the pistol on his desk. "Come on, Billy. Time to get the prisoners ready for tomorrow."

The young deputy looked like he had more questions, but he always had questions. Mackey was not in the mood to answer them. He and Billy still had work to do.

CHAPTER 2

James Grant sat up in his cot when he heard the rattle of keys at the door to the cells. He had heard the shouts and the gunfire outside. He hoped the mob had won, even thought it would mean death for him and Brenner. The trip to hell would be worth it if he knew Mackey was already there waiting for him.

But he was not surprised when the door opened and Billy trailed Mackey into the cells. Evil was tough to kill if it ever died at all.

These two men had dragged James Grant through all seven circles of hell in the year since he had come to Dover Station. And despite his current predicament as their prisoner, Grant had every intention of paying them back for it.

He hid his disappointment in their survival by applauding them. "Bravo, Aaron. You pushed back the horde and saved our lives in the bargain. I should have known better than to think a mob of shopkeepers and laborers could best the Savior of Dover Station. Al and I are in your debt."

"Speak for yourself," spat Al Brenner, the former police chief of Dover Station. Brenner was as mean as he was big, which said quite a bit, because Brenner was quite a large man. "I ain't in his debt nor anyone else's. I'd rather get lynched than let him have the satisfaction of watching me hang."

"You'll hang," Mackey assured him. "Both of you, but at the end of Judge Forester's rope, not theirs."

Grant forced a laugh. "I take it the temper of the townspeople is still a bit raw after news of Underhill's demise?"

"They'd be in here beating both of you to death right now if it wasn't for us," Billy told them. "But you'll have your day in court in Helena."

Grant admired the friendship between the marshal and his deputy. Other than Mackey being white and Sunday being black, there was little difference between them. Both were just north of thirty, a shade over six feet tall, and lean. They still had the military bearing they had acquired while serving in the cavalry together, where Mackey had been a captain while Sunday had been his sergeant. Their partnership had continued after Mackey had been drummed out of the army. When Mackey became sheriff of Dover Station, he named Billy Sunday his deputy. And when Mackey later became the United States Marshal for the Montana Territory, Sunday had become his deputy.

Grant had underestimated them when he had first come to Dover Station. He had tried to buy them out, and when that failed, he had tried to push them out. When they had outsmarted him at every turn, he had no choice but to hire men to kill them.

Now he was their prisoner.

Under other circumstances, James Grant might have admired their loyalty to each other. But as that loyalty had led to his arrest, wounding, and incarceration, he loathed the arrangement.

He decided there was no point in goading the lawmen

any further. He might say too much and tip his hand. That would only spoil his plans. Plans that were already in motion. Plans that would ultimately win Grant his freedom.

But for now, he had no choice but to endure the indignity of incarceration at the hands of his enemies Mackey and Sunday.

Mackey nodded to his deputy. "Best tell them what we came here to say, Billy. No sense in being around these two any longer than necessary."

The black man cleared his throat. "Tomorrow's the day we run you two down to Helena for your trial. Whether it turns out to be a good day or a bad day depends entirely on the both of you."

Mackey added, "The four of us will be taking the nine o'clock train to Helena. I'll expect both of you to be dressed and ready to leave by half-past eight. If you're not, it won't matter to us. We'll drag you onto the train naked if we have to."

"Oh, we'll be ready, Marshal." Grant grinned. "The only question is, will you?"

"Which brings us to the reason why we're talking to you two right now," Mackey said. "There's two of you and two of us. Those are even odds, and given Al's size here, we wouldn't blame you for thinking you could overpower us. Maybe make a run for it, even though you'll be chained together the entire time."

Mackey looked each prisoner in the eye. "Bet you've already got some kind of plan worked out between you."

Grant saw no point in denying it and was glad Brenner kept his peace for once.

But Brenner moved to the edge of his cot when Billy slipped the key into his cell door.

"Whatever you're planning won't work," Mackey went on, "and we're about to show you why."

As soon as Billy unlocked the cell door and pulled it open, Brenner charged toward his possible freedom, propelled by weeks of rage that had built up in his tiny cell.

Billy Sunday fired a straight right hand that struck Brenner flush in the jaw. The force of the blow, combined with the bigger man's momentum, caused the prisoner to drop like a sack of wet flour to the floor of his cell.

Sunday brought his boot down on Brenner's neck as he grabbed the big man's left foot and raised his leg. Grant watched Sunday pull a bowie knife from the back of his belt and hold it behind Brenner's knee.

Mackey leaned against Grant's cell door. "See how easy Billy did that? Brenner's a big man, way bigger than you, but he's still a Hancock. That means he's as tough as he is stupid. That's no match for our training and determination. Billy knocked your boy cold with one punch. He'll do it again if he has reason to. What's more, he's got his knife to the back of his leg. One flick of the wrist will cut Brenner's hamstring in two. He'll be a cripple for the rest of his life."

"Even though he won't be alive much longer," Billy added.

Mackey rattled Grant's cage door. "If either of you tries to escape, we'll cut both your hamstrings just to be fair. Prison's tough enough for a man with two good legs, Grant. It's even worse for a cripple."

Billy dropped Brenner's leg and tucked the bowie knife away as he stepped out and relocked the cell door.

Grant was disgusted by Brenner's stupidity. The big fool had played directly into Mackey's trap, but he hid his disgust as he said, "Consider us both sufficiently warned, Aaron. You've already tried to cripple me once." He rubbed the shoulder that still ached from Mackey's bullet that had almost cost him his arm. "I have no intention of giving you a second chance."

Mackey grinned. "I don't expect you to live long enough for it to matter one way or the other. Judge Forester will have you dancing at the end of a rope inside of a month at most. Guess you might as well try to keep as much dignity as you can in the few days you've got left."

"That's sound advice, Grant," Sunday added. "Why limp into hell when you can walk in on two good legs?"

"Why indeed?" Grant sat back on his cot and folded his hands across his belly. It was time to begin planting seeds of doubt in their minds. "In fact, who knows how much time any of us has left? Don't forget it's more than a day's train ride to Helena. A lot can happen between here and there. Weather problems. Trees across tracks. Bandits attacking trains. Mechanical problems. Engine boilers are fickle machines. Almost anything could happen to upset your plans. Anything at all."

Mackey leaned against Grant's cell door. "I know that brain of yours always has something cooking up, so I'll lay it out as plain as I can. If either of you try to run, you both get crippled. If anyone attacks the train, you both get shot in the belly. If the train makes any unexpected stops, for any reason, you both get shot in the belly."

Grant did not like the sound of that.

Mackey went on. "I know you ran the railroad in this part of the territory, Grant, and I know you probably still have some people loyal to you. I also know you've paid men to rob your trains and split the profits with you in the past, so Billy and I have decided not to take any chances. If the train stops, you die. Shooting you will be an abundance of precaution on our part."

"What if the train breaks down?" Grant asked.

"Better hope it doesn't," Billy said, "because like the marshal just said, you'll get shot in the belly if it does."

Mackey added, "We're bringing both of you to Helena for trial one way or the other. Straight up or over the saddle makes no difference to us."

Grant enjoyed the bravado of the lawmen. He would have enjoyed it more if they were not every bit as tough as they thought they were.

That was why bringing them down when they got to Helena would be so satisfying. He only hoped he saw the look on Mackey's face when it happened.

But that would come later. For now, as he sat in that cell, words were his only weapon. "I envy you your confidence, Aaron. Yours, too, Billy. I always have. The confidence to believe that your way of seeing things is the only way there is. You think there is only one way to convict me and one way to free me. Perhaps you're right. Perhaps I'm wrong. I guess we'll find out for sure when we get to Helena, won't we?"

Billy opened the door to the jail and walked into the office.

Mackey stayed behind. "Talk in circles all you want, Grant, but remember all the words in the world lead right back to you being a prisoner and me being a free man. By this time next month, I'll still be alive and you'll be rotting in the ground."

"Just like your friend Underhill." Grant smiled again, sucking his teeth. "It's a shame that such a good man should be cut down in the prime of life like that. And by a lowly drunkard, no less."

Mackey gripped the bar of the cell door a little tighter. "A drunkard you sent to kill him."

Grant shrugged. "So you've said many times, but still can't prove. I suppose it'll depend on Judge Forester's mood when we get to his courtroom, won't it?" He cocked his head to the side. "Or will it depend on more than that? I wonder. Territorial capitals can be such complicated places. I guess it's something for all of us to think about in the miles ahead."

Mackey pointed at the pile of clothing on the stool next to Grant's cot. "Be ready in the morning or you ride all the way to Helena in your drawers."

"But fly to my eternal reward on angel's wings," Grant called after Mackey as the marshal walked into the jail-house. "Enjoy the funeral. Give my condolences to—"

But Mackey had slammed and locked the door before he could finish his sentence.

It didn't matter much to Grant. The marshal had always been an easy man to read and even easier to rile. Grant had always had an uncanny ability to get under his skin, though he had never been able to figure out why. Perhaps it was because he—a stranger —had amassed so much power so soon in Mackey's beloved hometown?

Grant did not bother wasting time wondering about the reasons for Mackey's hatred. As the lawman had said, all the words in the world ended with Grant still being in jail and Mackey taking him before Judge Forester.

At least for now.

He looked through the bars of his cell at Brenner as the big man began to moan. The left side of his jaw was already beginning to swell and possibly was broken. It served him right. The big fool had run directly into Mackey's trap.

Just as Mackey was about to run into Grant's.

CHAPTER 3

Just before dawn the following morning, Mackey stood on the porch of the old jailhouse, sipping coffee as he looked up Front Street. A chilly night breeze picked up as the first rays of dawn began to crack across the horizon.

The funeral procession of Walter Underhill would start soon, as per the wishes of the dead man.

And as was his custom, Billy Sunday said what Mackey was thinking. "Sun's coming up." Like Mackey, he was clad in all black, save for a starched white shirt and the star pinned to his duster. "Guess they'll be bringing Underhill along any time now."

"Guess so." Mackey took another swig of Billy's coffee. His deputy had always made a fine pot. "That's the way Walter wanted it."

Billy cleared his throat and mimicked Underhill's deep Texas voice. "Put me in the ground just after sunrise, boys." Billy shook his head. "Don't know what's so special about getting planted at sunrise."

Neither did Mackey, but he saw no point in talking about it. "It's what he wanted."

"But he's just as dead now as he would be at a more sensible hour," Billy went on. "Like ten, maybe."

Mackey did not understand Underhill's reasoning, either. He did not understand why Underhill was even dead at all. Despite Doc Ridley's best efforts, the big Texan had finally succumbed to the knife wound that had festered in his belly for weeks. One day, he looked like he might finally be strong enough to get out of bed.

By the following evening, a raging fever had set in and killed him.

No, Mackey may not have understood Underhill's reasons for wanting a sunrise burial, but the dead did not need to explain their choices to the living. They were beyond all that now, and Mackey hoped they were the better for it. Especially in the case of his friend, Walter Underhill.

"The least we can do is grant his last wish," Mackey said, "seeing as how he was the town's first chief of police."

"Wonder if we'll get to be that lucky." Billy lit a cigarette. "About getting dying wishes granted and all."

"Given our line of work?" Mackey took another swig of coffee. "Probably not."

"Probably not." Billy let the smoke drift from his nostrils. "Don't know that Underhill deserves the privilege, either."

Mackey knew where the conversation was headed and decided it was too gloomy a morning for a debate. "Not now, Billy."

But Billy did not stop. "Walter was James Grant's police chief. He helped Grant get a lot of the power he had over this town. No reason to forget all that just because he went and died."

But Mackey had no intention of forgetting it. He could not forget it even if he wanted to. James Grant had done a lot of damage to Dover Station since the day he had come to town. He had won the confidence of Silas Van Dorn, the man who oversaw the town's expansion for the Dover Station Company. Grant had gone as far to poison the man so he could take control of the company and all of its investments in the Montana Territory. Grant had then set about getting himself elected mayor soon after.

Once he had appointed Underhill to head the new police force in town, Grant controlled all of the business and legal aspects of the town.

After bringing in the murderous Hancock clan to take over the criminal element of Dover Station, there was hardly a crooked or honest dollar spent in town limits that James Grant did not get a piece of.

Underhill had reluctantly helped Grant in the beginning before turning on him, but he had helped him just the same.

Mackey took another sip of coffee. No, he had no intention of forgetting the role Underhill had played in all of that. But when Underhill stopped obeying Grant and started enforcing the law in town, he had been killed on Grant's orders. Mackey was sure of it.

Now Grant was sitting in one of his cells, waiting for Mackey and Billy to bring him to Helena for trial. Underhill's ultimate defiance had bought him a lot of forgiveness as far as Mackey was concerned.

"Underhill was far from perfect," Mackey said, "but he was a friend to us when we needed him, especially during that Darabont business. And times since then, too."

Billy took another drag on his cigarette and joined Mackey in looking up Front Street.

Mackey knew Billy disagreed, but would not argue. The two men had never argued in the ten years they had known each other. Not while they had been in uniform and not as lawmen. They had always spoken their minds and, when there was a rare difference of opinion, let it sit for a while, gradually finding some kind of unspoken compromise before they picked up the conversation again. It had always been like that between them. It was why they were silent now.

They had saved each other's lives more times than either of them could count had they cared to try. And although neither man had siblings, Mackey figured Billy Sunday was closer to him than any brother could be. Their friendship was one made by choice, not blood.

Mackey took another sip of coffee as the sky began to slowly brighten with the rising sun. This had always been his favorite part of the day. The town was quiet. No echoes of the constant hammering from the new mill being built over on River Street. No drunken laughter or bawdy piano music from the saloons or joy houses that were now scattered all over town. No crowds milling along the boardwalks or heavy wagons of freight clogging the thoroughfare.

No trace of the mob that had threatened to overwhelm him and attack the jailhouse, either. The night had a wonderful way of scrubbing the town clean only to dry it anew each morning.

That early, quiet time of day reminded Mackey of the Dover Station of his childhood, back before the railroad came. Back when it had been called Dover Plains. It had been a booming town of loggers and ranchers back then. Miners and merchants, too. A place settled by men from both sides of the War Between the States. A place where the differences of the past had been set aside for the promise of a better future. The town had avenues named after Lincoln and Davis and streets named after Grant and Lee and Longstreet and Sheridan.

Men and women from North and South and across the oceans had been able to make a good living in the town they had hacked out of the wilderness. Even after the railroad came and the town changed its name to Dover Station, it had still felt like home to Aaron Mackey.

Now, because of the Dover Station Company, his hometown was a boomtown once again with all of the good and bad elements that came with such a place.

Many new buildings had gone up in the past year or so, with none more imposing than the Municipal Building directly across the street from the jailhouse. Its red brick walls and rounded turrets looked like a medieval castle he had read about in history books more than an office building for a small Montana town.

No, Mackey did not recognize his hometown anymore and wondered if he was supposed to. Towns were like people; living things meant to grow and change and, ultimately, die. No one ever got anywhere by standing still. He imagined towns were not much different.

Mackey figured Dover Station was no exception.

And neither was he.

Billy broke the silence that had settled over them. "Underhill was a good shot. Brave, too, when it came down to it. He was a fair horseman, too."

Mackey knew that was as close to a concession as he was likely to get from Billy. He decided to change the subject to something they could agree on. "Think Joshua's ready to go to Helena with us?"

Billy glanced back toward the jailhouse, where the young deputy was still sleeping. "He's getting enough rest for the journey, that's for sure. Didn't even stir when we walked out here. For a boy eager to get himself shot at, he sleeps pretty soundly. Maybe too soundly for the trail."

Mackey remembered how they had found young Sandborne half dead after Darabont's men had burned his ranch to the ground the year before. He remembered how Sandborne had handled himself when they had cornered Darabont's men and in the dustups they had endured against Grant and his men ever since.

"Spending time with us will do him some good," Mackey said. "And I feel better leaving Jerry behind to keep an eye on things."

"Jerry's a good man to have around," Billy agreed. "Reminds me of his daddy."

Jeremiah Halstead reminded Mackey of Sim Halstead, too, and made him miss his old friend all the more. "He'll give the Hancocks all they can handle if it comes to that."

"The Hancocks being Hancocks," Billy said, "it'll probably come to that."

Mackey heard the jangle of a bridle carried on the dying night wind blowing down Front Street. The funeral procession for Walter Underhill was almost certainly underway. He pulled out the pocket watch Katherine had given him from his vest pocket and checked the time.

"Almost seven. Right on time."

He turned the watch around to take a look at the inscription on the back. *To the finest man I've ever known. With all my love, Katherine.*

Jerry Halstead's presence in Dover Station may have made him miss his friend, but reading the inscription on the watch made him miss Katherine all the more. He had sent his father with her to Helena weeks ago for her own protection when things with Grant and the Hancock clan had gotten ugly. He could face them better if he knew the love of his life was safe. And under Pappy's protection, he knew she was as safe as she could be.

Billy said, "Still think we'll make that nine o'clock train to Helena?"

"Depends on how long-winded Doc Ridley will be when we get to the cemetery." In addition to being the town doctor, Ridley was also the closest thing to a preacher the town had. "If he sticks to the gospels, we stand a chance. If he starts with Genesis, we might have to catch the afternoon train."

Billy flicked his cigarette into the thoroughfare. "Then let's hope he starts with Revelation, because we've got a train to catch."

They could hear the hooves of the draft horse pulling the cart with Underhill's body plodding its way up Front Street. It had been a dry summer and the thoroughfare had dried into a passable muck.

Billy drained the rest of his coffee and set it on the porch railing before pulling on his black hat. "Here they come."

Mackey pulled on his hat, too, and walked down the steps to greet the procession.

Twenty-one men from the Dover Station Police Department led the somber procession up Front Street. The new chief, Steve Edison, led the way. All of his men held Winchesters at their shoulders, and their gold badges gleamed against their brown dusters. It wasn't a cavalry honor guard, but as proper as the reformed gunmen could muster.

The Clydesdale that Cy Wallach had brought all the way from St. Louis pulled the funeral wagon carrying Underhill's coffin. Jerry Halstead was in the wagon box, steering the big animal and its morbid cargo down Front Street.

Doc Ridley followed at a fair distance, his Bible clutched closely to his chest. A large number of townspeople filling the width of Front Street brought up the rear. They sang a warbly version of "Amazine Grace" as they made the pilgrimage up to the cemetery. What they lacked in tone, they made up for with enthusiasm.

The townspeople slowed their pace as they neared the jail in deference to Mackey and Billy, who took their cue to join the procession behind Doc Ridley. Mackey looked over the crowd for a familiar face but failed to see any. He did not recognize any of the men from the mob from the night before but was sure at least some of them were there. They would not try to lynch Grant and Brenner now, though. That moment had passed.

The big horse hauling Underhill took the steep incline up to Cemetery Hill with ease. When it came to a stop, Doc Ridley continued walking to the grave that had been dug alongside one of the few gnarled trees that occupied the hill of the dead.

Mackey and Billy stepped forward and opened the tailgate before pulling the coffin out. Four men Mackey did not recognize fell in behind them and helped lift the coffin onto their shoulders. The six fell into step as they carried Underhill's remains to the grave and lowered the coffin onto the sturdy leather straps that had been placed across the hole before solemnly backing away.

The crowd that had followed the procession filled in, taking up the entirety of the Cemetery Hill. Even the area that had come to be called Mackey's Garden was full of spectators. That part of the cemetery had been so named due to the number of men who had been buried there back when Mackey and Billy had still been the law in town.

Billy made his way through the gathering crowd to stand beside Mackey. "Fine turnout. Didn't think Underhill was this popular."

"Dead men always are," Mackey said.

He may not have recognized many of the faces in the crowd but noticed one man in particular who was standing behind them. He was a tall, fair-haired man who had stepped forward to carry Underhill's coffin from the wagon. Mackey decided he would make a point to find out who he was after the ceremony.

Doc Ridley eyed the eastern mountain ridge, waiting until the top edge of the sun rose above it before beginning the ceremony. When it did, he began, "Dearly beloved, we are gathered here today to deliver the remains of Walter Standish Underhill back to the dirt from whence all of us were made. A fine, yet flawed man, like many of us. But unlike any of us, this man gave his life to protect this town and its people. Walter Underhill's death came far too soon and at the hands of a murderous horde that has descended upon this gentle community like a plague of locusts from the days of old."

A ripple of murmurs went through the crowd just as Mackey heard something pop behind him.

Mackey and Billy grabbed for their pistols as they turned to face the sound. He thought it might have been one of the Hancock men trying to disrupt the service. He was surprised to find it was only a man with a camera on a tripod taking a photo of the service.

He had not known the town had a photographer, much less one who would be at Underhill's funeral. Charles

Everett Harrington, the publisher of *The Dover Station Record*, stood beside the photographer and quickly motioned for the lawmen to turn back toward the ceremony.

Doc Ridley read from both testaments of the Bible before closing the Good Book with finality and holding it once more to his chest. He closed his eyes as he raised his face to the rising sun.

"Into your gentle hands, O Lord, we commend the spirit of this faithful servant. May you receive him with kindness and mercy. Amen."

The crowd answered in kind.

Mackey, Billy, and the other pallbearers took the cue to grab the thick leather straps holding Underhill's coffin in place before slowly lowering the casket into the earth.

Police Chief Edison barked out a command, and his men snapped to attention. They brought their rifles to their shoulders, aimed at the sky, and fired three times. Old Underhill got himself a twenty-one-gun salute from the men he had once commanded.

Stifled sobs rose from the crowd as people began to line up to shovel spades of dirt from the pile beside the grave onto Underhill's coffin. Mackey and Billy had volunteered to fill in the grave once everyone had left, but Chief Edison insisted his men would do the honors. Given the number of mourners, Mackey figured Edison's boys would not have much work to do when all was said and done.

He turned when he felt a hand on his arm and saw the tall blond man holding out his hand to him. "Forgive me, Marshal, but we haven't had the chance to meet yet. I'm Paul Bishop, Mr. Van Dorn's replacement here in town. Mr. Rice told me to send you his regards."

In the wake of Underhill's sudden passing, Mackey had

forgotten about the telegram Mr. Rice had sent him to inform him that Bishop was coming to town.

He shook the man's hand, surprised by the strength of his grip. "Pleasure to meet you, Mr. Bishop. This is my deputy, Billy Sunday."

Some people paused before shaking the black lawman's hand, but Mackey was glad to see Bishop shook it eagerly. "An honor to meet you both, even under such sad and unfortunate circumstances. I never had the pleasure to meet Chief Underhill, but I understand he was quite an impressive man."

"Depends on your definition of impressive," Billy said. "But I suppose he was a better man than most."

Bishop smiled. "I suppose it takes all kinds to maintain law and order in this part of the world. But I don't need to tell either of you that. Both of you enjoy stellar reputations and not just from what Mr. Rice has told me about you, either."

"Depends on who you ask." Mackey was troubled by Bishop's friendly manner and slight appearance. He looked like a good wind might blow him over, which would not serve him well in Dover Station. But his handshake said there was more to him than that. For the town's sake, Mackey hoped so. "Mr. Rice tell you about what you're up against out here, Mr. Bishop? Montana's a long way from New York City."

"Call me Paul, please, preferably Bishop. I rose from the lowest rung of the banking ladder, where last names are barked out like commands to a dog. And although I might not have your skills as a lawman, I have other strengths that will serve me well here. And I can assure you that Mr. Rice painted quite a vivid picture before I agreed to take this assignment."

"The Hancocks are worse than even Mr. Rice could say," Billy added. "Grant gave them free run of the town for a long time now. They won't take too kindly to anyone who tries to put a stop to it."

Bishop looked toward Chief Edison, whose men remained standing guard on either side of Underhill's grave. "I've been told the new police chief is against the Hancock presence in town."

"He is," Mackey told him, "but he was one of Grant's gunmen before that. He can probably be bought if the price is high enough. If the Hancocks take a run at him, there's a good chance he'll throw in with them against you."

"All the better," Bishop said. "Besides, I never trust a truly incorruptible man, Marshal. And I have a feeling my company's pockets are significantly deeper than the Hancocks'. Besides, I have permission to send for a small army of Pinkerton men should the need arise."

Mackey had only just met Bishop, but he found himself liking him already. "Then maybe you've got a chance after all, Bishop. You've got a good town here. Could be a great one with the right people running it."

"And I know I can rely on your counsel should I fall short of the task." A new thought seemed to come to Bishop. "I understand you're due to take Grant and former chief Brenner to Helena on this morning's train."

Mackey checked his pocket watch again. It was just before eight. He was glad Doc Ridley had been short-winded for once. "We'll be bringing them to the station within the hour."

"Good," Bishop said. "Please tell Judge Forester that

Mr. Rice sends his regards to him, as well, and knows he has a bright future ahead of him as statehood approaches. If you find him too obtuse to understand what that means, feel free to tell him plainly that Mr. Rice wants Grant and Brenner hanging by the end of the month. He will be terribly disappointed if they don't."

Mackey had never smiled at a funeral before, but this was an exception. "We'll be sure to let him know."

"Oh, he already does." Bishop held out his hand to him. "But I'm sure you gentlemen can make a more convincing impression than any telegram or letter ever could."

After shaking hands with both of them, he bid them good day. Mackey and Billy watched the lanky banker manage the uneven ground of the graveyard with surprising ease.

"Looks like there might be more to that man than I thought," Billy admitted.

But Mackey was not so optimistic. "Talk's cheap where the Hancocks are concerned. Bishop might change his tune when they start pointing guns his way."

"At least Grant will be dead by then. That ought to take some of the fight out of the Hancocks."

"Only if they're smart enough to know they've lost." He slid his watch back into his pocket. "Come on. We've got a train to catch."

Both men paused to turn to face Underhill's grave and touched their brims before walking down the hill. They knew the Texan would have appreciated the gesture.

CHAPTER 4

When they reached the funeral wagon, they found Jerry Halstead leaning against it, waiting for them. His father's Anglo features and his mother's Mexican blood made some men mistake him for an Indian at first glance. His longish black hair did nothing to dampen the impression. But when he spoke, his accent was pure Texan.

"You two old ladies finally ready to go?"

"Sentimental," Billy observed. "Just like your old man."

"No reason to mourn him," young Halstead said. "From what I've heard, that bastard is a good chunk of the reason why Grant got so big in the first place."

Mackey knew he had gotten that from Billy. He had not been in the mood to debate the point at the jailhouse and he was certainly not in the mood to debate it at the man's graveside.

"We just planted the poor bastard. Let the dirt settle on him a while before you go dancing on his grave. Bring the wagon over to the jail. I want to get Grant and Brenner settled on that train before nine."

Jerry shrugged as he climbed up into the box. "Don't know why I've got to be sad. Hell, I never even knew him. Just drove his coffin is all."

Halstead released the hand brake and jigged the big Clydesdale alert as he brought the large horse around for the slow walk down the steep hill.

Billy laughed as they walked down to the jail. "Like I said. Just like his old man."

But Mackey did not laugh. In fact, he stopped in his tracks as soon as he spotted Mad Nellie Hancock and three of her kin walking up the hill in their direction.

Billy stopped, too.

Jerry brought the Clydesdale to a halt and threw the hand brake.

Nellie was wearing a man's black suit and a faded Plainsman hat to match. The three Hancock men with her were dressed like they had just come in from the field, though Mackey recognized them as bouncers from the several saloons her family now controlled in town.

And all of them had pistols on their hips.

Billy pulled his Colt and kept it flat against his leg.

Mackey stood at an angle, his right foot forward as he moved his hand to his belt buckle next to the butt of the Peacemaker he wore on his belly. That way, he could draw, aim, and fire quickly if he had to.

Behind them, he heard Jerry cock his Winchester.

The big Clydesdale sensed a change in the air and fussed, sweeping at the dirt.

Mad Nellie and her men stopped walking and held their hands away from themselves.

Nellie's smile showed teeth cracked and yellowed from years of tobacco juice and rotgut moonshine. "No need to get testy, Aaron. Me and mine are just here to pay our respects to poor ol' Walter Underhill. That's all."

Mackey's hand stayed on his buckle. "That why you came armed?"

"Dover's a dangerous town these days, Marshal. Lots of people would like us to wind up in a box like your friend up on that hill."

Billy said, "You and yours will wind up there soon enough if you don't clear out of town."

Nellie kept her hands raised as she shook her head in mock solemnity. "Now what kind of talk do you call that? Threatenin' a lady and her kin who've come in peace to mourn the passin' of a good man?"

Mackey gripped his belt buckle a little tighter to keep himself from pulling the Peacemaker. "A good man you paid to kill."

"You've told a few people that," Nellie said. "Now, I've never been much for book learnin', and I sure as hell ain't no lawyer, but I believe that's what they call slander, Marshal. I could sue you for that unless, of course, you can prove it." She winked at him. "But you can't prove it, now can you?"

Mackey knew she was right, but it did not make him feel any better. "I'd do a hell of a lot worse than slander you if I could. You'd be riding that train to Helena with your friends if I could make a case against you."

"You've already done enough damage, Marshal. Me and mine have had a lot of practice grieving lately on account of you." She tilted her head toward Billy. "And that black boy you've got over there."

Mackey heard the bones in Billy's hands crack as he gripped his Colt tighter but knew he would not draw, much less shoot. Not unless it came to that.

Mackey said, "I had paper on Henry Hancock when I killed him, Nellie. The rest of your people died because you sent them after me. Their blood's more on your hands than mine."

"You've got a fine imagination on you, Marshal. Why, I'm just a simple plainswoman doing the best she can to hold her family together and make sure her young ones grow up straight and strong."

"While running every crooked gambling parlor, saloon, and whorehouse in town," Billy added.

Nellie shrugged. "We fill a need. If we didn't do it, someone else would. And it pays way better than farming ever did. Allows us to buy things. Things that help me keep my family together and strong." Her eyes narrowed as she glared at Mackey. "Things that protect them from the likes of you."

Mackey did not like being threatened, especially by the likes of the Hancocks. "I hope that protection involves you trying to spring Grant and Brenner between here and Helena. We haven't killed a Hancock man in over a month. We wouldn't want to get rusty, would we, Billy?"

"No, we would not," Billy answered.

Nellie finally dropped her façade and pointed a gnarled finger at the marshal. "Al's last name might be Brenner, but he's a Hancock man as much as me and mine or any of us who bear the name. You'd do best to remember that before you kill him, Mackey. And be ready to face what's comin' if you do."

"He's on his way to getting a fair hearing in Helena," Mackey said. "It's up to a judge to decide if he lives or dies, not me."

"I hope you keep your word on that, Aaron." Nellie took a single step forward but stopped before getting close enough to cause any of the lawmen to raise their weapons. She knew exactly how far she could push them before being shot. "I truly do. Because you and I ain't done yet. Not by a long shot. We won't be done until you pay for what you've done to me and mine. And that's a bill that's coming due real soon. You can count on that."

Billy thumbed back the hammer on his Colt but kept it at his side. "How about you trying to collect right now? Seems as good a time as any."

From the wagon, Jerry said, "They won't pull, Uncle. It's only three against three. Everyone knows the Hancocks don't like a fair fight."

Mad Nellie glared up at Jerry. "This here's a debt that can be paid a lot of different ways, half-breed. And by a lot of people, too." She shifted her glare to Mackey. "How's that lovely gal of yours enjoying Helena, Marshal?"

Mackey drew and aimed the Peacemaker at her head before he realized he had done it.

Billy and Jerry aimed their guns at the two Hancock men before they could pull.

Nellie kept her hands away from her side as she took another small step forward and leaned into the Peacemaker's barrel. "Go ahead, Aaron. Shoot. Blow my damned fool head off. No one will blame you." She inclined her head toward the mourners on the hill. "You'll have plenty of witnesses that'll say I had it coming. But you'd better bring them black clothes with you to Helena if you do, because you'll be going to another funeral. Two, in fact. Your lady's and that loudmouthed old man of yours."

Mackey took a step forward and pressed the barrel against Nellie's head hard enough to make her take a step back. He saw nothing else. He heard nothing else. All he saw was Nellie's yellow, jagged grin.

All he knew was rage.

"Aaron."

It was Billy's voice that pierced the darkness.

"Aaron," Billy repeated. "Now's not the time. Not like this."

Mackey shoved Nellie backward with the barrel and lowered the pistol. "If she's got so much as a cold, I'll ride back here and end you myself."

"That part's up to you, Aaron." Nellie laughed before she hawked and spat on the ground between them. "Have a safe trip to Helena, boys." She wiped her mouth on the back of her sleeve. "But be careful. I hear that big city can be a mighty dangerous place. Busy, too. Never know who you might meet down there."

She beckoned her kin to follow her, and they moved wide around the three lawmen.

Mackey turned to watch them leave. "You and yours ever been to Cemetery Hill before, Nellie?"

The woman stopped but didn't turn around. "Can't say as we have. We always brought the men you've killed back to Hancock for a proper Christian burial."

"Take a look at the graves at the left side of the cemetery when you get up there. The part they call Mackey's Garden. Done a fair amount of planting up there myself. And I plan on doing a lot more when I'm done with Grant and Brenner."

Nellie wheeled to him. "No Hancock will ever be buried up there. Ever!"

It was Mackey's turn to smile. "That part's up to you."

Nellie's men urged her to join them as they kept walking up the hill toward the mourners.

Billy uncocked his pistol and slid it back in its holster. "The day I plug that hag is going to be one of the best days of my life."

Mackey glanced back at Jerry, who had already lowered his rifle. "Let's get moving. We've got a train to catch."

CHAPTER 5

Once Jerry parked the funeral wagon out front, Mackey thumped on the jailhouse door. "Open up, Josh. It's us."

He heard the bar across the heavy door lift before Joshua Sandborne opened the door; his double-barreled coach gun in his hand.

The twenty-year-old was not especially tall, and he still bore the open expression of youth, but what he lacked in years he made up for in grit. So far, he had been able to walk the fine line of cockiness and confidence, which was rare for a man so young with a star pinned to his shirt. "Glad you made it back okay, Aaron."

Mackey, Billy, and Jerry filed into the jailhouse, and Sandborne closed the door behind them. "The prisoners are all dressed and ready to go. Brenner's still a bit out of it from Billy busting his nose yesterday. He's awful shaky on his feet. Think he must've hit his head when he fell."

"Good." Mackey filled four mugs of coffee at the stove and handed them to each man. "A sore head and a busted nose will make them think twice before they pull anything on the way to Helena."

"I didn't think of it that way," Sandborne admitted as he accepted the cup. "But I guess you're right."

"Ay, chicito," Jerry teased him in Spanish as he pinched the young deputy's cheek. At twenty-three, the two young men were close in age and had developed a friendship since Jerry had come to town. "You have so much to learn."

Sandborne pushed his hand away. "At least I'm getting out of this jail for a few days instead of being stuck here like you."

That reminded Mackey of something. He said to Josh, "The horses loaded on the train?"

"I did it last night before I turned in," Sandborne said. "Billy's roan was no problem, but Adair is a spirited animal. She didn't bite me, but looked like she wanted to. Guess the mob got her worked up."

"She doesn't like trains," Mackey told him. "Likes people even less."

"Kind of like her owner," Billy observed.

Mackey ignored him and spoke to Jerry, "I don't like leaving you alone in town like this, but someone's got to stay behind and keep an eye on the Hancocks while we're gone. They've got a new man in charge of the company. A Mr. Paul Bishop. I know he's technically the responsibility of Steve Edison and his policemen, but it couldn't hurt for you to be around and lend a hand with things if they need it."

"I've handled worse," Jerry Halstead told him. "My coffee might not be as good as Billy's, but I'll make do until you get back. Maybe I'll get Billy to tell me what he does to make his coffee taste so damned good before you boys take your holiday in Helena."

"No chance of that," Billy said from over the rim of his mug.

Mackey checked the clock on the wall. It was almost half-past eight. "Time to get dressed and get these two loaded on the train. I'm going to need all of you to keep a sharp eye between here and the station. Pay attention to the windows high up and the rooftops. Brenner's a Hancock, and I wouldn't put it past one of them to try something."

"Especially with Nellie up at the cemetery," Billy added. "She's got a lot of witnesses up there who can prove she was nowhere near us if something happens. Be ready for anything."

Sandborne drained his mug and set it back on the table next to the stove. "Deputy Sunday. I was born ready."

Mackey and Billy smiled.

Jerry mussed Sandborne's hair. "You were only born yesterday, young one. How ready could you be?"

Sandborne nudged him toward the door. "Get out of here while we change clothes. I wouldn't want you to be embarrassed by seeing real men getting ready to ride."

Jerry laughed as he grabbed his Winchester and walked outside. "I'll be in the wagon when you boys are ready." He took his coffee mug with him.

As he sat in the wagon box waiting for Mackey and the others to bring out the prisoners, Jerry held his Winchester across his lap while he sipped his coffee. Billy really did make a fine pot, and he wondered what his secret was.

Jerry had watched him make coffee several times since coming to Dover Station but had never seen him do anything special. He'd grind the beans he bought from the store, dump them in the pot, and let it boil. That was it. He vowed to discover the secret one day, but for now, he was content to let it be an entertaining mystery.

Jerry was making a point of ignoring the four men who had gathered in front of the Municipal Building across Front Street. Their gold badges told him they were members of the town's police force under Chief Edison, but unlike the twenty men still up at Underhill's grave, these were not Edison men. They were Hancock men Brenner had hired during his brief time as chief.

The reason Edison had not fired these men yet was beyond Jerry. That was something he believed was politics, a topic he avoided whenever possible. Politics had cost him a star of his own and put him in jail. Since whoever Chief Edison hired or didn't hire was none of his business, he thought it best to put it out of his mind entirely.

But he paid plenty of attention to the four men in front of the Municipal Building. He did not look at them directly, but out of the corner of his eye. They had not been standing there when he had parked the wagon in front of the jailhouse, but they had been there when he climbed up into the box. That was why his Winchester was cocked and in his lap, casually aimed in their general direction.

One of the Hancock men cleared his throat and called out to Jerry, "Guess Mackey must be having a hard time finding men to help him. Him goin' and hirin' a half-breed and all. Heard he don't like half-breeds much."

Jerry knew ignoring them would only make them grow bolder, which could lead to trouble Mackey wanted to avoid. If he bantered with them a little, he might keep them distracted until Aaron got out here with the others.

"You've heard right, friend." He drank his coffee.

"Then why's he got you driving that wagon?" another man called out. "Seein' as how he's so down on breeds."

"On account of me not being a breed. My mama was Mexican, and my daddy was a Connecticut Yankee."

The third man said, "You sure look like a breed. That skin color and straight black hair and all."

Jerry glanced at the man and saw he looked like he was bald under his bowler hat. "Sounds like you might be jealous, friend."

The fourth man, who had been quiet until then, stepped forward. He was the biggest of the group and had sandy brown hair with a woolly beard to match. "We ain't jealous, and we ain't your friends. You're taking poor old Al to his death. Al's our kin, and we aim to do something about it right here and now."

Jerry set his coffee cup on the seat and slid his hand onto his rifle. "Then it's a good thing for you boys that I spent some time as a barber before I came here."

"A barber?" The men laughed as the woolly man stepped forward. "What good will that do you now?"

Jerry slowly turned the Winchester so his finger was on the trigger. "Because I'll part your hair if you make any sudden moves. You and the three idiots behind you."

Jerry kept his eye on the men when he heard the jailhouse door open and Mackey called out, "Everything all right, Jerry?"

"Just making some new friends while I'm waiting." Jerry's Winchester didn't move. "These fine officers were just checking on my well-being and wishing us a pleasant day, weren't you boys?"

The woolly man looked past him. "You bringin' out Al, Mackey?"

"And Grant." Mackey stepped off the boardwalk and moved to the side of the wagon. Jerry could see he'd changed clothes and held his Winchester at his side. "Hope you boys won't try something stupid when we do."

Jerry smiled at the Hancock men. "Speak for yourself, Marshal. I hope they do. Could get interesting."

The Hancock men were too proud to move, but too scared to do anything else.

Mackey grew very still. "Time for your boys to move along. Right now."

Jerry did not understand what exactly happened next, but something in Mackey's tone made the men sag just enough to show the fight had gone out of them. It was a quality that Jerry's father, Sim, had mentioned in his letters to him over the years. A grave finality, his father had called it, that made a man lose his sand quicker than any bullet or knife blade could. A tone that could also spur a man to ride into overwhelming odds with complete confidence that he would live to see another sunrise.

Whatever it was, Jerry watched the four men begin to move back toward the steps of the Municipal Building. The woolly one said, "You goin' with them, breed?"

"Nope. I'll be staying right here in town. It'll give us the chance to get to know each other better."

The four of them backed up the steps of the building and shut the iron door behind them.

"Don't back down from them," Mackey told Jerry, "but don't goad them, either. Edison might not back your play if you do, and there are a lot of Hancocks in town."

"No one ever backed my play before, Uncle." Jerry realized that sounded too harsh and quickly added, "Except for you. I don't know if I ever thanked you for that."

"You can thank me by still being alive when we get back." Mackey kept an eye on the Municipal Building as he called to the jail. "Bring them out, boys."

Jerry heard a great commotion and rattle of chains from

the jailhouse. With Mackey covering the street, he looked back and saw Billy pulling Grant out the front door backward. The barrel of his big Sharps was flat against the small of Grant's back.

Brenner followed, and it was clear to Jerry that the men's hands had been shackled so they faced each other. They moved at a snail's pace, but the awkward movement made it next to impossible for either of them to make a run for it.

Joshua brought up the rear with his coach gun pressed against Brenner's back. He shut the door and locked it. He tossed the keys up to Jerry, who caught the ring easily.

The two prisoners grunted and complained as they had to angle their way onto the tailgate and into the funeral wagon. Billy and Joshua followed them up. The wood creaked under the combined weight of the prisoners and the lawmen.

Mackey climbed up into the box next to Jerry. "Take it nice and slow. We've still got time to make that train.

Jerry rode the hammer down on the Winchester and set the rifle aside while Mackey and the others eyed the street.

He threw the brake and snapped the reins, spurring the Clydesdale toward the station.

It was good to have someone watch his back for once.

CHAPTER 6

Between spectators and passengers, the station was crowded, too crowded for Billy's liking. He thought most of the town was up at Underhill's funeral, but it looked like everyone else was here, waiting for a glimpse of James Grant and Al Brenner in chains.

Chief Edison had assigned a few men to keep the crowd back, but his best men were still up at Underhill's grave, and those who were here were not much good. At least they were not Hancock men.

"I wasn't counting on this," Mackey told them as they got close to the station. "Change in plans. Jerry, park the wagon at the back near the stock car. We'll board there where the crowd is thinnest. Jerry and I will hold them back while Billy and Josh get the prisoners on the stock car. We'll help Edison's men keep the crowd from swarming all over us."

Billy watched Jerry bring the Clydesdale to a halt and set the brake before hopping down and moving toward the crowd.

Mackey climbed down, too, and covered the crowd with

his Winchester. "Bring down the prisoners and load them into the stock car. Now."

"You can't do that!" Grant yelled as Josh and Billy pulled the prisoners to their feet. "I know those cars. There's no way through to the rest of the train from there."

Joshua opened the tailgate and jumped down. "Shut up and get moving. Time's wasting."

But neither prisoner moved. Brenner said, "You ain't locking me in a goddamned car with livestock all the way to Helena."

Billy grabbed hold of the shackles and yanked the chain up. "Get moving or we'll put these chains over the tail hitch of the train and drag you there."

The prisoners slid along their backsides until they got to the edge of the wagon, then slid down to the ground. With Joshua prodding them from the back, Billy climbed over the side and helped move the prisoners along as they crab-walked to the stock car.

Billy saw Mackey holding his Winchester low but ready as he watched the crowd that had finally spotted them and began to surge their way. Edison's men did their best to hold them back, but it was only a matter of time before the crowd broke free and moved toward the stock car. He had seen how mobs worked, and if he had forgotten, he had been reminded of it the night before. A group of people that large tended to take on a mind of their own, and there was no way of knowing what might happen next.

Billy saw the ramp for the stock car had been moved aside, and he called out to Jerry to help put it back in place. It would be nearly impossible for the prisoners to climb up into the car the way they were chained together, and there was no way he would take off their shackles now.

As Jerry jogged back to help him, Billy saw two men break free from the crowd and charge forward. One had a knife and the other had a pistol.

Men, women, and children cried out.

Billy shoved the prisoners to the ground, but before he could bring up the Sharps, Mackey raised his Winchester and fired at the approaching men.

Jerry dove out of the way just in time.

The man with the knife dropped to the platform. The right side of his head disappeared in a cloud of red dust.

The second man with the pistol stopped in his tracks as Mackey levered another round into the chamber.

The crowd surged again, only this time as far away from the train as they could manage. Billy had a clear shot at the man with the pistol, but knew at this range, the fifty-caliber round would go through him and several people behind him.

Besides, Aaron had the man in his sights. He was not going anywhere.

"Set your pistol on the platform nice and slow," Mackey ordered. "You don't have to die today."

"Shoot him, Andy," Brenner yelled to the gunman. "Shoot him now!"

But Andy did not shoot. He looked at Aaron and the prisoners. He looked at the people who had backed away from him and at all the guns aimed at him.

He was all alone and with only one way out.

Billy saw the shift in his eyes, and knew this could only end one way.

Andy yelled, "Remember the Hancock Boys!"

His pistol jerked up.

Mackey dropped him with a single shot to the chest.

Andy's pistol fired wide as he fell to the platform.

While the people on the platform cried out, Jerry scrambled over and helped Billy get the ramp back in place, then helped Josh drag the prisoners to their feet and into the stock car.

Billy covered Aaron as the marshal walked toward Andy, rifle still aimed down at the man he had just shot. He stepped on the dead man's wrist and plucked the pistol from his hand. He stood over the corpse and faced the spectators, his voice ringing loud over their screams. "Anyone else want to try us today?"

The crowd fell silent. No one stepped forward.

One of Edison's men slowly walked over to him. "I'm sorry about this, Marshal, but—"

Mackey handed him the pistol and walked back toward the stock car. Billy eyed the crowd in case anyone came at Mackey. No one did.

Jerry walked down the ramp as Mackey approached. "You know, I felt that bullet go right past my ear."

"You're welcome." He walked up the ramp and into the stock car.

Jerry helped Billy pull the ramp away from the train. "Aaron's awful handy with that Winchester, isn't he, Uncle?"

But Billy was not in the habit of discussing Aaron's shortcomings or his talents with anyone other than Aaron. Maybe it was from all the years he had spent hunting Apache and Comanche, but he was superstitious about certain topics. He had come to believe that a man was born with only a certain amount of medicine, and talking about such things could make him lose some of it, the way a glass of water gets empty if it sits too long.

"Cinnamon," Billy said.

The answer caught Jerry short. "What?"

"The secret to why my coffee's so good," Billy told him as he stepped up into the stock car. "I put a pinch of cinnamon in the water, let it boil until it's almost gone, then add the coffee and more water. It seasons the pot and gives the coffee a nicer flavor."

"Cinnamon," Jerry repeated as he helped Billy slide the stock door closed. "You two are a strange pair, Uncle. You and Aaron."

"Stay alive, Jerry Halstead," Billy said as he slid the door shut. "We'll send a wire when we get to Helena."

Billy would smile every time he thought of the puzzled look on his nephew's face on the long trek to Helena.

The light inside the stock car wasn't the best, but enough of the morning sun shone through the slats for the men to see what they were doing.

Enough for Billy to see Grant and Brenner dig in their heels at the straw outside Adair's stall.

"There's no way you're locking us in with that animal," Grant protested again. "There are rules, Mackey, and this is beyond the pale!"

The door to Adair's stall stood open, the biggest stall in the stock car. The black Arabian mare had her head over Mackey's shoulder as he stroked her neck. He kept his voice mellow for her sake. "Be quiet or you'll hurt her feelings."

Aaron's ability to be two different men at the same time still amazed Billy, even after all these years. He had just killed two men—three within the last twenty-four hours—but around his horse, he was as gentle as a lamb.

"I've seen what that animal can do," Brenner yelled.

"You should've thought about that before you sent two men to the station to kill us, Brenner. You don't get tea and crumpets after that." He patted the mare's neck. "Now you get to spend time with this sweet little girl right here."

Brenner balled his fists and punched his legs. "That damned hell beast of yours will kick us to death if you put us in there with her!"

"Not if you both stay nice and still." Mackey continued to soothe the mare and spoke in a gentle tone. "The rocking of the train always puts her to sleep, and she'll lay down in the hay like a newborn foal, especially since Billy or I will be here with you all the time. She'll stay that way for most of the trip, as long as you two idiots don't make a sound. That means no talking, no rattling those shackles. No trying to escape. One noise, even a whisper while she's sleeping, and you two will find yourselves busted up or worse."

"And what about when she relieves herself?" Grant asked.

"You're an old stagecoach man," Mackey told him. "What do you think? There's plenty of hay in the stall to soak most of it up. The rest is your problem."

"And what about when we have to relieve ourselves?" Grant persisted.

"Like I said, there's plenty of hay in the stall." Adair lowered her head even farther on Mackey's shoulder, drawing him closer to her. He stroked the mane on her neck. "Now's a good time to put them in, Joshua. She's good and quiet now."

Sandborne used the double barrels of his coach gun to prod them into the stall. The prisoners held the chains of their shackles to prevent them from rattling as they reluctantly moved inside and bunched up in the farthest corner of the stall.

Both men flinched when the stock car jerked as the train began to pull out of the station. Adair fussed a little, and her hooves sliding dangerously close to the prisoners, but Mackey kept stroking her mane and she quickly found her footing again.

Mackey patted her a final time before he slid out from under her and closed the stall door. She lifted her head over it and put her snout against her owner's head.

Mackey looked down at the prisoners. "You two behave yourselves, and we'll all have a nice comfortable ride to Helena."

Mackey walked to the back of the stock car, but Grant yelled after him from the corner of the stall. "I'm going to kill you for this, Mackey. As God is my witness, I'll make you suffer for what you've—"

Billy watched Adair swing her head around and butt Grant in the face. Not as hard as Billy had seen her do in the past, but hard enough to knock the man back against the wall. She kept her head an inch away from his, snorting loudly as she smelled his fear.

Billy held his finger up to his lips to remind both prisoners to be quiet and went to join the others at the far end of the car.

CHAPTER 7

Mackey was glad the railroad had followed his orders and gave them a clean stock car to house the prisoners. The train ride down to Helena would take a couple of days and, despite what he had said to Grant, he did not like the idea of sharing the space with a car full of livestock. The car was more than big enough for them to share with Billy's roan and Josh's bay, along with Adair.

"How are we going to work this, Aaron?" Joshua asked as they got situated in the three stalls at the far end of the car. "I mean, we weren't planning on getting stuck back here like this."

"This was the plan from the beginning," Billy told him. "Grant's got a lot of friends who depend on him. They've been known to rob trains before. Locking them up back here where there's only one way in and one way out is safer for all of us."

"But there's no way for us to get to the rest of the train from here," Sandborne continued. "We can't go back there to eat or sleep."

Mackey normally encouraged the young man's questions, but all the run-ins he'd had over the past several hours had put him in a bad humor. "We can't get out and no one can get in. That makes it safer for all of us. Sorry to ruin your dream of a grand rail adventure, Joshua, but you can have one on the way back. Maybe they even stock up on that soda pop you're so fond of."

The look of disappointment on the young deputy's face immediately made Mackey feel like a bully. And if there was one thing in this world he hated more than anything, it was a bully. Taking out his anger on Josh would not make him feel any better. It was like kicking a loyal dog who would just take the abuse and come back for more.

Which was why he tried taking some of the sting out of his words. "We'll make sure one of us is always awake and keeps watch over the prisoners. When we pull into a station, one of us will get off and grab something to eat. There are a couple of empty compartments on the train we can use to sleep in. You'll take first watch, Joshua, and when we pull into the station, you get first crack at going inside the train. Mr. Rice saw to it that the railroad set aside a compartment just for us. Billy will take the next watch, then me."

Young Sandborne brightened a little. "Didn't mean to sound like I was complaining, boss. I guess I'm just not used to all of this."

"That's your first lesson on being a lawman," Billy said. "Never get used to anything. Complacency is a good way of getting yourself killed."

The young man looked confused and Mackey asked him, "You bring along that dictionary I gave you?"

He patted his saddlebag. "Got it right here."

"Good. Go look it up and see what it means, then come back to us."

Joshua hauled his tack into his own stall across the aisle

and began digging through his saddlebag, leaving Mackey and Billy alone.

Billy leaned against the wall of Mackey's stall. "You're getting soft in your old age, Captain. I could be forgiven for thinking you almost apologized to that boy just now."

Mackey rearranged his saddle so it could serve as a pillow. The thick layer of straw would make for decent bedding. "Quit calling me Captain. We're not in uniform anymore."

"Kind of comes naturally when we're out in the field like this." Billy dug out some cigarette paper from his top pocket and patted his pockets for the tobacco pouch. "And don't go taking your bad mood out on me. I'm as bothered by what happened back at the station as you are."

Mackey knew he was. "It's not just that."

"It's what Mad Nellie said up at the cemetery. You're worried about something happening to Pappy and Katherine in Helena."

Mackey set the saddle aside and sat against the wall. As usual, Billy could practically read his mind. "Of course, I'm worried about them, but not as much as you might think. Sean Lynch works for us in Helena. He's keeping an eye on them, too, and from what I've heard of him, he's a good man."

"That dustup back at the station isn't bothering you, is it? We knew they were bound to try something before we loaded them onto the train. Hell, you handled it before any of us had the chance."

"What happened doesn't bother me," Mackey admitted. "How it happened bothers me."

Billy looked up from the cigarette he was building. "What do you mean?"

"A gunman and a man with a knife?" Mackey still could

not get his mind around it. "With all the guns we had on the platform? How far did two men expect to get against odds like that? Especially charging us the way they did."

Billy went back to building his cigarette. "Maybe they were the only two who showed up. After Grant and Brenner laid eyes on them, maybe they were too scared not to go through with it?"

But Mackey was not so sure. And he would not be sure until he got a wire from Jerry Halstead telling him who the men were. "It was a suicide mission, Billy. Hell, Custer had better odds at Little Bighorn. And why a knife? That man had a pistol on his hip. Between the two of them, they would've had at least twelve shots at three men. They could've gotten lucky, especially at that distance. But they stuck to their plan instead."

Billy stopped tapping tobacco into the paper. His eyes grew distant, as if he was watching what had happened again in his mind. "The one with the knife was heeled, wasn't he? I didn't remember that until you just said it."

But Mackey had seen it as it happened, and it had bothered him ever since. "We've seen Comanche do that. Apache a few times, but never a white man. Not a sober one anyway." He looked up at his deputy. "And them being Hancocks puts a whole different light on things, doesn't it?"

"Yeah." Billy lowered his tobacco pouch. "Doesn't make sense."

"It makes sense if the men knew they were outgunned and running to their deaths anyway. Makes sense if it means they were too scared not to come at us despite the odds." Mackey ran his hand over his face. "They either came at us because they were loyal to the Hancocks or Grant. Or because they were too afraid not to. Either way is a bad sign for us."

Billy went back to tapping tobacco flakes into the paper. "Think we'll have more of the same waiting for us when we get to Helena? Hancocks, I mean."

Mackey had thought about that, too. "Not Hancock men. They only travel in packs, and Lynch would sniff them out in a second. Besides, they'd blow whatever money they had on whiskey and women before we got there. They'd be too hungover to do any good."

"But . . ." Billy encouraged him.

"But it took Grant a couple of months to be healthy enough to make the trip," Mackey continued. "That gave him plenty of time to put something else together. I know we'll have plenty of marshals at the station to cover us, but after what just happened, I'll bet Grant probably has something else up his sleeve."

"We'll be ready for it no matter what." Billy tucked his tobacco pouch away and licked the paper sealed. "Always have so far."

Mackey knew the fact they were still alive was testament to that.

But he also knew there was a first time for everything. And they had never gone up against the likes of Grant or the Hancock clan before.

Josh Sandborne appeared in the aisle with the old dictionary Mackey had given him. "I found it!" He looked down at the dictionary and began to read, albeit slowly. In the two months since Katherine had been in Helena, the young man had fallen behind on the reading lessons she had been giving him, but he still practiced on his own every day. "Says here 'complacency' is a noun. Means 'a feeling of smug or uncritical satisfaction in one's achievements.'" He smiled at the lawmen, clearly pleased in his ability to read it. "Complacency."

"That's the word." Mackey stretched out and laid his head on his saddle. "Something we should all keep in mind for the rest of the trip." He glanced at Billy as he made himself comfortable. "That includes all of us."

Billy took the jibe well and patted Sandborne on the shoulder. "That was good reading, Josh. Now, you take first watch while the marshal and me get some sleep. If Adair takes to stomping them, give a shout."

Mackey felt himself slip away as his men took up their positions.

CHAPTER 8

By the time the train pulled into Helena two days later, Mackey, Billy, and Josh were well rested and ready for the second leg of their journey.

But James Grant and Al Brenner had not weathered the journey well. Both men had been fed hardtack and powdered milk that Billy had brought along for them, while they watched the lawmen eat three meals a day from silver trays the porters brought them at station stops.

At each stop, when the lawmen mucked out the stalls and laid down fresh hay, the men were doused with two buckets of water to keep the stench of their own mess down to a manageable foulness. Refusing to allow them to relieve themselves with dignity was part of Mackey's plan to keep them humble. The terror of Adair trampling them to death had served to keep them quiet.

When Grant gave Billy a hateful glare, the deputy said, "Don't worry. You'll be in hell in a week, and this will seem like paradise."

They had just doused the prisoners with two more buckets of water when someone pounded three times on the stock car door.

"Inside the car," came a booming voice from outside. "This is Marshal Sean Lynch. We're here to escort you and the prisoners to the courthouse."

"Is that so?" Mackey yelled back, waiting for the password he had telegraphed Lynch the day before they had left Dover Station.

"Oh, yeah. I almost forgot." Lynch cleared his throat and yelled, "Mr. Rice sends his regards."

Mackey threw open the latch and Josh helped Billy slide the door open.

The man he took for Lynch was of medium height, but barnyard strong. It was clear he was bald beneath the black Plainsman he wore and sported a full reddish moustache. The Winchester he held on his hip glinted in the sunlight and appeared to be kept in fine working order. Mackey began to feel better already.

The deputy U.S. Marshal did not waste time with pleasantries. "We've got a wagon right here at the back of the train to take the prisoners to the courthouse."

Mackey was glad to hear it. "Come take them, then."

Two of his men boarded the car, grabbed Brenner and Grant by the arms and crab-walked them off the car. It took a few steps for one of them to gag, then the other.

By then, Lynch had caught wind of them, too. "God in heaven, those boys are ripe. What happened to them?"

"Spent the whole ride in the stall with my horse. Didn't let them use the privy, either. Didn't want to take any chances after what happened at the station before we left."

Lynch gagged as he stepped back from the car and motioned for his men to get the prisoners loaded up. "Make sure you boys stay upwind from them on the wagon. Have Harry put the strap to them mules. Air those men out a bit before we bring them inside."

Mackey stepped out on to the platform and saw an even bigger crowd had formed here in Helena than in Dover Station. He did not look for Katherine or Pappy because he had already wired ahead and told them to wait for him at the Hotel Helena where they were staying. He did not want them caught up in any action that might pop off during Grant and Brenner's arrival.

Unlike the chaos at Dover Station, Lynch's men were doing a good job of keeping them penned in a good distance away from the stock car. "Looks like you have things well in hand here, Lynch."

Lynch cleared his throat of the stench and spat on the platform. "That supposed to be a compliment?"

Mackey did not like his tone. "It was, but it doesn't have to be, Deputy."

Lynch wiped his mouth with the back of his hand. "Once we get these prisoners settled, you and me are going to have ourselves a talk, Mackey. About how you treated these prisoners and about a lot of other things, too."

Billy quietly stepped between them, forcing Lynch to take a couple of steps back. "You will mind that tone when talking to the marshal, son. You're a deputy, same as me."

"I ain't your son." Lynch sneered as he looked Billy up and down. "You must be Billy Sunday. Inside of that car is dark. Guess I didn't see you coming."

Billy took a step closer. This time, Lynch didn't back off. "Didn't hear me coming, either. You'll have a harder time seeing me after I lay you out on that platform."

Before Mackey could intervene, Joshua led Adair out of the car, already saddled. The black Arabian's coat shined in the morning sun.

"Here you go, boss." Josh handed the reins to Mackey. "Figured you'd be anxious to ride behind the prisoners."

He clearly sensed the tension in the air and nudged Billy. "Anxious. That's another one of those fancy words I learned on the ride down here."

Then Josh Sandborne smiled at Lynch, who was still scowling at Billy. "Did I hear right that you're Marshal Sean Lynch? Out of Butte? The man who brought in Ed Kurtz alive?"

Lynch glanced at the young man. "Barely alive."

"I've read all about you, sir," Joshua gushed. "As much as I could read, anyway, on account of that I'm just learning how." He held out his hand to Lynch. "I'd be honored to shake your hand."

"Pleasure." Lynch begrudgingly shook young Sandborne's hand but kept glaring at Billy. "Nice to see someone in this outfit has sense enough to know their betters."

Mackey climbed into the saddle and brought Adair around. "You bring your own mount, Lynch, or did you ride the wagon?"

Lynch looked almost insulted. "I ride on my own everywhere I go."

"So do I," Mackey said. "Let's get you mounted and have that talk you mentioned. No sense in putting it off for later when we can settle it right now."

Lynch gave Billy a final glare as he went off to get his horse. "Suits me fine."

Billy went to go back inside to get his own roan, but Mackey angled Adair to block him. "I'd appreciate it if you'd head over to the hotel and check on Katherine and Pappy for me."

The deputy watched Lynch walk away. "Don't worry, Aaron. I won't kill him. Yet."

"Let's hope you won't have to do it at all," Mackey said. "We're going to need all the friends we've got. But after everything that's happened, I'd feel a whole lot better if you looked in on Katherine and Pappy for me."

Billy looked at the platform and toed it with his boot. "You working me, Aaron?"

"Lynch is just marking his territory," Mackey told him. "It's my job to handle him, not yours. Besides, knowing Katherine and Pappy are safe is more important than watching you and Lynch circle each other."

Whatever anger Billy had been holding onto seemed to evaporate as he patted Adair's flank. "In that case, it'll be my pleasure."

Mackey slapped him on the shoulder and set Adair moving. To Joshua, he said, "That was a sound tactical maneuver back there, Deputy. I'm impressed."

Mackey could almost feel the young man blush as Mackey rode away. Youth was not often good for much, but in this instance, he had put it to good use. He heard young Sandborne ask Billy, "Say, what's an 'ego'?"

As Mackey rode alongside Lynch behind the prison wagon, the marshal liked how Lynch did things. The prisoners were guarded by four men with rifles. Every rooftop had at least one rifleman looking down at the street and, Mackey imagined, at all the windows, too.

"Fine setup, Lynch," Mackey complimented him. "I'm impressed."

"Thanks."

Mackey realized the deputy would be a tougher nut to crack than he had thought. "What street are we riding on now?"

"Broadway. The big brown building up ahead is the courthouse. The smaller white building across from it is the jail.

A tunnel underneath links the two. We'll be keeping the prisoners there until trial."

He decided to try to soften up Lynch a bit with small talk. "Where are you from, Lynch?"

"Iowa. Place called Ames."

"I served with some good men from Iowa when I was in the cavalry. You in the army, Lynch?"

"Nope. Always been a lawman. My daddy was the town marshal back home. All my family were lawmen. My grandma even filled in as one once when my granddad came down with the fever."

"Sounds like tin runs in your blood. How'd you wind up in Montana?"

"On a horse."

Mackey shook his head. This was going to be harder than he thought. "You don't like me too much, do you, Lynch?"

"Let's get one thing straight right now," Lynch said. "I'm not a kid like that Sandborne boy back there. I know how to transport a prisoner and I know how to jail one, and I've gone up against more killers than you ever will, so you can stick your compliments where you're sitting. And I don't buy into that whole 'Hero of Adobe Flats' or 'Savior of Dover Station' business, either. Dover Station's a shitheel burg in the middle of nowhere, and you're not half the lawman I am. You've made your name shooting Indians and buffaloing drunk saddle tramps. You've only got this job because the papers think you're pretty, and you've got some rich friends back east who like you."

Mackey could see Lynch was in the mood to do more than just mark his territory. "Been waiting a long time to say that, haven't you?"

"Damned right I have," Lynch shot back. "Six whole

months. Wouldn't have had to say it at all if you'd been here where you belong instead of hanging your hat in that hellhole you call home. You're responsible for an entire territory now, not just carrying out some vendetta you've got against one man." He pointed at the marshal star on Mackey's duster. "That star is supposed to mean more than that."

"And you don't think I know that?"

"Don't seem to," Lynch told him. "You should've come here to Helena as soon as you got your appointment instead of waiting for the right time to nab Grant on personal business. Your job is here, and I've been doing it for you for almost half a year."

Mackey was trying to keep hold of his temper, but Lynch was making it awfully difficult. "I've been reading your reports and sending you orders, Lynch. You've been getting my telegrams and my orders by post. Me being in Dover Station hasn't hurt this office one bit."

"A man's got to be at his job in order to do his job," Lynch said, "especially one like this. Can't do it by post or telegram. It's about time you learn that."

"Sounds like you think you should be wearing this star instead of me."

"Then I guess I'm not making myself clear enough, because that's exactly what I think. I don't care if you don't like it, either. I was lined up for that job until your Mr. Rice stepped in and took it from me. I lost out on something I'd waited ten years to get because of politics. Lousy politics."

Mackey may not have liked the tone, but he was glad everything was finally out in the open. "If you've been doing this job for ten years, Lynch, then you know most of law work is nothing but politics. Mr. Rice may have talked to some people on my behalf, but the man who decided to put me in this job is the president of the United States. He could've made me a deputy marshal under you, but he didn't. A wise man would realize that says something about me." He looked at Lynch. "Says something about you, too."

Lynch pulled up his horse short.

Mackey brought Adair around in a half circle so he could face him.

Lynch's left eye twitched. "I'll be damned if I'll have my ability questioned by some hick with a name."

"And it sounds to me like you need to grow up. You're doing a hell of a job, Lynch. I mean that. My compliments might not hold much water with you, but you've got them anyway. You've kept my family safe for weeks, and for that, I'm personally grateful."

"You've got no call to thank me for that," Lynch said. "I'd have done that for anyone."

"But you did it for me, and I owe you. I've got plenty of faults, but ingratitude isn't one of them."

Lynch looked away.

Mackey didn't want to hold the point any longer and took a moment to look back at the prison wagon. It had stopped in front of a squat, white granite building with a turret that Mackey knew was the famous jail he had heard so much about. It looked like drawings he had seen of medieval dungeons and knew Grant and Brenner would not be enjoying their stay there.

He saw Lynch's men had pulled the prisoners off the wagon, and ten riflemen walked them in through a side door. They were well trained and put Chief Edison's men to shame.

The courthouse was directly across the street and resembled more of a church. The brown stonework and ornate cornices reminded Mackey of some of the town houses he had seen long ago when he had been assigned to a general's staff in Boston and New York. A massive clock tower rose high into the clear blue sky, and he could see it was now half-past ten in the morning.

It was too pretty a morning for such an ugly conversation, but it was a conversation that needed to be had.

Lynch surprised him by saying, "I won't work for you, Mackey. I resign my commission as of today."

"And I reject your resignation."

Lynch's eyes narrowed. "After everything I've just said?"

"You just aired six months of resentment," Mackey told him. "You're disappointed and angry, and you've got a right to be bitter about it. You don't respect me—yet—but I learned a long time ago respect has to be earned if it's going to mean anything. I would've thought ill of you if you weren't at least a bit sore about what happened and how it happened. You've done a fine job here, and I want you to keep on doing it. Not for me, but for this territory."

Mackey looked around at the bustling town. "Statehood's coming, and it's coming soon. A lot of people think that'll make our lives easier out here, but it won't. If anything, it'll make it harder, at least for a while. I'm going to need good men to help me keep order when things change. Good men like you. That's why I'm refusing your resignation. And it's why I think you're man enough to at least give me the chance to earn your respect."

Mackey held out his hand to Lynch. "Are you with me? Are you with Montana?"

Lynch looked at the hand for a long while before he shook it. "I'll give you a month, Marshal. One month and then we'll see."

"A month's more than I'll need."

The two men resumed their ride to the courthouse together.

Lynch said, "Judge Forester is anxious to see you. Said he wants to see you in his chambers after you get the prisoners settled. I wouldn't expect him to be friendly, though. He likes you even less than I do."

"He's a judge," Mackey said. "That's his right."

"Since it looks like I'll be sticking around for a while," Lynch said, "what's your first order, Marshal?"

"My first order is for you to keep doing the excellent job you've been doing, Lynch. If Judge Forester is the kind of man I've heard about, I'm sure he'll agree."

"And your second order?" Lynch asked.

"Loyalty," Mackey said without looking at him. "Absolute loyalty. If you've got a question, ask it. If you've got a better way of doing something, suggest it, but the decision is ultimately mine and mine alone. You can take credit for the good and blame me for the bad. I don't care either way."

He saw Lynch stiffen in the saddle. "Anything else."

"Just one thing. Everything you just said to me and about me stays out here. But if you ever talk to me like that again or run me down to anyone behind my back, especially to the men, I'll beat you to death. Wherever you are, no matter how many men you have with you, I'll leave you where I find you. Is that clear, Deputy?"

Lynch smiled. "It's clear you'll try."

"I don't try, mister. I do." He heeled Adair into a trot toward the courthouse.

Lynch followed.

CHAPTER 9

After seeing Grant and Brenner locked in separate cells of the basement jail, Mackey had Lynch bring him up to Judge Forester's chambers on the first floor.

The building had the same ornate wood-and-stone work that Grant's Municipal Building featured, but on a much larger scale. Where that building seemed like an imitation, the Lewis and Clark Building had the feel of the real thing. The halls were lined with marble and the walls adorned with wood paneling. Mackey noted the sound of their boots on the marble floor did not echo as loudly as they did back in the monstrosity Grant had designed.

Lynch pointed to a set of doors at the left side of the hall. "Those are our offices in there. Ought to be easy enough to find. It's got 'U.S. Marshal, Montana Territory' right there on the door. Entrance to the courtroom is in the middle and Judge Forester's chambers are to the right. He's got another door inside the courtroom that leads to the same place, but that door's usually locked when court's not in session, which it ain't now. You can head in over there, and his clerk will see to you."

The surroundings were a bit ornate for Mackey's taste,

but he could get used to them. He would have to, since he intended on spending more time here now that Grant was out of the way. "I take it you've been using the marshal's office for the past six months or so."

"You take it correct. I'll move back to my old office as soon as possible."

Mackey was glad he did not have to tell Lynch to do just that. He might have allowed him to keep the office, but after their exchange on Broadway, he decided his subordinate had to learn his true place in the pecking order.

Mackey broke off and entered the judge's chambers, quietly shutting the door behind him.

A fastidious-looking clerk with thick glasses popped up from behind his desk when Mackey introduced himself.

"I'm Mackey here to see the judge."

"The judge is enjoying a late breakfast, but asked that you be brought in as soon as you arrive. Please wait here."

Mackey looked around the clerk's office while the young man disappeared down a hallway and knocked on a door. Every square inch of shelf and desk space was cluttered with books and ledgers and papers. He had no idea how someone could keep track of it all and was glad he did not have to do it. If the marshal's office was in similar condition, he would have to make changes and quickly.

The clerk reappeared and beckoned Mackey to follow him. The marshal removed his hat and stepped through the swinging gate that led to the inner sanctum of the office.

Judge Adam Forester's chambers were even more cluttered than the outer office. Every surface, including couches, tables, and chairs, was overflowing with stacks of paper and law books. He imagined a stray ash from one of Billy's cigarettes would incinerate the place in a hot minute.

The only semblance of order was the judge's desk, where

a small space had been kept clear for the judge to eat and work. He was eating now, though all traces of whatever he had been eating had just been consumed.

Judge Adam Forester was a heavy man Mackey guessed to be at least three hundred pounds. His bald head bore a silver crown of unruly hair that spilled down into mutton-chops that stopped just short of his chin. His heavy face made his deep-set eyes look even more so and his round, reddish nose bore the evidence of his reputation as a man who liked his drink.

A dirty white napkin had been tucked into his collar to serve as a sort of bib to prevent his meal from staining his shirt.

Judge Forester looked up at Mackey when the clerk closed the door behind him. "Well, look at what providence has sent me. The prodigal marshal. The great Aaron Mackey has finally seen fit to grace my chambers with his presence. You'll forgive me for not rising to my feet to bow, but as you can see," he gestured with chubby hands at his plate, "I'm currently indisposed. I find subjugation is difficult on the digestion."

Mackey was beginning to think everyone in Helena was lining up to give him a hard time. But given Forester's status, he decided to give the jurist a little more leeway than he had afforded Lynch. "I can come back later if you're busy, your honor."

"And run the risk of you disappearing for another six months?" Judge Forester dismissed the idea with a wave of his hand. "Perish the thought. With your prisoners now delivered, I fear you might take it upon yourself to rush back to the Station of Dover, where I would have to wait even longer to be granted an audience with the Hero of Adobe Flats."

The judge motioned toward one of the chairs on the other side of his desk. "Pick whichever one has the least amount of papers and move them so you can take a seat. We have much to discuss today, you and I."

Mackey shifted a pile of papers from the chair on the left and set them on the floor. He took off his hat before he sat down.

The judge untucked his bib and patted his mouth with it. "Forgive me for being flustered, but it isn't every day a man in my position finds himself in the presence of such lofty company. Criminals and villains, yes, but rarely a hero such as yourself, much less a savior." He looked down at his empty plate. "Why, I've heard so much about your exploits, perhaps you could refill my plate with loaves and fishes, much like that other savior from so long ago."

Mackey realized he was gripping the brim of his hat too tightly and stopped. "You one of those judges who's cranky when he's hungover or are you always like this?"

Forester stopped smiling. "I like your tone even less than I like your lateness in attending to your duties here in Helena. You forget yourself, sir."

"And you forget that the only reason either of us are in Helena is thanks to one man." Mackey tapped the star on his duster. "The same man who got me this star and got you that black robe hanging on the back of your door."

"Ah yes. Our dear friend Mr. Rice." Judge Forester's chair creaked as he sat back and folded his hands across his belly. "Did he tell you to give me his regards? He's been sending me letters, too, you know. Veiled threats, more like it. He wants me to go easy on you about your absence from your duties here in Helena."

He picked up a bundle of telegrams and letters tied in string. "In fact, I have them all right here." And promptly dropped them in a bucket beside his desk. "You can see how much I value them."

Mackey enjoyed watching the judge's small display of power. It was easy to have contempt for a man who was almost three thousand miles away. "Pride goeth before the fall."

"Only if practicality fails to lead at all, young man." The judge wagged a finger at Mackey. "I keep forgetting you're not just another frontier tough with a star on his chest and a gun on your hip. You're an educated man. A West Pointer, no less, who knows his history and probably just enough of the law to be dangerous."

"I've picked up a few things," Mackey admitted.

"You've been taught in the ways of war and strategy and how to fight the red man," Forester went on. "That is why I am sure you must know a lost cause when you see one."

Forester's ability to dance around an issue with words was beginning to make Mackey's head hurt. "I'm used to fighting an enemy I can see, your honor, and I can't argue against a point you won't make. So, let's quit talking around things and put a pin in the map so we can figure out which direction where headed."

"That suits me just fine." The jurist folded his hands on the desk. "I hope you're prepared for a bitter disappointment, Marshal, because you have come an awfully long way and gone through a significant amount of trouble only to learn that the justice you seek is far more elusive than you imagined."

Mackey felt a coldness begin to spread in his belly. "Meaning?"

"Meaning, sir, that I have no intention of finding James Grant or Alfred Brenner guilty of anything, much less of the charges you plan on bringing against them in my courtroom this week."

Mackey almost came out of his chair, but controlled himself. "Every single one of those charges is valid. Every affidavit is completely legal."

"Yes," Forester said. "You're surprisingly thorough for a frontier tough, but my judgment stands. They're not worth the paper they're printed on."

Mackey tossed his hat on the desk before he crushed it. "You're throwing them out? All of them?"

Judge Forester took his time answering it. "The charges you've made against Grant and Brenner are tenuous at best, even if, by some miracle, they all happen to be true. Brenner refutes the confession you say he gave freely. He claims you made him sign that statement under great duress."

The coldness in Mackey's gut now stabbed him there. Yes, he had put a lot of guesswork into writing up Brenner's confession, but the man had signed it freely. "That is a sworn statement he made backed up by witnesses."

"That statement is all that ties Grant to the conspiracy you say he committed against the Dover Station Company," Forester shot back. "Without that confession, there is no basis to believe Brenner acted against you or played any role in the attempts made on your life. Yes, his confession was witnessed by Chief Edison and some of his deputies after he attacked you. The assault charge you have made against him will likely stand. However, since Edison assisted you in the coup that removed Mayor Grant from office—"

"Coup?" Mackey realized he had stood up. "That wasn't a coup. That was a lawful arrest. The son of a bitch tried to have Underhill killed. He ordered Brenner and the Hancocks to kill me and my deputies. Hell, he almost poisoned Silas Van Dorn to death."

Forester glared up at him from behind his desk. "You will control your vulgarity and your temper or I will have my bailiff arrest you."

"Then I hope you're not fond of him, because you'll lose him if he tries."

Forester shut his eyes and laid his head back against his chair. "You're not making this easy, Marshal."

"Sorry. Guess I've always had a hard time watching dirt get swept under the rug."

Forester's eyes sprang open. "There are no brooms in this chamber, Marshal Mackey, and certainly no rugs. Brenner's attorney is challenging the validity of his confession. That confession is the only evidence you have tying Grant to the criminal charges you have brought against him. Without it, you can't even place Brenner at the scene of any of the crimes of which you accuse him, and you have absolutely nothing on Grant. In short, you don't have a case."

Mackey could hardly believe what he was hearing. He had boarded the train with every belief that he was bringing Grant and Brenner to meet their fate at the end of a rope. Now it looked like they might be catching the next train back to Dover Station. "Men have swung with less evidence, your honor."

"Not in my courtroom." Forester sat back in his chair and shook his head, his chins wagging. "No, sir. I know you and Mr. Rice want me to be your hangman, but I'll not bend the rule of law for any man, not even him. And certainly not for you."

Mackey felt his body begin to shake and heard the quaver in his own voice. "This is rich. You're a flophouse drunk Mr. Rice wrung out and sent here to represent his interests five years ago. He only put you on the bench to protect those interests. Don't confuse the two, Forester. You're no better than half the people you put behind bars. You've only been allowed to think you are."

Mackey leaned forward until his hands reached Forester's desk. "And what do you think will happen when I tell him you're letting Grant and Brenner go? What do you think will happen when Mr. Rice changes his mind about you?"

Judge Forester looked down at his empty plate and pushed it aside with a heavy sigh. "How old are you, son? Thirty, thirty-one?"

"Thirty-five. What's that got to do with anything?"

"It means you've seen a lot of life in your time, but not as much as I have," Forester said. "You're a smart man and a brave one, too, but that's not going to be enough for you to overcome what lies ahead of you."

"I've seen more of life than inside a judge's chambers," Mackey told him. "I've led men in battle and put them behind bars for the rest of their lives."

"And a fair many of them in the ground, if myth is to be believed," Forester added. "Is what they say about 'Mackey's Garden' true?"

"Never liked that term myself," the lawman said, "nor 'hero' nor 'savior' neither."

"But they've stuck to you anyway," Forester said, "despite your best efforts to shun them." He held out his hand for Mackey to see, and it quivered as if he was riding in a bumpy coach. "You called me a drunk earlier, and you're right. I stand guilty as charged. It took me a long time to admit that to myself. But as the years go by, a wise man begins to forgive his own shortcomings and, eventually, embrace them. Maybe even put them to good use if he finds himself fortunate enough to do so."

Mackey's headache was beginning to return. "What the hell does any of this have to do with letting Grant and Brenner go?"

"It has everything to do with it." The fat man pitched forward and pushed himself out of his chair with great effort. He was taller than Mackey had expected, but not as tall as he. "You stand there, snugly cloaked in piety, youth, and bravery, and call me a coward and a drunk. You then revert to your true nature by threatening me with telling Mr. Rice about my decision that your case against Grant and Brenner is without merit. Yet you happily neglect to mention one simple, irrefutable fact."

Forester held his hands out from his side. "That no one cares about Grant and Brenner, Marshal." He held up a finger to caution Mackey. "And, before you say it, they care even less about justice, so don't bother trying to use that tactic on me."

"Grant's guilty," Mackey said. "He hired men to rob the same railroad he controlled. He robbed stagecoaches. He—"

"Prove it."

Mackey could almost see the bedrock of the case against his prisoners crumble before his eyes. He felt himself growing desperate, and he did not like the feeling. "He poisoned Silas Van Dorn."

"A matter Mr. Van Dorn wishes not to pursue for the sake of his family and business interests." His eyebrows rose. "Next charge?"

Mackey saw all of the cards he held against his prisoners disappearing in his hand and played the only one he had left. "He tried to kill me in his house."

"After you barged in there without a warrant and no credible reason to take him into custody. Yes, you claim to have Brenner's confession, but we're past that now. Grant was also severely wounded in the process and almost lost his arm. His attorney tells me he's still considering whether or not to sue over the affair. Not just you, but the United States government, as you were a marshal at the time of the incident."

Mackey caught something. "Grant's attorney wouldn't happen to be the same one Brenner is using?"

"It just so happens it is," Forester told him. "Mr. J. D. Rhoades himself. Finest attorney in the whole Montana Territory. Hell, maybe this side of the Mississippi, depending on who you talk to."

Mackey slowly lowered himself into his seat. He knew John David Rhoades and not from the articles he had read about the famed attorney's exploits in *The Dover Station Record*.

Mackey had known him when he was a major in the army.

He had defended Mackey at his court-martial at Fort Concho.

Grant had been keeping something up his sleeve this whole time after all.

Forester looked at him. "I seem to recall someone telling me that you are acquainted with Mr. Rhoades."

Mackey sank in his chair. "Yeah. I am."

Forester selected a cigar from a box on a bookshelf next to his desk and offered it to Mackey. "May I offer you one?"

"Only if I can use it to burn this place down."

"I've felt that way several times, my young friend." The judge clipped the end of the cigar, struck a lucifer off the side of the bookcase, and lit it. "And we are friends, you and I, or at least we will be."

Mackey looked at him. "You letting two guilty men go free isn't the best way to get on my good side, Judge."

Forester looked at him through the growing smoke as the flame took in the cigar. "I have no choice but to let them go free due to a lack of evidence on the charges you have leveled against them." He held up a hand to hold off another argument. "What you brought me might hold up against anyone else, but not against the likes of Grant and Brenner. They have crossed paths with plenty of influential people in this territory. Men who have their eyes on other interests, larger interests, than seeing Grant and Brenner swing."

Mackey had never fooled himself into believing he was a particularly smart man, but he was far from dumb. And although he despised politics, he was able to understand it when he saw it. "You mean statehood, don't you?"

Forester grinned as he puffed on the cigar tucked in the corner of his mouth. "I knew you were smart. Yes, statehood is coming. Before the year is out, or so they tell me. And the sooner men like Grant and Brenner are forgotten, the better for all concerned. Especially where our mutual benefactor Mr. Rice is concerned."

Mackey felt his temper begin to rise as everything Judge Forester had just told him slowly came into focus. "You mean his company. His investments. His money."

"Not just Rice's money," Forester allowed, "but that's the general gist of it. Men like Grant and Brenner remind people of this territory's wicked past. And men like our friend Mr. Rice wish to focus on the territory's future as well as the money that's to be made there." The judge opened his arms wide. "It's the way the world works, son. It's not always fair, but it's quite predictable if you know what to expect."

"Quit talking to me like I'm a kid," Mackey snapped.

"No, you're not a kid. That's the problem. You not a man with a death wish or a thug with a badge, either. You're a West Pointer, by God, and you'll always be a soldier whether you want to be one or not. You need a mission to carry out. A goal to achieve. That star on your chest doesn't change that. If anything, it lets you continue to be a soldier even out of uniform. There's nothing wrong with that. It's as much of your strength as it is your weakness, just like the bottle is mine. Why, it will serve you well until it gets you killed one day. But by then, you'll be old enough to see the bullet as a blessing."

Forester looked down at his shaking, spotted hand holding his cigar. "I used to think old age was something to which one should aspire. It isn't."

He squinted at Mackey. "But until that day comes, I believe you've got the makings of a fine lawman. Exactly the kind of man this territory is going to need when statehood comes. The kind of man who can see beyond Grant and Brenner and let them be swallowed up by the past."

"I'm not interested in hearing a recruitment talk, Judge. I had my fill of those in the army."

"These are far from empty words, son. These are facts. The governor won't last past statehood. The ranchers and the miners and the loggers will sweep that grinning idiot aside like old leaves when the time suits them. But men like you need to remain if this state has any chance of thriving. You're not going to last if you won't let go of the past and grab on to the future with both hands and never let go."

"You mean let Grant go. Give up on Dover Station." He shook his head. "Funny. I heard that speech from Mr. Rice a few weeks ago."

"And now you're hearing it from me but for a different reason. You and I owe Mr. Rice our positions, yes, but now that we have them, we owe this territory more. Mr. Rice is a good man but a wealthy man, and wealthy men are easily bored. They can afford to walk away when they get bored with things. He's bored now. Bored with me and with you and this whole Grant-Hancock-Dover Station business. He's built his fortune. He's making money in Dover Station even if Grant was stealing from him. He used Dover Station to solidify his foothold in the territory, as if owning the railroad wasn't enough. His focus is now on statehood, and nothing else matters to him. Nor, in all fairness to him, should it."

Mackey did not want Forester's words to make sense, but they did. "Why?"

"Because he has his role to play in statehood, just as you and I have ours. Important roles, if we have the wisdom to take them. If not, the same winds that blew in our favor yesterday will blow against us tomorrow. If Grant and Brenner hadn't secured such capable counsel, things might be different. But they're not, and Rhoades will use every means at his disposal to drag this out for as long as he can. At least until the referendum on statehood comes to pass. Powerful men want Grant and his kind forgotten, Marshal. And we need to forget them, too, if we're to have any hope of shaping the future."

Mackey felt his breath growing shallow. "And what kind of future will we have if men like Grant and Brenner can just walk away after all they've done? They're guilty, damn it!"

"I know they are," Forester allowed. "But I've read the brief Rhoades plans to present in court in a few days. Fine work indeed. Unless the prosecutor can come up with a convincing case, I'm afraid they'll escape the noose for now. But I wouldn't hold out much hope for their chances of a long life, particularly Grant."

"Why?"

Forester moved out from behind his desk and sat on the edge of it close to Mackey. "Grant's a clever man, but not nearly as clever as he believes himself to be. By bringing the Hancocks into Dover, he's the sheep who has allowed the wolves into the pen so there'll be more grass for him. But wolves do not eat grass. They eat sheep. And one day very soon, they'll eat James Grant, too. I know you want to see him dead at the end of a rope. For what it's worth, I believe he's guilty of every charge you have made against him, but you can't prove any of it."

He dared to pat Mackey on the shoulder. "His position with the Dover Station Company has been filled by Mr. Bishop. From what I've heard, Grant is unlikely to be allowed to resume his position as mayor of Dover Station, and his usefulness to the Hancock clan has come to an end. It's only a matter of time before they hang him for us. There are more ways to serve justice than in a courtroom, my boy. I should think you'd know that by now."

Mackey had learned that lesson long ago. He had learned in his days at West Point. He had learned it among the silent sands and spartan lands of Arizona and Texas and New Mexico. He had learned it long before he had handed Darabont over to the Blackfoot warriors who buried the marauder up to his neck and let the red ants eat him alive for butchering their women and children and old ones.

Yes, Mackey knew justice came in many forms. He knew there was more to justice than the white man's justice. But he had come to Helena hoping to find it anyway, because anything else had just been a waste of time.

Had he known it would turn out like this, he would have let Billy shoot Grant in his office all those months ago. Maybe Underhill would have still been alive. Maybe a lot of things would have been different.

"Maybe the prosecutor is better than you think," was the only hope Mackey had left.

"I wouldn't count on it," Forester said through the cigar smoke. "He's my son and not exactly the swiftest horse in the herd if you understand my meaning. But miracles happen every day, so maybe he'll surprise me."

It took a few moments for Mackey to realize the judge had worked his way behind him and opened his office door. "Our business is concluded for today, Marshal, but I still have plenty of work to do. I'll expect you in my courtroom the day after tomorrow, ready to give testimony should things get that far. I doubt they will, but it can't hurt to be prepared."

Mackey swept his hat from Judge Forester's desk as he stood. "Hardly see the point in it now."

"Point is that you've brought a matter to be considered before this court, son. It has to be officially adjudicated one way or the other. A lot of people are watching this case. They're watching it the way a greedy son watches his father's death bed. It can't end soon enough to suit them, and they shall rejoice when it does."

He actually patted Mackey on the back. "Don't worry. Grant will eventually die in the gutter where he belongs. And if we work together, we'll live long enough to see it. Come back tomorrow after you've settled in at the Hotel Helena. We'll talk about all of the other matters of your office that deserve your attention then."

The judge shut the door behind Mackey before he had a chance to ask him any further questions.

He found himself standing in the narrow hallway alone. Quiet. Like it used to be when he had led patrols through Arizona and Texas, hunting Chiricahua and Mescaleros and Comanche.

As quiet as it had been that fateful morning at Adobe Flats before the charge.

Alone with the finality of a closed door in his face.

He tucked his hat back on his head and made his way out of the office. The clerk did not bother to look up. And Mackey saw no reason to bid him good day.

CHAPTER 10

Mackey began to feel a little better as soon as he climbed back in the saddle. Everything always seemed clearer when he was on horseback.

He steered Adair in the direction of the Hotel Helena but let her move along the street at her own pace. He desperately wanted to see Katherine after so long apart, but he had a lot to get straight in his mind before he saw her. He had come to Helena a hopeful man. Now, everything he had been certain of was teetering on a knife's edge. It was as though the terrain had shifted around him in a blink of an eye. One second, he knew exactly where he was and where he was headed. But now, he found himself in a strange town where nothing was as he expected.

The ghosts from his past were mingling with his present. J. D. Rhoades had once saved him from a military prison, and now he was working for the man he despised. He knew Brenner's confession was legal, but since Judge Forester did not see it that way, that was no longer the case. He had expected Grant and Brenner to be dancing at the end of a rope after being convicted of murder.

Now it looked like they would be back in Dover Station

before the week was out. What would that mean for the town? What did that mean about the way Mackey did his job? He had not seen any of this coming? Should he have? Maybe Lynch was right. Maybe Mackey had used his federal office to avenge personal grudges. Maybe he was not fit to hold a federal post for an entire territory.

In a span of an hour, months of planning had been laid flat. Nothing was where it should be, and he found himself wandering. Lost.

Except for Katherine. She was the constant he kept his eye on as he moved through life. She gave him direction, and that meant everything to him.

He quickened Adair's pace to bring him to her. Everything felt better after a few moments in her arms.

Mackey saw Billy standing in front of the Hotel Helena. He was not standing on the boardwalk, but in the thoroughfare, next to his roan. Even from this distance, Mackey could see he did not look right. And the closer he got, the more he realized Billy did not look sick.

He looked scared.

Billy had never been scared in all the years they had ridden together.

Mackey heeled Adair into a gallop and raced toward the hotel, bringing the Arabian up short before his deputy.

Still in the saddle, he asked, "What's wrong? Is it Katherine? Pappy?"

Billy surprised him by grabbing Adair's bridle and pulling her into the street. "Keep riding, Aaron. Just keep on going. Head back to the train station and I'll be along in a minute."

Mackey looked at the hotel. "What's wrong? Where are they? Where's Katherine?"

"They're both fine," Billy told him, "and I'll explain

everything then, I promise, but I'm begging you to keep riding."

Mackey had never seen his deputy like this before and knew, whatever the reason, it was inside that hotel. "What happened?"

"Damn it, Aaron," Billy snapped. "I've never asked you for anything before. I've never had a cross word with you in all these years, but I'm telling you there's no good waiting for you in that hotel right now. Everyone's fine and they're going to stay fine if you just ride on for a bit and let me handle it. Please."

With Billy already holding on to Adair's bridle, Mackey swung his leg over the saddle horn and dropped down the other side. He drew his Peacemaker from his belly holster and began walking up the steps of the Hotel Helena.

"Stop, Aaron!" Billy called out. "It's Rigg."

Mackey stopped halfway up the stairs. He had not heard that name in over five years. He would have been happy to go the rest of his life without hearing it.

He had heard so much that day, he was not sure he had heard this right. "What?"

"Nathan Rigg," Billy repeated. "He's in the lobby waiting for you, and he's not alone. He's been here a long time, too. Maybe a couple of weeks from what I've been told. I wanted to ride down to the jail and tell you, but I wanted to keep an eye on him. I sent Josh to tell you, but I think he got lost or something happened because he didn't find you, did he?"

But Mackey doubted Josh Sandborne had gotten lost. Taken captive was more like it. Especially with a man like Nathan Rigg in town.

Billy tried one more time. "Katherine and Pappy are fine, Aaron. They're inside waiting for you. Got a special lunch planned for you and everything. But go in the back way, Aaron. Please. Be with your family and let me handle Rigg."

But Mackey knew it was no one's place to handle Rigg. It was his responsibility.

And, as everyone in Helena kept telling him, he had neglected his responsibilities for too long already.

With the Peacemaker at his side, Marshal Aaron Mackey walked up the steps of the Hotel Helena and walked inside. The front door was already open, and he did not bother to close it.

"Well now, honey, would you look at that!" Major Nathan Rigg's Virginia drawl filled the hotel lobby as he clapped from his spot on a plush red arm chair. "Aaron Joseph Mackey, as I live and breathe! I do declare, this is the best sight my sore eyes have seen in quite a while. And I hope you know I mean that with all possible sincerity, Aaron."

The late morning sun threw long rectangles of light across the lobby of the Hotel Helena. Mackey noticed the major's blond hair had become a little lighter in the five years or so since he had last seen him, but his blue eyes were as piercing as ever.

He had shaved off his chin-whiskers, but his moustache was fuller now. Longer, too, creeping down the sides of his mouth. He still cut an impressive and fashionable figure, even out of uniform. His black suit had probably been made by the same New York tailor who had made his uniforms when they had been in the army. For a gentleman of a proud Virginia family, Nathan Rigg had always sported a taste for northern comforts.

And as elegant as he may look now, sitting on a plush red armchair in a hotel lobby, Mackey knew Nathan Rigg was also just about the deadliest, cruelest man Mackey had ever known.

Mackey stopped about ten yards from him. "Morning, Major." Mackey looked him over for guns. He was not wearing a holster, but that did not mean he was unarmed. There had always been much more to Nathan Rigg than anyone could see on the surface. "What brings you to Helena?"

"It's Colonel Rigg, actually," Nathan corrected, "or at least it was before I left."

Mackey glanced around the lobby and saw four men trying hard not to be obvious about looking at him. They were undoubtedly Rigg's men.

"You left?" Mackey asked, "Or got thrown out? I heard different things."

"The years have dulled your senses some," Rigg laughed. "You're the one who got thrown out, remember? I know I can remember it as though it were yesterday. After all, I was at your court-martial."

"How could I forget?" Mackey gripped the Peacemaker at his side a little tighter. "You arranged it."

"And look at how much you've prospered since." Rigg nodded at the Colt in Mackey's hand. "You going to put that away?"

"As soon as you leave." He saw a fifth man leaning against the railing at the top of the stairs. He wagered there was probably a sixth man lurking around somewhere, maybe upstairs, too. Rigg was nothing if not careful, and he never came alone. "What are you doing in Helena, Nathan?"

"Why, I do believe that's the first time you've ever used my given name, Aaron. You're getting quite familiar in your old age."

"Impatient, too. I asked you a question."

"One that I'll be glad to answer as soon as you sit down." He nodded at a wingback chair across from his own. "Looking up at you is most straining on my neck, especially with the sun in my eyes. I chose such a disadvantageous location so you would know I came bearing no ill will toward you in my heart."

"The six men you brought with you say something different." Mackey sat but kept the Peacemaker on his lap. "Get to the point."

Rigg made a show of looking him over. "Yes, I must say you have certainly prospered since your cavalry days, Aaron. You hit a bit of a dry patch for a while as a common sheriff from what I heard, but I am glad to see you have finally found your level. The office of United States Marshal for the Montana Territory suits you much better. In fact, it's your new position that has brought us together here this very fine day."

Mackey sat quietly, waiting for his answer.

"You're not the only one who has prospered since his days in service to the nation, you know. Why, my military reputation has followed me into civilian life, where I have enjoyed a lucrative career as a special consultant to those who can afford my services."

"Special consultant," Mackey repeated. "That one of the new words they call butchers these days?"

Rigg did not flinch at the mention of the nickname he had acquired in the cavalry. He examined the sharp crease in his pants leg instead. "As a matter of fact, discretion is my calling card. I'm at my most successful when people have no idea I've had a hand in things at all."

The same headache Mackey had suffered in the judge's chambers was beginning to return with a vengeance. He'd had his fill of double-talk and empty speech for the day, but he did not dare let Rigg know he was getting to him. So, he asked the question he already knew the answer to. "Who are you working for now?"

Rigg looked up from the crease in his pants leg. "I am employed by several people throughout the country at the moment, but my employer here in the Montana Territory is none other than Mr. James Grant."

Mackey had known it the moment Billy had told him Nathan Rigg was there. It was impossible that his former commanding officer just happened to be in Helena at the same time he had brought James Grant to trial. Considering Mad Nellie's threat back at the cemetery, it all suddenly made perfect sense.

That did not make Mackey like it any better. "And what kind of work are you doing for Grant?"

"Why, freeing him from his present predicament of incarceration," Rigg told him. "In short, helping him obtain his release and regaining his freedom."

Mackey moved his finger flat on the Peacemaker, just above the trigger guard. "Jailbreaking part of your line of work now?"

"Oh, I doubt it will come to that," Rigg said. "We shall employ all legal means at our disposal first. That's why I've retained the counsel of J. D. Rhoades to help get my client's case thrown out of court. You remember old J.D., don't you? You should. He represented you at your court-martial. Did an admirable job as I recall." Then, that nasty grin. "Considering all of the evidence against you, that is."

"I remember J.D.," Mackey told him. "But let's move past that. What'll you do when Grant swings?"

Rigg's eyes flicked down to the Colt on Mackey's leg, then up to Mackey. "Then I'll try all means necessary to secure his release. It's what I'm paid to do, Aaron."

Rigg suppressed a yawn and rolled his neck, as though he was suddenly bored by the conversation. "But I don't think it'll come to that." He reached into his jacket pocket.

Rigg flinched when a fifty-caliber bullet tore through the chair cushion less than an inch from his left shoulder.

The women in the hotel lobby screamed. The men with them rose from where they sat and spirited them out of the lobby.

All of Rigg's men stood and drew their weapons, aiming them at Mackey.

Mackey kept his Peacemaker on his lap.

Rigg pitched to his left and took a close look at the smoldering hole in his chair. "Unless I miss my guess, I believe that looks like a fifty-caliber round."

"It certainly does."

"And that report sounded an awful lot like a Sharps rifle."

"That's because it was."

His examination of the hole finished, Rigg sat back and crossed his legs once more. "In all of my travels, I've only encountered two men so proficient with a Sharps rifle. I'm one of them. The second is that colored sergeant I seem to remember you took on as your dresser upon your promotion to captain."

"His name is Billy Sunday," Mackey told him. "And he was my sergeant, never my dresser. Now he's a deputy United States Marshal and it looks like he's got that Sharps aimed right at your head."

"An American success story," Rigg laughed. "He's like a dog. Still loyal to his master after all these years."

Mackey looked at the hole only an inch from Rigg's arm. "Still a hell of a shot, too. Good thing he didn't hear you say that, or his next shot would be two inches to the left and your consulting days would be over."

Rigg gestured back at the five men behind him. "As would your marshaling days only a few seconds later."

Mackey twisted his wrist and aimed the Colt at Rigg's belly. "Let's find out."

Rigg uncrossed his legs and placed his hands flat on his lap. "I'm afraid all of this is getting out of hand, Aaron. Let us take a moment's pause to gather ourselves before someone gets hurt."

"I couldn't agree more." Mackey thumbed back the hammer on the Peacemaker. "So why don't you boys gather yourselves right out of Helena while you still can?"

Rigg pinched the lapels of his coat and pulled them apart so Mackey could see he was unarmed. "Although I don't have a weapon, my associates do. I know you've gained great fame by riding into hopeless situations and coming out alive on the other side. But these men aren't the nomadic savages we hunted in Arizona, and they have you dead to rights."

"And Billy's got his Sharps aimed at one of their heads." Mackey would not take his eyes off Rigg. Just because he could not see a gun on the man, did not mean he could not have hidden one in his vest or somewhere else. A lot of men had met their eternal rest by confusing the elegant Nathan Rigg for being a pushover. "Can't say which one it is, but it's one of them. You might be comfortable with five-to-one odds, but are they?"

"Make that four to one." Brendan "Pappy" Mackey's familiar brogue filled the hotel lobby. Mackey saw his father had a pistol aimed at the back of the head of one of the gunmen at the far left of the lobby. "This boy's next move will be his last."

Mackey knew his father was supposed to be guarding Katherine but was glad he was there. Rigg might not know how important she was to him. "Tell your men to lower their weapons, and we can talk about how everyone gets to walk out of here today."

Rigg cocked an eyebrow. "But your man shot first."

"Call it negotiating from a position of strength," Mackey said. "Just like they taught us at the Point."

Rigg smiled. "Well played, sir. Well played." He motioned for his men to lower their weapons, which they did.

Mackey did not, and neither did Pappy.

Rigg said, "How about you boys go back to your rooms and let the good marshal and I continue our discussion in private? I'll send for you later if I need you."

"They stay right where they are," Mackey said, "until you release Joshua Sandborne."

Rigg held up his hands. "What makes you think I know where the young man is?"

"Because he's missing," Mackey said. "And no one said anything about him being young. Where is he?"

Rigg's blue eyes narrowed. "You've gotten much sharper, haven't you, Aaron? You were always such a blunt instrument before. A cudgel that knocked down anything in its way. Now, you're like a finely honed blade equally suited for either stabbing or surgery." He touched his brow. "My compliments."

Mackey raised the Peacemaker and aimed it directly at Rigg's head. "Release Sandborne. Now."

"I don't have him," Rigg admitted. "A couple of my men grabbed him before he reached the jail and worked him over a bit. They left him in a livery just off Broadway. A couple of bumps and bruises, but otherwise, he's fine.

And will remain that way as long as me and my men are allowed to leave unharmed."

"He'd better be," Mackey said, "because if he's not, you and I are going to continue this conversation real soon."

"We'll be continuing it soon enough, one way or the other." Rigg surprised him by quickly uncrossing his legs and getting to his feet despite Mackey having him covered.

"Now, while I have thoroughly enjoyed our reunion, I'm afraid my associates and I have other business to attend to at the jail. Mister Grant is expecting me to pay him a visit. And you have a rather pleasant luncheon waiting for you prepared by your beautiful fiancée, Mrs. Katherine Campbell. She's quite a woman, Aaron. You've outdone yourself, old chum."

He picked up his flat-brimmed hat and placed it on his head at a rakish tilt. "I'll be seeing you real soon, Aaron." He glanced at the front door. "Think it might be best if we head on out the back. Your boy is less likely to be covering that angle with his Sharps."

"Wonderful thing about a Sharps." Mackey tracked him with the Colt as he moved toward the back of the lobby. "Gives a man plenty of options."

Rigg touched the brim of his hat as he trailed his men out back. "Aaron."

Mackey kept his gun trained on Rigg's belly. "Nathan."

He only stood when they were gone and the back door shut behind them. He uncocked his Colt and went to his father. "Where's Katherine?"

"One of Lynch's boys is with her," Pappy said. "He wanted to come outside when they heard the gunshot, but I told them to stay with her. She's mighty upset, Aaron. Who was that man, anyway?"

Mackey watched the hallway to the back door as if his

old enemy might walk back through it at any moment. "Nathan Rigg." He holstered his pistol. "Colonel Nathan Rigg."

"You knew him from the army?"

"He was a major back then," Mackey said. "My commanding officer. My last commanding officer before—"

Billy rushed into the lobby, his Sharps in hand. "Saw them trail out the back and head up Broadway. He tell you where Josh is?"

"Livery off Broadway. Ride over there and see for yourself, but be careful. Rigg and his bunch could be waiting for you when you get there."

"I'll be ready for them." Billy looked at him curiously. "You're coming, too, aren't you?"

"No." Mackey began walking toward the bar. "You go on ahead. I'll be fine."

Pappy and Billy traded concerned looks as they trailed after him into the bar.

Pappy said, "Katherine'll be glad to see you, boy. Poor soul's been lost without you the whole time we've been here. I've missed you, too."

"Go see Katherine," Billy rushed to catch up with him. "Everything else can wait, especially the bottle."

"Not everything, especially the bottle." Mackey found a spot at the crowded bar and signaled for the bartender. The old hunger had been sparked deep inside him by seeing Nathan Rigg and the memories it brought back. The painful shame he had endured at the hands of that loathsome son of a bitch. The weapons of his own destruction he had placed in his hand. "Some things have been put off far too long already."

"Not the bottle, Aaron." Pappy forced his way next to his son, ignoring the curses he received from a drover he had pushed out of the way. The star on Billy's duster and the Sharps in his hand kept the man from doing more than grumbling. "Not whiskey. Not after you've been good for so long. There's not enough time left in the world for that to wait where you're concerned."

Mackey dug out a gold eagle from his pocket and slapped it on the bar. "Bottle of whiskey and a round on the house for me."

The bartender looked at the coin as though it was manna from heaven. "Who's buying, mister?"

"It's not mister. It's United States Marshal Aaron Mackey. The Hero of Adobe Flats and the Savior of Dover Station."

Murmurs among the patrons carried his name the length of the long bar in about a second. A man standing next to Mackey reached over and pushed the coin back toward Mackey. "Your money's no good here, Marshal. It'll be my honor to buy you a drink. Give the man a bottle. Put it on my tab."

Pappy eased the man back with a gentle shove to the chest. "We appreciate the offer, mister, but the marshal's got a fever. He won't be drinking today."

The man shoved Pappy's hand away. "Mind your business, old-timer, before—"

But there was no before and no after, either, as Pappy knocked the man cold with a short right hand across the jaw.

As the man fell back against his friends, Billy stepped in to prevent an all-out brawl from breaking out.

Mackey grabbed his father and pulled him away from the bar. "What the hell do you think you're doing? I'm a grown man and can have whiskey if I want to, damn it. I'm not a boy anymore."

But Pappy grabbed his son by the collar and pulled him

down until they were eye to eye. "You are a boy, Aaron. You're my boy, and you'll always be my boy while I've still got breath in me. Now come to your senses and let's go see Katherine like you should. There's nothing in the bottle for you but trouble."

Mackey grabbed his father's massive hands and gently pulled them from his collar. "Sometimes a man needs a certain amount of trouble to burn out a bigger trouble. And, Papa, Rigg is bigger trouble than you know. A little whiskey is just what I need."

Mackey turned back toward his space at the bar. He had hardly taken a step before the entire world went black.

Chapter 11

When the world came back to Aaron Mackey, it came back ever so slowly.

His head throbbed, and he did not dare open his eyes out of fear of the pain that would rush in when he did.

But he knew by the softness of the fabric and the smell of rosewater that his head must be in Katherine's lap. The gentle touch that could only be hers caressed his face.

"Poor thing," she said. "He's still asleep. What did you hit him with, Billy?"

"He didn't touch him," Pappy said. "I hit him."

"Was that really necessary?" she scolded.

"He's my son, and I can hit him if I want to, especially to stop him from doing something stupid."

"I'd hardly call ordering whiskey in a bar being something stupid," Katherine said. "Aaron never drinks and is entitled to one if he wants one."

"You're right," he heard Billy say. "Aaron never drinks. Not anymore, anyways. Hasn't touched a drop since the day we came back to Dover Station, and we aim to keep it that way. If you'd known him when he drank, you'd have slugged him, too, Katie. Only reason why I didn't do it was because Pappy beat me to it." Billy was quiet for a moment before adding. "You still hit like a mule, old man."

"You saw what happened to the last man who called me that."

Billy laughed, and Katherine scolded him. "This isn't a laughing matter, Billy. Poor Aaron's been out for almost an hour. I still think we should call for a doctor."

"He's awake now," Pappy said. "His legs have stopped twitching. He's just having himself a rest, is all. Let him be. The poor lad's earned it after the day he's had."

Mackey loved feeling her warm soft hands on his face. But he knew she would have questions when he finally opened his eyes. Questions he did not want to answer. Shame he did not want to admit.

"He never mentioned having a problem with drink," she said to them.

"Can't say why he would," Billy said. "It was an embarrassing time for him. For all of us, I guess. Happened when he got kicked out of the army."

"Kicked out?" she repeated. "But he was honorably discharged. I've seen the documents."

"That was part of the deal they gave him for keeping his mouth shut," Pappy told her. "Resign and nothing more will be said. It was out of deference for his service that they gave him that chance."

"And your medal," Billy said. "That's what got him into West Point in the first place."

"If it opened a door for him, so be it," Pappy said. "But he's the one who walked through it and earned his place on the other side. And those bastards had no right to take it from him like they did."

"Which bastards?" Katherine asked. "He doesn't talk much about his time in the army. We met while he was waiting for his promotion to captain. He didn't talk much about Adobe Flats then and hasn't since. And he never talked about why he left the army. He—"

Mackey's heart skipped a beat when she stopped talking. She had never been a stupid woman. In fact, she was one of the smartest people he had ever known.

He knew it would not take her long to add everything together to get a proper picture and he was right.

"He wanted to drink because of what happened in the lobby, didn't he? Because of that man who came to see him."

"Aye," Pappy said. "It's why I slugged him when I did. He's a different man when he's in his cups. A man you wouldn't recognize, Katie. A man you wouldn't care to know, much less love."

The damp cloth she put on his head felt good. Too good for him to open his eyes yet.

"There's nothing I don't know about this man," Katherine said. "Or love."

"You don't know the reason for his drinking," Billy said. "Neither do you, Pappy. And yes, Katie. That reason is Nathan Rigg."

Katherine dabbed his forehead with the cold cloth. "Why were his men pointing guns at Aaron?"

"That wasn't the first time Rigg has had Aaron and me in a bad spot. Probably won't be the last time, either."

"Captain Nathan Rigg?" Katherine asked, remembering. "I thought he looked familiar. He was an acquaintance of my late husband. He had been to our house in Boston several times. We always found him to be splendid company. I can't imagine he would cause anyone grief, especially a fellow soldier."

"Well, I don't have to imagine it," Billy said, "because I lived through it. At least the end of it, anyway. He was

Major Rigg by the time I came along, and when I did, that Rebel bastard had no use for a black sergeant like me."

"I won't say we agreed with all of his attitudes," Katherine said, "but the war—"

"The war had nothing to do with Rigg," Billy told her. "He just used being a Virginian as an excuse to treat people poorly. He's got fancy clothes and nice manners, but none of that hides the fact he was a man born crooked. That man had only one attitude and that was pure meanness. He had no use for any man below his rank nor for a man any color than his own. Black or red, he treated us all the same. A man like that has a way of drawing other men like that to him. It was like that in the army, and it looks like he hasn't changed any."

Katherine laid a warm hand on Mackey's forehead. "How did he ruin Aaron's life?"

"Don't," Mackey said without opening his eyes. "It's my story to tell, not yours."

Katherine cradled his head as she kissed it.

"It's as much my story as yours, Aaron," Billy told him. "And I've got as much right to speak on it as anyone, especially to family. Maybe I've got more of a right since you can't remember some of it." Billy paused before adding, "Unless you've changed your mind about me being family."

Mackey picked his head up from Katherine's lap, but the pain webbed from his jaw through his head, and he lowered it again. "You know better than that. All the family I've got is in this room right now."

Mackey didn't have the strength to tell him to stop again, so Billy laid bare his past.

"It started with an Apache buck named Diablo looking to make a name for himself by raiding ranches down in the Arizona Territory," Billy began. "His real name was Red

Moon, but he changed it to the Spanish word for 'devil' to scare the whites. His tribe wanted peace with the whites, so they banished him because Diablo was a troublemaker. He figured his only way to power was bathing himself in the blood of his enemies. Color didn't matter much, but preferably settlers, cowpokes on the trail, even members of rival tribes. Anyone he could kill, really."

"Good God," Katherine whispered.

"Killing was never enough for Diablo and his men. Each man he killed was a statement. Each kill more gruesome than the last. I know you're a nurse, Katie, but I'll spare you the details of what he did to folks. You can imagine what he did to men and womenfolk alike. You've heard some stories, I'm sure, but none like this."

Mackey felt a shudder go through her. He hated for her to hear all of this, but he supposed the time had come. "Go on, Billy."

"Rigg was our major at the time, and he ordered young Lieutenant Mackey over there to take twenty volunteers and two sergeants to hunt down Diablo as quickly as possible. Sim Halstead was one of the sergeants. I volunteered to be the other. No other sergeant at the fort would go with Aaron, and since Rigg didn't think highly of my kind, I figured I'd take my chances out on patrol.

"We had a half-breed Chiricahua scout with us called Eagle Eye to help us find Diablo and his men," Billy continued. "Don't know if that was his real name, but Rigg put great stock in Eagle Eye's tracking abilities. Eagle Eye also professed great hatred for Diablo, but I was never all that convinced. Neither was Sim. Aaron went along with it because Rigg ordered him to and was never known to question an order.

"We needed twenty men to do the job right. We wound

up with ten of the worst men in the regiment whose only skill was that they had no problem killing Indians. Got most of them straight from the stockade."

"This Eagle Eye," Katherine asked. "Did he do his job?"

"Depends on what his job was," Billy told her. "If his job was to lead us to Diablo, he certainly did it. Maybe did his job too well."

"He led them to Diablo," Pappy said, repeating the story his son had told him one drunken evening long ago, "but didn't tell them how close Diablo was. Luckily, Sim and Billy here were fine trackers in their own right and could read sign well."

"Is that true?" Mackey heard Katherine ask. "You mean this Eagle Eye led you into a trap?"

"He tried," Billy told her, "but we caught on to it just before he led us into a massacre. We were outnumbered at least two to one. The morning Eagle Eye disappeared, we were less than a mile from Diablo and his hostiles. I don't know if it was all Eagle Eye's doing or if he did it on orders from Rigg, but we came within a mile of getting killed."

"Why would a major order the massacre of his own men?" Katherine asked. "It doesn't make sense."

"So he'd have something to avenge," Pappy said. "Many a reputation has been forged in avenging the fallen, Katie. Could be he wanted to start another Indian War where he could be a hero. Could be he just didn't like Aaron. Men like Rigg do all sorts of things for all sorts of reasons, darlin'. Especially in uniform."

Billy continued with his story. "We realized Eagle Eye had disappeared in the middle of the night, and Aaron knew we didn't have much time before Diablo and his men rode into us. So, he ordered us to mount up just after dawn and attack. We cornered them at Adobe Flats, where they'd planned to ambush us and surprised them. We ran them down before they realized what was happening. Diablo and all of his men were killed. Seems like they'd never been in a straight-up fight before with men who knew how to fight back."

"So you accomplished your mission," Katherine said. "Rigg must have been pleased."

Mackey heard Billy choke on the words. "In a fashion."

"Tell her," Mackey said, his own voice hurting his head. "You pulled the cork out of the jug. Might as well drain the rest of the bottle."

"Major Rigg had issued Aaron an order before we rode out," Billy said. "If we found Diablo and his men, we were to 'visit the same horrors upon them as they had committed against the innocent men and women and children who had been their victims.' That's an awfully elegant way of telling us to hack them to pieces."

Mackey smelled tobacco and knew Billy had lit a cigarette.

"So," Billy continued, "we got to visiting. Just three of us had the stomach for it. Sim Halstead, Aaron, and me." Mackey heard Billy take a long drag on his cigarette and let the smoke drift out through his nose. "Yes, sir. We visited the hell out of those savages that day. Guess we became savages ourselves in the process."

Mackey had expected Katherine to shove his head off her lap and run out of the room in horror. Instead, she cradled his head carefully and kissed his forehead. "My poor love."

"When we got back to the fort," Billy went on, "Major Rigg wasn't happy that Eagle Eye got away. He'd ordered us to go right back out and get him, but the men were wiped out, and none of us were in much shape to travel.

Sim and me and all of the other boys praised the lieutenant for his bravery in battle. Eagle Eye swore there were only fifteen braves with Diablo. He had more than thirty when we hit them. Aaron's tactics cut them down to size in short order. We would've been killed if it hadn't been for him. We even put it in writing, but Rigg wasn't impressed."

"I still knew a few graybeards in Washington," Pappy said, "who looked into the matter and decided Aaron deserved his captaincy. But by the time he'd finished his training, Aaron was sent to serve under Rigg again. That was when you met him, Katherine darlin', before he was shipped out west again. Rigg reissued his order to find Eagle Eye."

"Aaron only wanted to take me and Sim, but Sim was sick and it wound up just being the two of us. Took the better part of a year, but we found Eagle Eye in the nations and dragged him back to the fort. When we brought him in, some of the junior officers set to beating on him. Aaron stopped it, but hit one of the men a bit too hard and turned him into a vegetable. The boy's father was a senator from a southern state. Things were still raw along the Mason-Dixon line following Reconstruction and Mackey was court-martialed. His trial was supervised by Major Rigg himself. Rigg wanted Aaron to be hanged, but the generals allowed him to resign instead. They'd spent so much time building him up as the Hero of Adobe Flats that tearing him down would've made them look bad. Rigg was furious, always vowed to get even. Never heard what happened to him after we left the army, but I guess now we know."

"We saw Rigg come to town a couple of days ago," Pappy said, "him and that pack of wolves he brought with him. He was quiet, but obvious. Drew a lot of eyes and seemed to like the attention. I never knew his name, but if I had, I would've put a bullet in him before you got here."

"Then you'd be in jail right along with Brenner and Grant," Mackey said as he sat up from Katherine's lap. Katherine fussed over him as he regained his senses. "You'd be in there longer than they'll be, too, because Judge Forester is letting them go."

Billy took a step backward as though he had been hit. "Are you sure? Your eggs got scrambled pretty good just now."

Mackey rubbed his aching jaw. "Not enough to get that wrong. He told me so himself, right before my run-in with Rigg."

"How can he let them go?" Billy said, close to yelling. "We've got them dead to rights."

"Judge Forester sees it different." Mackey tongued a molar loose and spat it into his hand. He tossed the tooth to his father. "Your prize for winning the fight."

Pappy held the tooth up to the light. "If it knocked some sense into you, then I gladly accept. If not, I'll belt you again. Maybe wind up with a tooth necklace. Walk around wearing it proudly like one of them heathens you used to hunt."

But Billy was still on the Forster business. "Did the judge tell you why he was letting them go?"

Mackey spent the next couple of minutes laying out his conversation with the judge point by point. When he had finished, Billy looked more disgusted than Mackey had ever seen him. His deputy was not known for showing much emotion.

"That name Rhoades sounds familiar. Where'd I hear it from?"

"He used to be an army lawyer," Mackey said as he got

to his feet. He thought he would still be dizzy after being out for so long, but his mind was clear. Maybe the old man was losing his touch after all.

"Rhoades was the lawyer at my court-martial," Mackey reminded him. "Looks like he and Rigg have thrown in together, because they're both working for Grant."

Billy leaned against the wall as the entirety of the situation sat upon him. "Looks like Grant wasn't lying about having a plan. Did it right, too. He managed to use your past against you in the bargain."

"Looks that way." That was when he noticed Joshua Sandborne sitting on a couch at the far end of the room. The young man did not have a scratch on him, but his eyes looked like he had taken a brutal beating.

"You all right?"

The young man simply nodded.

The look in his eyes said more than the young man ever could. "Sorry you had to hear all that, Joshua. About me. Guess I'm not the man you thought I was."

"You're not." The young man stood up. "You're more than I thought. What are we going to do next, boss?"

Mackey walked over to the window and parted the curtains. A man leaning against a gas lamp across the street quickly looked down and walked away. Rigg had someone watching him.

"Stay alert," Mackey told him. "And stay alive."

"Complacency," Josh said. "Right boss?"

"Right." Mackey dunked his aching head in the bowl on the dresser. The young man did not know how right he was.

CHAPTER 12

After the four of them had an early dinner in the dining room of the Hotel Helena, Katherine insisted that Mackey take her for a walk around town. Alone. Billy, Josh, and Pappy did not like the idea of the two of them being off on their own, but Katherine was clearly not in a mood to argue.

Her stern expression when she ordered them to stay had made Mackey smile. He had seen Pappy and Billy face down men twice their size, but one look from Mrs. Campbell fixed them in place.

She slipped her arm through his as they strolled along the boardwalk together. The heat of the day had already faded, and the afternoon air hinted at the promise of a cool evening to come. The brief Montana summer was already preparing to give way to autumn and the harsh winter that followed.

"I missed you, Aaron" she said as they walked past the other couples on the boardwalk. "I missed you terribly."

He put his hand over hers. "I missed you, too, but sending you away was the best way I could keep you safe from the Hancocks."

"I know. But a woman can still miss her fiancé, can't she?"

He smiled at the thought of their marriage. He had not properly proposed to her, but after all they had been through since his wife Mary had left, the idea of marriage was only a formality to him. In his mind, they were already man and wife. "You still want to go through with that? Even after what you heard back there?"

Her reply was immediate. "Now more than ever."

"Even after knowing what I did."

"To men who had done it to innocents dozens of times over," she said. "You were following orders, and even if you weren't, whatever you did probably put the fear of God into any other young men like that Diablo fiend who were looking to do the same thing. You did good, Aaron, even in something horrible, so yes, I still want to marry you."

"Even after I saddled you with Pappy for two months?"

"He was a delight," she laughed. "A perfect gentleman. Always charming and sweet. And he never allowed me downstairs without looking the lobby over first. It's a shame he never married again after your mother died."

Mackey did not have the heart to tell her that Brendan Mackey had never lacked female companionship. There was always some lonely widow or unhappy housewife in Dover Station who gladly welcomed his attentions. Mackey had always been amazed that none of Pappy's illicit relationships had never become a scandal, but they had not. If anything, his lovers had always remained admirers without their husbands becoming any the wiser. Or if they did, they were wise enough not to demand satisfying their honor.

Mackey rubbed his jaw. At almost sixty, the old man still kicked like a mule.

Katherine hugged Mackey's arm. "There you go again, disappearing inside that head of yours."

Mackey felt himself blush. "Sorry. I've got a lot on my mind."

"You always have a lot on your mind. Back in Dover Station, it was Darabont, or Grant, or Mary, or any of the dozens of thugs you went up against. Now it's Nellie Hancock and Judge Forester and being marshal of the territory. You're a brooding man, Aaron, which is why I love you. You never do anything lightly. Not even loving me."

He found himself gripping her hand even tighter. "I'm glad you noticed."

"I noticed clear enough to know I want to be your wife. Not just your woman, Aaron. Your wife. I want to have your name. Legally."

"My name might not be worth much for much longer," Mackey admitted. "I've got a territorial judge who doesn't like me, two prisoners who are going to be looking for blood the second they're freed from jail, and every blood relative of the Hancock clan who wants me dead. I wouldn't want to make a widow of you again, Katie. I wouldn't want you to live with the heartache."

"I'll live with it anyway." She surprised him by stopping and taking his head in her hands. "But I won't have to. I can remember a time after Darabont took me when I was too afraid to leave my own hotel. You helped me through that. I can remember a time when I didn't know where I fit in this world anymore, but I came out here and you helped me through that, too. You haven't just saved my life, Aaron. You've shown me how to live. I'd be a fool to let that go, and I want it to last for however long it can. And for however long it is, I want to spend the rest of it with you."

Mackey felt his face grow warm and his throat close. "Okay, Katie" was all he could manage to say. "Okay."

She pulled his head down and kissed him. He put her

arms around her and kissed her back, ignoring the gasps such a scandalous public display of affection caused among the townspeople.

She eased his head away and threw her arms around him. "And I'm not worried about becoming a widow, Aaron Mackey, because you ain't gonna let that happen."

He eased her back an inch to get a better look at her. "Did you just say 'ain't gonna'?"

"I certainly did," she said proudly. "And I meant it, too."

Mackey turned when he heard a man begin to clap. "Well would you look at that, J.D.? True love blossoming right here before our very eyes."

Mackey recognized Rigg's voice and drew his Colt as he pulled Katherine behind him.

Nathan Rigg was leaning against a porch post, cheroot hanging out of the corner of his mouth, grinning at them. "Now that's the second time you've drawn on me today, Aaron." He made a show of opening his jacket to show he was still unarmed. "And for the second time today, I'm not heeled."

Mackey did not lower his Peacemaker. "You're always heeled. Probably have a hideout gun tucked in the back."

"What a scandalous accusation." Rigg looked down at Rhoades. "You're a lawyer, J.D. That's a scandalous and libelous charge, isn't it? Why, I could sue the marshal here for besmirching my good name, couldn't I?"

"Only if it isn't true," the lawyer said, "which it is." He looked at Mackey. "He's got a Remington tucked in the back of his pants."

Mackey could see Rhoades had aged some in the years since Mackey had last seen him. He'd grown rounder since leaving the army. Balder, too, and he wore a pair of thick, wire-rimmed glasses. "Good to see you, Aaron."

Mackey did not take his eyes off Rigg. "Wish I could say the same for you, John. Wish you chose your clients better."

"I'm a lawyer. I go where the clients are, and I don't always have the luxury of picking who I represent."

"Especially when they pay so well."

"I didn't take an oath of poverty, Aaron. You make your living with a gun, I make mine with the law."

"So do I," Mackey said. "By enforcing it, not by letting guilty men like Grant and Brenner go free."

"Everyone's entitled to a defense," Rhoades sighed. "You ought to know that better than anyone. I defended you once upon a time."

Mackey was about to say he was not a murderer, but the words died in his mouth. He kept looking at Rigg instead. "Your taste in friends isn't the best, either."

"You'll get no argument from me there." The attorney looked back at Rigg, then at Mackey. "But we're not friends. We're partners. There's a difference."

"Not to me."

Rigg laughed. "You're getting virtuous in your old age, Aaron. I can remember a time when there wasn't much of a difference between you and me." He looked around Mackey at Katherine. "But I wouldn't want to discuss such things in front of your beloved here." He touched the brim of his hat. "Evening, Mrs. Campbell. You might not remember me, but I had the honor of being a guest in your home back in Boston many moons ago. Forgive me for being somewhat forward, but I must say the years have been most kind to you."

"I remember you, Captain Rigg," she said as she stepped out from behind Mackey. He tried to hold her back, but she avoided his grasp. "It was Captain Rigg, back then, wasn't it? Then Major Rigg and finally Colonel Rigg from what I understand."

"You're surprisingly well informed," Rigg remarked. "You seem to have followed my career with some interest." He looked at Mackey. "Guess you're not the only man in uniform who made an impression on Mrs. Campbell during one of her famous parties."

"No," Katherine said as she took another step forward, "you didn't leave much of an impression at all. But I have seen you many times in the years since."

"You have?" Rigg's brow furrowed. "That's strange. I haven't been to Boston in years, and this is my first time in Montana. You must have me mistaken for another dashing Virginian."

"No, it's you. Or, rather, men like you. Men who stood exactly where you're standing right now, so confident. So sure of themselves that they had Aaron all figured out. That they had the drop on him, as I believe men like you say when they feel they have an advantage on a man."

She stopped just before blocking Mackey's line of fire and looked Rigg up and down. "Men who have talked a good game and made all sorts of threats on Aaron's life. Some of them veiled, like yours. Some of them overt. Either way, it didn't matter. All of them poked and prodded him as far as they thought they could until that one, brief moment when they pushed him just too far. I've lost count of all the men like you who stood before him, but the number doesn't matter because they've all ended up the same. In a pine box in a shallow grave."

Katherine smiled. "Yes, Colonel Rigg. I've seen you many times since Boston, and I see no difference between you and all the others who've stood where you're standing right now. You'll make the same mistake all of them did, too, and when you do, he'll put you down just like he's put down every other cur who thought they had him cornered. And not because he's the Hero of Adobe Flats or the Savior of Dover Station. And not because he has men like Billy to watch his back, either. It's because he's Aaron Mackey. And you're nothing."

Rigg's jaw tightened as his left eye twitched.

And so did his right hand, ever so slightly, toward the back of his coat.

Mackey raised his Peacemaker and aimed it at Rigg's head.

Katherine held her ground, without fear, smiling up at the mercenary.

Rhoades laid his hand on Rigg's arm and said, "We have to be going, Nathan. We have an appointment, remember?"

Rigg's jaw loosened and his fake smile returned. "Why, thank you, J.D. I'd almost forgotten about our prior commitment." He touched the brim of his hat again. "Lovely chatting with you, Mrs. Campbell, and please forgive us for intruding on your special moment. I find true love so enchanting."

Rhoades shot Mackey a relieved look as the two men turned and walked away.

Mackey uncocked the Colt and slid it back in his holster.

Katherine turned and looked at him, quite pleased with herself. "I think that went rather well, don't you?"

Mackey laughed in spite of himself. "Mrs. Campbell, you've got some mouth on you."

"It'll be Mrs. Mackey soon." She slid her arm back in his and pulled him along to resume their stroll. "And it's one of the many reasons why you love me."

"Yeah," Mackey said. "I guess it is."

CHAPTER 13

Judge Forester's courtroom was filled beyond capacity and swelteringly hot. Everyone who was anyone in Helena had come to see justice dealt in the matter of the Territory of Montana versus James Hollister Grant and Alfred Hancock Brenner. The newspapers had billed it as the most significant event in Helena since its selection as the territorial capital and no one intended on missing it.

Mackey stood next to Sean Lynch next to the door to the judge's chambers. Grant and Brenner sat shackled at the defendant's table. Rhoades was wearing a gray suit and regularly dabbed at the beads of sweat on his bald pate. Rigg was in the gallery behind the defendant's table where two of Lynch's men stood guard with Winchesters.

My men, Mackey reminded himself. *I'm the marshal now.*

The prosecutor was a spindly-looking young man, thin as a broom handle. Sebastian Forester was the judge's son but looked nothing like his father. He looked like a slight breeze might bowl him over at any minute, and Mackey knew from experience that John Rhoades was no slight breeze. He was a thunderstorm in a courtroom, or at least had been when he had represented Mackey in his court-martial all those years ago.

Katherine and Pappy sat behind the prosecutor's table. Katherine looking proud and elegant in her pink dress and wide-brimmed hat despite the outcome they all knew was coming.

"Look at them all," Lynch said to Mackey out of the corner of his mouth. "I'd give a month's wages to be anywhere but in this sweatbox, and they've been lined up for hours just to get in here."

Mackey did look out at them and saw about half a dozen Rigg men spread out among the crowd. Men wiped away sweat with their handkerchiefs while women batted warm air at themselves with hand fans.

"Your boys see Rigg's men?" Mackey asked.

"They're your boys now, Aaron," Lynch reminded him, "and they've seen them." He nodded up at the upper gallery. "And I see you've brought some men of your own, too."

Joshua Sandborne stood at the railing of the upper gallery, his Winchester resting on his hip. Billy stood at the highest point in the courtroom with his Sharps at his side. If any of Rigg's men so much as scratched their leg near their pistols, they would catch a fifty-caliber round for their trouble. His Winchester was leaning against the wall beside him.

"They're our boys now," Mackey told him. "Remember?"

"Glad to hear you say it." Lynch seemed to mean it, too.

The door to the judge's chambers opened and Lynch stepped forward to bellow, "All rise!"

Everyone in the courtroom not already standing got to their feet.

"This court is now in session. The Honorable Adam Forester, Federal Magistrate for the Territory of Montana, presiding."

"Be seated," Forester said as he climbed into his bench.

Mackey had to admit that Forester looked much more respectable in his black robe than he had in his chambers a few days before. In the army, he had seen how men changed when the mantle of responsibility was placed on their shoulders. He was glad to see it now.

As the people retook their seats, Lynch resumed his place next to Mackey. "This ought to be good. Don't let Seb's appearance fool you. The boy's got more sand than he looks."

"That boy's going to need all the sand in Arizona to go up against Rhoades."

"You'll see."

Judge Forester cleared his throat and said, "Mr. Forester, what are the charges presented against the defendants here today?"

Seb Forester got to his feet and read from his notes. "Your honor, James Grant and Alfred Brenner stand accused of attempted murder of a peace officer and conspiracy to commit the murder of a peace officer. Mr. Grant is also accused of attempted murder by means of poisoning, your honor."

"Are these all of the charges these defendants stand accused of, Mr. Forester?"

"No, your honor."

The courtroom burst into murmurs.

Rhoades and the defendants exchanged panicked looks.

Mackey almost had to steady himself against the wall. Almost.

The prosecutor continued. "Upon further examination of the charges brought against the defendants by Marshal Aaron Mackey and his deputies, my office has decided to level additional charges against the defendants of assault against a peace officer, disturbing the peace, unlawful resisting of arrest, and interference of a peace officer in the lawful execution of his duties."

Forester turned his large head toward the defendant's table. "These are very serious charges, Mr. Rhoades. How do your clients plead?"

Rhoades leapt to his feet. "Innocent, your honor. Furthermore, I protest the additional charges that have been made against my clients at this late date. As you know, I prepared a detailed brief outlining the specious nature of the preliminary charges leveled against my clients. Dover Station Chief of Police Brenner absolutely denies the confession Marshal Aaron Mackey submitted to this court as being given under great duress during his unlawful incarceration by Marshal Mackey."

"I've already considered that, counselor," Forester told him. "Do they also plead not guilty to the assault charges the prosecutor has made against them just now?"

For the first time, Mackey saw J. D. Rhoades stuck for an answer.

Forester leaned forward and bore into Rhoades, just as he had with Mackey in his chambers a few days earlier. He was glad he was not the subject of the jurist's ire now. "It's not a hard question, Mr. Rhoades. Enter a plea for your clients on these secondary charges brought by the prosecution. Guilty or innocent." He raised a stubby finger. "But, keep in mind that I'm inclined to go much easier on your clients if they plead guilty now as opposed to forcing the expense and bother of a trial."

Rhoades asked, "May I have a moment to confer with my clients, your honor?"

"You can have several moments," Forester told him. "Then you should confer with the prosecutor before talking to me. This court demands swift justice and abhors delaying tactics. And the men who use them."

Lynch elbowed Mackey. "See? I told you there's more to Seb than you think. He's a damned fine lawyer."

But Mackey was already thinking two steps ahead. "Hope him being the judge's son doesn't complicate things later."

"Not a chance. The judge asked twenty lawyers in the territory to prosecute the case. None wanted to touch it out of fear that Grant will go free and hold it against them later."

Mackey was not surprised to hear it. "All the more reason to lock the bastard up."

"There's more than one kind of prison, Aaron," Lynch said. "And don't discount the judge, either. He's an old drunk, but a crafty old drunk who's usually right."

Rhoades had to practically hold his hand over Brenner's mouth to keep the big man from yelling while Grant sat quietly, listening to his attorney.

At the opposite table, Seb Forester shuffled papers and made an occasional note.

Rhoades crossed over to the prosecutor's desk and looked annoyed, as if his opponent was interrupting something important. Mackey liked the young man's style more with each passing minute.

The two men spoke for a while longer before the frowning prosecutor reluctantly nodded.

Their conference ended, Rhoades said, "I believe the prosecution and the defense have reached a fair compromise, your honor."

Forester bristled. "I'll be the judge of what's fair in my

courtroom, Mr. Rhoades." Over the subdued laughter that trickled through the galley, Forester said, "What sort of compromise has the prosecution agreed to?"

Seb set his pen aside and stood. "Your honor, the prosecution has agreed to accept the not-guilty pleas of the defense on the initial charges brought by Marshal Mackey, and to accept the guilty pleas of the defense on the assault charges brought by the Territory of Montana. The defendants have also agreed to waive their right to a jury trial and request your honor's indulgence in passing sentencing as soon as possible."

Mackey watched the courtroom erupt in another round of murmurs, only to grow quiet just as quickly when Judge Forester scowled at them. "There'll be no more of that in this courtroom. I want silence during these proceedings. Church mouse pissing on cotton silence, or, by God, I'll throw everyone out of here!"

When total silence resumed, Judge Forester look at the defendants. "On your feet, the both of you."

Grant quickly got to his feet while it took a nudge from the guard's Winchester stock to get him to stand.

With both defendants and attorneys standing, Judge Forester began. "Mr. Grant, I find you to be one of the most deplorable human beings ever to have been brought before me in over forty years of practicing law. I believe you are guilty of poisoning your employer, stealing from the company you controlled, and of inviting a criminal element into Dover Station for your own aggrandizement. However, I can't convict a man on what I believe, only what the prosecution can prove. Your counsel has provided a detailed brief explaining why Mr. Brenner's confession is unreliable at best and was, at worst, coerced during his incarceration.

Therefore, while I am personally convinced of your guilt, I must reluctantly find you not guilty of those charges."

Mackey's hands balled into fists. The old bastard on the bench had lost his nerve after all.

"However," Judge Forester continued, "I find the territory's additional assault charges against you have much more merit. Alfred Brenner, you are hereby found guilty of assault and sentenced to no less than five years of incarceration in the territorial jail. Any infraction during your incarceration will add an additional five years to your sentence up to a maximum of twenty-five years. Given your mercurial disposition, I am confident you will undoubtedly spend the rest of your life behind bars."

Brenner's shackles rattled as he tried to flip the heavy table over. The deputy behind him slammed the butt of his Winchester deep into Brenner's right kidney, causing the big man to buckle and drop down into his seat."

The judge turned his attention to Grant, who had not budged an inch despite Brenner's outburst. "James Grant, I find you guilty of both assault charges that the prosecution has brought against you. However, you have already suffered greatly as a result of your actions. You have limited use of your arm, thanks to Marshal Mackey's bullet, have been held in miserable conditions for months, and have lost every position you have held in Dover Station. You are sentenced to time served and released under the following conditions."

He held up a single stubby finger. "First, you are hereby forbidden from holding any elected or appointed office in this territory for the remainder of your natural life. This order will be carried over into statehood should that blessed event occur."

Another digit popped up. "Second, you are forbidden

from holding any position of managerial responsibility in any corporation doing business in the territory and eventual state of Montana. That includes any position on any board of directors. Third and finally, you are hereby ordered to pay a fine of fifteen thousand dollars to the court to cover the costs of your incarceration and travel here to Montana."

Grant had to steady himself on the table before he fell over.

"Your honor," Rhoades protested. "Such a fine would practically bankrupt my client. While we appreciate the court's generosity in sentencing, we ask that it reconsider such an onerous amount of money."

But Judge Forester would not be moved. "Your client's been suckling from the Dover Station teat for quite some time, counselor. He's probably stolen twice that amount. Now, I might not be able to hang him based on the evidence brought before me here today, but I can make sure he walks out of here a shell of the man he used to be."

The judge cleared his throat and regained his composure. "Of course, you have the right to appeal my ruling, at which time I will order these men remanded to the custody of the federal marshals, who will be more than happy to confine these men until we set a trial date. Probably sometime next year."

Rhoades began to protest, but a glare from Judge Forester froze him in place.

Rhoades swallowed hard before saying, "We will not be appealing the decision, your honor."

"Wise decision," Forester said. "The marshals will take Mr. Brenner into custody. Grant, you're free to go. Court adjourned."

Without banging a gavel, the judge simply got up and

stepped down from the bench. Lynch stepped forward and once more bellowed, "All rise."

By then, Al Brenner had regained enough strength to fire an elbow into the guard's stomach. The blow doubled the guard over as Brenner brought down his shackled hands on the back of the deputy's neck, knocking him to the floor.

Rhoades was knocked out of the way, and the gallery erupted into a sea of chaos. Mackey saw Pappy and Katherine were still seated as he and Lynch scrambled to subdue Brenner.

The second guard rushed to help his partner, but Grant sat down and pushed his chair back, blocking his way just long enough for Brenner to swing his shackled hands like a club. Fist and chains rocked the second deputy's head and sent him flat on his back.

Lynch slid across the table and drove his boot into the back of Brenner's left knee, causing the big man to buckle. The deputy wrapped a thick arm under Brenner's jaw and wrenched his neck backward.

Mackey yanked Grant out of the chair and threw him to the floor to get him out of the way.

Just as Brenner was about to smash Lynch in the head with his shackles, Mackey kicked Brenner in the groin with all of his strength.

The fight went out of Brenner, and Lynch rode the big man down, pinning his face to the courtroom floor. More deputies surrounded them, some carrying more shackles to help secure the prisoner better.

Mackey let the men go to work and found Grant struggling to get to his feet. Mackey grabbed him by the arm and yanked him to his feet just as Rigg had one leg over the railing to help his employer.

"Get back," Mackey warned him.

Rigg remained where he was. "Mr. Grant's a free man, Aaron. Let him go."

"There's still a few things we need to tend to before we just let him go," Mackey said. "We'll spring him as soon as we can. Until then, you wait."

Rigg clearly did not like that idea.

Mackey hoped he disliked it so much that he tried to do something about it.

"It's fine, Nathan," Grant said as Mackey pulled him behind the crowd bringing Brenner back to jail. "Head over to the Hotel Helena. I'll meet you there as soon as I'm free."

Mackey pulled Grant's chains tight enough to make the prisoner cry out, though it was drowned out by the shouts and curses Brenner was causing. "Why'd you pick the Hotel Helena to meet?"

"Because I hear it's the finest hotel in town." Grant smirked. "And attracts all the best clientele. Never know who you might run into or what might happen, especially after a few drinks in celebration of my freedom."

Mackey pushed the prisoner through the doorway where Lynch held the door open. "This here's a tunnel that leads back to the jail across the street. We use it for prisoners we figure might have some friends who'd try to break them out." He looked down the steps at the bellowing Brenner, who still yelled despite being hog-tied with shackles.

Mackey waited until the group was out of the way before he threw Grant down the stairs.

Lynch quickly pulled the door shut to mask Grant's screams.

"Looks like he slipped," Lynch said. "Shame."

Mackey liked the way Lynch thought. "Guess I must've lost my grip on him in all this excitement."

"Guess so." Lynch looked down at Grant, moaning and feebly trying to roll onto his knees at the base of the stairs. "Hope the poor man isn't hurt. Him being this close to freedom and all."

Lynch went back out into the courtroom as Mackey went down the steps to help the prisoner to his feet. "A man can hope."

Mackey pulled Grant upright and slammed him against the stone wall of the tunnel.

"You can't rough me up like this," Grant panted. "I'm free to go. The judge said as much himself. The same judge you and Rice paid to kill me." He laughed through bloody teeth. "No one likes a sore loser, Aaron."

Mackey grabbed his collar, pulled him off the wall, and slammed him against it. "You're not going anywhere until I know you understand that your days of killing people and ruining their lives are over. Once we let you out of these chains, no matter where you go in this territory, you'll always be a convicted criminal. That'll follow you wherever you go."

"Convicted on a phony charge by a drunken judge and a thug with a badge." Grant spat a mouthful of blood onto the tunnel floor. "When statehood comes, I'll just get the new governor to commute my sentence. Or the next one after him. You think you ended me today?" Grant laughed. "All you did was make me a folk hero. Hell, by the time all is said and done, maybe I'll have a few phony titles after my name like you've got."

Mackey punched him in the gut, which doubled Grant in half. Mackey would not let him fall and eased him back upright.

"Unless you want a lot worse to happen to you before I let you go, you're going to do one last thing for me."

"Go to hell!" Grant yelled, his voice echoing in the long, stone tunnel.

But when he flinched when Mackey brought his hand back to hit him again, the marshal knew he finally had him cowed.

"When I take you back to the jail," Mackey continued, "you're going to send word to Rigg and his men to clear out of the hotel and move somewhere else. If I see you or any of Rigg's men anywhere near that hotel, I'll start shooting out of self-interest. Do I make myself absolutely clear?"

Grant laughed. His teeth still bore a trace of blood. "Rigg really has you scared, doesn't he? I didn't believe it at first when he told me you two had a past. I figured he was just another hired gun full of hot air looking for a payday. I honestly thought nothing on God's green earth could scare the great Aaron Mackey. But it looks like I was wrong." He laughed again. "If he has you shaking, then he's worth every cent. I can't wait to hear the story of why you're so scared of him."

Mackey grabbed him by the throat with his left hand and squeezed as he said, "The only story you need to hear is the one that ends with you leaving me and mine alone. You stay the hell out of Dover Station. You leave Montana as soon as you can, or I promise I'll plant you here."

"It's a free country, Marshal," Grant strained to speak through Mackey's grip on his throat, "and I'm a free man. I can live wherever I chose. What's to stop me from picking Dover Station?"

Mackey released him again with a shove. "Listen to some of those stories Rigg tells you about me around a bottle of brandy tonight. You might think differently after that."

Mackey snatched Grant by the collar and walked him

down the long tunnel beneath Broadway to the jail. A couple of deputies called out to him from the other end of the tunnel, and Mackey told them to come ahead.

They took hold of Grant and marched him back to the jail. The convict gave him a bloody sneer over his shoulder before the deputies jerked him by the chain and pulled him forward.

Mackey stood in the tunnel, alone while he listened for the echoes of the men and prisoners to die away. The few moments of solitude helped him put his mind in order as the events of the day sank in. He had gotten almost everything he had wanted. Brenner would be locked up for close to ten years or more after today. Grant was free, but his life was ruined in Montana. Judge Forester had proven to be a man of his word and a crafty one at that.

Mackey knew he should have felt happy, but he could not shake the feeling of dread that had settled over him the moment Forester had made his ruling. It was as if a part of him had just died while something new within him struggled to life.

He did not want to admit it, but his life had changed because his pursuit of Grant had finally come to an end. He remembered having read Melville's *The Whale* when he had been at West Point, which made him wonder if he had become so obsessed with chasing Grant that actually bringing him to justice was no longer its own reward?

No, he decided. That was not it. He had seen men in the army who had allowed the love of the chase to cloud their judgment in the field. Men who had been too taken with the moment to question themselves or their decisions.

Mackey knew this was something else. A feeling that an old part of his life was fading into the fog of the past while a new life was coming into view.

A feeling that told him he would have to ride through a maelstrom before he reached that new life that beckoned him. A storm stirred up in some way by James Grant and Nathan Rigg.

He only hoped he would weather this storm better than Captain Ahab had.

He set the dark feeling aside and began walking through the tunnel toward the jail.

CHAPTER 14

Mackey was in the middle of watching his deputies muster Grant out of chains when one of the junior deputies came rushing into the jail to find him.

"Marshal Mackey." The boy was so out of breath, he could barely stand. "Judge Forester wants you in his chambers. Immediately, if not sooner. His very words, sir. Not mine."

Mackey immediately thought Rigg must be up to something, maybe some kind of bid to free Brenner. "Is he in trouble?"

"No, sir. He's fine. He just said he needs you in his chambers immediately."

Mackey saw he did not have much of a choice, so he walked outside and climbed into Adair's saddle. Although the courthouse was just across the street from the jail, he decided to ride instead of walk. He was new in this town, and impressions were important if he was to have their respect. He knew the black Arabian mare always made a distinct impression on strangers. Besides, he was a cavalry-man, and no cavalryman worth his salt walked when he could ride.

He brought Adair about and let her move at her own pace through the guarded gate of the prison and across Broadway to the courthouse. Yes, the judge had sent word for him to hurry, but he had never been of the mind to put the heels to Adair's flanks unless it was necessary. That was why he had always gotten the best out of her when he needed her most. The horse knew that if Mackey was urging her on, there was a good reason.

A request from an eccentric judge did not qualify as a good reason to Aaron Mackey.

The street was still filled with spectators gathering to discuss what they had heard and seen in the courtroom. He knew from experience that most of them would get it wrong, of course, and by nightfall, several different accounts of the same event would have spread throughout Helena's drawing rooms, dining halls, and saloons. The morning papers might contradict some of what they had heard from their neighbors, friends, and acquaintances, but gossips rarely allowed facts to get in the way of a juicy story.

Mackey rode Adair into the stable at the rear of the courthouse, where the black liveryman ducked his head to him as he took the reins from him as he climbed down from the saddle. "I'll look her over and give her a good rubdown if she needs it, sir."

But Mackey had something else on his mind. "Why'd you do that just now?"

The liveryman looked confused. "Do what, sir?"

"Duck your head like that when you came outside?"

The liveryman seemed startled by the question. "No cause, sir. Just something I do."

"What's your name?"

"Name's Charles," he said with pride. "That's always been enough of a name for me, so I don't have a last one."

"Don't ever duck your head to anyone ever again, Charles. Not to me. Not to anyone who comes here. They're no better than you. You're the man who takes care of their horses. That's an important job. Act like it."

"Yes, sir," he said with a bit of newfound pride in his voice. "I believe you're right."

"Don't forget it. And don't let them forget it, either. Anyone gives you trouble, you come see me."

"I will, sir. And thank you."

"You can thank me by keeping Adair here separated from the rest of the horses in there. She's doesn't get along well with other animals, especially mares." He was glad she did not mind Charles holding her reins. "She seems to have taken to you, though."

The liveryman patted her neck. "I have a special way with animals, sir. Always have. Comes in handy for a liveryman."

He watched Charles lead Adair into the livery.

Mackey turned and walked up the back stairs of the courthouse. He had no idea why he had felt compelled to tell Charles not to duck his head. He had no idea if what he had just told him would make a difference, but he felt it still needed saying.

When he reached the judge's chambers, Mackey was surprised that the front desk was empty, but he could hear voices coming from Forester's office. Not only voices, but something that sounded like it might be laughter.

Now he was really beginning to worry.

Mackey pushed through the gate and slowly walked back toward the judge's office. None of this fit with the man he had come to know as Adam Forester.

When he walked into the chambers, he immediately saw the reason for the laughter.

He saw Billy and Joshua holding small glasses of something that looked like champagne. Pappy was there, too, decked out in a red, white, and blue sash across his morning coat, a top hat tucked under his left arm.

And Katherine was standing next to Judge Forester. She was still wearing the same beautiful pink dress and broad-brimmed hat she had worn in court, only now she had pinned a matching veil to it.

The colorful bouquet of flowers she held told him the reason why Judge Forester had sent word for him to hurry.

Katherine's smile confirmed it. "Glad you finally decided to come to your own wedding, Marshal."

The rest of the ceremony was a blur to Aaron. Katherine had arranged everything with Judge Forester a few days beforehand, asking that the wedding take place immediately after the trial.

"I knew a new life would be starting for us now no matter what the verdict," Katherine said to him as the wedding party took their places in the now-vacant courtroom. "What better way to sweep the past clean than with a wedding?"

Mackey felt himself blushing. He was not used to this kind of attention. "But I didn't get you a wedding ring."

"I've already got one." She took off her old wedding ring and handed it to him. "This time, it'll be from you and like a whole new ring again. Your father is giving you his. He's also been kind enough to offer to give me away."

Mackey handed Katherine's ring to Billy. "Keep an eye on that until the time comes."

"I did the last time, didn't I?" Billy reminded him.

Mackey had thought less and less about his marriage to Mary in the years since she had left. He had forgotten almost every detail about their wedding day, even that Billy had been his best man then, too. "Let's hope the second time's a charm."

"It is." Billy took Katherine's gloved hand and kissed it. "It really is."

Mackey had the chance to take a better look at his father and the colorful sash he was wearing. "Why's Pappy in that getup? He wasn't wearing a sash and a top hat at the trial." He noticed another detail troubled him even further. "And why the hell is he wearing gloves? He doesn't even wear gloves when he's unloading freight."

Katherine suppressed a smile and looked away from her future husband.

Mackey asked Billy, "What's going on?"

Billy replied with a wince.

"Is someone going to tell me," Mackey asked, "or just stand there making funny faces all day?"

"A boy from the telegraph office found him right after the trial," Billy said. "Mr. Bishop of the Dover Station Company pushed for the town to hold an election for mayor today. Looks like they elected Pappy as their new mayor."

Katherine giggled.

Now Mackey knew why Billy was wincing. "They finally did it." He closed his eyes. "He'll be worse to live with than ever after this."

"At least you'll know Dover Station will be in good hands." Katherine took her fiancé's hands. "All the more reason to stay right here in Helena, isn't it?"

"Music to my ears," Judge Forester said, interrupting the couple. He held up a key and an envelope to Aaron and

Katherine. "I almost forgot. An early wedding present from Mr. Rice of New York."

Mackey took the envelope and key from the judge. "What is it?"

"The deed to the Hotel Helena. Says he was so impressed with what Katherine had done with the Campbell Arms in Dover that he knew she could do wonders here with her own hotel. I know she'll turn that tired old place into a palace, starting with the kitchen."

Katherine giggled again as she brought her hands to her face, barely able to control herself. Mackey had never seen her so happy.

Joshua stepped forward and took the envelope and key from him. "I'll keep them safe for you until after the ceremony, Aaron. You look like you might drop them."

Judge Forester cleared his throat. "Now, let's hurry up with these proceedings so I can swear your daddy in as mayor of Dover Station. I'm not sure if it's legal or not, but, by God, it'll certainly be fun!"

Mackey found himself being jostled into place by Katherine and Pappy and Billy. He was not accustomed to being flustered or rushed but realized he did not mind the bother.

Only young Sandborne stood back on the fringe, but Mackey beckoned him to stand next to Billy before the judge. "You're part of this family now, Joshua, whether you like it or not."

Josh seemed to like it just fine, given by how quickly he stood next to Billy.

Satisfied that everyone was in place, Judge Forester cleared his throat and began the proceedings.

"Dearly, beloved, we are gathered here today to witness

the joining of Aaron Mackey and Katherine Campbell in holy matrimony."

The ceremony went on like that for several more minutes. Words being said by the judge and Aaron and Katherine. Vows repeated and rings exchanged and none of it seemed real to Mackey until he heard the judge say, "I now pronounce you Mr. and Mrs. Aaron Mackey. You may now kiss the bride!"

And Mackey did kiss her, and as she kissed him back with what he knew was all of her heart, he realized the great whale had swum away beyond his notice or care.

CHAPTER 15

Although Rhoades told him the suite of rooms he had acquired for him at The Frontier Palace were much nicer than his single room at the Hotel Helena, James Grant did not care.

"It's the principle of the thing," he said as he tried to rub feeling back into his wrists. He had been released from jail several hours before, but the feeling of the shackles was still there. He imagined it would be a long time before he forgot how they felt, if ever. "I'm a free man, J.D. I should be able to stay where I please."

"You may be free," the attorney allowed, "but you're a convicted felon in the eyes of the law, so when the territorial marshal tells you to do something, I advise you to do it. Changing rooms is a small price to pay, James. You won. I thought you'd be happy."

Grant glared at him. "How can I be happy with Al Brenner rotting away in a cell for the next five years? The Hancocks will be furious I let him get locked up."

"Ten years," Rigg added from the chair in the corner of the suite. "Old Forester tacked on an extra five for what he did in his courtroom. That stupid bastard will probably rack up the full twenty-five years by this time next week. I doubt his kin will shed a tear for him, especially after we get you back to Dover Station."

"What?" Rhoades exclaimed. "You can't go back there, James. The judge told you as much."

"He said I can't sit on a board or work for any large companies," Grant told him. "He didn't say I couldn't start my own company."

"Start it with what?" Rhoades asked. "That fifteen-thousand-dollar ruling pretty much cleaned you out." The attorney sat up a bit straighter. "And there are my fees to consider."

"I've considered them," Grant said. "Yours and Rigg's, too. You'll get your money, and the judge will get his fine." Grant smiled. "That old drunk was right, you know. I stole a lot more than fifteen thousand from Silas Van Dorn while I was running things. More than he or anyone else knows."

"I don't want to know," Rhoades said. "But as your attorney, I strongly advise you to stay away from Dover Station. Mr. Rice has sent out a replacement for Silas Van Dorn. Paul Bishop. I've heard a lot about him. He's not sickly and he's not a fool, James. You won't be able to control him like you controlled Van Dorn. He's a Quaker, in fact, and doesn't drink or gamble. The man doesn't even curse. You won't be able to corrupt him."

Grant absently moved his hands over his red brocade vest. It was good to feel such finery again. "There's more than one way to corrupt a man, J.D. If you can't do it by being next to him, then you take the ground out from under him." He looked at his attorney. "Believe me, I know. And I know just how to do it, too."

Rhoades stood up. "I believe every man is entitled to a

defense before the law, but I won't help you break it, and I won't sit idly by while you put yourself in jeopardy. If you won't follow my counsel, then you have no further use for my services. I believe our association has come to an end. I'd like my payment now before I leave."

"I'd give him his money, Mr. Grant," Rigg said. "You don't want him coming after you in court for it."

"It's your money too, Nathan. Don't forget that."

Rigg examined the crease in his pants leg. "Well, if it's all the same to you, J.D., I think I'm going to hang around for a while. See if Mr. Grant has any use for me in his future plans." He looked over at Grant. "That is, if you'll have me, sir."

Grant smiled. He had expected the mercenary to stay with him, knowing a wise bet when he saw one. He was glad his time in Mackey's jail had not dulled his instincts. "You're welcome if you have a mind to stay, Mr. Rigg."

The retired colonel looked at the attorney. "Guess you're on your own from here, J.D. I've got myself another partner."

"I can't say I'm surprised," Rhoades said, "or particularly disappointed. Now, about my fee?"

"I have your bill," Grant told him. "As soon as I get back to Dover, I'll have my bank send the money to your offices in Chicago. It'll be waiting for you by the time you get there."

"I certainly hope so." Rhoades picked up his leather bag and walked to the door. "I'd wish you luck, Mr. Grant, but I don't think it'll do you much good. Going up against the likes of Aaron Mackey is no one's idea of a successful venture."

"I went up against him," Rigg said. "And I'm still here to tell the tale."

"For now," Rhoades said. "But I got to know him fairly well when I represented him in his court-martial. What the Campbell widow told you about him on the street is true. You won because you were his superior officer. There wasn't much he could do to stop you in a military court-room. But you're not in the army anymore, Nathan, and Mackey doesn't answer to you. He answers to Judge Forester and, more than that, to himself. If you cross him, I don't hold out much hope for your chances."

Grant watched how Rigg would handle the attorney's rebuke. He half expected him to shoot him where he stood.

But he just returned to examining the crease in his pant leg. "I've always known I'll die in my bed, J.D. I think I even saw it once on a particularly warm day on my family's plantation in Virginia. I like to think of it as some kind of prophecy. Nothing Aaron Mackey can do will change that."

"For your sake, I hope not," Rhoades allowed, "but like I said, I don't hold out much hope for your chances." He looked at Grant. "Either of you. Good luck to you. You're going to need it."

He walked out of the suite, leaving Grant and Rigg alone.

Grant watched the door long after Rhoades had left. "That man gives Mackey too much credit."

"And you don't give Mackey enough," Rigg quickly said.

"Don't tell me you're afraid of him, too." Grant was beginning to have second doubts about his new employee. "He's not God, Nathan, and a good part of his current celebrity came from me. I'm the one who cooked up that Savior of Dover Station business, not *The Dover Station Record*. Figured building him up would be good for my investments, and I was right, too. But I know the man behind the legend I created. He's still a two-bit hick from the middle of nowhere. He might be some kind of war hero, but he's still just a man, and any man can be killed."

"That's where you're wrong, Mr. Grant." Rigg uncrossed his legs and picked up his chair as he carried it over to be closer to his new employer. "He might be just a man and any man can be killed, but he's no hick. I sent him up against the worst raider Arizona had seen in years with a ragtag force of convicts and every ne'er-do-well in the stockade. I made sure he was undermanned and outgunned. Even gave him a crooked scout to help balance the odds against him. He not only returned alive, he returned a hero."

"I've heard all about that story," Grant said, "and it never impressed me. I'm no sand savage."

"No, you're not." Rigg set the chair down next to Grant and took a seat. "So when they elevated Mackey to captain against my wishes, I sent him after the scout who betrayed him. Just him and Sergeant Sunday. I figured two men would be no match for a Comanche with a good year-and-a-half head start on him. It took him a year before he returned back to the fort, and when he did, he had that scout in tow. When I ordered some of my officers to kill the scout before he talked, he stepped in and stopped it single-handedly."

He leaned forward, and Grant found him uncomfortably close, but refused to move.

"A man like Mackey," Rigg went on, "doesn't stop. He doesn't quit. He doesn't get discouraged, and he doesn't go away. You have to make a man like that go away and the only way you can do that is by breaking him. You don't break him with bullets or violence. You break him by cracking his very soul. And if you're willing to do that, then you and I are going to get along just fine, because I'm the man to do it."

He held out his hand. "And my price is a sixty-forty split, Mr. Grant. A sixty-forty split of everything, and, together, we end Aaron Mackey once and for all."

Grant looked at the hand before him. Was this the hand that would finally rid him of Aaron Mackey once and for all time? "That's an awfully steep price to pay to get rid of one man."

"Don't think of Mackey as one man," Rigg said. "Think of him as the only man who can bring you down, because he'll never stop trying until he does. You know I'm right, too. Hell, I'll even throw in that colored deputy of his for no extra charge." His hand remained steady. "What do you say?"

Grant did not like the idea of cutting in a practical stranger on so much of the empire he planned to rebuild. An empire that would dwarf anything Frazer Rice or Silas Van Dorn had dared to dream. An empire he intended on building as soon as possible.

But he had no doubt he could find a use for Rigg and his men. If anything, they could be useful in bringing the Hancock family to heel. After that, he could always have an accident, just like Walter Underhill.

He shook Rigg's hand. "Why do I have a feeling I've just made a deal with the Devil himself?"

The colonel laughed as he pumped Grant's hand with enthusiasm. "Oh, Mr. Grant, with your money and my men, we'll do things the old Devil himself would shy away from."

James Grant liked the sound of that. He liked the sound of that very much.

CHAPTER 16

A week later, Jerry Halstead was sitting on a bench, sharpening his bowie knife on a whetstone when Chief Edison and three of his men arrived at the station.

"Morning, Ed," Jerry said without looking up from his knife. He had taken to calling the man Ed, even though he knew that was not his first name. "Looks like rain's coming."

"Rain's not the only thing coming." Edison sat on the other end of the same bench. "I suppose you and me are here for the same reason."

Jerry spat on the stone and moved his blade across it. "Guess that would depend on what your reason is."

"Mayor Mackey is due in on the eight o'clock train from Helena," the chief said. "We're here to escort him over to the Municipal Building to show him his new office."

"That's a coincidence, Ed, because I'm here to do the very same thing."

Jerry held up his knife so it caught the dull morning light. The knife was the last present his father had ever given him. He had given it to him on the very day he had been shipped off to missionary school in Texas. It was in better condition now than it had been the day he had taken it from the box it had come in. It had served him well in the years since, and he took pride in keeping it in fine condition.

"Heard Grant is back in town," Edison said, "though I haven't seen him myself. They say he's holed up in an upstairs bedroom at The Ruby, though no one has seen him. No one who'll admit it anyway." The chief shrugged. "Could be just a rumor, I guess."

"I heard that one myself," Jerry said. "It's one of the reasons why I came down here this morning. Figured you boys might not mind having another gun hand on your side."

"Couldn't hurt," Edison allowed, "especially after hearing he's got a new man with him. Nathan Rigg. Heard he was a colonel in the cavalry, but he's something of a mercenary now. Now him I've laid eyes on. He's a dandy, all right, but looks like he knows how to handle himself."

Jerry had seen Rigg standing in front of The Ruby saloon on Lee Street a few days before, though he had not known his name. To Jerry, Rigg had the look of a man who had put an awful lot of work into looking dangerous. As to whether or not he was as dangerous as he looked would be a matter to be decided at a later date.

Perhaps today, here at the station. Yes, Jerry decided, that would be a fine way for them to make each other's acquaintance.

The police chief swallowed as he looked at the big knife Jerry was admiring. "My name's not Ed, you know. It's Steve."

Satisfied that the blade was sharp enough, Jerry leaned forward and tucked the knife into the sheaf on the back of his belt. "I know, but you look more like an Ed to me, so I'll go on calling you Ed, if you don't mind."

Something in the chief's face told Jerry that he did, in fact, mind, but not enough to make a big deal about it. At least yet. "I suppose I've been called worse. You're a mighty tough man to get to know, Halstead."

"I've been told that a time or two," Jerry admitted. "I've been called distant and even aloof depending on the company I keep. I had to look that one up the first time someone pulled that word on me. Aloof. It's a good word. Wish I could use it more in my kind of work, but so far, I haven't found a way. I get called 'uppity' a lot, too. That's usually by folks who take me for a half-breed."

He made a point of looking at the chief. "What about you, Ed? You think I'm uppity?"

"I know you're not a breed," Edison admitted. "Always saw Mexicans as white as far as I'm concerned, but I'm not concerned much when people form their opinions. But there's no denying you're definitely a strange one. In the short time you've been here, you drink alone, eat alone, and haven't made any friends, at least none that I can see."

"Lawmen aren't too popular in boomtowns, Ed," Jerry said. "People shine you on because they want a break when they step out of line or they want you to back their play when they find themselves in a tight spot. When you let them down, things tend to get awkward after that. Being distant saves a lot of disappointment all around."

He flicked the deputy marshal star pinned to his chest. "Being a lawman is a lonely business, but it's the only business I know."

"Heard something about you finding yourself on the other side of the law." Edison looked up the tracks to see if the train was coming. "Heard you served your share of time in a Texas jail."

"You heard right," Jerry said. "Didn't run afoul of the law, though. Just one man's version of it. But I served three years before they realized I was right, so here I am."

"Sounds like you've been around a couple of boomtowns in your time," Edison observed. "You look kind of young to have that much experience."

Jerry smiled. "But I've got an old soul, *amigo*. A very old soul indeed."

"Then you ought to know friends are important, especially in a boomtown like this."

Jerry shrugged as he joined Edison in looking up the tracks, waiting on the train to show up. "I've got friends."

"They're in Helena, and Helena's a long way from here."

Jerry considered that. "You're my friend, aren't you, Ed? You and your deputies."

"I wouldn't go that far," Edison warned him. "I mean, I don't have a problem with you. Hell, I don't know you well enough to know if I even like you or not. But even if I did, I can't speak for all of the men in my department."

"I wouldn't expect you to. But I guess you're talking about your Hancock deputies."

"You guess right," Edison told him. "They're still pretty raw about Al Brenner being locked up and Grant going free."

Jerry had figured that would be the case. "I had nothing to do with that."

Edison laughed. "You had plenty to do with it. Hell, you were part of the shoot-out at the jail that killed plenty of those boys. I don't know if you or Billy or Aaron planted more Hancock boys in the cemetery, but I'd hate to have my life depend on the difference."

Jerry hoped the train got there soon. He had never enjoyed making small talk with anyone, and Edison was turning out to be a talker. "I never killed a man who didn't have it coming, Ed. You'll just have to take my word on that. And as far as the Hancocks go, I hope they've learned their lesson and know enough to leave me alone."

"Hancocks don't stop," Edison told him. "They keep running at something until they tear it down. I've done a lot of traveling in my life, too, and I've never seen a family quite like them. And there's a hell of a lot of them, too. Bastards breed like rabbits."

"Guess it's a good thing for me that I've got lots of bullets." He elbowed the chief. "But let's hope it doesn't come to that."

Edison shook his head. "Well, my conscience is clear. I've said what I came here to say. Whatever happens next between you and them, you can't say you weren't warned."

"I knew it before you said it, Chief, but I appreciate the effort just the same." He was relieved when the sound of the train horn echoed in the distance. "And it looks like our new mayor is almost here."

Both men stood up to stretch their legs before the train pulled into the station.

Jerry Halstead found himself liking Steve Edison. From what Mackey had told him, the bowlegged former gunman was just corruptible enough to be trustworthy. Jerry had always gotten along with that sort, and he imagined the same would hold true in Edison's case. He never trusted a man who was not at least a bit crooked, except of course, for Aaron and his Uncle Billy.

As the train came into view, Edison said, "Wish you'd get your damned hair cut, though. Can hardly blame some people taking you for a breed."

"I suppose I can't," Jerry said. "Not until they're foolish enough to try to do something about it."

* * *

After the train pulled in and the passengers began stepping down from their cars, Jerry spotted Pappy right away.

The spectacle of him brought a smile to Jerry Halstead's face.

Pappy was sporting a top hat and black suit with a red, white, and blue sash across his chest. He wore gray gloves and had a porter in tow carrying his bags. He had trimmed his iron-gray beard to a much more manageable, close-cropped affair that made him look like a man of importance.

The new mayor was clearly so pleased with his new position that even Jerry could not help but be happy for him.

"Mr. Mayor." Jerry swept off his hat with a flourish. "Welcome home to Dover Station."

"Jerry, my boy!" The Irishman locked him in a bear hug and lifted Sim Halstead's boy off the ground as if he was still a youngster. "It's great to see at least one friendly face to greet me after so much time away."

Edison extended a hand to the new elected official. "Congratulations, sir. Me and my men look forward to working with you."

Pappy pumped the chief's hand enthusiastically. "Not all of them, I'm sure, but we'll be settlin' that soon enough. Now, when's the swearin'-in ceremony?"

"Got Doc Ridley and his Bible waiting for you in your office right now," Edison told him as they began to walk the length of the platform. "The town wanted to wait until you got back to decide on a date, but they're itching to have it soon. Tomorrow, in fact. Some men are building a platform the width of Front Street right now. After everything that's happened, a celebration like this is exactly what this town needs."

"As do I, Chief," Pappy said. "As do I. And I have wonderful news. Aaron and Katie have finally wed."

Jerry laughed. "So Aaron finally found someone who could take a joke. Good for them!"

"Guess that means they'll be making their home in Helena now," Edison said.

"Looks that way," Pappy said. "Judge Forester is anxious for Aaron to focus on his marshalin' duties, which is fine by me. It's time he took hold of that job and made something of it." He snapped his gloved fingers. "I almost forgot. I've brought cigars for the occasion. The finest in Helena, or so they told me."

He summoned the porter with his bags to hold one while he opened it and handed out enough cigars for Jerry, Edison, and the two deputies he had brought with him. "And I've got a few boxes more comin' on the next train. I've got to say, I never had a taste for these things before, but now, I find 'em quite enjoyable."

Jerry took one and drew the cigar under his nose. Pappy might not know a good cigar when he had one, but Jerry did. And this one seemed fine. "What good is a politician without a cigar?"

Pappy feigned insult. "Heaven forbid I ever become a politician. I'm a public servant, boyo, and don't you go forgettin' it. And don't go lettin' me forget it, either. If I ever get too big for my britches, tap me on the back of the head and remind me I'm still just an old dirt farmer from Longford."

"Spoken like a true politician," Jerry observed.

Even Edison had to laugh at that one.

Jerry sensed someone behind them and turned in time

to see the doors of the station building slam open before five men walked out onto the platform. They all had the short faces and deep-set eyes Jerry had come to recognize as the common look of the Hancock clan.

And all of them had pistols on their hips.

Jerry put himself between the mayor and the newcomers. "Can I help you boys with something?"

Edison and his men formed a tight ring around Pappy. The porter moved behind them with his bags.

"Sure can," said the Hancock man in front. "You can tell me what you bastards think is so funny."

"Bastards, is it?" Pappy bit off the end of his cigar and spat it onto the floor. He edged his way around Jerry and dug a box of matches out of his pocket.

"Now, I can't say much for the lineage of these men, save young Halstead here, but I'll have you boys know I'm no bastard. Patrick and Rose Mackey were wedded according to the rites of Rome in St. Michael's Church in Longford almost sixty years ago."

The new mayor thumbed a match alive and brought the flame to his cigar, before waving it dead. "So, you might want to watch where you throw that word around, son."

"I know where I'm throwing it and who at," the Hancock man said. "And I'm throwing it at you, you donkey bastard."

"Well, in that case, I suppose I'll have to do somethin' about it." He tucked his cigar into his mouth and tossed his hat to the porter, who struggled to catch it before it hit the platform. He unbuttoned his coat and held the flaps open for the Hancock men to see. "But, as I'm unarmed, we'll have to settle this the old-fashioned way? With fists. I'll even leave me gloves on so as not to cut up your pretty faces."

Jerry again moved between him and the Hancock men. "They look like the kind of men who fight fair to you, Mr. Mayor?"

Pappy eyed the men. "They can fight however they want. The result'll be the same."

Jerry never took his eyes off the men. "You've got bigger business to attend to, Mayor. Chief, escort Mayor Mackey to the Municipal Building so he can get started on his new duties."

Pappy looked up at Jerry and spoke in a low voice. "What are you doin'? For God's sake, there's only five of them. Little ones at that."

"Wouldn't do having the mayor getting into a brawl on his first day back, now would it?" Jerry grinned at the Hancock men. "And like you said, there's only five of them. Little ones at that. I'll be just fine."

Pappy frowned as he took his hat back from the porter. "If I knew bein' mayor would be so borin', I never would've taken the job."

Pappy reluctantly let Edison and his men walk him back to the Municipal Building, leaving Jerry on the platform to face the five men alone.

The leader pointed at him. "You're that breed Mackey left behind to mind the store for him, ain't ya?"

Jerry casually bit off the end of his cigar and, like Pappy, spat the end on the platform. "I'm not a breed, but yeah, I'm the one Mackey left behind."

"Guess that means you're not any good," said the blond man standing behind the leader, "seein' as how he didn't seem fit to bring you with him."

"I suppose I've always been good enough." Jerry dug out a match from his pocket and struck it on his belt, bringing the flame to his cigar without taking his eyes off the men. "Guess there's only one way for you boys to find out."

He waved the match dead and flicked it onto the platform. "But you're not going to find out by talking me to death. You came here to do something, so you might as well get to it."

The five men flinched as if they had all been slapped at the same time, but they did not go near their pistols.

Jerry took a good draw on the cigar and removed it from his mouth with his left hand. His right was flat against the holster of the Colt Thunder on his hip.

The leader pointed at him again. "You and your friends are the reason why Al's not coming home any time soon. Said they locked him away for five years for that phony charge you pinned on him."

"Five?" Jerry grinned. "I heard it was up to ten after he acted up in the courtroom."

"Might as well be fifty, for all the difference it makes to us."

"Makes a big difference to me." Jerry let the cigar smoke drift from his nose. "Means one less Hancock boy I'll have to kill. Too bad, too. I was kind of hoping for the chance to plug him myself. Figured it would set the rest of your bunch back on your heels. But, I guess I'll have to make do with you boys."

Jerry was not smiling anymore. "So, let's drop the ring and set to pulling."

The men looked around at the few men and women who had remained on the platform to watch what happened next.

"You hear that," one of the other Hancock men called out to them. "This man threatened our lives. Anything that happens now is within our rights. We're defending ourselves, and you're all witnesses."

"They're witnesses, all right." Jerry took another puff on his cigar. "Witnesses to you boys pulling your pistols and dying soon after. Might get my name in the paper. Maybe get a fancy name like they hung on Mackey. Get myself famous."

The leader's shoulders twitched as he reached for the pistol in his belt.

Jerry drew and fired before the Hancock man cleared leather. His bullet hit his target in the throat.

The remaining four Hancock men parted as their leader stumbled backward, dropping his pistol as he clutched his bleeding throat. He fell backward, landing on his rump as life leaked between his fingers. Slowly, he sagged back and gurgled as he fell limp on the platform.

The four men looked down at their fallen relative, then at Jerry.

And at the smoking Colt that was still aimed at them.

"Go on," Halstead encouraged. "Any of you boys want to join him?"

But he knew the remaining men were too scared by what they had just seen to do much of anything. And how fast it had happened. But Jerry also knew men were at their most unpredictable when they were scared.

The blond one said, "Mister, you've got no idea what you've started here today."

"Then why don't we finish it?" He smiled. "It's still four on one. Who knows? One of you might even live."

But the men backed away from their fallen relative, keeping their hands away from their sides.

Jerry aimed at Blondie. "Where do you think you're going?" He nodded down at the dead Hancock. "Dover

Station's a clean town, boys. Pick up your trash and take it with you."

The four Hancock men reluctantly came back, picked up their fallen relative, and carried him inside the station house.

Only when the men were out of sight did Jerry holster his pistol and sit back down on the bench to resume smoking the cigar Pappy had given him. It was a good cigar and worth the time it took to enjoy it properly.

The stationmaster, a man whose name Jerry could never remember, popped out of the station house. His round face already red, he pointed down at the dark bloodstain left by the dead man on the platform and yelled at Jerry. "Are you responsible for this?"

"Depends on how you look at it." He pondered the question as he smoked. "I'm the one who shot him but wouldn't have done it if he'd just walked away." He decided that was just about right as he looked at the stationmaster. "Yes, sir, I suppose responsibility is an awfully tough idea to nail down when it comes to something like this."

"Not when you've got a bloodstain the size of Texas on my platform it ain't." He waggled a finger at Jerry. "I just had four Hancock men carry a dead man through my station. My customers are fit to be tied over it. One woman fainted at the sight."

But Jerry had never been concerned about customers of any kind. "They'll get over it, especially if they've got a round-trip ticket."

The little railroad man only grew redder. "And what about that bloodstain on my floor?"

"I suggest you get a porter to come out and clean it up while it's still fresh. It'll be twice as hard to get rid of when it's dry."

"I have half a mind to—"

Jerry looked at him the way he had always looked at men who were about to say too much or go too far. He had never seen his own look himself, as there had never been a mirror around when he did it.

But he did not need a mirror to know the result was always the same. The man barking at him either backed down or threw down.

And given that the stationmaster was unarmed, Jerry imagined he would back down.

Which he did, but not without a final word before stomping back into the station house. "You're a cold piece, Deputy. A very cold piece indeed."

Jerry puffed on his cigar. He saw no reason to argue with a fact.

CHAPTER 17

Two weeks later, Lode Star, Montana

Mackey ducked his head back inside the barn, just as a round hit the frame.

"Those boys can shoot."

Billy stole a quick look at the crooked log cabin where the miners were holed up as he fed a fresh round into his Sharps. The Winchester was propped up against the wall next to him. "You mind telling me again why we're here?"

They'd had this discussion several times on the two-day ride out of Helena to the mining town. "Judge Forester's got paper on Brett Colburn. You know that."

"I do know *that*." Billy switched to the Winchester and began feeding rounds from his belt. "I'm wondering why *you and I* are out here. You're supposed to be in an office reading papers and spending time with Katie."

They flinched as another miner fired into the barn. "Lynch is better at that kind of thing than I am. He's happier in Helena, and I'm happier here. And Katie knows I've got a job to do."

Both men ducked as a double-barreled shotgun boomed before buckshot peppered the gaping entrance to the barn.

The shooting from the cabin had started as soon as they had ridden into range. Mackey and Billy had barely had enough time to tie their horses behind the barn and enter through the back door. They had not even been able to announce themselves as the law before the shooting started.

Mackey looked around the barn and saw a ladder leading up to the ceiling. "Think you could make it up to the hayloft if I give you cover?"

Billy shook his head. "Not with the kind of fire they're laying into us. The ladder's exposed, and you can't give me cover while I climb it. Like you said, those boys can shoot."

Mackey knew Billy was right and cursed himself for voicing such a stupid idea. He wondered if, after two weeks of marriage, he was already beginning to lose his edge.

Then he had an idea. "Use the Sharps to blow a hole in that door. A little less cover might change their thinking a bit."

In a single motion he had practiced countless times, Billy drew the big rifle to his shoulder, aimed, and fired. The fifty-caliber round obliterated the latch on the wooden door, causing it to swing open.

The boom of the big-bore gun served to quiet all firing from the cabin, giving Mackey a chance to yell out, "You in the house. Stop firing. We're United States Marshals. We've got a warrant to take in Brett Colburn for murder."

"That was a fair fight," a man from inside the cabin called out. "Go away and leave us be."

"Can't do that," Mackey yelled back. "We've got paper on him. Colburn, if you're in there, come out with your hands empty and walk into this barn. We won't shoot, and none of your friends will get hurt."

Mackey ducked back inside as the men in the cabin opened up on them again, once more peppering the barn with bullets. A few rounds pierced the walls, sending beams of dusty daylight into the barn.

Then the shooting stopped as quickly as it had started. They were reloading.

Mackey did not need to tell Billy what to do next. The two men had been through enough dustups like this over the years to be able to read each other's minds.

Mackey fired into the cabin just below the windows where the men were likely to be taking cover.

Billy slung the Sharps on his back and scrambled up the ladder, holding the Winchester in his free hand.

Mackey stopped firing after six shots and waited for a target to present itself. He heard moaning coming from inside the cabin, so he knew he had hit at least one of them during the last volley. He judged the moaning to be coming from the left side of the house, so he shifted his aim to the right side.

"Come out now," Mackey called out again. "No one else needs to get hurt. I just want Colburn. The rest of you can go, even after all of this. You've got my word on that."

A burly man appeared in the doorway and brought up his shotgun to fire, no doubt running to aid his fallen friend. Mackey snapped off a shot and saw the fat man spin as he fell back from view. His shotgun went off as he fell. The blast went through the roof of the cabin. The walls of the cabin were thick, but the roof looked mighty thin.

He had no doubt that Billy had seen it, too, and would use it to his advantage.

"Last chance," Mackey called out, "before we rain hell down on all of you."

He was answered by two rifles that poked through the

shattered windows on the right side of the cabin. Mackey ducked back for cover as shots pounded the barn and barn floor. Their angle was getting better, and he had to hold himself flat against the wall as bullets zipped by him. It was only a matter of time before one shot got lucky and found him through the thin walls of the barn.

Then Billy's Sharps boomed from the hayloft. A second later, a man screamed.

The firing let up, and Mackey chanced a look. He saw a large hole in the roof over the shooter's positions.

A man popped up in the window and brought his rifle up.

One shot from Mackey's Winchester struck him in the chest and put him down for good.

Mackey waited for more shots to come from the cabin, but all he could hear was the broken door creaking on ancient hinges across the courtyard.

Mackey reloaded the Winchester, finishing the last of the cartridges on his belt. He had plenty more ammunition in Adair's saddlebags, but did not dare go back for it. He doubted he would need it anyway. "You in the cabin," Mackey called out. "Is it over?"

As he listened, Mackey was answered with groans and muffled cries of pain. He knew it was as over as it was going to get without taking a look inside the cabin for certain.

He switched his rifle to his left hand and drew his Peacemaker, holding it against his leg as he moved. He did not have to tell Billy to cover him as he moved in. He knew what to do.

Mackey walked slowly but steadily toward the cabin, listening and watching for any sudden movements. But the closer he got, the more agony he heard from the wounded men inside.

He walked up on the porch and crouched when he heard the unmistakable cocking of a hammer from the left side of the cabin. A single shot rang out through the doorway.

It was followed by Billy emptying his Winchester into the left side of the roof.

Mackey remained still while he heard a roof beam strain and creak before it cracked and caved in.

Mackey got to his feet and stood flat against the left side of the doorway. He saw the man he had shot in the chest was still alive, but lying flat on his back, struggling as if he was pinned to the floor.

The second rifleman was slumped next to him. Half of his head was gone thanks to Billy's round.

Mackey took a quick look around the doorframe. The fat man with the shotgun had been half buried beneath the rubble of the collapsed roof, his belly still bleeding from Mackey's bullet. He risked a further look into the house and saw the entire left side of the roof had completely caved in, burying whoever had been over there beneath hundreds of pounds of wood. If anyone had survived it, they'd be hard pressed to get off a shot without Mackey hearing them first.

His Peacemaker leading the way, Mackey stepped into the cabin and moved right. Now he could see that side of the cabin was empty except for the dead man and the dying man flat on his back.

The dying man lifted his head and felt blindly for the rifle that was well out of reach. Mackey approached him slowly and took a knee beside him to get a better look at his wound. Mackey's bullet had hit him dead center in the chest. The blood beginning to pool beneath the man told Mackey the bullet had gone straight through.

"Can you talk?"

The dying man's breathing grew rapid. "Enough to tell you . . . to go to hell."

"Don't waste your breath." Mackey tapped the man's side with the barrel of the Colt. "You're dying. Could be a few minutes, could be the rest of the day. You might last more than that. No way to know for certain with a wound like that. You might even be alive when the coyotes get wind of the stench from your friends. Or the buzzards come in through that hole in the roof. If I was you, I wouldn't want to live to see that."

The man shut his eyes and looked away. A tear streaked down his cheek.

"Tell me if Colburn's here and, if I believe you, I'll end you now. If not, I'll leave you here to take your chances. That might not sound like much of a deal, but it's the only one you have."

The man slowly shook his head.

"Is Colburn here?"

The man kept shaking his head. "He's up at the mine."

Mackey knew there were several mines in the area. He knew the one Colburn worked, but he needed to hear the dying man tell him so he knew he was telling the truth. "Which one? And remember, the truth or I walk away."

"The Lode Star." The dying man coughed and a thin stream of blood spilled from the corner of his mouth. "That's his claim. Got a lot of men working it with him." Another cough drowned out what he had said before, "All of them hardcases like us. Hate . . . lawmen."

Mackey believed him.

He stood up and aimed the Colt down at the man's head. "It didn't have to end like this."

The man smiled, baring reddened teeth. "Sure, it did."

Mackey squeezed the trigger and kept his word.

* * *

When he got outside, Billy had already brought around the horses. Neither of the mounts fussed about the stench of blood and death from the cabin. Both animals had grown used to the smell long ago.

"Any of them left alive?" Billy asked.

"Not anymore." Mackey fed fresh rounds from his saddlebags into his Winchester and stuck it in the saddle scabbard. He dumped the spent bullet from his Peacemaker and replaced it, too, before climbing into Adair's saddle.

He took the rein from Billy. "Last one said Colburn isn't here. He's up working the Lode Star mine."

As they rode away from the cabin, Billy said, "That's good news."

"Nothing good came out of what happened back there today."

Billy seemed to give that some thought before saying, "At least we don't have to dig Colburn out from under all that rubble."

Mackey could not argue with him there. "There's that, I guess."

Mackey knew from reading the map back at his office in Helena that the Lode Star mine was set deep in a hillside just outside the town that bore its name.

Mackey had been hoping Colburn would be in the cabin. Now, he and Billy would have to ride through town to reach the mine. Most of the townspeople probably would not welcome the men who had come to arrest the owner of the biggest mine in town, but that was a chance he and Billy would have to take.

The town of Lode Star was made up of hastily built wooden buildings that had settled unevenly in the Montana mud. Mackey could not see a straight line in any structure along Main Street, where the ground had risen to buckle the sorry attempts at boardwalks that had been laid down long ago.

A man could walk from the Lode Star to the main street if he wanted to and, given the number of tents and shanties he saw lining the thoroughfare, Mackey figured most of the miners did exactly that.

The only people on the street at that time of day were women. None of them wore fancy dresses or carried parasols like they did back in Helena or even Dover Station. These were hardworking women who lived with their men in the tents and shanties that comprised the mining town. They froze in the winters and broiled in the summers and did their best to keep a good home for their children and husbands, who could never quite scrub the grime of the mine from their clothes, no matter how hard they tried.

They were women who did not see strangers much and were wary of them when they did. Mackey could not blame them. He had never been fond of strangers, either.

Mackey had been surprised when Lynch had told him that Lode Star had itself a sheriff and a deputy. So, when he saw a faded hand-painted sign that read TOWN JAIL, he rode toward it. Billy followed.

They tied off their mounts and walked up the crooked steps into the jail. The door was open, and they found two men with their feet up on their respective desks, dozing in their chairs.

Mackey cleared his throat, snapping both men to consciousness. The older of the two, a thin red-boned man with a wild moustache, quickly got to his feet. "What the hell do you want?"

Mackey and Billy stood silently as they waited for the sleep to clear from the sheriff's eyes enough for him to see the stars pinned to their dusters. "Marshals. I didn't know you boys were coming."

"I'm Aaron Mackey, and this is Deputy Billy Sunday."

"Mackey?" the man repeated in a whisper. "Sunday? I've heard of you boys. You're the new marshal out of Helena."

Mackey was beginning to lose patience. "Who are you?"

"I'm Sheriff Larry Sweazy," the red-boned man said, "and that drowsy feller over there is my deputy, Mike Bray."

The thin deputy yawned as he stretched his limbs.

Billy said, "Sorry to interrupt your nap, boys, but the marshal and I need your help."

Sheriff Sweazy flattened down his shirt. "Must be awfully important business to bring out the likes of you two."

Mackey walked over to the peg board where the wanted posters were pinned. Half the men up there were either captured or dead. He recognized one or two who had died from old age.

"You get mail in this burg, don't you? Where are the wanted posters you've been sent?"

"Got 'em right here, Marshal." Sweazy fumbled with the top drawer of his desk and pulled out a thick sheaf of papers. "Look at them every day, like a parson reads his

Bible. I don't bother posting them on account of me not wanting to let the bad guys know we're on to them."

Billy took out the folded wanted poster he had in his back pocket for Brett Colburn and showed it to him. "This man in that Bible of yours?"

Sweazy squinted as he peered at the poster Billy held. "That old Brett? Why no, I don't believe he is. What would he be doing on a wanted poster anyway?"

"He shot a deputy in Virginia City," Mackey told him. "And gunned down two more in the posse that rode out after him."

"Brett?" Sweazy continued shuffling his sheaf of papers. "Not a chance. He's a model citizen. Always has been, ain't that right, Mike? Hardest-working man I know and as honest as the day is long. Him and his men work the Lode Star mine, the biggest concern we've got in these parts. Law-abiding men, the lot of them. Live outside of town in a nice cabin, too."

"We just came from there," Mackey said.

The marshal's tone made Sweazy look up from his papers. "That so?" The papers in his hand began to rattle and he quickly set them back in the drawer. "Everything fine?"

"It wasn't a nice cabin before we got there," Billy said. "Can't say we left it in better condition."

Sweazy's mouth quivered a bit while Deputy Bray gave an exaggerated yawn as he got up from his desk and shuffled toward the back.

Mackey glared at him. "Where do you think you're going?"

"Usin' the privy," Bray said as he scratched his belly. "Always need to go after a nap."

"Or run down to the mine to warn Colburn we're here," Billy said. "You'd best stay where you are."

Deputy Bray turned and faced the marshals. Mackey noticed he wore a Remington '75 too high on his belt. "I don't have to take orders from the likes of you."

Mackey grew very still. "You'll be taking a bullet from him if you take one more step toward that back door." He pointed at the deputy's desk. "Sit down. Now."

Deputy Bray found his chair without looking at it and sat back down.

Sweazy slowly came out from behind his desk, hands raised. "Now hold on just a minute, boys. We're all on the same side here."

"No, we're not," Mackey said. "You got Colburn's wanted poster in the post and you chucked it. You knew Colburn was wanted and you turned a blind eye because he owns The Lode Star. We came here to ask for your help in going to the mine and arresting him. But we're not asking anymore. Both of you get up. You're coming with us."

Sweazy tried a smile. "I've got to say, Marshal, your tone ain't exactly friendly."

"Neither am I. Don't make me tell you again." He nodded toward the back door. "We'll go out that way. Past that privy you were going to use. Looks like the quickest way to the mine."

The sheriff and his deputy shuffled toward the back door and opened it. Mackey and Billy followed.

When they stepped outside, they saw the footpath down to the Lode Star was in spitting distance.

And there was no privy out back.

Billy smiled. "Well look at that, Marshal? That mine's real close. Don't see a privy, though."

"Imagine that." Mackey pulled Bray's Remington from its holster and tossed it back into the jail. Sweazy didn't have to be told to unbuckle his gun belt. He did it on his own and left it next to the back door of the jail.

Mackey shoved him toward the footpath. "Get going."

CHAPTER 18

The entrance to the Lode Star was down around the bend at the end of the footpath. Four miners black with dust were pitching rocks from a rail car into a flatbed wagon.

They stopped what they were doing when they saw the four lawmen approaching. If they were intimidated, they did a good job of hiding it.

One of the miners asked, "Who are your friends, Larry?"

"They're no friends of ours," Deputy Bray said. "They've come for Brett."

One of the miners quit pitching rocks and walked toward them. "That so? Well, they may have come for him, but they're not going to get him."

"Got paper on him," Mackey said. "He's wanted for three counts of murder in Virginia City."

Another miner stood next to the first. "Well, Brett's down working the mine, boys. He's not the kind who likes to be bothered while he's working."

"Then you're going to have to go down there and bother him for us." He kept Sweazy and Bray in front of him and his hand on his buckle, within easy reach of the Peacemaker. "And you're going to do it right now."

Billy had already walked well away from the group, giving the miners more than one angle to worry about.

Sweazy said, "Now everyone just stay easy. There's no reason for anyone to get their heads broken over this." To the miners, he said, "They're federal marshals out of Helena, boys. Their warrant is legal. I saw it."

"Legal's got nothing to do with it," a third miner said, joining the other two. "Brett owns this mine. If he's not here to pay us, we don't get paid, and our families don't eat. It's that simple."

"And not my concern," Mackey said. "Go get him like I told you."

A fourth miner laughed. "Mister, if one of us goes down that mine, we're not coming back alone. We'll have twenty men with us. Every single man jack among them will be carrying pickaxes, shovels, and damned near anything else they can use to pound you boys into dirt."

The miner pointed at Mackey's pistol. "Now, you and your friend over there might pick off some of us. I figure you'll get maybe six of us with those peashooters of yours if you're lucky. But you won't get all of us, and when we catch you, God His own self won't be able to save you."

"But you'll be dead." Mackey's hand did not move from his buckle. "A job's not much good if you're dead."

"Best take your own advice, lawman," said another miner. "This mine is our lives. You take Brett, we've got nothing to live on anyway. So, twenty against two are odds any of us are willing to take if it keeps us from starving to death."

"Maybe we can thin those odds down a bit." Billy walked out of a wooden shed to the far left of the mine.

And he was holding two sticks of dynamite.

The miners backed away.

Billy set both sticks against a rock outcropping and began building himself a cigarette. "I don't know about all of you, but the marshal and me have had a real nasty day. Nothing relaxes me more after a trying time than a good smoke. So, either one of you gets real smart real fast and run down that mine and fetch Brett Colburn for us— alone—or I set one of these firecrackers alight and throw it in that shaft. Maybe it kills Brett and maybe it doesn't. But it'll seal up your livelihood for a long while. And those twenty men you say are in there with him won't be much good to anyone, much less their families."

The miners looked at each other.

Mackey saw Deputy Bray's bladder go.

Sweazy looked at Mackey. "You wouldn't."

"Probably not," Mackey said, "but Billy sure would. He's right about the kind of day we've had, and he's in a pretty bad mood."

"Damn you," one of the miner's yelled. "Colburn's the only thing keeping us alive."

"I've got paper on him," Mackey yelled back, "and we're taking him in. Straight up or over the saddle, makes no difference to me."

"Won't be nothing to put over your saddle if he's buried under tons of rock," Sweazy said.

"I'll take what I can get." He pointed at the lead miner. "You. Bring Colburn out here. Alone. Now."

"And only Colburn." Billy set the cigarette in his mouth and thumbed a match, lighting it. "And be quick about it. Before I finish my smoke. If I see anyone else come out of there, or if you're not back by the time I'm done, I set this butt to a stick and start chucking."

The lead miner ran back into the mine. The others stood around the ore car, arms folded across their chests.

Sweazy turned to face Mackey. "You, sir, are a son of a bitch."

Mackey ignored him and watched the mine entrance.

Billy had long since finished his cigarette but was keeping a match ready when the lead miner appeared at the entrance. He was followed by a burly man whose face was as black as his beard.

He pushed his way past the group of miners and stood alone before Mackey. "I'm Colburn."

Mackey looked at the man as he asked Sweazy, "That him?"

"Yeah," the sheriff looked at the ground. "That's him."

"Brett Colburn," Mackey announced, "I hereby place you under arrest for the murders of three people in Virginia City, Montana. Deputy Sunday and I will be bringing you back to Helena to stand trial. If you behave yourself, you'll be treated well. If you try to escape, we'll cut your tendon and bind you in shackles the whole way back."

"Mackey," Colburn squinted. "Yeah, I suppose you would. I've heard of you."

"Then you know I mean what I say." Mackey stepped to the side and beckoned him to come his way. "Prison's hard enough on a man with two good legs. It's worse when he's a cripple. Get moving. We've got a long ride back to Helena."

Colburn lumbered toward him. "It's a hangman's noose for me either way. I won't get no fair trial."

"It'll be fair." Mackey could sense the man was storing up energy as he moved and got ready to duck. "Judge Forester's a good man."

"Maybe," Colburn said, "but I'm not."

When he got close enough, the miner tried to rush Mackey. The marshal stepped aside and tripped the big man, sending him face-first into the dirt.

Mackey closed in quick and kicked him in the head, then drew his pistol to keep the miners or Sweazy or Bray from getting any ideas about helping their boss.

But Billy already had them covered.

Mackey spoke to Sweazy. "Colburn got a lawyer who handles his business?"

"I believe he does. Why?"

"I want you to talk to him and see to it the mine stays open while Colburn's on trial. Tell him to make sure these men get paid. Just because Colburn's in jail doesn't mean the mine closes. He'll have plenty of time to settle his affairs before he hangs."

Sweazy glared at him. "I thought you said he'll get a fair trial."

"He will," Billy said. "Then he'll hang."

Mackey pointed at the sheriff and his deputy. "You two pick him up and drag him back to your jail. Billy will sit with him while I get his horse. I take it he's got one in that livery we passed on the way in."

"He does," Sweazy said as he beckoned his deputy to help him lug Colburn back up the hill. "A chestnut Morgan."

Mackey was glad it wasn't something smaller that might falter on the trail. "Good horse for a long ride. Now move."

Sweazy and Bray grunted as they dragged the unconscious Colburn back up the foothill to their jail. Mackey held his pistol at his side as he followed them.

Billy walked backward, eyeing the miners as they went. None of them made a move.

CHAPTER 19

Dover Station

James Grant sat on the edge of the bed, still too drunk to rise to his feet to greet such an important day.

He had spent the past week of his return to Dover Station awash in future glory to come. He had made a great show of spending money among some of the more important people in town who had prospered in the months since his incarceration. Businessmen, shop owners, saloon keepers, and bankers who had prospered independent of the Dover Station Company's blessing. People who had despised him when he tried to run them out of business, but now that he had won his freedom, looked upon him as the best hope to break the stranglehold the company had on the town.

None of them were much on their own, but together, they represented a base of the population that could propel him back into power when the time came. He had spent the past week or so wining and dining them, showing them a good time and allowing them to partake in the female companionship The Ruby offered in their cribs out back.

He did not expect their undying loyalty to him. He only

needed it for as long as it took him to regain power over the town. To do that, he would need to be as lucky as he was prepared. And, with Rigg's help, he happened to be both.

Through his hangover, he could hear a great many people outside who had gathered along the alleyways and byways off Front Street all the way to Lee Street. He checked the pocket watch he had cast on the nightstand before falling into bed alone in the early hours of the morning. There were no shortage of Hancock whores who wished to bed him, but save for the times he was securing new allies in his bid for the town, he lived a solitary existence. He feared he might say too much when he had drank too much, and the wrong people might hear his plans.

The success of his plan hinged on one absolute certainty.

Secrecy.

He knew the weight of his plan would collapse in on itself if anyone was to learn of it too early. Fortunately, today was the day it was scheduled to begin.

He opened his pocket watch and saw it was almost noon. He had not slept past the dawning of his new destiny after all.

He would have to be content to sit by the window and watch the aftermath from above. To do anything more would be dangerous. To do any less would rob him of his first taste of revenge against the town that had given him so much and had been only too happy to take it all away.

He closed the pocket watch and held it tight in his fist. "By this time tomorrow," he said to the empty room, "the town will be mine again."

James Grant fought off the wave of nausea that washed over him as he got to his feet and stumbled to the door. He pulled it open and yelled to the bar three levels down. "Coffee! Bring the whole pot! Now, damn you!"

He slammed the door shut and began to get dressed. He pulled a new black suit out of the wardrobe he had made in Helena for this day. It would show solemnity for the coming tragedy, but also convey the power he had acquired once again.

One of the soiled doves who worked the place knocked before opening the door and placing a pot of coffee and cup on the dresser. She looked him up and down in his new suit and said, "Lookin' mighty spiffy, Mr. Grant."

But Grant was too busy knotting his tie just right to take compliments from a whore. "Get out."

When she did, he took a step back and looked at himself in the mirror. *Yes, I suppose I do look spiffy at that.*

He raised his chin, disappointed by how the collar seemed too big for him. The months he had spent recovering from the bullet that had almost taken his shoulder followed by the time in Mackey's jailhouse had caused him to look gaunt and thin.

He would avenge every second of the pain he had felt. He would avenge every moment he had spent in prison. He took a final look at his pocket watch and saw it was five to noon. His vengeance would begin soon.

He slid the pocket watch into his vest pocket and walked over to the chair he had placed by the window. He pulled the drapes apart and took a seat, prepared to watch his destiny unfold before him.

"My time," he said to the empty room. "My time."

This is almost too easy.
From his perch in the turret of the Municipal Building,

Colonel Nathan Rigg sighted his Sharps on the platform that had been built across the middle of Front Street. He had spent the past week or so watching the fools from the Dover Station Company build it from wood cut from the company's new sawmill.

Paul Bishop, the new manager of the company, had made sure every piece of lumber was stamped with the ornate DSC symbol, designed for all the town to see. Red, white, and blue bunting had been hung from the platform. Across the length of Front Street, a canvas sign billowed in the wind that read, "God Bless Mayor Mackey, God Bless Our Town and God Bless the U.S. of A."

Front Street was packed with townspeople and other spectators who had come from miles around to witness history in the making. He doubted a field mouse would be able to find enough of a path on the thoroughfare to scurry across.

Dover Station was set to throw itself the biggest party it had ever seen. Bigger, as he had been told by several drunks in The Ruby, than even James Grant's swearing-in ceremony the previous year.

That day, the people told him, had been marred by the new mayor's disappointment that he had not been able to get rid of Mackey and Sunday. They had gone and gotten themselves appointed U.S. Marshals.

Everyone was confident that Brendan Mackey's swearing in as mayor would be a much more festive celebration. An event the town would not soon forget.

Rigg grinned at the memory, for he knew no one would be forgetting this day any time soon, but not for the reasons they thought.

The simplicity of it would have made Rigg laugh had

he not been hired to put James Grant's "Grand Plan," as he was fond of calling it, in place.

Right now, part of that job was to sit and wait for the festivities to begin. A glance at the Bank of Dover Station clock tower told him he had five minutes to go.

As he sat with his back against the turret, Nathan Rigg pondered the road that had led him here. He had spent the last week or so looking the town over and could not understand Grant's fascination with the place.

It was no different than any of the other dozens of towns sprouting up west of the Mississippi. Its only virtue was that it was far enough from the other big towns to seem like more than it was. The buildings Grant had built when he had been in charge were overdone and overly built. He supposed that had been by design.

No, Dover Station was no different from the other towns Rigg had seen except in one respect. None of them had been controlled by James Grant.

And by the same time tomorrow, the town would be his once again. Nathan Rigg would see to it personally.

During one of Grant's many drunken nights since returning to town, Grant had told Rigg repeatedly that he envisioned Dover Station growing into the ornate buildings he had built. He wanted it to becoming its own city-state, as it were, where no county or state or even federal government would dare question its authority. Let Helena be the capital, but Dover Station would remain the most important city in Montana. "Albany may be the capital of New York," Grant often slurred at the top of his lungs, "but Manhattan is its power. Dover Station is destined for the same greatness."

Nathan Rigg had been a soldier and an officer long enough to understand that power did not come from places or things. It came from men who knew how to wield it. And no number of fancy buildings could ever change that.

James Grant had envisioned himself to be one of those men. He claimed the only difference between him and Frazier Rice or Silas Van Dorn or Carnegie or Morgan was money and position. Judge Forester may have taken a large chunk of his fortune, but not all of it. Barely a third. And Grant remained confident that Rigg and the men he had brought with him, combined with the Hancock family, would be enough to help him regain the town that had been taken from him.

But Rigg knew Grant had lost far more than his position. His run-in with Mackey had cost him his mind. He was already beaten but had just enough money to convince himself otherwise for now.

J. D. Rhoades may have washed his hands of his client, citing the fact that Grant's delusions made it difficult for him to continue to take the man's money. If Grant was intent on wasting his money, Rigg saw no reason why he should not take as much of it as Grant was willing to part with. Nathan Rigg had always considered himself a practical man.

Which was why Rigg had tolerated Grant's drunken ravings, listening dutifully to his nightly assurances that a single bullet would set the wheels of progress in motion that would return his fortunes to him once again. And when the calamity settled, he would regain his rightful place as the man in charge of Dover Station.

Rigg had nothing to lose in finding out if Grant might be right. It was far from a gamble on his part. His deal with Grant was for forty percent of every new enterprise in town. He had already been paid handsomely for his alliance with

Grant, so if the Grand Plan worked, all the better. Grant may have lost his mind, but his plan was surprisingly sound.

Rigg knew that after he took the fatal shot, Front Street would descend into chaos. No one would notice him in the panic as he slipped out the back door of the Municipal Building, out through the secret back stairs behind the bookcase Grant had built for himself in the mayor's office.

Rigg certainly was not concerned about Chief Edison or his men. They were already positioned too far up Front Street to reach the building in time before he escaped. And even if someone happened to see him run from the building, which was a distinct possibility, he would have a saloon full of witnesses at The Ruby who would swear Rigg had been there the entire time.

The fact that every witness would be a Hancock man would seem convenient to some, but would stand up in any court in the land.

Not that anyone would be making any arrests immediately after Rigg had accomplished his mission, for the assassination was only the first part of Grant's Grand Plan. The second part would come later that night, during something that Grant called the "Purification."

Rigg looked out at the crowd of revelers again. Every square inch of Front Street was filled with spectators jealously guarding their tiny piece of real estate to watch that blowhard Mackey take the oath of office.

Rigg, for his part, was glad of it. He had always been a frustrated showman. He had often wondered if he might have been successful had he followed his fellow Virginian John Wilkes Booth in a career upon the stage.

He only hoped his assassination would be just as obvious but, unlike Booth, end in anonymity.

The crowd below stirred and rose to a roar as Brendan

Mackey, Doc Ridley, and Chief Steve Edison walked out of the Municipal Building and ascended to the stage. That Yankee popinjay Paul Bishop was with them, too. That was no surprise. Dover Station belonged to his company lock, stock, and barrel. He had no doubt Brendan Mackey would be in his pocket, too, if he was not already.

He would not be there long.

Rigg ducked once more behind the balustrade of the turret. He held his rifle loose and listened for the precise moment when the ceremony began.

Then he would strike.

And the new Dover Station would begin to be born.

Jerry Halstead eyed the crowd from his spot on the jailhouse porch. He had done a good job of keeping the porch clear of spectators in general but allowed some of the smaller kids to climb all over it in the hopes of getting a good look at the platform. He doubted any of them cared what was going on, much less understood what was happening. But it was something to see, and kids always liked to be part of things.

With his Winchester on his shoulder, Jerry was glad to see Chief Edison had spread his men around the fringes of the group. The deputies Edison could trust were closer to the platform. He had made sure the Hancock deputies were farther back and on the edges. No sense in tempting fate. The rivalry between the Hancocks and the Mackeys was becoming the stuff of local legend. What better way to cement a legend than taking a shot at their rival's old man as he was sworn in as mayor?

But Jerry had seen enough Hancock men shoot to know they would probably miss even if they were standing right next to them. But they were a mean and stupid bunch, and sometimes, that was enough to put a man down. He was sure Walter Underhill would have attested to that had he still been aboveground.

His killing of a Hancock man at the station a week ago had not won him any friends among the clan, but they had given him plenty of space in the days since. He figured one of them might make a run at him today once the whiskey started pouring and family pride took hold.

Jerry looked to the platform when the crowd began to cheer. Pappy, Doc Ridley, Mr. Bishop, and Chief Edison were walking down the stone steps of the Municipal Building and making their way to the platform.

Pappy looked as proud as a Mexican general. His black morning coat buffeted in the cool breeze blowing along Front Street. Only the white sash he wore with the word "Mayor" stitched into it kept it closed. He had to hold on to his black top hat to keep the wind from carrying it away.

He was glad the town committee had decided against having the stage in front of the Municipal Building. It had to be the gaudiest building Jerry Halstead had ever seen. The round turrets on the corners and the balustrades atop it made it look more like a castle than an office building. Maybe that had been Grant's idea when he had built it? A king surveying his kingdom from his castle.

Now, the word was that he was holed up in The Ruby and well on his way to becoming the town drunk. No one even bothered to talk about him anymore except to remark about how far the mighty had fallen.

As soon as he drank his money away, Jerry bet the Hancocks would throw him out on his ear. He would probably wind up sleeping beneath the back stairs of the very castle he had built for himself.

Jerry looked over the crowd again, wondering if Grant might be there. It was almost impossible to pick out any one face among the mass of people who had packed Front Street for a glimpse at town history.

The crowd roared as the men stepped up onto the platform. He half expected trumpeters to begin playing from the Municipal Building's turrets. Maybe American flags unfurled from the top.

He looked up at them in the hopes Pappy might have asked for that kind of theatrical flair. He would not put it past him.

Instead, Jerry Halstead saw something else.

Something had moved up there.

It could have been a bird landing or a branch blowing in the breeze. But he knew no birds would come near Front Street that day, for the crowd was too noisy. And he knew there were no trees that grew that tall in Dover Station.

Someone was up there.

Jerry looked around the crowd for a path that could get him to the Municipal Building, but even though it was just across the street, the knot of humanity was impossible to get through. He tried to shout a warning to the deputies in front of the building, but his voice was drowned out by the roar of the crowd.

He waved at them to get their attention, but they were too busy craning their necks to get a look at the spectacle on the platform.

No one was looking up at the turret.

Knowing there was nothing else he could do, Jerry brought his Winchester to his shoulder and aimed up at the top of the turret. The building was tall and the angle impossibly steep, but he figured the Winchester should have enough power to at least get close if he fired.

He only hoped he could get close enough if he had to.

Jerry stood rock still, the crowd ignoring him as he aimed as steadily as he could, hoping to God his eyes had been playing tricks on him. That it had been a bird, or a puff of smoke, or nothing at all. He wanted to be wrong but knew he had been right.

Then, one of the children on the porch pulled on his pants leg. "Hey, mister. What're you aiming at?"

Jerry pushed the young boy away with his boot, keeping his aim on the turret. "Get away from me."

"Hey!" called out a man who must have been the boy's father. "You can't kick my son like that." He pulled himself up onto the porch to confront Jerry, who pushed the man away, causing him to fall back into the crowd, who suddenly turned away from the platform to the jailhouse to see what the ruckus was all about.

Jerry cursed and took aim again at the top of the turret.

Now he saw it.

The same thing he had seen before.

A tuft of blond hair blowing in the wind.

And a shape that could only be a man aiming a rifle.

Jerry fired.

The crack of his Winchester echoed loud, too loud for his to be the only gun fired.

The bastard had gotten off a shot after all.

The crowd descended into madness.

Jerry racked in another round and fired again as men and women and children broke into panicked runs all around him. The boardwalk bounced as children jumped off and ran to the arms of their mothers and fathers.

Jerry did not have a target but fired again. Another piece of turret cracked and threw up dust into the air. If he could not hit the rifleman, he could damn near block his shot while Pappy and the others got to safety.

He kept his aim up at the building, half expecting one of Edison's men to take a shot at him. But out of the corner of his eye, amid the screaming and sea of people crashing into each other, he saw three officers run into the building. He hoped they would get inside in time to trap the gunman and put a bullet in him.

Seeing no movement from the turret for several seconds, Jerry decided to wade into the crowd to get to the Municipal Building. He used his Winchester to knock people out of the way. Men and women, he did not have the time to care. He could not allow the gunman to escape into the crowd.

After almost losing his footing several times, Jerry bounded up the stairs of the Municipal Building and skidded to a stop on the marble floor. "It's Jerry Halstead," he yelled, his voice carrying throughout the cavernous building. "Did you get him yet?"

One of Edison's officers stuck his head over the third-floor banister. "Nothing here. No one at all."

"Did you check the roof?"

The man's quick disappearance told Jerry he had not.

Knowing the rifleman could already be on his way out of the building, Jerry ran through the empty courtroom and out the back door next to the judge's chambers. He jumped down the three steps to the ground and looked around for any sign of the gunman fleeing the building.

He did not see anyone with a rifle. All he saw was a herd of people running in all directions along Lee Street.

But he stopped when he saw something on the ground.

The same kind of crater he had just left in the soft dirt when he had jumped down the stairs. And a single set of footprints heading down Lee Street before they were muddled by the hundreds of feet from panicked spectators.

It was a thin trail, but it was the only trail he had, and he decided to follow it.

He leapt onto the boardwalk, out of the fray of people in the street, and moved as quickly as he could through the jostling crowd. He looked all around for anyone who might be holding a rifle close to their side. Someone running. Someone trying not to run. Someone who looked too scared. Someone who did not look scared enough. Anything that might look out of place.

He caught a glimpse of someone in the middle of Lee Street, walking at an even pace as he dodged the frightened people charging toward him. Walking stiffly with his right arm not moving.

Jerry knew the man might have been just another spectator trying to get away from the scene, no different than any of the other people on the street that day.

Except this man had blond hair. And he had to keep flattening it against the wind.

With his left hand.

Because, although Jerry could not see it, he knew the man held a rifle in his right.

He pushed his way to the edge of the boardwalk and brought the Winchester up to his shoulder. "You with the blond hair. Stop!"

But the man did not stop, for Jerry's words were drowned out by the screams and shouts of the frightened people clogging Lee Street.

Then someone either knocked into Jerry or pushed him. He did not know which. All he knew was that he had fallen and had to grab onto someone to keep from falling on his face.

But he had kept hold of the Winchester.

He quickly regained his footing and moved against the tide of humanity to walk in the same direction as the blond man had been headed.

A walk that should have taken him five minutes even at the slowest of strolls had taken him fifteen. He jumped up every so often to try to see the blond man over the heads of the crowd, but only caught glimpses of him now and then still heading north.

Jerry pushed and pulled and shouldered people to the side, jumping up again when he reached the last place where he had spotted the man.

Each time, all he saw was a man who might be him. Maybe. Even if he was the rifleman.

He finally found a clear space on the boardwalk near the last place where he had seen the blond man and rushed for it. Upon climbing it, he held on to the porch post and searched the crowd of heads in the hopes of seeing the man again. But all he saw was the worried and sometimes bloodied faces of people still caught in the throes of panic.

And not a blond head in the bunch.

Jerry had lost him.

He resisted the urge to curse and yell. To punch the porch post. His rage compounding by the second, he looked for someone, anyone, who might be looking to start a fight with the man they called a half-breed.

But as he looked around, none of his tormentors were in sight.

Jerry looked up at the sky and closed his eyes, drawing the air deep into his lungs in a bid to calm himself down. Now was not the time for anger. Now was the time for calm. To think. Because the gunman was still out there, and he was very calm indeed.

And when Jerry opened his eyes again, he found what he was looking for. Not the blond man, but something that told him he had been right all along.

A sign read THE RUBY SALOON.

Of course, this would be the last place he had spotted the blond man. For this was a Hancock saloon. And who better to want Pappy dead than a Hancock man?

CHAPTER 20

The weather might have been cool outside, but inside, Jerry found it was full-on summer.

The packed saloon was thick and humid in the way small spaces tended to get when they were too crowded with drinking men. The place was swamped with people who had just run in from the swearing-in ceremony. All of them were anxious to relate their version of events at the same time, though no one was really listening.

Jerry bumped his way through the tight, crowded space. Some of the men turned to protest but, when they saw the star on his vest and the look in his eye, thought better of it.

The jostling caught the notice of the man in the lookout chair. Although his rifle remained across his lap, Jerry could feel him watching him.

Jerry looked at every head he could see for any trace of the blond man he had just chased up Lee Street.

And when he found it, the man he had been looking for was sitting alone at a table by a thick wooden beam that held up the roof.

The same fair-haired man he had seen strolling around town from time to time for the past week or so.

The man people called Nathan Rigg.

Jerry pushed his way through the crowd toward the table where Rigg was sitting. The closer he got, the clearer it became that the man had just gotten there. He was winded, his clothes were disheveled, and his hair was wild despite his repeated attempts to pat it down with his hand. Thin beads of sweat peppered his brow.

The man was still trying to flatten down his hair when Jerry reached his table.

"The wind's mighty bad out there, isn't it?"

Rigg looked up at him. "Excuse me?"

"Your hair. It got messed up by the wind just now."

Rigg stopped trying to flatten his hair and flashed a smile. "I'm afraid you've had too much to drink, my friend. I haven't left this table all morning."

"That so? You're sweating awfully bad for a man whose been in a nice, cool bar all morning."

"Far from it." Rigg looked at the star pinned to Jerry's vest, but did not comment on it. "I've always been a sucker for sentiment, and despite the fact that I despise every member of the Mackey clan, I took it upon myself to venture out to see the ceremony. How often does a man get to witness history in the making? I had no sooner rounded the corner off Lee Street when I found myself carried backward by a tide of humanity. Why, it's only by the grace of God Himself that I found safe harbor here or I might have been trampled to death."

Jerry watched Rigg smile. He was back in control. "Ever see a man trampled to death by a mob, Deputy? I have, and I assure you it's an ugly sight you won't soon forget."

Rigg seemed to remember himself. "All of this excitement has made me lose my manners. Forgive me for not offering you a drink. You look just about all done in."

Jerry ignored the offer. "You mean you were just off the corner of Lee Street here. No closer to the platform than that?"

Rigg laughed. "Heavens, no. I was taken by a rash impulse to take a look for myself and it almost cost me my life. No, sir. I never got closer than the corner just outside that door."

Jerry Halstead had been watching Rigg the entire time he had been talking. He had all the mannerisms of some Virginian gentlemen he had run into in Texas. The breezy way he spoke. He showed a lot when he spoke, probably charmed a lot of people, too.

Most people were easy to charm, but not Jerry Halstead. He had been charmed enough in his young life to see his way through the show. Families who had promised to adopt him, only never to be seen again. Sheriffs and townspeople who had said they would back him in a gunfight, only to stay back in the jailhouse when the ring finally dropped. Judges who had promised him a slap on the wrist for doing his duty and sent him to prison for three years.

Yes, being gullible had cost Jerry Halstead dearly. It had almost cost him his life. He had learned how to spot the truth and how to smell a lie. The stench of lies coming from Rigg just then was almost overwhelming.

Rigg raised his hand and snapped his fingers to get the barman's attention, only to frown when he had failed to do so. "Fred," he called out. "I'll have another, and my friend here will have—"

Rigg's smile infuriated Jerry.

"Forgive me, Deputy. I forgot to ask what you wanted."

"How about the truth?" Jerry said. "In fact, I'll take a bottle of it. And not from the barman, either. From you."

Rigg casually lowered his right hand. "I'm afraid I don't follow the implication."

"Maybe, but I was the one following you. All the way up Lee Street. All the way from the Municipal Building where you had taken a shot at Pappy."

He gripped the Winchester tightly in his left hand. The crowd in the saloon was too packed to raise it, but he had plenty of room to go to work with his pistol if Rigg gave him cause.

Rigg sat quietly, or as quietly as a man could in the raucous saloon. "I think you have me confused with someone else. Why, I don't think I've fired a gun in some time, and certainly not today. Why would anyone want to shoot at such a charming man like Mayor Mackey?" He laughed. "He's quite the colorful character, isn't he?"

But Jerry was beyond listening. The truth of what he had seen was too clear now to be anything else. He began looking around. "Where'd you stash it?"

"Stash what, Deputy?" Rigg asked. "I believe I'm the only man in this entire saloon more confused than you at the moment."

"The rifle you used. Where—"

Jerry saw a Sharps hanging on two pegs above the back of the bar. That explained the loud boom that had echoed a split second after his own. The kind of sound a fifty-caliber round made when it was fired.

He had to admire Rigg's craftiness. "That's a neat trick you pulled. Hiding it in plain sight for the whole town to see above the bar. Another time, I might even be impressed."

Rigg slumped theatrically in his chair. "Now you have me at a complete loss, sir. I think you may need that drink more than I do. Fred," he yelled out above the din of the crowd, "another one for me and make it a double for my friend here, if you please."

He looked at Jerry. "I'm sorry, Deputy, but I am afraid I've forgotten your name, assuming I ever knew it in the first place."

"The name's Jeremiah Halstead. And my name's not the only thing you've forgotten."

"Oh?" Rigg said. "Enlighten me? What else have I forgotten, sir?"

Jerry looked at the clear table. "You've forgotten your glass."

Rigg's eyes narrowed. "I'm afraid I don't understand."

Though the quick glance he threw at the table told Halstead he understood. He knew he had been caught in a lie. "You can't order another drink if you never had one in the first place. Your table is clear."

Rigg laughed it off. "I suppose one of the girls must've cleared it off."

Jerry kept his eyes on Rigg. "What girls? There's not a woman in this entire place. They're all upstairs working. And it's too crowded for anyone to clear a glass."

Rigg shifted in his seat. "Why do I have a feeling you're working up to making a rather ugly accusation, Deputy Halstead."

"I'm not working up to anything." He was glad his hand was already close to his holster. "I'm stating a fact. You're a liar."

Both men drew their respective Colt Thunderer revolvers.

Later on and in the years that followed, the men who

had been watching what had taken place that early afternoon in The Ruby disagreed on who had drawn first. All of the Hancock men said it was clearly Rigg. Their friends and a few impartial observers said Halstead had edged him out.

None of the men who had seen it happen, though, were willing to stake their life on the claim. The winner was debatable. The fact that it had been close was undeniable.

And so was the fact that, less than a second later, every pistol in the saloon—except his own—was aimed at Jerry Halstead.

Jerry slowly raised his Winchester to his hip and aimed it in the general direction of the men around him.

Except for the sound of hammers being thumbed back, a humid silence fell over the saloon.

Jerry did not budge. "Nathan Rigg, I'm placing you under arrest for the attempted murder of Mayor Mackey."

Rigg flashed an infuriating smile. "I'm afraid you have found yourself at quite a disadvantage, sir. Not only are you outgunned, but every man in this saloon here and now is more than willing to swear that I was here the entire time, save for my brief excursion along Lee Street." He raised his voice for the whole saloon to hear. "Why, I haven't left the premises all morning, have I, boys?"

All the men in The Ruby mumbled some form of agreement.

"Did you hear that, Deputy?" Rigg asked. "A saloon full of unassailable witnesses. Why, I'd even wager a few of them are capable of writing out their statements and even signing their names."

"We're here for you, Colonel," a man called out from the crowd.

But Jerry did not look around at the men pointing guns at him. He did not dare. He was a federal lawman with federal authority. He knew if he faltered now, there would be no way he could live in this town. He also knew his chances of making it out alive if he lowered his gun was slim. Rigg would shoot him and claim self-defense, backed up by a saloon full of witnesses.

Jerry had made his choice when he walked into the saloon. He was willing to live with it or die for it, whatever happened. But however it went, he would be taking Rigg with him. "You can add resisting arrest to the charge. Now get up."

Rigg laughed and soon every man in The Ruby laughed with him.

Rigg may have been laughing, but his eyes were not. "I suppose now is where you threaten to kill me. 'Straight up or over the saddle. Makes no difference to me.' That's Mackey's favorite saying, isn't it? What's yours?"

Jerry held the Colt steady. "Last chance, Rigg."

Jerry heard someone behind him yell, "That's enough! Everyone lowers their weapons right now or my boys start cutting loose on the whole lot of you."

He recognized the voice as belonging to Chief Steve Edison. He heard several Winchesters being cocked and figured he must have brought some of his officers with him.

Jerry heard all of the men in the saloon began uncocking their pistols as they lowered them.

Only Halstead and Rigg were left aiming at each other.

Rigg called out, "How good of you to join us, Chief Edison. I hope your presence will prevent a rather nasty turn of events."

"I told everyone to lower their guns, Rigg," Edison said. "That means you."

"As soon as the deputy here lowers his."

"He's the law," Edison said. "You're not. Put it away."

Rigg slid the Colt back into his shoulder harness and slowly moved his hand away. "Let there be peace."

Jerry heard Edison shove people out of the way to clear a path to him. When he got close, he spoke directly into Halstead's ear.

"Put it away, Jerry. We've got bigger problems now."

Jerry kept the Colt on Rigg. "The bastard shot at Pappy, Ed. There's no way we just let that go."

"No one's letting anything go," Edison whispered. "But now ain't the time. None of us will make it out of here alive if you don't put it away. We'll get him later. He's not going anywhere."

Rigg brought two fingers to his right brow and saluted the chief. "Now I know why Mr. Edison was selected as chief of police. He a smart man, Jerry. One to whom you should listen. You'll live longer if you do."

Jerry still did not lower the Colt.

"Damn it, Halstead." Edison struggled to maintain a whisper. "The town's pulling itself apart right now, and I need every able-bodied man I've got to keep order. This isn't over. It's just over for now."

Jerry gritted his teeth. "Is the mayor alive?"

"He's fine," Edison told him. "Got some scrapes in the panic, but he's alive. He's waiting for us in his office right now. Let's go."

Reluctantly, Jerry slid the Colt back in its holster as quickly as he had drawn it. He lowered the Winchester, too.

Rigg crossed his legs and smirked. "I admire your

choice in pistols, Deputy. The Thunderer has always been a particular favorite of mine."

"You won't have the chance to look at it as long next time."

Jerry let Edison lead him as he backed out of the saloon.

CHAPTER 21

The chaos on Lee Street had quieted down some, except for a large crowd that had gathered in front of The Ruby when word spread about Halstead's standoff with Rigg and the Hancock boys.

Edison's men cleared a path through the spectators to let Halstead and the chief pass. When they had gotten well clear of the crowd, Edison asked, "You mind telling me what you were aiming to do back there besides almost getting yourself killed?"

"Rigg took a shot at Pappy," Jerry said as they threaded their way through the thinning crowd on Lee Street. "He was up in the turret of the Municipal Building with a Sharps. The same damned Sharps that's hanging over the bar back there."

"Are you sure?" Edison asked as he struggled to keep up with him. "Are you sure it was Rigg?"

That was the problem. Jerry *knew* it was him, knew it in his bones, but he could not swear to it. "The gunman had wavy blond hair, just like Rigg. I followed a man with wavy blond hair from the building through the crowd, but I lost him in front of The Ruby." He realized he had not seen him actually enter the saloon, but it was close enough to the truth. "Then I see Rigg sitting there, winded and sweating. He says he was there the whole time, but he's lying. He said he was drinking, but his table didn't have a glass on it."

The more he thought about it, the angrier he got. "He's lying, Ed. He's lying, and I let him go."

"The Ruby's a Hancock saloon, and they answer to Grant," Edison reminded him. "Every man in there's a Hancock man, and there's no way they would've let you walk out of there with Rigg. No way."

But Jerry had not walked into The Ruby expecting to arrest the rifleman. He expected to kill him for trying to kill Pappy. Edison may have been convinced Jerry would have died, but Jerry had been in spots like that before. The Ruby as crowded as it was, he could have shot Rigg and taken down twenty of them before he had to resort to using his bowie. He would have gotten hurt, maybe even shot, but he had figured he had a better-than-even chance to make it out of there alive in the confusion once the shooting started in such a packed room. And even if he did not, at least Rigg would be dead.

But Rigg was alive. Probably buying rounds for the house and laughing about how he got Mackey's deputy to back down. How Edison had saved him and how half-breeds just did not have enough sand for a fight.

"I could've taken him, Ed."

"Well you're not taking him today," Edison told him. "In fact, I'm the one who's taking you. To the Municipal Building. Right now."

Jerry stopped walking, ignoring the people who bumped into him.

Edison stopped, too. He was careful to keep his hand away from his pistols and keep his Winchester at his side.

"I don't like the sound of that," Jerry said. "You taking me in for something, Chief?"

"Of course not," Edison said. "It's just that the town elders want to talk to you about what happened is all."

Jerry started walking again and Edison fell in alongside him. The townspeople had calmed down considerably since the shots rang out and were eager to move out of the way of the lawmen, who appeared to be in a hurry.

"Which elders?" Jerry asked.

"The new mayor for one," Edison told him. "Doc Ridley and Mr. Bishop for another."

"Bishop's not an elder," Jerry said. "He sits behind a desk and makes money."

"He runs the company that runs the town," Edison answered. "Guess that makes him the eldest elder we've got, even over old Pappy."

But Jerry had been led into a room with powerful men after another dustup and had not breathed free air for three years afterward. He did not like the feeling that was beginning to creep into his bones. "When do they want to see me?"

"Immediately if not sooner," Edison said. "Those were Mr. Bishop's exact words."

"He giving you orders now?"

"The mayor agreed. Stands to reason they'd want to talk to you," the chief explained, "seeing as how your shot started the whole thing off."

Jerry started to argue but the words died in his throat. He supposed he had shot first, otherwise Pappy would be dead. "But I wasn't the only one who got off a shot, Ed. Rigg shot, too."

Edison's silence made the feeling creeping into his bones turn into a full-on ache. "You did hear the Sharps go off, didn't you?"

Edison's frown told Jerry all he needed to know. "Let's talk about it up in the mayor's office. It'll be better for everyone if we have the same conversation once. Better for everyone."

When they got closer to the Municipal Building, Jerry stopped at the alley leading back to the old jailhouse. He wanted to point out the spot in the mud where his feet had landed when he had jumped down the stairs. He wanted to point out where the gunman's feet had landed, too.

But all traces had been pounded out by the feet of fleeing citizens.

He needed time. "I'm not going up there, Ed. Not now and not like this."

The chief closed his eyes and lowered his head. "They're up there waiting on us. Let's just get this over with."

But Jerry had no intention of going anywhere. Not just yet. "I need some time to work something through. An hour at most. Tell them I'm shook up. Tell them anything. Just give me an hour. That's all I'm asking."

Edison looked at his men, who had formed a loose circle around them. They looked like they were keeping the townspeople away, but Jerry wondered if they were not also keeping him from leaving, too.

Which was why he decided to try a little humility. "Don't make me say please, Ed. I've had to eat dirt once in public today. Don't make me eat it from you, too."

Edison said, "You've got your hour. But I'll feel better about it if you let some of my boys hang around you to watch your back. I'm gonna have to insist on that."

"To watch my back?" Jerry asked. "Or watch me?"

"Same difference." He ordered two of his men to stay with the deputy to keep him safe, before he walked toward the Municipal Building. "One hour, Jerry. Not a second longer." He touched Halstead's arm. "Now I'm the one saying please."

Jerry began walking back to the old jailhouse. Edison's men followed.

Jerry sat alone behind Mackey's desk, drinking coffee that had gone cold hours ago. He had brewed the pot according to Billy's instructions and, although it was not as good as his uncle's brew, it was still a better pot than he normally made.

For the first time in as long as he could remember, Jerry Halstead felt alone. More alone than he had felt in prison. More alone than he had felt in all of the days he had spent by himself on the trail after he had been released.

He found himself wishing Mackey and Billy were there. Young Sandborne, too. He imagined things would be much different if they were.

But they were in Helena, and he was sitting at a desk that was not his in a town that was not his. Outside, one faction wanted him dead, and the rest despised him for what they believed him to be. Half-breed was only a name to pin on him for what he really was. A stranger. An outsider. Federal badge or no, he was not one of them, and they were lining up against him.

Edison had only heard one shot, and they thought it was his. They thought he panicked and caused a riot.

He had found himself in the same situation three years before in a boomtown called El Paso. The railroad had just come to town, drawing men looking to make their fortune quickly any way they could. Men like young Jeremiah Halstead.

But instead of his fortune, he found himself wearing a tin star as Town Marshal Roy Halbeck's deputy. The marshal's office got a piece of every business in El Paso and, although Jerry knew he would never be rich as a lawman, he was making more money than he had ever dreamed a half-Mexican, half-Anglo boy could.

It was not long before factions began springing up in town, and Halbeck had found himself on the wrong side. A group of businessmen had hired a gunman to kill Halbeck and, after several tries, they succeeded.

The town council was up in arms over the cold-blooded murder and immediately promoted young Halstead to town marshal. They gave him a single mandate: Kill the man who had gunned down Halbeck. Jerry had planned to do that anyway, but having the support of the town made it a bit easier.

Or so he had mistakenly believed.

He did not have any trouble finding Big Dave Farley at the ranch of his employers. After it was over, six men laid dead in the Texas dust with Marshal Halstead the only survivor.

The town elders and the newspapers were quick to praise him for avenging their fallen hero. But the rancher had plenty of friends in town, and despite the assurances of the council, Jerry was arrested by the county sheriff and convicted of six counts of murder. He was supposed to serve twenty-five years but was released after three. The reasons were murky, even to Halstead.

Now, Jerry Halstead found himself with another star pinned to his chest and another room full of powerful men looking to speak with him about something he had done to defend a town. Montana might be a long way from Texas, but powerful men were the same everywhere. They became powerful by using men and throwing them away. Men like Jerry Halstead.

He finished his cup of cold coffee and set it on Mackey's desk. He stood up and drew the bowie knife from the back of his belt as he walked toward the jailhouse door.

He had placed his faith in powerful men once before. He would be damned before he made that same mistake again.

He threw open the jailhouse door and stepped outside, determined to make his own luck or die trying. The same way he had always made his luck. On his own terms.

The two officers Edison had watching him shifted uneasily when they saw him walk out of the jailhouse with the big knife in his hand but did not approach him. He was not coming for them.

He was walking toward the ruined grandstand instead.

CHAPTER 22

Less than an hour later, Jerry Halstead sat next to Chief Edison in the deep leather chairs of the mayor's office of the Municipal Building.

Pappy Mackey sat behind the big desk with an enormous painting of Dover Station above his head. His top hat and sash were nowhere in sight, and he stroked his beard while Mr. Bishop ranted.

"A mess," the businessman said as he paced back and forth in front of the window overlooking Front Street. "An absolute, unmitigated disaster. An embarrassment that has set this town back at least ten years."

"Paul," Pappy said. "It's been a long day for everyone, and it ain't even past lunchtime yet. Yellin' about it won't make it any better."

Bishop turned on him. "There's a time for whispering, Brendan, and a time for yelling. The *Record*'s reporters tell me ten people were trampled to death and dozens more were injured. Dozens! If this isn't a time for yelling, then I don't know what is."

Bishop glared at Jerry, who had decided it was best to look at the painting. He was not accustomed to having people yell at him. He was not fond of it, either. "Well, Deputy Halstead, what do you have to say for yourself?"

Jerry knew Bishop was in no mood for details, so he kept it simple. "I saw a blond-headed man with a Sharps rifle up in the turret of this building. I saw him aiming down at you people on the platform. I shot at him just as he shot at all of you."

Bishop seemed to be waiting for more and grew frustrated when more did not come. "That's it? That's your answer?"

Jerry was getting annoyed by his tone. "That's what started everything, so yeah, that's my answer."

"And what is your answer for the fact that none of Chief Edison's men found anyone up in the turret, even though they were up there in a matter of seconds?"

"Not seconds," Jerry said. "They got here as fast as they could, but the crowd held them up. It took them a minute or two to get in here. It took me even longer to make it through that mess. That's plenty of time for a gunman to get clear of a building."

"Assuming there was any gunman at all," Bishop sniffed.

"My boys did find boot prints up there," Edison said. "I saw them, too, and they looked mighty fresh."

Bishop did not look convinced. "You sure they weren't from your men, Chief? Are you willing to stake your job on that?"

Edison looked away. "They looked fresh, but I'm no expert. No one is."

"That's just wonderful!" Bishop yelled. "I've got dozens of people hurt and killed and all I can get from you is muddy footprints you think are 'mighty fresh.'"

Jerry looked at Bishop, meeting his glare. "There was a gunman, mister, or I wouldn't have fired. I'm not one for cutting loose with a Winchester in crowds unless I have a reason."

"Is that so?" Bishop asked. "Then how do you account for the fact that no one else appears to have seen this gunman you claim was in the turret?" He looked at Edison. "Any of your men see a man with a rifle up there, Chief?"

Edison shifted uneasily in his seat. "My men were looking at the crowd. We were afraid of the Hancocks trying to take a shot at Pappy. We weren't paying much attention to the rooftops."

Bishop turned on Jerry. "Seems like you're the only one who saw anyone on that turret, Deputy Halstead."

Jerry went back to looking at the painting. "I can't account for what other people saw or didn't see. I only know what I saw. A blond man in the turret with a rifle. A Sharps, from the sound of it."

"A sound only you seem to have heard, because I only heard one shot," Bishop said. "From a Winchester. Your Winchester."

Jerry's temper slipped out from under him. "They got a lot of Winchesters back in Manhattan, Mr. Bishop? Because I'm betting they don't, so I figure you couldn't tell the difference between a rifle shot and a shotgun blast. Well I do know the difference, and I'm telling you it was a Sharps."

Bishop clasped his hands behind him. "I may not be able to tell the difference, Deputy Halstead, but there are plenty of people in town who can. Including Chief Edison here. No one heard two shots. They only heard one. One that came from your rifle. How can you explain that?"

"Enough," Pappy said from behind his desk. "If Jerry said he saw a rifleman, then he saw a rifleman. His word is good enough for me."

Bishop looked at the mayor. "Brendan, I think you're allowing your friendship with the deputy's late father to cloud your judgment here."

Pappy stopped stroking his beard. "My friendship with Sim isn't clouding anything. A man can't help who his father is, good or bad. My boy would tell you that if he was here. And if he was here, he'd be tellin' you he knows and trusts Jerry with his life like I trust him with mine. He trusted him enough to leave him here to keep an eye on the Hancocks instead of taking him to Helena with him where he could've done more good. If Aaron trusts him, then so do I."

Pappy went back to absently stroking his beard. "If he says there was a man with a rifle in the turret, that's good enough for me. I don't know how he got away, but he did. And if he said there were two shots, then there were."

"Even though you didn't hear them, either," Bishop said.

"I was a bit busy at the time," Pappy fired back. "And so were you. The crowd cheerin' like that. How could we know? The shot could've gone wide."

Bishop looked at Jerry. "Or there wasn't a second shot at all. Maybe the deputy here just panicked."

Jerry had been hoping it would not come to this. He had been hoping his word would be enough, but it obviously was not. He decided it was time to lay his cards on the table.

He dug into his shirt pocket, pulled out a slug, and tossed it on Pappy's desk. "To use one of your phrases, Mr. Bishop, how do you explain that?"

Edison and Pappy pitched forward in their chairs to get a closer look at the lump of lead on the desk.

"Looks like a bullet to me," Pappy said. "Fifty-caliber to my eyes."

Edison picked up the leaden bullet head in his fingers and examined it as if it was a gold nugget. He looked at Jerry. "Where'd you get this?"

"I dug it out of the mud in front of the platform," Jerry told them. "It took a lot of prodding with my bowie to find it, but I did. Just to the left of where all of you were standing." He looked at Bishop. "The shot went wide when I shot at him."

Pappy sat back in his chair. "Well, it sure looks like Jerry was tellin' the truth, just like I said he was."

Edison said nothing, examining the bullet instead.

Bishop did not bother looking at it. "How convenient. He probably placed it there to cover himself."

Jerry felt his anger beginning to build and it took everything he had to remain in his chair. "And just how the hell could I have done that?"

Bishop shrugged. "You could have planted it to support your story."

Jerry would have laughed if it was not so ridiculous. "That's right, Bishop. We've got a whole box of old fifty-caliber slugs just sitting in a sack over at the jailhouse. I tucked it in my pocket and brought it over here just to satisfy you."

Edison gently placed the slug back on Pappy's desk. "I think you owe the deputy an apology, Mr. Bishop, and so do I. There's no way he could've planted that. A spent round up on the turret? That's easy. But to fake this, he would've had to grab a Sharps and fire it into the thoroughfare. My men were watching him the whole time, so that leaves only one conclusion. There was someone up there, and Jerry saved our lives."

Edison extended his hand to Jerry. "I'm sorry for not backin' you stronger."

Jerry shook his hand as Bishop fumed. "He could've fired it days ago and palmed it, claiming he found it just now."

"Why would he do that?" Edison said before Jerry could answer. "He had no cause to want any bloodshed today."

Bishop surprised him by having an answer ready. "He had a run-in with the Hancocks at the station a few days ago. Killed one of them. Probably wants to pin this on them."

Jerry sprang out of his chair and faced the businessman. "You taking the Hancock clan's part already, Bishop?"

Bishop took a step toward Jerry, his hands still clasped behind him. "I want that bunch wiped from the streets of Dover Station forever. Every last one of them. But the bad blood between you and that family is no secret. And, according to Chief Edison here, he narrowly saved your life today when he pulled you away from Nathan Rigg at The Ruby."

"I said I pulled him out of there," Edison said. "Never said I saved his life."

"But you did just the same." Bishop pointed at the slug on Pappy's desk. "That may very well be the evidence you claim it is, Deputy. It may not be. I don't know. But I do know we've got at least ten people trampled to death and dozens more hurt and dying. I know that word of what happened here today will be in every paper in the territory by this time tomorrow. And, within a week, every paper in the country. That means New York. That means Mr. Rice and Mr. Van Dorn will be very upset, which means I'll be upset. They may reconsider their investment in this town, which would cause irreparable damage to my career and reputation."

Jerry finally saw the truth. "You don't care about the dead and the dying, do you? You only care about yourself."

"I care about what happens to this town!" Bishop yelled. "I care about the investment my company has made here. I care about my betters calling me home and abandoning this place to the likes of Grant and the Hancocks. And I don't want that to happen. None of us do."

He took another step toward Jerry, his hands still behind his back. "So no, Deputy Halstead. I don't just care about my career. I'll always be able to find employment elsewhere. But I didn't come all the way out here from New York City just because I was told to. I came here because I wanted to help build something that lasts. And what happened here today puts all of that in grave danger."

Pappy eased out from behind his desk and laid a hand on Bishop's shoulder, breaking the tension in the room. "What happened here today was a tragedy, but not of Jerry's doin'. Lay the blame at the feet of those behind it. The same people who've been tryin' to undo all that good work you just talked about. James Grant and the Hancock clan. And, while you're at it, you might want to thank Jerry here for savin' your life."

Bishop unclasped his hands from behind him and let them drop at his sides. For the first time since he had walked into the office, Jerry thought Bishop looked exhausted and much older than he really was.

"That's the problem, Brendan," Bishop said. "It's not up to me to lay this at anyone's feet. I'm not the sheriff or the chief of police or a judge." He looked at Jerry. "And no, I don't really think you planted that slug in the dirt, Deputy, but I'm an attorney by training. I don't think you knew that about me. I have a habit of asking questions, even the most wild, baseless questions, because I need to be ready to answer them. And everything I said here today will be repeated in every saloon and every parlor and around every dining table in town, so we need to be ready to answer that kind of talk when it starts. Because, if we don't, it'll take on a life of its own that not even I will be able to stop."

Bishop let out a long breath. "Now, if you gentlemen will excuse me, I have a telegram I need to send to Mr. Rice about what happened here today, followed by a detailed report that will be carried back to New York on the next train."

He walked around Jerry and Edison but stopped when he placed his hand on the office door. "I'm not going to apologize for what I said here today, gentlemen, but I'm grateful to Deputy Halstead for probably saving our lives. Now, let's pray I can find a way to save this town."

He opened the door and closed it quietly behind him.

The two lawmen sat again as soon as Bishop left the office.

Pappy sat on the corner of his desk. "Damned mess, boyos. The lot of it."

"I want you protected," Edison said to Pappy. "I'll have five of my men guarding you every minute of the day from now on."

"You'll do no such thing." He opened the cigar box on his desk and selected a cigar. He motioned for Edison and Jerry to take one, too, but neither felt much like smoking. "I'm the mayor of this town now, and I can't run things behind a line of gunmen. I do that, I'm no different than that ninny Grant."

"Someone tried to kill you today," Jerry said. "If you don't want Ed's men around, then let me watch you."

"As if I could stop you." Pappy bit off the end of his cigar and spat it into the cuspidor beside his desk. "But I have a feelin' you boys'll be plenty busy with other things for the time bein'. The Hancocks don't like me bein' mayor, and they'll be lookin' to raise as much hell as they can."

He thumbed a match alive and brought the flame to his cigar. He looked at Jerry as the flame took. "You really think Rigg was the one who tried to shoot me?"

"I'm sure of it." Jerry punched the arm of his chair. "But I didn't see his face, so I can't swear to it in court."

Pappy waved the match dead and dropped it in the cuspidor as he pushed himself off the desk and walked to the window. "All the more reason why we should keep this out of a courtroom, wouldn't you say?"

Edison and Jerry traded glances before the chief said, "You mean you want me and my boys to take on the Hancocks?"

Pappy parted the heavy drapes and looked out on the ruin that was Front Street. "No, Stephen. I want you to take them down once and for all."

Pappy puffed on his cigar as he looked out the window. "Good name, Stephen. Patron saint of horses and coffin makers. Both'll come in handy with the work that's before us now. Got a church to him in Ballykilmore back in the old country."

He glanced back at the lawmen. "Know the best thing to come out of Ballykilmore? The road to Dublin." He laughed at his own bad joke. "Gets me every time."

Edison did not laugh. "What you want will mean more men."

"Hire them." He took a long puff on his cigar. "Hire as

many as you need. Just make sure they're good and know what they're hired to do."

Edison grinned. "Don't worry. Grant didn't hire me because I'm pretty. They'll be killers, every one of them. I can have them here within a week."

Pappy nodded. "See to it, then."

But Jerry had shorter goals in mind. "The Hancocks will be coming after you a lot sooner than a week, Pappy. I won't let that happen."

Brendan Mackey went back to looking out the window again. "The whole Rebel army tried to kill me and Old Sherman once and look at where it got them. We burned Atlanta down."

He looked back at Jerry and winked. "Don't worry, son. I'm not so easy to kill. But we'll kill them for what they did here today, won't we, boys?"

CHAPTER 23

Grant placed the coffee cup back in its saucer before he threw it at Rigg. "You missed."

"Just barely," the Virginian said. "It won't happen again."

Mad Nellie Hancock sat quietly in the corner, slumped in her chair as she sipped a mug of beer.

Grant balled a fist and brought it slowly down on the table. Rigg's calmness could be infuriating sometimes, but he dared not lose his temper. Not in front of the likes of the Hancock crone.

"You aren't getting forty percent to miss, Rigg, and you aren't getting forty percent for 'barely.' You're getting forty percent to succeed. Now Mackey's guard is up. He'll have men around him constantly. If you had killed him like you were supposed to, his death would have been lost in the fog of all that happened. We'll turn him into a martyr if we kill him now. You know what they do to martyrs, Nathan. They build churches to them."

He made a conscious effort to open his fist. There was a time for anger and this was not it. "I needed that old man dead so I could put my plan in place. Now, the Purification will look too obvious. Too naked."

"It's my experience that people are embarrassed by nudity, Mr. Grant. They look at it when they see it, but are quick to look away out of modesty." Rigg grinned. "At least outside of a whorehouse."

Grant had finally had enough of Rigg's smugness. "Everything was supposed to happen in the aftermath of the assassination! How will it look now if I put my plan into action?"

"Just like it would have if Pappy was lying on the mortician's worktable," Rigg said. "Nothing needs to stop. If anything, it should go on exactly as you planned. No one will remember when it started or how. They'll be too taken by what happened to care, and you'll be too powerful for them to dare question you by then."

Grant ran his hands over the arms of his chair. Perhaps Rigg was right. Perhaps his plans were not ruined after all. "You really think we can still pull it off like we planned?"

"Like *you* planned, Mr. Grant. And yes, I do." He glanced back at Nellie, who was sipping her beer like it was warm milk. "Madam Hancock, are you still ready to proceed?"

She looked up as if awoken from a sleep. "What'd you just say to me?"

"Are your people ready to start?"

"I've got my boys all over town, boss man," Nellie slurred. "One nod from you and I'll set them to work, so long as you promise none of my places get lost in the goings-on. I'll need your word on that now."

"You have it, my good woman." Rigg casually opened his hands as he looked at Grant. "See? No harm done. At least, not until you give the order.

Grant suddenly began to wonder if this was a good idea. He was placing the fate of his future in a windbag dandy and a drunken crone in charge of an inbred horde of mongrels. But men had forged empires with less.

A feeling of excitement sparked deep in Grant's belly. Perhaps all was not lost after all.

He pulled out his pocket watch and saw it was half-past three. "Spread the word, both of you. Have them start at six. A good hour, six." He closed the watch and slid it back into his vest pocket. "Yes, a very good hour indeed. A good hour for the Purification to begin."

Had he not been so consumed by his own thoughts, Grant would have seen the look of concern on Rigg's face.

Despite his best efforts and a full pot of coffee, Jerry Halstead struggled to stay awake.

He had intentionally selected the least comfortable chair in the Mackey General Store to stand guard while the town's newest mayor slept in the back room.

But the events of the day were finally catching up to him, and he found himself nodding off several times.

A shotgun blast and a bloodcurdling scream were enough to bring him to his feet. They were followed by several more yells and gunshots.

He scrambled behind the counter, grabbed the coach gun he had stashed there, and placed it on the display case. He had taken care to stash several rifles throughout the store in case he and Pappy needed them.

He set his Winchester against the counter beside him and aimed the sawed-off shotgun at the door. The scream and gunshots might be a Hancock distraction designed to bring him outside to investigate, but he was not going anywhere.

He and Pappy had spent the better part of the afternoon

nailing all of the other doors in the general store shut, even the loading door in the back. If trouble came, it would come through the front door.

He had no intention of walking into a trap. He had every intention of killing anyone who kicked down the store's front door.

He thumbed back the hammers of both barrels when he heard someone pounding on the door. "Jerry!" a familiar voice called out. "It's Steve. I mean Ed. Open up, quick!"

"How do I know it's really you?" It sounded like the chief, but he had to be sure. "What did I show you today?"

"A slug from Front Street," the voice called back. "Open up, damn it. There's trouble. Bad trouble."

Deciding it really was Edison, he left the coach gun on the counter and grabbed his Winchester as he rushed to the door. He found the police chief outside with five of his men behind him. All of them looked nervous.

"What's wrong?"

"All hell has broken loose on the north end of town," Edison told him. "We've got a riot on our hands. Fistfights, looting, the works. Everyone's been drinking since this morning and they're goin' wild. A bunch of my men are pinned down in the Campbell Arms and need our help."

Jerry turned when he heard a noise behind him. Pappy was trudging out of his bedroom at the back of the store in his faded long underwear. "How bad is it?"

"Plenty bad," Edison told him. "Ten of my men are holed up in the Campbell Arms holding back a crowd, but another group is smashing everything in sight. There's talk of raising a group to hang Mad Nellie Hancock for what happened today."

But Jerry did not believe it. "The Hancocks run the

north end of town. No one's looking to hang that hag. They're trying to draw us out."

"Whatever it is," Edison said, "I've got most of my men trapped and only five to try to get them out. I need you, Jerry."

"And you'll have him." Pappy pushed the deputy toward the door. "Go with them, boy." He grabbed the coach gun from the counter and began hurrying back toward his room. "I'll be along in a minute."

Jerry did not like the idea of leaving Pappy alone. "I'll wait for you."

"Those boys in the hotel don't have that much time," Pappy yelled. "We haven't a moment to lose. Now move! That's an order. Don't worry. I'll be right behind you."

Jerry still did not want to leave Pappy alone, but knew the trapped officers were the only hope the town had to keep it from tearing itself apart. "You're sure?"

"I haven't needed a nursemaid in sixty years," Pappy said. "Now get goin' like I told ya!"

Jerry held off as long as he could, hoping Pappy would be ready, but the shouts and gunfire had erupted into a low thunder echoing through the streets. He knew every second counted.

"Hurry up, then!" he shouted back before joining Edison and his men as they ran up Front Street toward the sounds of chaos.

Pappy tossed the coach gun on the mess of bedclothes as he pulled up his pants and slid the suspenders over his shoulders. He sat on the edge of the bed, fumbling to pull on his boots. The rush of excitement was pumping hard through his veins. He hated the idea of what was happening, but the old soldier in him still craved the thrill of action that awaited him. *Just like the war.*

He froze when a voice from inside the store said, "I thought they'd never leave."

Pappy's head snapped around and he saw a stranger standing in the doorway of his bedroom. It was not Rigg, but one of the men who had been with him in the hotel lobby in Helena.

Pappy could not see well in the low light of his room, but could see more men in the store behind him.

"Who are you?" was all Pappy could think to say.

"To you?" the man grinned. "Death. Yes, sir. Nothing more pitiful on God's green earth than the sight of a helpless old man in his drawers. A pitiful sight to behold indeed."

The man's eyes widened when Pappy raised the coach gun that had been hidden among the sheets. "Behold this."

He fired. Both barrels caught the man in the chest, sending him flying back into the store.

Pappy dropped the empty shotgun and rolled across the bed as gunshots began ringing out from the store. Round after round struck the wall and floor around his bed. He ignored the fire burning in his calf as he dove for the door and slammed it shut. More bullets slammed into the door. He had just managed to throw the bolt before his leg gave way.

Slumped against the side of the doorway, he looked down at his leg and saw a gaping wound in his left calf. He almost cried out when he saw blood pouring from the place where his heel used to be.

The gunfire stopped as he caught the unmistakable smell of what every shop owner in the world feared most.

Smoke.

The bastards planned on burning him out if they could not kill him outright.

He eyed the Winchester that Jerry had given him to keep in his room. As bullets began to pierce the door, he knew that rifle was his only hope. He tried to get to his feet, but the pain in his leg and foot was too great. He knew if he tried to stand again, he would black out from the pain and die in the fire.

He crawled to the bed and used all of his strength to pull himself up. With one good leg under him, he hopped over to the dresser and grabbed hold of the rifle. He put all of his weight against the dresser in a bid to move it so he could block the door. But with only one good leg under him, the task was impossible.

And the smoke from outside was getting thicker and beginning to roll under the door.

The store he had built with his own two hands was burning around him.

It was at that exact moment that Brendan Mackey knew he had a choice. He could leave this world as a cowering old man, either gunned down in the corner of his bedroom and found choked to death by the smoke, or he could leave this world the way his dear old mother had told him he had come into it, kicking and screaming with everything he had.

In the end, he realized he had no choice at all.

Using the Winchester as a poor cane, Pappy hobbled to the door. He managed to keep his balance, even as a bullet pierced the door and caught him in the left shoulder.

He paused beside the door a moment to catch his breath. This was not the end he had envisioned. Not on the long, interminable boat ride from Ireland. Not at Rocky Face Ridge. Not at Adairsville. Not when he had fought the very land itself to help build what had become Dover Station.

It may not have been the end he had planned for, but

it was the only one he had. Might as well make the most of it.

He slid the bolt aside and threw the door open. He screamed the name of the one thing in the world that meant everything to him. Words he had never been able to bring himself to voice before.

"I love you, Aaron!"

With that, Brendan Mackey stumbled into the smoke and gunfire, brought up his rifle, and killed the first man he saw.

CHAPTER 24

From the cover of an overturned wagon on the north end of town, Jerry Halstead shot a man who had charged at him brandishing a chair leg. Edison covered him as he quickly reloaded his Colt.

"They're thicker than flies," Edison said as he shot a man who was about to throw another flaming bottle of whiskey at the Campbell Arms. The top floor of the hotel was already engulfed in fire. Flames lapped out the broken windows and climbed up at the roof.

His Colt reloaded, Jerry holstered the pistol and grabbed up his Winchester. The mob in front of them had finally been pushed back close enough to Lee Street for Edison's men to start making their way out of the hotel. The ten men dashed out the front door and joined Edison and the other deputies behind the overturned wagon.

Jerry took careful aim at the center of the mob and fired. A man cried out as he spun around and fell to the ground. The mob turned toward the direction of gunfire and, now that they had re-formed, howled as they ran toward their position.

All fifteen men were in place by then and opened up

on the crowd. Their rifles cut down dozens of men in one volley. The crowd quickly ducked and broke at a dead run back toward Lee Street.

"We've got 'em turned, boys!" Edison cheered before turning to one of the men who had been trapped in the hotel. "You ready to get back some of your own?"

"Just say where, boss."

"Right here and now. Take five of you and head down the next street. Hit them on Lee Street from the side, but don't get boxed in again. Fall back to Front Street if you need to. We'll hit them from the north end and finish them off."

The men took off in the direction where Edison had ordered them to go.

Jerry had never seen action like this before, so he was more than happy to let Edison take the lead. "Where do you want the rest of us?"

"With me. Let's keep pushing them back toward Lee Street," Edison said. "We'll keep them boxed in over there."

Jerry followed Edison as he and his ten men broke cover and ran toward the head of Lee Street. They cut down a few stragglers who had fallen behind the main body of the mob like they were stepping on bugs.

One man brandished a knife, but Edison shot him dead before he got close enough to use it.

Another man popped out from a storefront and charged Jerry from the side. Jerry slammed him in the face with the butt of his Winchester, stopping him cold. Another swipe of the butt connected with the man's jaw and put him down for good.

By the time he caught up with Edison and his men, they had already formed a line that stretched across Lee Street. Their open brown dusters billowed in the breeze.

Jerry looked down Lee Street and caught a glimpse of what he had always envisioned hell would look like.

The street was packed with people breaking everything there was to break and shooting at everything there was to shoot. Every storefront he could see had been shattered and its contents pulled out into the street. The boardwalk was littered with clothing and baskets and broken glass.

People who had been caught in the fray, or those who had been part of it, were slumped against buildings and in the street. No building had escaped the wrath of the mob except one.

The Ruby stood as untouched as the day it had first opened. A few Hancock men stood guard from the second-floor balcony, looking down at the scene the way one might watch a prizefight.

That was when Jerry's deepest suspicions had been confirmed. The Hancocks had to have been behind all of this. Grant had probably planned it, just as he had planned on shooting Pappy.

The thought of raising his rifle and cutting down the men on the balcony where they stood suddenly seemed like a wonderful idea. He had no doubt The Ruby was packed with Hancock men who would be quick to finish him off, but suddenly, that did not matter.

The waste, the death, the bloodshed they had caused that day overwhelmed him, and killing as many of them as possible was the only thing that made sense to him, even if it cost him his own life.

Edison's voice from the center of the line of gunmen snapped him out of it. "Boys, we weren't lawmen when we got here, and we ain't lawmen tonight. Not after this. Let's show these animals what the Edison gang is all about."

The men raised their rifles in unison and began firing

into the crowd as they began to move down Lee Street at a slow, measured walk.

Jerry wanted to follow them. He wanted to join in the killing. He wanted to help them match blood for blood. Hate for hate.

But in that moment, he found himself rooted to the ground where he stood as if he was chained there. For over the shouts and screams and gunfire, he could have sworn he heard a high-pitched cackle come from The Ruby. The same cackle he had heard in the graveyard all those months ago, the day they had laid Walter Underhill in his grave.

The cackle of Mad Nellie Hancock.

And as he watched Edison lead his men on their murderous walk down Lee Street, Jerry Halstead saw something else. Something that he knew could only be one thing, but his mind was too slow to understand.

Flames shooting high into the Montana night like a dark sunrise, the darkest sunrise he could imagine. Flames rising from the Dover Station General Store and Mercantile.

"Oh God. Pappy."

He broke back toward Front Street and ran faster than he ever run before.

The heat from the burning store laid Jerry Halstead flat in the middle of the street.

About a dozen townspeople had gathered to throw buckets of water on the building, but they could not get close. Jerry wondered where the fire brigade wagon was, but he knew it would not come.

It was the same overturned wagon they had used for cover in front of The Campbell Arms.

And although there was no way for him to know for

certain, he knew Pappy was still in there, somewhere among the flames.

He slowly got to his feet, leaving his rifle on the buckled mud of Front Street and began to pull off his shirt. He would wrap it around his face and run into the building. Maybe Pappy was still in there, in a closet maybe, or a cellar though he had no idea if the store even had a cellar. He did not know anything, and that was the problem. He had to know for certain.

He had just pulled his shirttails free and was about to cover his face when he felt a bony hand grip his arm. He brought his free hand back to strike, but lowered it when he saw it was Doc Ridley. His thin face was blackened from the smoke. A thin trickle of blood flowed from a deep cut in his scalp.

"Don't, son. Don't. It's no use. I already tried to get in as soon as I saw the flames. It was too hot then and it's much worse now."

His hand fell away from Jerry's arm and dropped to his side. He looked around him and Jerry did, too. Everywhere he looked, fire danced in the darkness. "It's gone, son. It's all gone. Everything we did. All that we built. All gone. Ashes to ashes. Dust unto the dust."

Doc Ridley looked at the flames that reached ever higher into the night. Jerry realized that for all his skill, for all of his bravery, he had no choice but to stand there and watch along with him.

"He's gone," Doc Ridley whispered among the shouts of the dying and the killing. "Brendan Mackey is dead. He was supposed to be indestructible. He was a force of nature. He can't be gone but—." He raised a trembling hand to his mouth. "My God. My God."

He was sobbing when Jerry watched him walk away from the flames.

The ammunition in the store caught fire and exploded. The sudden burst of heat and force launched Jerry backward through the air until he found himself on his backside in the middle of the thoroughfare.

He wanted to get up. He wanted to make one last run at the burning building. He wanted to believe Pappy still had a chance. Doc Ridley was right. The man was a force of nature. The man was tough.

But for all of his toughness, Pappy was still just a man. And no man could survive that. Not even Brendan Mackey.

Jeremiah Halstead drew his knees up close to his chin, hung his head, and wept.

CHAPTER 25

Billy sat up in bed when he heard someone knocking on his hotel room door. The Creole woman lying next to him—whose name he could not remember if he had ever known it at all—was still too drunk from the previous evening to stir.

Billy sat on the edge of the bed and reached for his pants as the knocking turned into pounding.

"Damn it, Sunday." Billy recognized it as Judge Forester's voice. "I know you're in there. Open this door right now. This is a matter of vital importance."

The judge? Billy buttoned his pants and pulled his braces over his shoulders as he paddled barefoot to the door. He pulled the Colt from his gun belt hanging over a chair. No sense in being careless.

Judge Forester whisked off his hat as he pushed his way into Billy's room before the deputy had a chance to fully open it. Billy quickly shut the door behind him in case someone had forced the jurist to set him up at gunpoint. With Grant on the loose and vengeful as he was, Billy saw no harm in an abundance of caution.

"What's the urgency, your honor?"

"I have news." Then Forester caught sight of the sleeping Creole woman in his bed. Based on his expression, it was clear to Billy that Forester recognized her. Billy imagined he had been a customer of hers from time to time.

The judge took his eyes away from the soiled dove in Billy's bed. "I need you to sit down, Deputy, because I'm afraid what I've come here to tell you is going to come as a shock."

But Billy did not sit down. "Is it Aaron?"

Forester's chins wagged as he shook his head. "Dover Station had a riot last night. A bad one. The worst this territory has ever seen."

Billy thought of Jerry and of Edison and of Pappy and wondered what had happened to them. "How bad was it?"

"Bad. About fifty people killed. Nearly every businesses and home burned out from what I've been told. The governor is waiting for another telegram this morning once Chief Edison has had a chance to survey the damage properly."

Forester cleared his throat. "Brendan Mackey was killed in a fire that broke out in his store."

Billy heard the words. He understood everything the judge had just told him. But the true meaning of those words had failed to reach him.

It was the same kind of distance he had experienced with people who had tried to describe the ocean to him over the years. He could not grasp the enormity of something so large without seeing it for himself. He had no scale to appreciate something so large.

Billy Sunday had always known Pappy would die. He was a man, after all, and all men ultimately died. But Pappy had always been more than a man to him. More in every sense of the word. Just like he knew the ocean existed although he had never seen it, he knew death would one day come for Pappy. He just never thought he would see it. And now that it had happened, he did not quite know what to say.

"You said it was a fire?" was all that came to mind.

"One that was still smoldering as of an hour ago when the last telegram came through," Forester told him. "The ammunition he sold blew up and caused the fire to jump Front Street and Lee Street. Burned down a good portion of the town, or so they think. Like I said, they'll be giving more definite reports once the sun's up. I'll pass along every bit of information to you as soon as I get them."

Dover Station burned. Pappy dead. It did not seem possible. Not all at once. Not after all the town had survived. Something else did not make sense, either.

He looked at Forester. "Why are you telling me this? Does Aaron know?"

Judge Forester once more shook his head. "Everyone who knows is too afraid to tell him. No way of knowing how a man will react when he learns his daddy's dead. I knew they liked to fight with each other, but it was also clear to me that they were very close." He looked down at the hat in his hands. "I figured you should be the one to tell him, Billy. It just didn't seem right for anyone else to do it."

Billy had pegged the judge to be a lot of things, but thoughtful had not been one of them. "I'll get dressed and tell him right now. He needs to know this right away."

Forester remained where he was while Billy got dressed. "I wanted to tell you about all of this first for another reason. Part of it is selfish, I'll admit, but part of it is for Aaron's own good."

Billy pulled his shirt over his head and began tucking it into his pants. "Can't say as I follow you, your honor."

"I think you do," the judge said. "You know Aaron Mackey better than anyone, so you know what he's capable of doing once he finds out his father burned to death in a riot. That man's got hellfire in his blood, Deputy, and I need you to keep a tight grip on him. Not just for me, but for his own good, too."

"You've got a point there." Billy pulled on his boots. "I know Aaron better than any man alive. Even better than Pappy did. Maybe even better than his wife does, so you can take it as gospel when I tell you that no one can stop Aaron from doing what he sets out to do. I can try to move him in a certain direction. Katherine, too, maybe better than me now, but he's not going to let this go, your honor. I imagine Grant was behind the trouble in Dover Station somehow, and I figure Aaron will come to the same conclusion. He'll want Grant to answer for that, either in your court or his own."

"That's why I was hoping you might be able to move him a little," Forester tried. "Move him to let the law take its course in this matter. It's too soon to know what really happened yet. Maybe Grant is dead, too. Maybe he played a role in what happened. Either way, we'll probably know more by the time Aaron boards the train to go bury his father."

Billy tucked in his shirt tails. "He'll be going as soon as possible. There won't be moving him off that score. And don't forget he's the law in this territory, because he won't be forgetting it."

Forester bristled. "He's not the law, only part of it!" The

Creole woman stirred, and he quickly lowered his voice. "And he only has his badge because I allowed him to have it. I can unpin it as quickly as I pinned it on."

Billy grabbed his gun belt and wrapped it around his waist. "The president gave him that star, your honor, not you. And even if you take it from him, it won't make much of a difference. We'll be heading to Dover Station as soon as he's of a mind to go. Sooner rather than later, I'd imagine. And when he goes, I'm going with him, even if that means going against you."

"I'm not a fool, Sunday," Forester said. "I know I can't stop him, and I don't think any man in town would try. Not even Lynch. But I'm afraid of what he'll do once he gets to Dover. He's a man capable of raising hell when he has a mind to, and I'm praying to God you know how to keep him from doing that."

Billy buckled his gun belt. "I've never found a way of telling Aaron what to do. Never even tried. But I'll do my best to keep him safe, same as I've been doing for the past ten years. Didn't need you asking me to do it, either."

Forester surprised him when he grabbed Billy's arm. "Damn it, Deputy. I don't want to have to hang him for what he's liable to do to Grant in a fit of rage."

Billy looked at the judge's hand until he had the sense to remove it from his arm. Then Billy walked to the door. "You won't hang Aaron Mackey, your honor. No need to worry about that."

Forester fidgeted with his hat. "I can't say that I like how you said that, Deputy."

Billy moved to the door. "No reason not to like the truth, Judge."

* * *

Billy closed the door behind him and walked down the hall and up the stairs that led up to Aaron's room. Aaron and Katherine's room. The bridal suite they had called home ever since the day they had been married about a month before. Since Mr. and Mrs. Aaron Mackey now owned the hotel, he imagined ownership had its privileges.

Billy had sensed a shift in Aaron in the past month, even when they had gone to arrest Colburn. He had lost a certain amount of restlessness that had always been in him. He seemed more at peace with himself and who he was. Aaron was just a touch slower to anger and a little easier to talk to, even for Billy. He supposed he had Katherine to thank for that. He was almost like the Aaron he had known in the cavalry. The strong, confident man who could lead others into battle against impossible odds. The kind of leader who could make a man forget his fear of losing his hair to an Apache blade because Aaron Mackey was in charge.

And Billy knew all of that progress would be undone the moment he learned that his father had been killed in a riot. Burned to death in a fire in the very store that had helped settle a town. The store Pappy had built with his own hands.

Billy knew Pappy would not have been found in bed, overwhelmed by smoke and flames in his sleep. He would be found shot to death or worse, because no fire alone could kill the likes of Brendan Mackey. He had helped Sherman set too many fires for him to be caught in one by surprise.

Billy had no doubt the great man had been murdered. He had been taken from them by the Hancock clan. By James Grant. By Nathan Rigg. Aaron would know that, too. And nothing on earth or heaven would stop him from setting things right.

Billy stopped just outside Aaron's door to steady himself. The room Aaron now shared with Katherine as they began their new life together. A life that had been off to a beautiful start, only to be ruined by this. By something ugly. By something that was as final as it was unnecessary. Another death resulting from James Grant's greed.

Billy felt a fly land on his face, but when he went to swat it away, he found it was not a fly at all. It was a tear. The top part of his shirt was damp, and he realized he must have been crying the whole walk up to Aaron's room.

For Pappy had been the first white man besides Aaron to treat him as an equal. No matter the occasion, no matter the circumstances, Brendan Mackey had never looked at him differently than he had looked at any other man. He had come to see the old man as something of a father figure. A man who had always been there. A man to rely on for a laugh or a kick in the backside, whatever was needed at the time.

A man who was not there anymore.

He drew in a ragged breath and prepared to knock on Aaron's door. He knew once he did so, he would be changing his best friend's life forever and not for the better. He would be destroying his world. And he was the only man who could possibly do it.

He knocked on the door and prayed his friend enjoyed the last few seconds of happiness before he opened it.

Aaron was smiling, really smiling when he opened the door. Billy had not seen his friend smile so much since the day he had been married.

And Billy watched that smile—and all the joy that went with it—fade when Aaron saw the look on Billy's face. The dried tears. The dampness of Billy's shirt.

Billy's breath became ragged again as he watched Aaron's face change ever so slightly.

Billy wanted to speak, but his throat was so tight, the words just would not come out.

Aaron took a step backward into the room and his shoulders sagged.

From somewhere inside the suite, Katherine called out cheerfully, "Is that Billy? Invite him in for coffee, silly. There's plenty left."

Coffee. Somewhere in this world, someone still cared about civility and coffee.

Billy saw Aaron's lip tremble as he, too, struggled to breathe. Billy did not have to tell him what had happened. It was clear there was only one reason in the world why Billy Sunday would look like that.

And when Aaron did speak, his voice was smaller than Billy had ever heard it. "Poppa?"

Billy closed his eyes and felt more tears flow.

He grabbed Aaron before he fell and held his best friend close. As close as he had the last time he had seen him weep. The day they had returned to Dover Station after he had been forced to resign from the army. The moment he had seen his father for the first time since Rigg forced him from the only life he had ever wanted. The last time he had been given no choice but to admit defeat.

As Mackey wept, Billy saw Katherine standing by the window. She was holding her hands in front of her face. She was not at the point of crying yet, but Billy knew she would be soon. Seeing Aaron betray emotion was not an easy sight to get used to, so he did not blame her for not rushing to his side to comfort him. After all, Aaron did not need comforting. He did not have emotions or sadness or fear. He was a rock.

But Billy knew better.

Mackey bit off his tears and gripped Billy tighter. It was only when Billy said, "Let go of it, Aaron," that his tears finally came.

CHAPTER 26

For reasons that none of the three of them could explain, Billy, Aaron, and Katherine had gotten dressed and sat in the hotel's main parlor alone.

The door was not locked. Neither Billy nor any member of the hotel staff had barred anyone from entering the room. But no one had dared to go in, either. Not Judge Forester or the mayor or even the governor.

Billy imagined part of the reason they had all kept their distance was out of respect. The territorial marshal and his wife were in mourning over the death of his father. He deserved some degree of privacy at such an awful time.

But Billy knew that most people were not so thoughtful. Most people craved spectacle, to be able to say they had been there to comfort the great man at the time of his greatest loss. They would share those stories with the other people who lived in Helena. Those who could claim they had comforted him would see their status in town rise, for they had been one of the few the marshal had allowed close to him in his hour of need.

But no one had entered the parlor. Not because they had been told not to or because they felt it was wrong.

They stayed away because something told them to do so.

Something they could not quite comprehend or, if they did, often discounted as nothing more than a bad feeling.

Billy knew better than that.

For as he sat in the corner of the parlor, away from his friend and his wife, he knew something in Aaron had changed. Katherine, clad in a black dress and veil, sat next to her husband as if he was a stranger. Perhaps because that was what he had become upon learning his father was dead. He had become something else.

Mackey was also clad in black, save for the white shirt he wore and the silver handle of the Peacemaker holstered to the left of his belt buckle. Billy had seen him strap on another Colt holstered on his right hip, though it was hidden under the black duster he wore. The broad, flat brim of his Plainsman threw a shadow over most of his face in the darkened parlor.

Billy had sensed this same change in him before, back when Darabont had laid siege to the town. When he had found out that Darabont had taken Katherine with him. When he had found Sim Halstead dead. And when he realized James Grant was trying to kill him.

Billy could only describe it as rage. Rage emanated from Aaron Mackey like heat from a stove. Rage filled the room with a feeling that was every bit as dark as fire was light. Rage so strong that every fiber of his being told Billy to run and get as far away from the source of it as soon as possible. A force that could not be touched, only felt.

But it was a rage Billy felt himself, and therefore knew there was no way of escaping it. The only way to stop it was to extinguish the source of it. That day, the source of it was James Grant.

Neither Billy nor Katherine moved when Aaron finally spoke for the first time since learning his father was dead.

"There's something in me."

His voice was still hoarse from the screams of rage that had been muffled by Billy's shoulder.

"It's something that crawled inside me and tucked itself away in my soul," Mackey went on. "I don't know how long it's been there, but it's been there for as long as I can remember. I used to think I could control it. Most times I can. But I can feel it now. I can feel it boiling over, and I don't want it to burn you. Either of you. I don't want it to get into you, too."

Katherine took his hand and laced her fingers with his. Mackey did not respond to his wife's touch. "I love you, Aaron. So does Billy. That's why we're here, and we're not going anywhere."

"You don't love me. Not this me. This part of me. You don't even know this me. Billy does. He's seen it, but not you. I don't want you there to see what it does to me. I don't want you to see what I can do. What I really am. I want you to stay here in Helena while we go to bury my father."

But Katherine only grabbed her husband's hand tighter. "Now you listen to me, Aaron Mackey. I'm damned near forty years old. I'm not like Mary. I'm not some child who doesn't know what life is. I know the way men are. I've always seen that darkness in you, and I married it when I married you. There's nothing you can do or say that will ever make me stop loving you. There's no amount of men you could kill and no reason you could give me that would dim my love for you even a little because I know exactly what you are."

Mackey's voice remained flat and raw. "You're not coming on the train with me."

"No, I'm not," she agreed. "And not because I'm afraid of you or because of what you're going to do in town, but because I don't want you worrying about me. I want you to do whatever you need to do to get whatever that thing inside you is back into whatever box you keep it in. And when you come back to me, we're going to starve it to death, Aaron Mackey. You and I are going to starve it out by loving each other the rest of our lives so it never, ever comes back."

Billy could not see through her black veil but could tell she was crying.

"Do you hear me?" she repeated. "You're going to come back to me, and we're going to go on with our lives. Do you hear me?"

Billy saw the brim of Mackey's hat imperceptibly move up and down. Then he felt Mackey look at him, though his eyes were in shadow. "You ready?"

"Always," Billy said.

The two lawmen stood. Katherine stood with her husband and wrapped her arms around him. She buried her face in his chest, though Mackey barely moved.

When she finally let him go, he walked slowly but steadily toward the pocket doors of the parlor and slid them open. Billy tipped his hat to Katherine before following him out the door.

The hotel of the lobby was filled with all of the leading citizens of Helena who had come to pay their respects to the marshal. Billy saw Judge Forester and the mayor and the governor along with their wives.

But Mackey did not bother to look at any of them. He walked past them, ignoring their condolences as he headed out to the front porch of the hotel.

Billy and Mackey stopped when they saw twenty riders

lined up on the street in front of the Hotel Helena. They were all United States marshals, and Sean Lynch was on the horse in the middle.

Joshua Sandborne was standing by the hitching rail to which Billy's horse and Adair were tied. Billy's horse was made restless by the presence of so many animals behind her. Adair stood stock still and looked at her rider.

Mackey said to Lynch, "Forester send you to stop me?"

"No, sir," Lynch told him. "We're going with you."

Mackey took Adair's reins from Joshua. "No, you're not."

"I'm afraid this ain't about just you anymore, Aaron," Lynch said. "It doesn't matter much how you got here, but you're one of us now, and if Grant and the Hancocks can get away with doing something like this to your family, then they can do it to any one of ours. We can't let that stand, so we'll be riding to Dover Station with you."

"The judge won't like that," Billy said. "He believes in law and order."

"Law and order don't always go together," said a marshal Billy recognized as Johnny Boggs. "Can't have any law without some order to go along with it. And we intend on bringing about some order to this territory right quick."

"How?"

The marshal Billy recognized as Larry Martin out of Butte said, "We're going to help you boys to wipe out the Hancocks in Dover, then ride up to Hancock to kill this at the source. Rip those bastards from the earth, root and stem, just like any other weed. Then set a torch to everything we see. Burn it into their memory so they remember that no one does this to one of us and gets to live after."

Billy noticed Mackey had not moved since he had taken Adair's reins. He stood stock still as the men spoke. Billy thought Boggs and Martin made good sense. He knew they could certainly use the extra guns.

But, as was his custom, he also knew what Mackey would say next.

"No."

Lynch looked confused. "What do you mean 'no'?"

Boggs added, "You don't aim to ride into Dover Station alone, do you?"

"Won't be alone," Mackey said. "I'll have Billy with me. And Jerry Halstead, too, if he's still alive. Maybe Steve Edison's men."

"Then I guess you ain't heard," Lynch said. "Edison left town before sunup. Pulled out with all of his men. And word is the Hancocks have Jerry Halstead pinned down in the old jailhouse. Poor bastard will probably be dead by the time you get there."

"Jerry?" Mackey shook his head. "Not likely. Not that soon."

"The town's just about burned out," Boggs said. "The Hancocks got you outgunned fifty-to-one, counting you and Billy. I know you're good, Aaron, but no one's that good."

"We'll find a way," Mackey said. "Always have."

"Always will," Billy added.

"It ain't that simple," Martin said. "Word is that big company is pulling up stakes and heading back to New York. Every friend you've got in town might already be dead, Aaron, not that they were worth much anyway. No offense to them meant."

"They've got law. Chief Edison's got fifteen men loyal to him."

Lynch continued, "Word is they shot twenty rioters last night, and not one of them was a Hancock boy. Not one.

They probably did all this so they could take the town back for Grant. No one left in town is going to help you against odds like that."

"Doesn't matter what they do," Mackey said. "It only matters what I do." He looked at the line of men. "It matters what we do, too. I'm not ordering the slaughter of women and children, even if they bear the Hancock name. This territory's filled with men who have paper on them. You want to help? Go out and bring them in while Billy and I tend to Dover Station personally. That's an order."

"No, Aaron," Lynch said. "That's suicide."

Billy answered for him. "Not the way we do it. It's our fight. We'll fight it our way. Same as always. The marshal has made up his mind. You boys best be on about your business. We appreciate the gesture just the same."

The line of twenty men looked at each other, unsure of what to do next.

Lynch frowned and nodded at Boggs, who reluctantly led the men back up Broadway to the courthouse. Only Lynch remained behind.

"You sure about this, Aaron?"

"I'm sure. Keep an eye on things here until I get back. I know you'll keep on doing a fine job."

Lynch looked at Billy, maybe hoping the deputy might get him to change his mind. But Billy knew when Aaron's mind was made up, and it was made up now.

"God go with you, then." He brought his horse about and followed the others back to the courthouse.

Sandborne untethered Billy's horse from the hitching rail and handed him the reins as Mackey climbed into Adair's saddle.

"I'm sorry about Pappy, Aaron," the young man said,

choking back tears. "I sure wish you'd let me go with you, but you won't, will you?"

"You've got the biggest job of all," Mackey told him. "You're staying here to protect my wife. Don't let anything happen to her."

"I won't," Sandborne said. "I'll defend her with my life."

"I know you will. You're family."

Billy patted Sandborne on the back as he climbed into the saddle and rode behind Aaron to the train to Dover Station.

CHAPTER 27

Mackey and Billy were situated in their own sleeper car, having rejected Mr. Rice's offer of sending his private car for them. It would have taken too much time to bring it to Helena, and Mackey was anxious to get back to Dover Station as soon as possible. If Jerry really was holed up in the jailhouse, they did not have a moment to lose.

They were more than five hours out of Helena before Mackey saw fit to say anything. The silver pot of coffee on the narrow table had gone cold, and his own cup was unfilled. He had spent the entire ride looking out the window, though Billy doubted he had seen anything except his own reflection in the glass.

"You check the train for Hancock men?" Mackey asked.

"I did. Didn't see anyone who looked like the family, but a couple of men are definitely heeled. Could be Pinkerton men. Could be just travelers. My guess is they're Rigg's men."

"Rigg's men is a safer bet," Mackey agreed. "How many?"

"Five possibilities," Billy said. "None of them were sitting together. All of them eyed me as I walked through the cars.

I tend to get that when they see a man of my persuasion walking through a train not wearing a uniform or carrying a silver tray."

"All of them look you over?"

"All except one," Billy said. "Lean man in a moustache and a bowler two cars ahead. Was awfully interested in the paper he was reading, too. Got the feeling he was working real hard not to look at me."

"Probably because he already knew who you were. Find out where he got on."

"Already did. The conductor said he boarded the train after us in Helena. He's the one I pegged for a Rigg man."

Mackey kept looking out the window. "Might be best if you took another look around, see where he is now."

"Sounds like a good idea." Billy stood up and moved to the door. "You want anything?"

"Nothing that's on this train." He looked away from the window for the first time in hours. "Take your time walking through the train. Make sure they see you're alone. Maybe it'll make them think now's their time to take a run at me."

Billy figured that was what Mackey had in mind. "Hopefully, it's just my nerves talking. Maybe it's nothing."

"It's something." Mackey went back to looking out the window. "Your nerves have saved our lives more times than I can count."

Figuring his friend was done talking for now, Billy went off to tend to the business at hand.

Billy found he drew even more looks from the passengers this time around as he slowly made his way through the train cars. They all quickly looked away.

Couples quickly whispered to themselves as he passed. Under other circumstances, Billy would have enjoyed the attention. But for now, he saw everyone as a threat. Rigg could have hired any one of them to try to take their lives, even the women. The retired colonel was nothing if not crafty.

Billy spotted the man in the bowler hat still seated where he had found him before, two cars ahead of their compartment. He was no longer reading his paper and sat with his eyes closed. But he did not have the relaxed look of a man asleep.

He looked like a man who was waiting for something.

Billy took his time walking past him and into the next car. Knowing the man would probably be looking to see if he stopped, Billy kept moving until he got to the farthest car in the train. He found the conductor, a roundish man with a round head that had a conductor's cap perched unevenly atop it. He was the same conductor who had told him the man in question had boarded the train in Helena.

"I need you to go back there and see if the man we're interested in is still in his seat."

"Was he there when you walked through just now?" the fat man asked.

"He was, but I want to make sure he didn't get up since then. He looked like he was sleeping, but I think he might've been faking it for my benefit."

"I don't see why he'd get up now. I'm sure he's still where you found him, enjoying the ride."

Billy knew train conductors were famous for their laziness, but this one was working awfully hard at living up to the reputation.

He grabbed the fat man and shoved him toward the

door. "Get moving. If you get to his spot and he's not there, take off your hat. I'll worry about the rest."

The conductor scrambled to open the door and got going.

Billy stood by the door and watched the fat man keep his balance with surprising ease as the train rocked back and forth along the rails. The conductor had just made it to the car in question, when the cars moved out of alignment as the train went around a curve, obscuring his view of the conductor.

Billy punched the door in frustration. *Come on!*

It took a few seconds for the train cars to align again before Billy could see through to where the conductor was. He was well past the section of the car where the bowler man had been sitting.

And the conductor was not wearing his hat.

The man in the bowler was gone.

Billy bolted into the next car and began running up the aisle. People gasped and leaned out of his way as he ran past them. He opened the doors to the next car and continued through that one and to the next, finally catching up to the conductor and knocked him out of the way, sending the fat man onto the laps of the couple who had whispered about Billy when he had passed through a few minutes before.

He cut through the last car between him and Aaron and saw the man, without his bowler now, reaching into a bag as he walked closer to Aaron's compartment.

He opened the door and was ready to barge into the last car when the train hit another turn, and the cars went out of alignment again. Billy almost lost his footing and spilled out of the train but managed to grab onto the door to keep himself upright.

By the time the cars once again straightened out, Billy saw Aaron had his attacker pinned against the window by the throat. A coach gun had fallen to the floor at the man's feet.

Billy opened the door and rushed to join Aaron. The bowler man's eyes were bulging and his face had turned beet red. He feebly slapped at Mackey's arm in vain, trying to break his grip before he strangled to death.

But Mackey's arm could not be moved, and his grip did not falter.

Billy reached his friend's side just as the attacker gurgled his last breath before life slowly left him. When his eyes went soft and his body sagged, Billy knew the man was dead.

Mackey let go, and the dead man collapsed to the train floor.

The fat conductor gasped when he saw the sight of the dead man on the floor of the train car. His train car.

"Good God. What have you done? What's going on here?"

Mackey did not look at the conductor when he said, "Billy, take care of that." He grabbed the dead man by the collar. "I'll take care of this." He looked at his deputy. "Give me your knife before you go."

Billy could usually figure out what Mackey would need before he asked for it, but he had not figured on this. "What do you need my knife for, Aaron?"

"Already told you. To finish up here." He held out his hand and waited for his deputy to hand him his knife. "Time to remind Colonel Rigg that old habits die hard, Sergeant."

A chill went through Billy at the sound of his old rank, for he suddenly knew why Aaron wanted the knife.

He pulled it from the scabbard on the back of his belt and handed it over, handle first.

Mackey took it from him and dragged the corpse into their compartment. "Tell the conductor this compartment stays shut until we reach Dover Station, or I won't be happy."

Mackey slid the compartment door shut.

The conductor was holding his hand to his chest, his eyes full of horrible questions.

Questions Billy did not dare answer.

Chapter 28

Early the next morning, Colonel Nathan Rigg cleaned his nails with a telegram envelope as he waited at the station for the train from Helena to arrive.

He was in wonderful humor, for today was a special day. One that would be long remembered as the day he would finally see the end of the insolent Aaron Mackey and his colored boy Billy Sunday. It had been a day he had waited a long time to see. He had even taken a bath, shaved closely, and put an extra shine on his boots and pistols for the occasion.

This was a moment he wanted to savor alone, which was why he had ordered his men to carry out other tasks. There were not many of them left after the fire, and there was much for them to do to bring order back to town.

Rigg looked up from his grooming and was warmed by the sound of chains snapping all over town as teams of horses took to clearing away the debris of what was left of the old Dover Station.

The odor of burnt buildings had always been a pleasant smell to him. It meant renewal. For Rigg, it meant forty percent of the future that was to come.

Some of the old-timers who had survived the fires, like Doc Ridley, had denounced what had happened as God's vengeance for the town's decent into wickedness and villainy at the hands of James Grant. Ridley claimed the rioters and looters had merely been the tools of the Almighty for smiting the town just as He had done to Sodom and Gomorrah.

Mr. Grant had ordered Rigg to personally shoot the mouthy old fool several times, but Rigg had decided to let him live. He enjoyed the Bible-thumping doctor's rants, especially when they were aimed at him whenever he walked down the street.

Every able-bodied man still in town was working day and night to clear the burned-out buildings and dead bodies from the streets, while Doc Ridley clutched his Bible and hurled insults at him. Words were all he could hurl. The notion of trying to kill him had probably never entered his saintly mind.

Rigg was glad Doc Ridley had not done anything foolish enough to force his hand. He found the doctor's impotent rage entertaining, and he imagined entertainment would be in short supply in Dover Station for the foreseeable future.

Rigg had enjoyed reading *The Dover Station Record's* detailed account of the "Fall of Dover Station." He especially enjoyed the widely differing death counts that seemed to grow larger the farther away the other papers that covered the story were located from the scene. *The Record* reported forty dead, a number that did not include the ten who had died during the panic at the mayor's swearing-in ceremony. Papers as far away as San Francisco said the entire town had been swept away in a firestorm that had taken hundreds of lives, leaving Dover Station a virtual ghost town. He had not read papers from back east yet, but imagined the New York dailies would say it was the worst tragedy since the burning of Atlanta.

Let them speculate, Mr. Grant had said. All the more glorious for our cause when we rise like a phoenix from the ashes.

All the more profitable for Rigg, too.

But paradise, Rigg decided, was a bit farther in the distance than he would have liked. Mr. Grant's newfound sobriety following the fire had served to make him particularly tedious as far as Rigg was concerned. But he could tolerate a certain amount of tedium while his money still spent well with the promise of more to follow.

Grant seemed intent on living up to his promise of including him in on forty percent of what the newly formed Grant Land Office Company brought in. As a man who had always owned one hundred percent of nothing, Rigg liked the idea of having a piece of the future. A future he and his men now controlled.

Almost all of the old wooden buildings in town had burned to the ground after the General Store exploded. The ammunition old Mackey stored was set off by the fire, sending burning cinders across half the town. Without a fire brigade to combat it, the flames had spread quickly. Not even Mr. Grant had expected so much damage.

Rigg laughed at the irony of it all. The store of the man credited as one of the settlers of the town had played a key role in its ultimate destruction. And it had taken the man himself with it.

Rigg's only regret were the six men he had lost in the fire. Not one of them had made it out alive. When the pile had finally cooled down enough for the draft horses to sift through the wreckage, he found them all scattered throughout the store. Each of them had been shot at least once. Most more than that.

Brendan Mackey had been found, too, still clutching the Winchester he had used to kill his own murderers. Under different circumstances, Nathan Rigg imagined the old man would have been someone he would have liked to know, maybe even respect.

Rigg sighed and went back to cleaning his nails. Alas, fortune had other plans.

He smiled again when he saw the headline of *The Record* folded beside him on the bench.

JAMES GRANT VOWS TO REBUILD!

FORMS NEW ENTERPRISE
FOR THAT PURPOSE

Grant's words still thundered in his ears as he addressed the stunned townspeople from atop the rubble of Mackey's store. He was freshly shaven and reasonably sober, wearing a black suit that was appropriately solemn given the occasion.

"The old Dover Plains may have burned away, but the heart of the town still beats within each of us stronger than ever. Our bank building, our Municipal Building, our sawmill, our rail station, and our newspaper building are all still standing defiant in the face of defeat. These are the buildings I helped build when I first led this town. And I vow, with your help, to replace every business and every structure with new buildings that will withstand any fire or torment visited upon us. Let us forget the past and begin anew to forge a new Dover Station that will be the envy of any town this side of the Mississippi!"

Yes, Rigg had to hand it to Grant. He was a pretty good speaker when he was sober, and he had been sober for several days now. Part of him thought Grant might even make good on his promise. Rigg certainly hoped he did. After all, forty percent was nothing to blow one's nose at.

He looked up from cleaning his nails when he heard heavy footsteps on the station floorboards. He feared it might be one of his men to tell him Jerry Halstead had found a way out of the jailhouse. Having to hunt down the gunman would only serve to ruin this special day.

Rigg was glad to see it was only Paul Bishop, lugging his own bags as he waited for the train.

The tall, dignified banker did not look so dignified now. He looked pale and frail, as if he had aged twenty years and lost twenty pounds since the riots had broken out two days before.

Another man might have left Bishop to dwell on his defeat in peace, but Rigg was unlike other men. He never passed up an opportunity to gloat.

He tucked the telegraph envelope he had been using to clean his nails into his coat pocket and stood to approach Bishop.

"What a sight indeed," Rigg smiled. "The cock of the walk slinking out of town. Except he's not a rooster. He's just a common cur summoned back to his master in New York City with his tail between his legs. My how the mighty have fallen."

"Shut your filthy mouth, Rigg," Bishop spat without looking at him. "Shut it right now."

"Your manners, sir." He pulled back his jacket and placed his hands on his hips. The handle of the Colt Thunderer glinted proudly in the morning light. "Us gentlemen must not forget ourselves, no matter how dark the hour might be."

"You're no gentleman," Bishop said. "You're a butcher. A common thug. A cancer that will keep growing until it kills the very thing it lives on." He straightened his coat, as if to salvage some degree of dignity. "My only regret is I won't be here to see you get what you deserve."

"Been called back to New York City, have you?" Rigg asked, though he already knew he had been. One of Grant's first actions after things settled down was to regain control of all the enterprises he had lost in the previous year. He focused on reestablishing control over the telegraph office first. Information was power, especially in times like these. "Guess your bosses don't have the stomach for a fight."

Bishop finally looked at him. "They don't have the stomach for carnage, Colonel Rigg. They don't see any value in continuing their association with a town that seems so intent on destroying itself. They intend on divesting their holdings in Dover Station immediately."

Rigg had already known that, too. Bishop had received the telegram from Mr. Rice late the previous night, recalling him to New York. He thought news of his triumph over Mr. Rice and Mr. Van Dorn might send Grant jumping back into the bottle in glorious victory.

Rigg had never been so glad to be wrong. Now that power was shifting back his way, Grant acted like a man reborn.

"It's a shame you have to return home like this." Rigg beamed. "I was hoping you'd stick around for a while, sir. See what we can make of this place with your own two eyes."

"I've already seen enough to last me for a lifetime,"

Bishop said. "You, Grant, and that mad Hancock woman are welcome to have this place. Mr. Rice and Mr. Van Dorn will invest their money in more civilized locations in the territory, where their holdings will be secure from the likes of you."

"Secure," Rigg repeated, "for now. But don't count old Jimmy Grant short. He's a man of vision and determination." He dropped his voice to a theatrical whisper when he said, "Not to mention the small fortune he managed to siphon off you morons back when he was running things. Yes, sir. Swiped it right out from under your high noses."

Rigg looked out on the wreckage of the town and injected a dose of pride in his voice as he said, "Yes, sir. It'll take us a year or two before we have this place back on its feet. Maybe three on the outside. But we'll get it done, then move on to the next town and the next. We are a force of nature, Mr. Bishop. Grant and Rigg. You'll be hearing from us again real soon."

Rigg's heart skipped a beat when he heard the train whistle echo through the valley. He had been so busy gloating, he had nearly forgotten his real purpose for being at the station. The train from Helena was almost there. His glory was riding the rails and nearly at hand.

He was suddenly in a generous mood. "You're not exactly my first choice to share this moment with, Mr. Bishop, but when the train comes, I'd like to show you something. Something that will prove to you the depth of our resolve and the length of our reach. Something you'll be proud to tell your fancy bosses about in New York City. A glimpse into Montana's future."

"I'm afraid I have other commitments," Bishop sneered, "though I thank you for the kind offer."

Rigg patted the Colt on his hip. "It wasn't exactly an invitation."

The businessman looked away from him. "A gentleman indeed."

When the train grinded to a halt at the station, Rigg pulled Bishop on board before the conductors had a chance to step off the train. He pushed aside the passengers who were waiting to disembark, shoving them aside as he rushed headlong toward the compartment where he knew Mackey and Sunday were lying dead. The telegraph he had received from Chidester Station had given him the compartment number where he could find them.

He paused to compose himself outside Mackey's compartment. It was easy to spot the compartment. It was the only one whose door was still closed.

He rested a trembling hand on the door. "Behold the future, Mr. Bishop!"

He tried to pull the door aside but found it locked.

Bishop smiled. "The future seems barred to you, Mr. Rigg."

"That's Colonel Rigg to you!" Anxious to see the bodies, Rigg drew his Colt and put a bullet through the lock. He slid the door open with his free hand.

Inside, he saw his best operative, Charlie Gates, lying on the floor, propped up beneath the window. His eyes bulged from their sockets. His skin was blue. His black tongue hung loose from his gaping mouth.

And his scalp was gone.

It took Rigg a few moments to notice something had been written on the corpse's white shirt. Something written in the dead man's blood.

I'M COMING.

Bishop laughed as he patted the stunned Rigg on the shoulder. "From where I stand, *Colonel* Rigg, the future looks awful bright, indeed."

Rigg would have shot the banker in the back as he walked away, had he been able to take his eyes from the scalped man in the train compartment.

And the bloody words written on the dead man's shirt.

I'M COMING.

CHAPTER 29

Mackey and Billy had left the train at Chidester and sent the telegram from there. Now they made their way through the mountain pass where the Blackfoot tribe had once lived. It was almost nightfall by then, and Mackey knew they would need to make camp before they headed into Dover Station the next day.

Billy once again broke the silence that had fallen over them. "You think Wolf Child still lives around here?"

"If he's still alive," Mackey said, "then he still lives here. He bled for this land. He won't give it up so easy."

Billy pointed at the scalp hanging from a string on Mackey's pommel. "You going to get rid of that thing? It's likely to give Wolf Child the wrong impression if he sees it."

Mackey had forgotten it was there until Billy mentioned it. "If anyone could understand why it's there, it's Wolf Child. Why do you want me to get rid of it?"

"It's grisly."

"It sets a tone," Mackey told him. "Besides, since when have you been bothered by a scalp? I recall a time when you had more hanging from your pommel than I did."

"Those were Apache and Kiowa scalps," Billy reminded him. "Different time and different reasons. We were different men, too, Aaron. We did all of that on Rigg's orders."

"We did it because it needed doing," Mackey said. "Rigg just happened to give the order. Another officer might've done the same. Maybe even me."

"Maybe," Billy allowed, "but like I said. We're different now. And you're a better man than the kind who takes scalps."

"Would be nice to think so," Mackey said. "Wish it was true, but it's not."

Both men drew up short when they heard a crack off to the side of the trail. Someone else would have mistaken it for a snapping twig or a branch. Maybe a porcupine scurrying through the overgrowth.

But Mackey and Billy had both heard a hammer cock enough times to be able to tell the difference.

A man spoke to them in Siksika. "You used to be more careful, even for a white man."

Mackey recognized the voice and responded in the same language. "We are not here to harm you, Wolf Child."

"If I thought otherwise," the man said, "you would not still be alive."

The old Blackfoot chief stepped out from a stand of trees onto the narrow path. Had the light been better and if they had been paying more attention, Mackey knew they might have spotted the old man among the overgrowth. But in better conditions, Wolf Child would not have been standing there. He would have found another spot to greet his visitors.

"If you still remember where my village was," Wolf Child said, "go there. I left some game in the woods I have to bring for supper. Unless you have become too important to eat with an old man, *Máóhk Ki'sómma*."

The old man never had been able to say his name properly, even the rare times he had chosen to speak the Devil's Tongue. "Wait and let us help you with the animal you killed."

"Go to my village and wait," Wolf Child said. "Accepting help from the white man only makes us weak."

The old man disappeared back into the overgrowth.

Billy understood the language, but not well enough to speak it. "Still a nice old Blackfoot, isn't he?"

"We're off to a good start." Mackey kept riding. "At least he didn't shoot us."

At the old Blackfoot camp, the three men ate venison and drank a pot of Billy's coffee. People usually made a point of complimenting Billy on his coffee, but Wolf Child did not. If he liked it, he hid it well.

As they ate, Mackey spoke to the chief in his native tongue. "I did not think we would find anyone here."

"Figured," Wolf Child replied, "seeing as how you made enough noise for a deaf boy to follow. The vengeance trail has made you careless, *Máóhk Ki'sómma*."

Mackey stopped eating. "How did you know?"

He gestured toward Adair, who joined Billy's mount in eating the tall grass that had sprung up around the old village site. "The scalp you have dangling from your saddle tells me so. A man like you does not do something like that without purpose. That purpose for you would be a vengeance trail."

"I told you to get rid of that thing," Billy said from the other side of the fire.

Mackey went back to eating. "Never could get much past you, Wolf Child."

"That is true." The Blackfoot motioned to get Billy's attention and spoke at him. "When his father first showed him this place, *Máóhk Ki'sómma* used to sneak out here at night and watch our customs and see our ways. He used to hide behind that large rock over there. All he would do is watch, but never approached the village. We came to call it Watching Rock for the young boy who looked at us."

Mackey bit into another hunk of venison. "Didn't know you knew about that."

"A wise chief knows everything about his village. And all that is around it." He regarded his own hunk of meat. "I was a good chief."

Billy asked in English, "If you knew Mackey was there, why didn't you invite him in?"

"Because it was not our place to invite him. Our village was always open to the people of his village. At least to those who came in peace. His father, Barking Dog, was always welcomed in our village and brought He Who Follows with him many times."

Mackey almost spat out his food. He had forgotten the Blackfoot tribe used to call Pappy "Barking Dog" because his brogue sounded like a dog barking to them. Sim Halstead never had the heart to tell Pappy the truth, back when Sim still spoke, so he told Pappy it was their term for "Great Chief."

Mackey smiled at the memory, but the smile did not last long. Both of them were gone now. Sim and Pappy. Taken from him from men not fit to empty their toilet water.

Mackey felt Wolf Child's hand on his leg. "I know what happened to your father. I saw the flames from the high place and heard the screams of your people. A man leaving this place stopped to say goodbye to me and told me all that had happened in your village. I mourned your father. I mourn him still. He was a fine white man."

"Yeah." Mackey set his venison aside, suddenly losing his appetite. "He was."

"And you have come this way to avenge him. You and the Dark One here."

"Not just him," Billy said in English, "but that's part of it."

Wolf Child set aside his own food on the blanket and grew quiet. When he felt he had been quiet enough, he said, "What you seek to do is a dangerous thing, *Máóhk Ki'sómma.* You already have a great blackness in you. This is clear. But the blackness can grow blacker still if you water it with blood. You have killed white men and Apache and Comanche and Kiowa and Lakota. These were good things, because these are bad men who caused many of my people to fall under their blade. But what you seek to do now is different. What you seek to do now is for yourself, to stop your own pain. I fear what will happen to you when you find blood only makes the pain harder to cure."

Mackey watched the fire dance. "I look forward to finding out."

Wolf Child shook his head. "You may think the blackness inside you cannot grow any darker, but it can. I have seen it grow in good men, both white and red. I have seen how a spirit can be poisoned by the blackness, growing blacker until it no longer lives. I do not wish this for you, *Máóhk Ki'sómma.* Your father was a great man, and no great man wishes such a thing for his son."

"The men we hunt have blackness of their own," Mackey said. "A blackness that threatens my village and all of my people. Maybe even you, some day."

The old man looked up at the stars high above the fire. It was a clear night, and there was much to see. "I am near a place where the blackness cannot follow me. It no longer holds any power over me. But both of you are young men. You have much time before you become as I am now. You have many things to see and do, for yourselves and your people. But you cannot do these things if your eyes are blinded by darkness, just as we could not see the sky if it was covered by clouds."

Mackey looked to his left and saw a dead prickly bush with what appeared to be a pale rock beneath it.

But Mackey knew that was no rock. "And what do you say about your friend over there?"

Wolf Child pitched forward to see the place where Mackey was looking. "Ah, that is, as the white men say, my 'chamber pot.'" He seemed pleased with himself to be able to pronounce English words so well. "That is my enemy. I remind him of his shame each morning when I make my water."

Mackey knew that was the spot where the Blackfoot tribe had buried Darabont alive after he had turned the outlaw over to Wolf Child's scouts. They had buried him up to his neck and poured honey over his head to attract the ants. Mackey had no idea how long it took for a man to die from something like that, but however long it had taken, it still was not long enough for Darabont.

"I used to make my droppings there, too, when my people moved on to another place. But the prickly bush grew and I could no longer do that."

Billy had been able to follow the conversation well enough to say, "Sounds like a fitting end for him."

"I will do it," Wolf Child said, "as long as I can make

water. When I die, I hope a skunk or a possum will do the same. Maybe a wolf, though that is too noble for him."

"You have your chamber pot," Mackey said. "I have my scalp and my vengeance. How are they different?"

"Because I knew when to stop." Wolf Child looked at him for a long time. "Do you? Or will the blackness blind you until you have wandered too far within it to find your way out again? Until you cannot see the stars above or the good ground around you."

The chief grabbed Mackey's arm with a strong, bony hand. "The dead are lonely and beg us to follow them. Do not do this, *Máóhk Ki'sómma*. Not even for your father. Kill who you must, but not all, for all need not die to avenge him."

For the first time since Billy had told him Pappy was dead, Mackey felt different. It was not peace. It was not comfort, just different.

It was why he said, "I'll kill enough to end it once and for all." He watched the fire dance among the logs. "As many as it takes, but no more than that."

Wolf Child joined him in watching the fire. "I hope that number is small enough for you to escape the blackness."

Billy sipped his coffee and watched the fire with them.

CHAPTER 30

By the time Billy and Mackey woke the next morning, Wolf Child was gone. There was no sight of the old chief, and neither Billy nor Mackey intended on looking for him. He had been roaming the plains and these hills for longer than either of them had been alive. If he had decided to leave, they knew it must have been for a good reason. Mackey knew better than to question a Blackfoot's reason for doing anything.

But their conversation about the blackness had remained with Mackey throughout his sleep and had remained with him still now that he was awake. The talk had left an impression on him like a bruise, for the wisdom had come from within him, not from anything Wolf Child told him.

He imagined that was a gift of the wise, to be able to make other men better by leading them to their own conclusions. He had not shoved Mackey in the right direction. He had not even pointed it out. He had just kept talking until Mackey decided what he had to do.

The coals from the previous night's fire were still hot enough to warm up the coffeepot. Since neither he nor Billy was hungry, they simply finished their coffee, packed up, and rode out toward Dover Station.

Neither man had spoken a word, either, until Billy once again broke the silence. "Mind telling me what you've got in mind? I'd kind of like to know before we get there."

Mackey realized he had not been very talkative since leaving Helena. He had not told Billy much of anything that was on his mind the whole way to Dover Station.

They had ridden together for so long, he always imagined his deputy knew what he was thinking. But this time was different. Everything was different about this.

"We're going to do what we were trained to do," Mackey said. "Observe, plan, and attack."

"I figured that," Billy said. "I'm just wondering about how do you want to handle the observing part. We can see some things from the ridge around town, but not everything."

Mackey had already given that plenty of thought on the train. "We'll set out at opposite sides of the hillside, meet up in the middle, and figure out what we need to hit and when. Freeing Jerry and taking down Grant and Rigg need to be the priority. Mad Nellie's death won't stop the Hancocks from coming at us, so killing her is low on the list."

"Rescuing Jerry and killing Grant and Rigg is going to be a tall order for two men," Billy pointed out. "Unless they're in the same place, we're going to have to choose which one is more important. I say rescuing Jerry's more important."

"It is," Mackey agreed. "We'll figure out who'll be easier to kill once we look over the town. The only advantage we have is the element of surprise."

"If you wanted the element of surprise," Billy said, "you probably shouldn't have left Rigg's man in our train compartment. Even if the conductor kept his mouth shut about it, Rigg has already found him by now and knows we're coming."

Mackey wanted to feel some kind of emotion about what he had done. Not so much about killing him, but about how he had scalped him. How he had used the man to send a message to Rigg. He knew he should feel regret or remorse. The soldier in him should be furious how a theatrical display had cost him a tactical advantage.

But Mackey did not feel anything at all. And he had not felt anything since the moment Billy had told him his father had been murdered.

"Rigg knew we'd be coming anyway," Mackey decided. "He had people watching us in Helena. He thought he knew when we'd get there. But now he doesn't, and that's going to be the difference."

He hoped Billy was not going to ask him more about his plan because he did not have one. He knew the town had burned quite a bit and the landscape was probably much different than when they had last seen it. He had no idea where Grant or Rigg were staying. He imagined they'd spent a fair amount of time at the Municipal Building, but he did not know where either man was living. The Van Dorn house? The Ruby? He had no idea what they were riding into.

All he knew was that he regretted rejecting Sean Lynch's offer of bringing twenty deputy marshals into Dover Station. A show of force was exactly what the Hancocks needed. A pile of Hancock dead would remind the town what happened to those who aligned themselves with Grant and Rigg.

But when Mackey returned to his senses, he knew that was the darkness talking. Since he assumed Grant had re-gained control of the telegraph office, he had not dared to wire ahead from Helena to ask questions. He and Billy would have to find their answers on their own.

Billy pulled him out of his own mind by asking, "What was that name Wolf Child kept calling you?"

Mackey looked at him as if he had been shaken awake. "What name?"

"It sounded like your name, but wasn't," Billy said. "I've never heard him call you that before, and I couldn't catch the meaning."

Mackey remembered. "*Máóhk Ki'sómma.* It's as close as he can get to saying 'Mackey.' It's the name he gave me when he felt I was a man. It was to honor my father, who had always been pretty fair to his people over the years."

"What does it mean?" Billy asked.

"It means Red Sun." Mackey thought about it as they rode. "Always thought it was a pretty silly name until now."

"Red Sun," Billy repeated as if he was trying it on for size. "Seems fitting, especially now."

Adair skittered as she caught the first whiff of dead smoke on the wind from Dover Station. Mackey patted her neck as he urged her forward.

"Wolf Child always had a knack for seeing the future."

The lawmen tied their horses to a tree and belly crawled to the rim of the ridgeline that surrounded Dover Station. Mackey realized they were doing exactly what Darabont and his men had done when he had laid siege to the town more than a year before.

Upon crawling up the rim and seeing the town, Mackey realized there was not much left of Dover Station.

"Damn," Billy swore. "It's worse than I thought."

Mackey found himself unable to speak.

A thin haze still hung in the late morning air, but Mackey could still see the devastation.

Almost every wooden building in town was gone. His father's store was a ruin of scorched wood. Not a single post remained standing.

Most of the buildings that had been left over from the original settlement were gone, as well. The stores and shops and saloons from his childhood had been erased from the townscape as if they had never been there. The upper floors of the Campbell Arms had been burned away and the roof had fallen into the building. The first floor looked untouched, but he was sure the entire hotel was a mess. He hoped all of the guests had been able to get out in time.

That made him think of Katherine and how she would take the news of her hotel being destroyed. But he quickly pushed her out of his mind. He could not afford to think of her now. He had to remember his training and remember his mission, no matter how difficult it was to look at.

The only remnants of Dover Station still standing were the buildings that James Grant had built when he had been in power. The sawmill and the *Record* building and The Bank of Dover Station, and the station itself had all been left untouched by flame.

And, of course, the Municipal Building was still standing, looming over the ruined town like a medieval castle. Mackey had grown to hate that building and all it represented.

But his hatred died away when he saw the old jailhouse was still standing, as if in defiance to the destruction around it. It was still as squat and ugly as ever, but its stone walls and slate roof had protected it from the flames.

He could see the door to the jail was shut. And five men

were keeping an eye on it from behind an overturned wagon in front of the Municipal Building across Front Street. He knew that was where Jerry Halstead must be holed up.

Billy cleared his throat and, had Mackey not known better, would have sworn he wiped away a tear. "What do you want to do next, Captain?"

He normally hated when Billy referred to him by his old title, but under the circumstances, it seemed to fit. They were reconnoitering an enemy camp, just like they had back in their cavalry days.

"Let's split up and look everything over on foot," Mackey told him. "You head north toward the old Van Dorn house up on the hill while I circle back to the sawmill. We stay among the rocks and meet in the middle. We report on what we see and figure out what we do next. I think they've got Jerry pinned down in the jailhouse, so let's not worry about him for now. Keep an eye out for Grant and Rigg. If we can peg down where they are, we can plan what to do next."

"Sounds good to me," Billy said. "Let's meet back here in two hours." He nodded at the clock in the tower of the Dover Station bank building. "Might as well put that thing to good use for once."

They moved back away from the rim and set off to carry out their respective missions.

CHAPTER 31

Billy had never disobeyed a direct order from Aaron Mackey. Not when they had been in uniform and not since they had pinned on their badges. But he would disobey his last order and for good reason.

He had scouted enough enemy positions to know there was only so much a man could see from afar. Sometimes, he had to get closer to see what was really happening.

Billy moved around toward the old Van Dorn house, keeping among the large rocks along the ridgeline to avoid being spotted by anyone who might be living in the house. He did not know if Mr. Bishop was still living there, or even if he was still living. He kept out of sight in case the place was guarded.

He stopped moving when he reached Cy Wallach's mortuary. The old wooden building was far enough from the main part of town to have avoided being burned. After being fairly certain no one had spotted him, Billy took a risk and quickly scrambled down among the rocks toward the mortuary.

He paused at the base of the rocks, checking to see if

anyone was on the street to spot him. No one was looking his way, so he darted through the back door of the mortuary.

Cy Wallach looked up from his desk, startled by Billy's sudden appearance. "My heavens! Billy! You're here."

But the deputy had no time for pleasantries. "Good to see you, too, Cy. Where's Doc Ridley?"

"I don't know," Cy told him. "I know he survived the calamity, which is more than I can say for many of us. I take it you know of what happened to poor Brendan?"

"That's why I'm here." Cy was a simple soul, and Billy did not want him to know Mackey was with him. He might tell the wrong person. If Billy found himself against Grant's men, at least Mackey would still be out there somewhere. "I need you to find Doc Ridley and bring him here. Quietly. Can you do that?"

"I can certainly try. When should I get him?"

Billy wondered if the new embalming fluids he had brought to town were starting to rot his brain. "Now, Cy. As soon as possible. Go."

The mortician scrambled to find his hat and pulled down the shade to his front door before heading out into the street. Billy wheeled the mortician's chair to a dark corner of the room and sat down among the shadows.

He listened for any sound that might tell him someone was coming. He watched the windows and saw wagons and the crews of men moving along the streets. Most of the men were either hauling wreckage or new timbers fresh cut from the sawmill. None of them looked toward the mortician's place. If anything, they made a point of looking away from it. He imagined they had all had their fair share of death for now.

The town was still Dover Station, but Billy knew it was no longer his home. It belonged to James Grant now and always would. To Grant and Nathan Rigg. Billy felt like he had snuck into an enemy camp because that was what he had done. There were no reinforcements waiting to ride down to rescue him. He had no idea of the nature of the enemy he faced. He had no idea if Jeremiah Halstead was still alive in the jailhouse or if he was injured.

Billy felt himself getting jumpy and decided now was the time for a smoke. He pulled out a paper from his shirt pocket and tried to fold it, but his hands were shaking so much, he dropped the paper. He picked up the paper and stared at his hand, willing it to stop shaking.

You survived Alton Canyon. You survived Greely Pass. You survived Adobe Flats. You hunted down Darabont. You brought Grant to justice once. You will do it again. You and Aaron. Same as always.

His hand stopped shaking and he pulled his tobacco pouch and began to build himself a cigarette.

Billy had just snuffed out his cigarette when he saw Cy and Doc Ridley approaching the mortuary. They were alone.

Doc Ridley looked as if he had aged a decade in the month or so since Billy had last seen him. His hair had gone from gray to an unruly shock of white. His clothes were stained from ash, and his face was thick with stubble. He shuffled along at a stoop and Cy had to help him up the stairs that led to his office.

Ridley's eyes were vacant when Billy emerged from the shadows. "Billy?" He clutched his Bible as if it were a blanket. "Is it really you?"

"In the flesh, doc." He shook the man's hand gladly, which seemed to pump new life into the doctor. "We're here because of what happened, but I need you to tell me where we stand."

Billy rolled the chair around so the doctor could sit before he fell down. Billy was content to sit on the floor. Cy set about pulling the drapes closed.

"Aaron with you?" Ridley asked. "He knows what happened to Brendan?"

"He knows. And we're here to make things right, but we need to know what we're up against. Where's Edison and Jerry Halstead?"

"Gone," Ridley stammered. "All gone. Edison's bunch left the morning after the fire. Just climbed up on their horses and rode out of town. Said there was no town left to defend and no way for them to get paid. Figured they'd cut their losses and move on. Can't say I blame them."

Billy was not surprised Edison and his men did not stick around. They were mercenaries, after all, and no badge could change that. "What about Jerry? Is he in the jailhouse?"

"Cornered like a rat," Ridley said. "But he's got no way of getting out, and they've got no way of going in. They've tried everything to pry him loose, but he always managed to put a few of them down every time they took a run at him. After a while, they got smart and decided to wait him out. They've been perched in front of the jailhouse for the past day or so like they're sitting a vigil. I suppose they are, in a way. A vigil of death." The doctor's eyes grew far away. "I've been sitting a vigil of my own, you know. For Brendan. For Dover. The town's gone, Billy. All gone."

Billy could see the doctor was beginning to fade back into the horrors he had witnessed over the past few days. Billy needed to pull him out of it until he learned all he could. "What about Grant and Rigg? Where are they staying?"

"Bishop's gone," Ridley told him. "Was summoned back to New York yesterday. Now, it's as if Grant was never arrested. Rice's company is selling off everything it owns in town. Word is that they have a willing buyer in Grant. He's moved into the Municipal Building. He lives there now in that damned castle of his. Rigg has become the sheriff. Grant gave him the old Van Dorn place. Both of them look down on the town from their high perches like a couple of vultures, while the rest of us are here in the middle, left with nothing."

Billy knew Doc Ridley was fading quickly, so he pumped him for everything he could before the well ran dry. "And what about the Hancocks? How many are here?"

Doc Ridley's eyes grew even more vacant. "More come in every day. Must be over a hundred by now. The Ruby is the only wooden building in that part of town still standing. All of their other saloons and hotels, too. God, how could one family be so big so fast? And that horrible Nellie and her infernal cackle that echoes in the street all day and all night. Even worse at night. That demonic laugh haunts my dreams, Billy. Haunts everything around it."

The doctor looked at Billy with wet eyes. "There was nothing I could do for them, son. Nothing at all. There were no sick to heal. Not in time for me, anyway. There was only the dead and dying. So many dead and gone. So many gone now."

Doc Ridley rubbed the Bible on his lap and finally slipped away, muttering verses and passages from the good book. Billy wanted to know more, but knew he had gotten all he could from this poor man. Or what was left of him.

He pulled himself up from the floor and laid a hand on the man's shoulder. "You rest now, Doc." He wanted to tell him everything was going to be fine, but he did not have the heart to lie to him.

Ridley surprised him by covering Billy's hand with his own. He looked up at him and said, "You'll kill them, won't you? You and Aaron? Promise me you'll avenge us. You'll avenge Brendan. You'll kill them all, just like you killed Darabont, won't you?"

Billy did not know what to say, so he simply squeezed his shoulder and moved to the door.

He pulled Cy aside and whispered, "Take him back home and stay with him. Make sure he rests. He's in a frail way. And remember, you can't tell anyone I was here."

Cy seemed to understand. "What will you do now, Billy? You and Aaron?"

Billy left without answering him. He did not know what to say.

Chapter 32

When they met again an hour later, Mackey told Billy all he had seen from the ridgeline.

"All of Lee Street is gone except for The Ruby. I saw a lot of Hancocks walking around, and I have a feeling that's where the Hancocks are working out of. They're all toting rifles and bossing the work crews. There's got to be at least a hundred of them from what I saw. Didn't see Grant or Rigg, but their people are watching the jail, so my money's on Jerry being in there, if he's still alive. Maybe some of Edison's men, too."

Judging by the look on Billy's face, Mackey could tell he already knew everything he had just said. "You went into town, didn't you?"

Billy said he had. "Took a chance and headed into Cy's place. Talked to Doc Ridley, or what's left of him. Poor man's out of his mind with grief." He took a long drag on his smoke. "I know he was hard on us over the years, Aaron, but it's a shame to see such a proud man laid so low."

But Mackey had more on his mind than Doc Ridley's health. "I thought we agreed to keep our distance. To recon—"

"I reconnoitered, Captain," Billy snapped. "I reconnoitered

the hell out of that place, and all I saw was a bunch of burned-up buildings and scared men, same as you saw. But it didn't tell me anything except what I already knew when we got on the train in Helena. We're outgunned, outmanned, and Grant controls the town again. I couldn't learn any more than that by peeking around a bunch of rocks, so I took a risk. I disobeyed your order, and I'm not the least bit sorry, either, so don't go expecting an apology."

Mackey sat quietly, making sure the storm had passed. In all the years they had known each other, in all the trouble they had faced together, neither of them had ever raised their voice to the other.

But Mackey knew this was different. Everything was different now. Nothing was the same and never would be again. Mackey was beginning to think it might even be for the best.

And arguing with Billy would only make everything worse.

Mackey toed the ground. "I suppose reconnoitering could mean going into town. And I never ordered you to do anything. It was more like a plan. Guess you just made it better. Like you always do."

Billy finished his smoke and flicked away the dead butt. "That your way of apologizing? Because if it is, it's a lousy apology."

"No need for anyone to apologize because you didn't do anything wrong and neither did I." He forced the first smile in days and nudged his deputy in the shoulder. "Good work, Sergeant."

Billy looked at him. "Damn, you really are sorry."

Mackey did not want to talk about it anymore. "What did Ridley tell you?"

After he finished hearing everything the broken man

had told Billy, Mackey had a clearer picture of what they were up against. "Bishop's gone. That's bad. And Jerry being cornered is worse. How long has he been holed up in there?"

"Since it happened, I suppose," Billy said. "The doc didn't say, and I got as much out of him as I could. But he's got to be low on food and bullets by now. At least the pump is still working unless they figured out a way to cut that."

Mackey was already turning that over in his mind. "I rode in here hoping we'd get Grant and Rigg. But with Grant up in the Municipal Building and Rigg on the other end of town, that splits our objectives."

He felt Billy looking at him, almost like he was testing him. "What's our main objective?"

Mackey was surprised he asked. "Getting Jerry out of there alive, of course."

"Glad to hear you say that," Billy said. "But you've got a choice to make, Aaron, and it's not an easy one. We can go after Grant or we can go after Rigg. You'll only have one chance to get one quietly. I can raise a distraction to a point, but not before every gun in town gets pointed at us. That's when things will start to get nasty."

Any trace of a smile disappeared from Mackey's face. "I can kill both."

"Not quietly," Billy told him. "And not publicly, either. It'll look like murder if you do, and Judge Forester will see you swing for it. He told me so the morning he told me about Pappy and he means it, Aaron. I saw it in his eyes. He'll hang you for murder if he has to."

Mackey knew Forester would do it, too. He would do it because he would have no choice. He would do it because he said he would.

But Mackey had made a promise to himself when he left Helena that he would avenge his father and his town. And he had every intention of living up to his word.

Maybe there was a way of doing both after all.

The more Mackey thought about it, the more sense it made. It might even work. "I've got a plan, if you'd allow me to present it, Master Sergeant Sunday, sir."

"I wasn't an officer," Billy reminded him. "I worked for a living, remember? Now what's the plan?"

CHAPTER 33

Later that evening, Nathan Rigg walked out of The Ruby and stretched. The dying sunlight felt good, and he welcomed the approaching night. It was harder for a man to spot him as he walked the darkened streets of town, and he knew Mackey was gunning for him.

He looked up at the hills that surrounded the town and wondered if he might already be up there, somewhere in the coming darkness. He might be up there waiting his turn or he might be rallying some men outside of town. He had spies camped out near the telegraph lines throughout the day. None of them had reported seeing anything on the outskirts of town.

Rigg had no doubt Mackey would show up soon. Perhaps tomorrow or the next day, but not tonight.

Rigg walked down the steps of The Ruby and began to walk home. Grant had wanted him to attend yet another one of his torturous meetings in the mayor's office at the Municipal Building; this time with members of The Bank of Dover Station to review his grand plans for the town. Grant insisted that Rigg attend since this was the meeting that would decide the future of the town.

But the only meeting Rigg had planned for that night

was between his backside and a chair on the porch of his new house. The locals might call it the Old Van Dorn house for now, but there would be a new batch of locals soon. And by the time he was through with this town, they would call it Rigg's Mansion. Yes, he rather liked the sound of that.

He imagined he would like the sound of rain on the roof even more. His roof. He had never had one over his head that he could call his own. He had grown up on a plantation owned by his grandfather and had been forbidden by his father from ever returning. The old fool had always been a prude.

After his appointment to West Point came through, Rigg had lived in quarters paid for by Uncle Sam for most of his life. The time since he left the army had been spent in hotels or lodging houses.

This was the first night in his life that Nathan Rigg had a place to call his home, and he intended to enjoy every second of it. Grant's grand plans would have to wait.

As he walked home, Rigg had to admit there was a certain rough charm to the place. He could see why old man Mackey and his friends had picked this spot to make a life and build a town. The rocky outcroppings that surrounded it protected it from the wind, and the rocks themselves kept the town from being swamped by a flood. The ground pitched away from the town, and into the river for which River Street was now named. It was good land, and he was glad Pappy had been able to die in the place he had built. He did not hold much stock in the Mackey name, but he figured Pappy had died the best way any man could want. He had taken the men who killed him with him to hell on the ground of his choosing.

From the time he had been a boy on his family's plantation, Nathan Rigg had always known he would die in bed.

He was certain of it, just as he was certain the sun would rise in the east each morning and set in the west each night. It was why he had taken so many chances in battle and why he had never lived in fear of any man. White, black, or red. He only hoped, that when that day ultimately came many years from now, that he would show as much grit as Brendan Mackey had shown when he faced the reaper's scythe.

Rigg could feel the people watch him as he walked across Front Street. Laborers clearing out the debris and shopkeepers who no longer had shops to keep. Men building tents in the burned-out lots that had already been cleared of charred wood. New buildings were already beginning to go up, with credit extended by James Grant and lumber provided by his sawmill.

The townspeople who dared to look at him did not look upon him with admiration. They looked at him in fear. Rigg drank in that fear as happily as he had forced down Mad Nellie's rotgut that passed for whiskey at The Ruby. The time to enjoy fine spirits would come soon enough, but for now, the wretched drink reminded him he still had much work to do.

Keep at it, you damned fools, he thought as he passed another work crew. *I own forty percent of your labor.*

He laughed to himself as he passed by the burned-out husk of The Campbell Arms. The place had been the pride and joy of Aaron Mackey's woman, Katherine Campbell, the Boston whore who let a good man die so she could be with her lover. He had known and admired Major Campbell as the only officer he had ever met who could match his own brutality. His wife's betrayal had practically forced him to charge the Comanche the fateful day he lost his life. At least he had died honorably, if foolishly clouded by notions of honor.

Honor was a luxury that outcasts like Rigg could ill afford.

Yes, Rigg was glad the rioters had burned the hotel to the ground. It was a fitting blow to the vain widow and a fitting price to be paid by any ally of Aaron Mackey. He only wished he had ordered it burned himself.

Grant had wanted the ruin pulled down immediately, claiming the plot where it stood was a prime location for a grand hotel. But Rigg had ordered the workers to clear other lots first. He wanted to be able to sit on his porch for a while and gaze upon the fallen hotel as a trophy to forever casting out Mackey and his ilk from the town he now controlled. Yes, he would enjoy the view from his porch indeed.

He tipped his hat to a wagon full of church women who rumbled past his house, but the women all turned away. He imagined they must be the women of the men at the logging operations on the outskirts of town. He wondered why a wagonload of church mice would be coming to town at this hour. It was not Sunday, and there were no sick left to attend to. The violence that accompanied the riot had been as efficient as it had been destructive. The dying were all dead, and the living were all who remained.

He wondered if the church women would throw in a good word with the Lord for him, though he doubted it would do much good.

He walked up the steps of his house and opened the door. He had not been able to spend much time there since Bishop had moved out and Grant had given the house to him. Grant had decided to move into the Municipal Building lock, stock, and barrel; preferring to live and breathe the future of Dover Station. The constant presence of armed guards in a fortified building to keep the townspeople at bay did not hurt, either.

But Nathan Rigg had refused to allow any guards near his place, especially while he was not there. He knew the five remaining men he had brought with him to town, and he would not trust any of them to be near something so personal to him. He was enough to face down any threat to him, including Aaron Mackey.

Besides, he believed being surrounded by gunmen exuded weakness, not power. Grant's ego dictated that at least one guard be with him at all times, even though Grant was fairly good with a firearm himself. Rigg was happy to oblige. They were all Rigg's men and would keep him apprised of Grant's activities. It was almost as good as being there himself.

He closed the door behind him and set the latch. He took off his hat and tossed it into the front parlor. He did not bother to see where it landed, for wherever it landed, it was in the house that now belonged to him.

He would take his time to explore the house later, but he was anxious to change out of the clothes he had been wearing for two straight days. He might even call over one of the ladies from The Ruby later to draw a bath for him to christen the new house.

His hand glided along the smooth handcrafted railing as he went upstairs. Silas Van Dorn may not have been much of a man, but he had impeccable taste. Rigg would make it a point to enjoy the house he had left behind.

At the top of the stairs, Rigg opened the door to the large bedroom that was now his. The thought of lounging in the soft four-poster bed delighted him.

But he stopped short when he saw something hanging from the canopy.

A scalp.

Mackey.

He reached for the Colt on his hip just as the bedroom door slammed behind him, and he felt four sharp blows to his kidneys.

An intense pain webbed through his body as he sank to his knees. He felt the Colt being ripped from his hand before he was struck with the butt of the pistol in the back of the head.

The blow sent him flat on the floor. The room was now spinning, but instinct replaced his dulled senses. He flopped over on his back and reached for the second Colt at his left side.

But Mackey had beat him to it; snatching the pistol from its holster and tossing it to the other side of the room.

Rigg gripped the small blade he kept tucked beneath the holster and drew it, slashing out at Mackey's throat.

But the younger man was fast enough to pitch back just in time for the blade to slice across his chest.

Seeing the blood of his assailant gave Rigg new energy as he scrambled to his feet and lunged at Mackey, blade first.

But Mackey parried the swipe and followed up with a vicious left hook that caught Rigg square in the jaw.

Rigg staggered, but kept his feet, intending to stab Mackey when he drew closer.

But Mackey followed up with a savage uppercut that shattered Rigg's nose and sent him flying back onto the bed.

Dazed and bleeding, but not out of the fight yet, Rigg bounced off the bed and roared at Mackey as he plunged the blade at his assailant's face.

But Mackey grabbed his right hand, stopping the blow, and fired an elbow into Rigg's ruined face. Stars exploded before his eyes, and he fell back on the bed empty-handed and exhausted.

His head was throbbing, and he shut his eyes to keep the room from spinning lest he throw up. He would not give Aaron Mackey the satisfaction of seeing him be sick in his own bed.

Rigg's eyes sprang open, but he saw nothing. He remembered his own prophecy.

I will die in my own bed.

A searing pain in his left leg caused him to cry out as he shut his eyes again, followed by an equal pain in his right.

He did not have to reach down to know what had happened. Mackey had used his own knife to cut the tendons at the backs of his legs. Just as he had taught him to do to fleeing Apache prisoners.

His eyes bulged when he felt Mackey grip him by the throat and raise him from the bed. He expected to see rage in the man's eyes. Hate, even.

Instead, he saw nothing. No spark of humanity or emotion at all as he dropped Rigg higher up on the mattress.

"You coward!" Rigg screamed, though his voice was barely a rasp. "You didn't give me a chance."

"You got more of a chance than Pappy had."

Rigg watched in horror as Mackey took a lamp from the side table and began to pour the kerosene over the length of Rigg's body. "At least you'll die the same way."

Rigg gagged as some of the fluid found its way into his mouth. He clawed at the bedclothes that pulled free as he gripped them. "I'll see him in hell and spit in his face."

"Remember what you used to say, Nathan? How you

always wanted to die in bed?" Mackey thumbed the match alive. "You've got your wish."

The last thing Rigg saw, as the flames began to consume him, was Aaron Mackey standing in the doorway. He could not see his killer, only the vaguest outline of him as he watched the fire take hold.

And then the pain began.

CHAPTER 34

Mackey sat atop Adair in front of Rigg's house as flames began to shoot out from the bedroom. His chest hurt from the blade that had sliced across his chest, but at least it was not a deep cut. It could wait. He bit off the pain it caused by gripping the Peacemaker tighter.

Adair ignored the inferno that was beginning to consume the top floor of the old Van Dorn house. Other flames had ruined the town. Mackey hoped these might begin to purify it.

Mackey didn't have to wait long before six Hancock men came at a dead run to see what was happening.

And they stopped just as quickly when they saw the black Arabian and its rider standing stock still in the middle of the street.

"You boys are too late," Mackey said. "Your boss is dead."

The man in the middle went for his gun first.

Mackey raised the Colt and gunned the man down before he could clear leather.

Then, he shot the man to his left.

Then, the man at the far end.

As the three Hancock men fell, the remaining three backed off and broke toward Lee Street.

Mackey did not have to urge Adair to chase them. The warhorse knew what had to be done.

She easily ran them down as Mackey drew close enough to shoot two of three fleeing men. The last one managed to turn and snap off a quick shot before he stumbled backward into the choppy mud of Front Street.

Mackey brought Adair around, took careful aim down at the cringing Hancock man, and ended him.

Adair shuddered as Mackey reined her in and dumped out the empty cartridges onto the dead man. The mare's blood was up now. She had caught the scent of gunpowder and blood and was anxious to get back to work.

Mackey felt the stares he had drawn from the few townspeople and workers on the street. They were too tired to run and had seen too much to look away.

He slowly fed six new bullets into the Peacemaker. He felt relief course through the growing crowd as they recognized him.

That's right, he thought as he slid the last bullet into the cylinder. *Aaron Mackey has come home.*

He looked up when he heard the boom of Billy's Sharps echo through the dead town like a thunderclap.

He had barely touched the reins before Adair bolted down Front Street toward the sound of thunder rolling down the hills.

Billy had been lying prone among the rocks for fifteen minutes when he saw the flames shoot out from the upstairs window of the Van Dorn house. Six shots followed, and he knew Mackey had stopped at the top of Front Street to reload.

Billy had kept the Hancock officers crouched behind the wagon dead in the sights of his Sharps the entire time. When one of them popped up to see what was happening at the north end of town, Billy fired.

The fifty-caliber slug hit the Hancock man in the side of the head. What was left of him was still twitching as it fell back against the Municipal Building.

Billy ejected the round and fed a new one into the chamber before drawing a bead on one of the men who had crept over to the dead man's side. Most of him was still under the cover of the toppled wagon, but enough was exposed. His next shot took off the man's hat and the top of his head with it. He landed atop his fallen kin, just as dead.

Knowing they had probably marked his position by now, Billy moved at a crouch to his left just as a bullet ricocheted off the rock he had just been using as cover. He dove for the next rock over, where he had stashed his Winchester.

Another round pinged off that rock, quickly followed by another that struck the dirt to his right.

He did not need to look to see the shots were not coming from the Hancock men below. They were coming from a much higher position.

Someone in the Municipal Building had seen him.

And now, Billy was the one who was pinned down.

James Grant had been reviewing the plans for the town with the men from the Dover Station bank when he heard the gunshots carry down Front Street. The three bankers backed away from the window and fled his office as Grant rushed to see what was happening.

Two Hancock men lay dead in the street as a rider on a black horse circled back and finished off a third. The rider and horse stood still in the middle of the thoroughfare as the killer appeared to slowly reload his pistol like he did not have a care in the world.

Grant could not see the rider clearly from this distance, but he saw the flames curling out of the old Van Dorn house and knew Rigg was probably dead.

That meant the rider had to be Aaron Mackey.

And where Mackey was, Billy Sunday was sure to be close by.

Grant flinched when he heard a thunderclap roll down from the rocky hillside. He looked down at his men keeping Jerry Halstead holed up in the jailhouse in time to see one of their heads disappear in a cloud of red mist.

Grant knew that would be Billy Sunday and his damnable Sharps rifle.

Grant scrambled back to his desk and snatched up the Winchester he had propped up against the wall for protection. He had just gotten back to the window in time to see a second Hancock man fall atop the first. The remaining three remained low behind the wagon.

Cowards.

But James Grant had cowered under Aaron Mackey's gun once before. He had made a silent vow to never do it again.

He dropped to a knee and poked the barrel of the Winchester out the open window. He had seen the spot among the rocks from where the Sharps had been and fired in that direction.

The bullet hit where he was aiming just as the black

deputy dodged from his position to the safety of another rock.

"I've got you now!" Grant roared as he levered another round into the chamber and fired. The bullet smacked off the rock Billy was hiding behind. He shifted his aim and sent the next round into the dirt. He had expected Billy to jump from cover.

But the lawman remained hidden behind the safety of the rock. Grant knew Billy would only remain hidden for so long before he stole a glance at the Municipal Building to see where the shot had come from.

And when he did, Grant would be ready. He would never be caught short by Mackey or Sunday ever again.

He did not have to wait long. He saw a flash of movement to the right side of the rock. Something darting past. He fired two shots at it before he realized it was not the deputy.

Just his hat.

He aimed his Winchester back at the rock as he levered in a new round.

Just as he barely glimpsed the outline of a man above the rock, the windowsill and frame exploded in his face.

Grant cried out as he fell back into his office. The Winchester skittered across the floor.

A searing pain filled the left side of his head as he pawed at the wound with a trembling hand. The entire left side of his face was peppered with shards of splintered glass and wood. He felt for a hole at the back of his head, fearing he might already be dying, but he only felt his own hair.

Grant began to pluck the splinters from the skin closest to his eye. He managed to get a few out before the pain grew too great, and he feared he might pass out.

But James Grant would not allow himself to pass out.

Not yet. Not with the destruction of Aaron Mackey so close at hand. He would see that for himself with whatever eyesight he had left.

As he crawled across the floor toward his Winchester, more gunfire rose up from the street, and Grant knew the end was near, whatever that end might be.

This time, Aaron Mackey would be the one to falter beneath the gun. The guns of the Hancock family that lived to see him dead.

CHAPTER 35

Gunfire rang out all around Mackey as he and Adair raced down Front Street.

None of the bullets struck him, and none of them sounded like they had even come close as he sped toward the jailhouse to rescue Jerry. But there was no doubt the Hancocks knew he was in town.

Mackey steered Adair to the right side of Front Street, toward the wagon where he knew the Hancock men were hiding. He saw two dead men slumped against the Municipal Building and knew three more were likely still in hiding.

One man rose from behind the wagon to shoot at him, but Mackey fired first and put him down. Adair bolted past the wagon as Mackey fired another shot down at another Hancock man, but he had no idea if he had hit him.

A shot rang out from the front door of the Municipal Building. Mackey saw one of Rigg's men crouched behind the building's heavy metal doors.

Mackey's shot hit the door, but Billy's shot from up

in the rocks struck the man in the chest and sent him backward.

Well past the Municipal Building now, Mackey brought Adair around and heeled her back toward the jailhouse. He pulled his Winchester from the saddle scabbard as he dropped from the saddle and headed for the jail. Adair ran off down the alleyway toward the back of the jail.

The jailhouse door opened and Mackey dove inside as round after round began to slam into the boardwalk and walls all around him. He felt a fire in his left side as he hit the floor and heard the heavy door shut behind him.

"Hot damn, Aaron!" Jerry exclaimed. "I'm glad to see you."

But Mackey was in no condition to enjoy the reunion. He patted his left front side and his hand came up bloody. "I'm hit."

Jerry dropped to a knee beside him and noticed the blood on the front of Mackey's shirt. "You got lucky, amigo. It's just a graze. That one could've ended you."

"That's a knife wound." He took his hand away from his left side and showed him the blood. "This is a bullet wound."

Jerry moved to take a closer look as the sound of bullets slamming against the jailhouse died off. "Looks like a ricochet took a small chunk out of you above your hip. It's a nasty scratch, but it's better than a hole in your belly. Got anything in this dump by way of medicine?"

Despite his condition, Mackey resented his jailhouse being called a dump. "This dump has kept us alive more times than I can count. And no, we don't have any medicine. Doc Ridley always came by whenever we needed tending to."

Jerry stood up and looked around. "Looks like I'll have to make do with what we've got."

With the initial shock of his wounds wearing off, they began to hurt like hell. "You sure this is just a flesh wound? That's an awful lot of blood."

"Of course, I'm sure," Jerry said as he walked over to the stove. "To listen to you, you'd think you've never been shot before."

"Because I haven't."

Jerry turned to look at him. "That so? After all the scrapes you've been in?"

"Sorry to disappoint you." Mackey had not thought much about it until that moment. "Guess it's only fitting that my last day in Dover Station is also the first time I've been shot."

Jerry went back to the cells and came out tearing a sheet in half. "If you die, it won't be from that paper cut on your side." He grabbed the coffeepot from the stove and crouched beside the marshal.

Mackey shied away from the hot pot. "What are you doing?"

"You don't keep whiskey in here and you don't keep medicine," Jerry said. "Best I can do for you is to pack that wound with coffee grinds to help ease the pain and soak up the blood."

Mackey began to object, but remembered the Apache and Comanche often used poultices to mend gunshot wounds and cuts. "Those grinds must be boiling."

"Ran out of firewood for the stove yesterday." Jerry dumped out the damp coffee grinds into his hand and packed them on the wound. "But coffee's still coffee, even when it's cold."

The grinds stung at first, but the pain quickly died away

as Jerry folded one half of the torn bedsheet over and over to place on top of the grinds and used the other half to tie it around Mackey's waist to hold it in place. "I've only got enough grinds to pack the wound in your side. That cut on your chest will have to wait."

"At least I'll smell good," Mackey said. "Always did like the smell of coffee."

Jerry inclined his head toward the door that continued to be peppered by bullets. "Hope you like the smell of gunpowder, because we've got plenty of that coming our way."

Mackey held out his hand to Jerry. "Help me up."

But Jerry pushed Mackey's hand aside. "You're not getting up until that bleeding lets up some. Give the grinds a chance to stop the blood. I've got enough to worry about around here without you passing out on me. A few minutes won't make much of a difference. I've been holding them off for a day or so."

Mackey had no intention of passing out or sitting down while Billy was outside fighting for his life. He tried to get up on his own power, but the lightning flash of pain that coursed through his body sent him flat.

Jerry eased him back against the wall. "I told you not to move. What's your hurry?"

Mackey spoke through clenched teeth. "We need to distract the Hancocks while Billy gets clear of the rocks. He's out there all by himself."

"I thought I heard his Sharps banging out from the rocks," Jerry said. "He'll be fine, Aaron. This isn't his first dustup."

"But he's up there all alone, damn it! We need to give him cover while he makes a break for it." Mackey reached for his Winchester, but it was too far away. The effort left him winded as sweat broke out on his forehead. "Can't let him get pinned down behind those rocks. They'll be riding after him soon."

Jerry eased him back against the wall again. "And you're no good to him in the shape you're in. You're hurt. Give yourself time to heal. I'll mind the door. They haven't been able to get in here yet, and I'm not going to let them get in here now."

That was when they heard the first thud hit the jailhouse door. And despite his growing delirium, Mackey knew that was not a bullet.

It was from something much bigger.

Fresh sweat broke out on his forehead when the second thud came. "The bastards are ramming the door."

CHAPTER 36

Billy knew he had hit Grant, but there was no way of knowing for certain if he had killed him. And he could not afford to stay where he was long enough to find out.

Grant had no sooner disappeared from the window when Billy picked up his rifles and scrambled back up the incline toward the tree where his horse was tied off. He slid the Sharps into the scabbard before climbing into the saddle, keeping the Winchester in hand.

He brought the horse around away from the trees so he could see any riders coming his way while he fed more cartridges from his saddlebag into the Winchester. He was far from empty, but doubted he would have the chance to reload once the Hancocks came riding after him.

The rifle fully loaded, Billy stood up in the stirrups to get a look at the scene on Front Street. Six men were darting across the thoroughfare from the alley next to the Municipal Building lugging a large log from the sawmill. They were headed straight for the jailhouse.

They were going to ram the door.

Billy brought the Winchester up to his shoulder and snapped off a quick shot at the men. The bullet missed and struck the log instead. One of the men at the back flinched and fell back, letting go of the makeshift battering ram. But it was not enough to stop the momentum of the others.

He levered in a fresh round and aimed at the prone man in the thoroughfare when bullets began to whizz past him from right to left. But none of them had found their mark, and Billy still had a shot to make. He aimed carefully down at the fallen man and fired. The shot struck his target in the chest and laid him flat in the mud.

Billy dropped back into the saddle and snapped the reins. His horse broke into a dead run away from the gunfire toward the town cemetery. He did not bother to look back at his pursuers. He imagined there was a lot of them and there was no time to lose.

He heeled his mount into a full gallop. The horse responded by giving him everything she had. The ridge behind him filled with rifle and pistol fire, but all of the bullets sailed wide of him. *They're firing at a dead run*, Billy thought as he opened the distance between them. *Good. Let them waste their bullets. My shots will count.*

For he knew however many of them were chasing him, it was that many fewer Hancock men firing at Jerry and Aaron in the jailhouse.

The gunfire behind him continued to fall short and wide as he sped toward the cemetery.

He had just about reached the low iron fence that enclosed the cemetery when his horse shuddered from the impact of a bullet in its left flank. The mare reared up from the shot but tried to keep her footing as her left leg failed.

Training and instinct led Billy to spill off the right side of the saddle as the mare collapsed to the left. He hit the ground hard but kept his grip on the Winchester as he rolled free. He got to his feet and kept running toward the cemetery.

He hurdled over the low iron fence before sliding to a stop behind a large gravestone.

His fallen horse began to scream in pain as Billy aimed his Winchester at the mass of horses and riders bearing down on him. He judged them to be about twenty or so, clustered together in the narrow path along the ridge above Dover Station.

Clustered together would be their downfall.

Billy's first shot put his mare out of her misery with a single round to the head. She had been a good horse to him and did not deserve to suffer.

He levered in a fresh round as he shifted his aim to the approaching riders, intent that her death would not be in vain.

He shot the lead rider in the chest, sending him tumbling backward out of the saddle. The Hancocks were so bunched together on the narrow trail that the falling man caused chaos for the men and horses behind him.

Billy watched several of the horses falter as they trampled the rider in their charge toward the cemetery. But there were still plenty heading right for him at a dead run.

Billy aimed at the next man in the lead and fired. The bullet caught him in the right shoulder and sent his rifle back across the face of the man riding next to him. Both fell from their horses, causing even more of a knot of confusion on the narrow pathway.

Two startled horses shied away from the knot and brought their riders with them as they slipped over the ridgeline and tumbled down among the rocks. The screams of injured horses and men would have bothered Billy if he had the time to hear them.

But he did not have time, for two riders pressed on beyond the fray and kept coming at him.

Billy cursed as his next shot went wide, but his next shot hit the second rider low in the belly. The man cried out and dropped his rifle.

But the lead rider kept coming, kicking his horse into a full gallop.

The horse was faster than it looked and closed the distance quicker than Billy expected. His next shot only nicked the rider in the side as he tried to get the frightened animal to leap the low iron fence surrounding the cemetery.

But the horse was not a jumper and its front hooves caught the fence, sending it and its rider tumbling into the cemetery, bowling over a few gravestones at the edge.

He decided the fallen man would be out of the fight for now and shifted his aim back toward the main body of Hancock riders who had come gunning for him.

The knot of horses in the middle of the path was beginning to loosen as another mount lost its footing and tumbled off the ridgeline.

One of the riders managed to get off a lucky shot that struck the gravestone Billy was using for cover. The men were clustered so tightly together that Billy had no trouble picking them off as they tried to regain control of their mounts.

Three more Hancocks fell before the remaining men brought their horses around and rode away from the killing ground as fast as they could.

They had given up the fight, but Billy had not.

He rose and drew careful aim at the last rider in the bunch, but his shot went wide as he was tackled by the Hancock man who had tumbled into the cemetery.

The Winchester clattered among the gravestones as Billy was knocked off his feet. His attacker straddled him as he pummeled him with a flurry of blows that mostly struck the deputy's back and shoulders.

When the Hancock man finally stopped, he looked toward his escaping kin and was about to call out when Billy threw a right cross that connected with his attacker's jaw.

The man smacked his head off a gravestone as he tumbled back.

Billy pulled himself up into a crouch and drew his bowie knife from the back of his belt. He was ready to plunge the big knife into his attacker's heart when the man twitched as his last breath escaped him. His eyes fluttered before the last spark of life left them forever.

The man was most likely dead, but Billy had learned most likely was never good enough where the Hancocks were concerned. He brought down the knife anyway, just to be sure. No sense in wasting a bullet. He would need every round he had left.

Billy snatched his Winchester and took cover behind another gravestone. The Hancocks were still riding away from him, back toward the burning Van Dorn House and town, where he imagined they would come up with another plan to hit him.

If they were smart, they would split their force and charge the cemetery from two directions at once. One from the ridgeline they had just fled and one from Front Street. Maybe bring more men with them this time.

Billy knew that not even he could cover two positions at once. If he stayed where he was, he would never leave the cemetery alive. *At least they wouldn't have far to carry me.*

But one Hancock man had laid hands on him that day, and that was one too many.

He might not be able to fight them all off before they got him, but if he had to go, he would bring as many of them with him as possible.

If he was going to die that day, he might as well die among friends. His life after the cavalry had begun in the crooked old jailhouse on Front Street. He could not think of a better place to end it, if it came to that. Among friends. Among Aaron and Jerry.

Not friends. Family.

He tucked the bowie back in his belt and began to run down the hill toward the jailhouse when a loud boom carried on the wind from Front Street.

The men were ramming the jailhouse door.

Billy ran as fast as his legs could carry him.

CHAPTER 37

"That door won't hold for long," Mackey yelled over the rhythmic pounding of the door.

Boom. Stop. *Boom.* Stop.

Each blow shook more grout and dust from the wall around the door. Mackey knew the entire front side of the jail would cave in if they did not do something soon.

Jerry ran to Mackey's desk and tried to push it toward the door, but Mackey knew it was no use. The desk was too heavy for two men to move, let alone one man and another with a hole in his side.

Mackey edged himself over to the rifle rack on the wall above his head and stabbed at the coach gun cradled there. He ignored the fire in his left side as he grabbed the shotgun.

Boom. Stop. Stop. *Boom.* Stop. Stop.

The blows were coming slower now. The men were tiring.

Mackey did not have to check to see if the shotgun was loaded. His guns were always loaded.

Jerry saw what he was doing and stopped trying to move the desk.

"After the next strike, throw the door open and get the hell out of the way."

Jerry ran to the door.

Boom.

A beam in the ceiling cracked.

Jerry slid the latch open and threw the door open wide.

Mackey flopped onto his belly as Jerry fell back.

The attackers staggered in the doorway to keep control of the log.

Mackey cut loose with the right barrel of the coach gun.

The heavy log slammed down into the boardwalk as the men on one side of it were cut down in a cloud of gunsmoke.

The two men on the left side of the log fell toward the doorway, carried by the momentum of the falling ram.

Mackey fired the left barrel of the shotgun.

The men who fell past the door did not get up again.

The heavy wooden beams in the ceiling cracked again, and Mackey ignored the fire in his side as he cast away the coach gun and got to his feet.

He drew his Peacemaker from his belly holster and scrambled toward the door. He caught a Hancock man running away from the jailhouse toward the shelter of the Municipal Building.

The Colt bucked as Mackey shot him in the back. The fleeing man fell to his knees before skidding to a halt at the bottom step of the Municipal Building.

Mackey's pain was gone. So was his fear. So was his rage. All he could see was that damnable fortress across Front Street. The gaudy monstrosity that had meant the death of all that he once held dear.

His town.

His childhood.

His life.

His father.

No, he was not afraid and could not feel pain as he stood on the boardwalk and yelled, "Is that all you bastards have? Send Grant out here and let's finish it! Right now!"

He heard his own voice echo in the quiet street save for something else. Something that almost sounded like singing. He wondered if he might already be dead, when the pain from the wound in his side told him he was still very much alive.

But he bit off the pain as he yelled at the men he could see still crouched inside the doorway of the Municipal Building. "Are you going to send him out, or do I have to come in there and drag him out?"

The man in the doorway disappeared and, over the roar of his own blood in his ears, he heard the sounds of a scuffle from inside the building. He wondered if Grant was trying to come outside, only to be held back by his own men.

He kept watching the Municipal Building as he heard Jerry walk out onto the boardwalk beside him. "He still in there?"

Mackey would not take his eyes off the door. "Looks like. Anyone else on the street?"

"No," Jerry told him. "But Billy's walking up on your left."

Mackey looked and saw his deputy come around the side of the jailhouse, his Winchester aimed at the Municipal Building entrance.

"Put it down for now," Mackey said. "Sounds like they're making up their minds."

Billy reluctantly lowered his rifle, but kept watching the entrance, too. "Looks that way."

Mackey suddenly felt tired and leaned against the doorframe for support. "How are you fixed for bullets?"

"Nearly out." Billy stepped up to the boardwalk and looked at the five dead men scattered in front of the jail-house. The log they had been using to ram the door had fallen and broken the steps. "You boys have been busy."

"You too, from what I heard. You all right?"

"Fine." He stopped when he saw the blood on Mackey's shirt. "Damn it, Aaron. You've been shot."

"I'm fine. Jerry patched me up using some old coffee grinds."

Billy looked at Jerry. "Comanche teach you that trick?"

"I've picked up a few things along the way. Say, anyone else hear singing?"

Mackey was glad someone else had heard it, too. "Thought it was just me."

The three lawmen looked up Front Street and saw a group of men and women walking toward them through the encroaching darkness. Many held torches as they moved along the width of the thoroughfare.

They were singing "Amazing Grace."

Doc Ridley led them, his Bible clutched against his chest just as it had been when he had led Walter Under-hill's funeral procession a month before.

Was it only a month ago? Mackey wondered. It seemed decades ago.

Gunmen began to file out from the Municipal Building and the three lawmen crouched behind the log and the doorway of the jailhouse for cover.

"This is it," Mackey told his friends. "This is how it ends."

But the gunmen did not fire and neither did Mackey or Billy or Jerry. They all took cover behind the overturned wagon but watched as the ragged procession made its way toward them.

Hancock men filed out around both sides of the Municipal Building. All of them were armed, but none of them were raising their guns toward the jail.

Doc Ridley stumbled up to the ruined boardwalk as the procession of singing townspeople moved between the two buildings. He was still singing when he gripped Mackey's arm and pulled him out from behind the doorway.

Mackey kept the pistol at his side as he found himself pulled down into the tide of humanity slowly moving along the thoroughfare. Billy followed. So did Jerry.

Mackey tried to see if Grant had come out of the building, but the crowd was too thick for him to see much of anything. They kept warbling through the old-time hymn as they moved past the buildings and up the hill that led to the cemetery.

That was when Mackey saw where they were taking him.

A mound of fresh dirt stood alone in an untouched part of the cemetery, just outside the patch of dirt that had become known as Mackey's Garden.

There was no gravestone, just a wooden cross stuck in the ground with the name "Brendan Mackey" scrawled across it in black paint.

Doc Ridley held on to Mackey's arm as the singing townspeople filled in around him. Billy was on his right. Jerry was on his left.

Mackey waited for the sight of his father's grave to impact him, but it did not. He had been too accustomed to death to place much value in the resting place of earthly remains. Not even the place where his father had been buried could change that.

But what the townspeople had done certainly reached

him. They had done the only thing they could do to end the carnage. They had come together to save him and Billy and Jerry. They had come together to save themselves from further bloodshed, too.

The people had just begun to sing the last part of the mournful hymn when James Grant was shoved to the front of the group ringing his father's grave. The left side of Grant's face was a bloody ruin, peppered with splinters and glass. Two Hancock gunmen were on either side of him.

Mackey tried to raise his pistol, but Doc Ridley's grip on his arm was surprisingly strong for a man so frail.

"Dearly beloved," the doctor called out, "we are gathered here this evening to bid a sacred farewell to a man who helped build the town we have been so humbled to call our home for these many years. A man whose grit and humor and determination helped forge a town out of the wilderness. A man whose courage was an example to all of those who were wise enough to see it and fortunate enough to bear witness to it."

Doc Ridley closed his eyes and kept his grip on Mackey's hand. "Heavenly Father, we commend the spirit of Brendan Mackey into thy hands and hope you will hold him in the palm of your hands."

The people said, "Amen" as one.

Doc Ridley let go of Mackey's hand.

Mackey raised his Peacemaker and aimed it at James Grant.

So did Billy. So did Jerry.

And every Hancock man in the cemetery aimed their guns at them.

Billy surprised Mackey by saying, "James Grant, you are under arrest for the attempted murder of a peace officer in the execution of his lawful duty."

Grant looked at him with his good remaining eye. He smiled as the blood continued to trickle down his face. "You couldn't prove it before, and you can't prove it now."

"Sure, I can. You shot at me up in the rocks, and I shot back."

"Prove it."

"Your face is all the proof I need," Billy said. "And this time, I can swear to it in court with a clean conscience."

"You're talking about a courtroom?" Grant looked around at all the Hancock men aiming their guns at the lawmen. "What makes you think you'll leave this place alive?"

One of the women in the group stepped forward and stuck a pistol against Grant's belly.

Mackey almost dropped his gun.

It was Katherine.

"They've got more chance of making it out of here alive than you do, you son of a bitch."

"Enough!" cried out Mad Nellie Hancock as she pushed her way through the crowd and into the clearing. "Everybody just hold on, here."

No one lowered their guns.

Nellie said to Mackey, "I've lost enough of my own on account of you, Mackey. If we give you Grant, do you promise to leave us alone, for good and for all?"

"I'm taking him one way or the other," Mackey said. "Straight up or over the saddle. It makes no difference to me."

"But it makes a difference to me and mine," Nellie said. "You kill him, all of you die. Thanks to your fancy lady here, now some of mine will die in the shootin'. You want Grant? I don't want any more of mine dyin'. Not today. Not tomorrow. Not next month or next year, either. I want it over for good and for all. What do you say?"

Mackey felt the weight of every eye in town upon him. He knew what he should do. And he knew what he had to do.

Unfortunately, they were not the same thing.

"Tell your men to lower their guns and move away," Mackey said. "They'll have no more problems from me."

Nellie leaned forward. "I've got your word on that?"

Mackey gripped the Peacemaker tighter. "Any of yours play a hand in killing my father?"

"The Hancocks always claim their dead proudly," Nellie told him. "If a Hancock had been killed along with your daddy, you'd have heard about it. We knew what Grant and Rigg were up to. We didn't stop 'em. But we had no hand in it, either."

Mackey imagined that was as close to the truth as he could expect Mad Nellie Hancock to get.

"Tell them to lower their weapons and go home. You'll have no trouble from me and my men, but they lower their guns first."

Nellie glared at the men as she gestured for them to lower their guns.

All of them did and began to slowly walk away from the cemetery.

One of the townspeople handed Billy a rope. He and Jerry set about tying Grant's hands behind his back while Katherine kept her pistol against his belly.

"You damned fool!" Grant yelled at Nellie. "I'm the only chance you have in this territory. Without me, who's going to rebuild this place? Who's going to line your pockets? Cut these bastards down and let's get back to work."

"Enough Hancock blood has been spilled on your account, Grant. We'll make do with what we've got."

She looked at Pappy's grave, then at Mackey. "I hope

you ain't expectin' condolences, Marshal. I never did like that mouthy old bastard anyway."

With Grant secured, Mackey holstered his pistol. "The feeling was mutual."

Mackey waited for her to say more, but she did not. She simply melted in with the crowd and headed back home with her people.

Katherine rushed to Aaron and threw her arms around his waist. He jumped from the pain that spiked in his left side and she moved away from him. "Honey, are you hurt?"

"I'll be fine." He eased the pistol from her right hand. "Where'd you get this?"

"Lynch gave it to me before I got on the train to come down here," she said as she lifted his shirt to look at his wound. "He didn't want me to come but knew there was no sense in trying to stop me. I'm only glad I got here when I did."

He pulled her close to him and wrapped his arms around her. She stopped worrying about his wound and embraced him, too. "You are some kind of woman, Mrs. Campbell."

"Mrs. Mackey," she said into his chest. "And don't you forget it."

"How touching," Grant sneered as Billy and Jerry pulled the rope tighter around his wrists.

"What do you want me to do with him, Aaron?"

"Stick him back in the jailhouse where he belongs," Mackey said. "Our jailhouse. Jerry, check on when the next train's headed back to Helena. I've got a feeling Judge Forester won't be so anxious to kick him loose this time around."

Grant struggled as the two deputies yanked him in front of them as they walked down from the cemetery.

Doc Ridley touched Mackey's arm as he joined the rest of the townspeople who trailed away from the cemetery. He did not say anything, and Mackey did not expect him to. He had already said plenty without saying anything at all.

As the last of the townspeople walked back down the hill to whatever was left of their town, Mackey and Katherine stood alone beside his father's grave, holding each other as another night descended on Dover Station.

CHAPTER 38

Two weeks later, Mackey and Billy stood at the window of Judge Forester's office, looking down at the gallows in the yard of the jail across the street.

"Do you agree with the newspapermen, Marshal?" the judge asked. "Do you think I'm a fool for not allowing them to cover James Grant's hanging?"

Mackey had never liked hangings. He thought it a morbid way to kill a man. The waiting to die. The building of a gallows. The rope hanging there waiting to be employed for only one use. He knew some people needed killing and figured a bullet in the belly in the middle of nowhere was cruel enough punishment for any offense at hand. But hanging just did not sit well with him.

"I'm under the impression that my opinion doesn't matter to you one way or the other, your honor."

The judge looked at him through cigar smoke. "Your opinion matters when I ask for it."

Mackey looked back at the gallows. "Never liked hangings personally, so I'd say you were right to keep it private."

Judge Forester looked at Billy, who was also looking out the window at the gallows. "Do you agree, Deputy?"

"I wished I'd shot him six months ago when I had the chance," Billy admitted. "But I think a man deserves some dignity when he dies, especially when it's the court doing the killing."

Forester grunted as he puffed on his cigar. "Justice is supposed to be blind and bare for all of the world to see."

"Justice would've been me letting Billy shoot the son of a bitch like he said. The papers just want pictures for their readers," Mackey said. "But like Billy said, a man deserves some dignity in death, even James Grant."

"It certainly would have saved a great deal of bother, all things considered. Then, of course, I would've had to hang you two for murder." The judge glanced back at the large clock in his office. It was almost eight in the morning. "Five minutes until the proceedings start. You boys sure you don't want to be down there and look him in the eyes one last time before he's shown across to the other side?"

But Mackey had decided the last time he would look at James Grant was that moment the deputies led him from the courtroom after Judge Forester handed down his death sentence. To go down there now would only be self-serving. If the events at Dover Station had taught him anything, it was that he should try to be above such things if he wanted to be marshal of this territory.

"Lynch can handle it," Mackey said. "Besides, my place is up here in case you or the governor decide to delay the execution, remember."

"No one's going to be delaying anything," Forester said. "We want this skunk dead and buried before he stinks up the territory any further than he already has." The judge winced. "I've got to admit, I thought you'd be the one who'd be swinging today, Mackey. I didn't think you had it in you to let him live after what he did to your daddy. I don't know if I could've done it myself."

Mackey had tried not to think too much about his father's death since returning to Helena. It had been better for him. Better for Grant's prospects of meeting the hangman's noose, too, lest Mackey decide to do something stupid. "I try not to think about it, sir. There was enough killing to last that town for a long while."

Forester took another puff on his cigar. "I've heard people say they don't know if the town will ever come back. With Mr. Rice putting everything up for sale, who knows what'll happen to the place?"

Mackey could feel the old questions and the old anger beginning to rattle around in his mind. Was he angrier at Mr. Rice for abandoning the town or building it up in the first place? If he had been scared off by Darabont that first week he was in town, none of this would have happened. Dover Station would have gone on being the sleepy Montana town it always had been, and Pappy probably would still be alive.

But he would not have been the territorial marshal, and Katherine would not own the nicest hotel in Helena. Billy would not be a federal lawman, either, nor Jerry Halstead nor Josh Sandborne. They'd all be growing stale on the front porch of the old jailhouse on Front Street, watching the world ride by.

And, as was his custom, Billy Sunday filled in the silence left by Mackey's brooding. "Dover Station's not our town anymore, Judge. Helena is. Everything that counts is here now."

Forester looked at Mackey. "He speak for you, too, son?"

"He's the only man who can," Mackey said.

"Glad to hear it." Forester leaned against the window

frame as they watched Sean Lynch and his men lead James Grant out from the jail and into the yard. One deputy with a rifle led the way while another trailed behind him. Lynch brought up the rear where the preacher would normally be, but Grant had declined to have one present at his hanging. In fact, he had not spoken to anyone since Forester had handed down the sentence of death the previous week.

Mackey watched them lead Grant up the thirteen steps to the platform before Lynch placed him squarely in the middle of the trapdoor that would open beneath his feet once the rope was secured around his neck.

Although they could not hear anything from so far away, he could see Lynch pause and ask Grant if he had any final words before his sentence was carried out.

Mackey imagined he must have said something along those lines, for Grant's head snapped up toward the window where Mackey and Billy and the judge now stood. He glared up at them with all the hate and fury a condemned man could possibly muster.

But hate and fury were all he had left, and neither could hurt anyone any longer. And Mackey knew that with one nod of Judge Forester's head, James Grant would never hurt anyone ever again.

Obviously realizing Grant had nothing to say, Mackey watched him slip the burlap hood over Grant's head while two deputies tied his feet. That task done, Lynch slipped the noose over Grant's neck and pulled it tight. The knot was just above his right ear and appeared to have just enough give in it to end Grant's life quick once he threw the lever.

Lynch took five steps back and put his hand on that lever before looking up at the window where Billy and Mackey and Judge Forester were standing. He needed final confirmation before he pulled the lever that dropped James Grant to his doom.

Mackey began to step aside so Forester could move in and signal the order, but the judge placed a hand on the marshal's back. "The honor belongs to you, Marshal Mackey. God knows if anyone has earned the right to send him to hell, it's you."

Mackey remained where he was. He tried to feel something for all Grant had done. All of the killings and all of the pain he had caused and all of the blood he had spilled in his quest for more. He was never content with the generous wages Mr. Van Dorn had paid him. He was not satisfied with a healthy share of power. Because men like him were never satisfied. They wanted all of the money and all of the power, and when that ran out, they would find something else to desire so they could have it. Men like Grant built things up just so they could tear them down and start all over again, just as he had done with Dover Station.

Men like Grant drew men like Nathan Rigg to their side, men who desired the same thing.

More, whatever that meant.

But on that particular morning in Helena, Montana, James Grant's days of wanting more were about to come to an end.

The marshal of the Montana Territory gave one curt nod.

Deputy Marshal Sean Lynch pulled the lever.

And James Grant dropped through the trapdoor before jerking to a halt. The angle the noose snapped his neck, left no doubt that he was dead.

Mackey closed his eyes.

And did not feel a thing.

Judge Forester popped the cigar into his mouth as he

turned away from the window. "Good way to start the day, don't you think, boys?"

Billy turned away from the window, too. "Don't know about good, your honor. But it sure was necessary."

"Certainly was, wasn't it, Mackey?"

He decided it was time to stop watching Grant's body dancing at the end of the hangman's rope. He was as dead as he was ever going to be. No sense in gawking at it.

He moved away from the window and approached the judge's desk. "Like Billy said, it was necessary."

Forester resumed signing the thick stack of warrants he had piled on his desk. "Glad you think so. If you'd like to take some time off, spend it with your wife, I'd be amenable to it. You probably could use a few days to yourself, now that it's over."

Billy stepped forward and picked up some of the warrants Judge Forester had just signed. "Looks like we've still got plenty of work to do, your honor. As long as you've still got paper on people, nothing is over. Not by a long shot."

Forester looked up as he folded a warrant closed. "Billy speak for you on that, too, Marshal?"

Mackey grinned at his deputy, who grinned back. "Always has. Always will." Mackey nodded at the sheaf of warrants Billy was holding. "Who's next?"

*Keep reading for a special excerpt of another
thrilling Western adventure by* TERRENCE MCCAULEY . . .

DARK TERRITORY
A SHERIFF AARON MACKEY WESTERN

*In the boomtown of Dover Station, Montana, tracks
have been laid and everyone's looking to make a fortune,
lawfully or not. And the law has something to say about it—
one bullet at a time . . .*

DOVER STATION—WHERE DEATH RIDES
FASTER THAN THE WIND

A rash of deadly train robberies has the chief investor of
Dover Station feeling itchier than a quick draw without a
target. And he wants Sheriff Aaron Mackey to scratch
that itch with every bullet his battered badge authorizes
him to shoot. When Mackey and his men gun down four
kill-crazy bandits, they uncover a plot cooked up by a
respected citizen of Dover Station—someone who can
pull enough strings to replace Mackey with a disgraced
marshal from Texas. Now Mackey's badge may not say
much, but his gun defies all fear. Anyone who stands
between Mackey and the future of Dover Station is
about to become buried in the pages of history . . .

Look for **DARK TERRITORY** *on sale now.*

CHAPTER 1

Sheriff Aaron Mackey and Deputy Billy Sunday came running when they heard the shotgun blast from Tent City.

Mackey was not surprised to find one of the Bollard twins blocking the end of the alley between the new Municipal Building under construction and the old bakery on Second Street.

Since the man was facing the other way, Mackey could not tell which Bollard twin it was, not that it mattered. Both buffalo skinners were as big as they were mean, with the same bald head and long greasy black hair that hung practically to their shoulders.

Whichever twin this was, he was holding a smoking double-barreled shotgun at the end of the narrow alley. He was most likely drunk, too, given the way he was swaying.

The crowd that had gathered booed when the sheriff ran toward him and slammed the butt of his Winchester into the back of the bigger man's skull. Bollard timbered forward into the dense mud of Second Street. Mackey yanked the shotgun from beneath the fallen man and handed it to Billy.

His deputy opened the shotgun. "Both barrels are spent." He cast the shotgun aside. "I'll cover you from here."

The sheriff stepped over one Bollard twin to confront the other on Second Street, the heart of what had become known as Tent City. He almost gagged at the stench of overboiled meat and drying laundry filling the cold air as he pushed through the bedraggled crowd that had gathered to watch the spectacle.

The rapid growth of Dover Station thanks to investment from the Dover Station Company had attracted too many people looking for work and not enough places to live, hence the creation of Tent City. Many who lived there had plenty of money in the bank, but nowhere to spend it except the saloons and joy houses. Such squalor tended to breed a misery of its own devising, and Tent City was no exception. They never had much occasion to cheer and made the most of it when they did.

They were cheering now.

Mackey saw the other Bollard brother was putting on quite a show, standing over a man bleeding from the kind of chest wound only a shotgun blast could make. Surprisingly, the victim was not dead yet and was doing his best to squirm free from the giant looming over him with a skinning knife.

Mackey, tall and lean, turned sideways to make himself harder to hit if Bollard pulled a gun. It also made it easier for Mackey to draw and fire the Peacemaker holstered next to his buckle if it came to that. But the sheriff made a point of keeping the barrel of the Winchester down. No sense in forcing Bollard to act and make a bad situation worse.

"Drop the knife and step away from the man, Bollard," Mackey called out. "Right now."

The crowd booed, and the big man held his ground. "Not

on your life, Sheriff. Not after what he done. Stabbin' my brother? Sneakin' around, stealin' other people's goods? T'aint right and you damn well knows it."

Mackey kept his eyes on Bollard when he heard Doc Ridley yelling from the boardwalk across the thoroughfare. "That man is still alive. I might be able to save him, Aaron. Get that animal away from him!"

Bollard pointed his knife at the acting mayor of Dover Station. "Don't go calling me no animal, you little bastard. Check on my brother's wounds if'n you want to be useful."

Then he pointed the knife at Mackey. "And you had no call to buffalo my brother like you done. Tom's already hurtin' and was well within his rights to shoot this son of a bitch I got right here."

The crowd of Tent City grumbled in support. Keeping his eyes on Bollard, Mackey spoke over his shoulder to his deputy. "Check on Tom for me."

"Already did," the black man whispered. "Given the amount of blood pooling into the mud around his belly, I'd say he was gutted. Can't tell for certain, but I think he's dead. Slamming that rifle butt into him probably didn't help much, though."

The sheriff was glad Billy had kept his voice down. The crowd might riot of they knew Tom was already dead, and the situation would quickly spin out of control.

Despite Mackey and Billy's best efforts, the law had a tenuous grip on Tent City. A riot would make him lose control of the ragtag settlement forever. He had no intention of allowing that to happen.

"I told you to do something, Bollard." Mackey raised the Winchester and placed the butt of the rifle on his right hip, careful not to aim it at him. "I won't tell you again."

"And I ain't heeled like you," Bollard yelled. "Toss yer guns and we'll talk."

"That's not going to happen." Mackey switched the Winchester to his left hand, once more keeping it aimed down at the mud. But his hand was on his buckle, near the Peacemaker holstered at his belly. "Now we're even. Drop the knife like I told you."

But Bollard refused. "Not good enough. I seen what you can do with a pistol and that cross-belly draw you got. You and that Negro ya brung with ya."

Emboldened by a cheer from the crowd, Bollard said, "Both of you toss all yer guns and we can parlay." He grabbed a handful of the dying man's hair and yanked up his head to the delight of the crowd. "Or, so help me, I take me the scalp I intend on gettin'."

Doc Ridley jostled to keep his place in the bustling crowd. "Aaron, there's no time for this!"

Mackey agreed.

In one fluid motion, he drew his Peacemaker and fired. The shot slammed into the center of Bollard's chest and sent the big man tumbling backward into his makeshift tent, snapping the post as he fell. He was quickly buried by the scraps of tarp and rags and animal hides he had used to make his home.

Mackey aimed the pistol at the crowd of men barring Doc Ridley's way. Every one of them froze. "Step aside and let him through."

The crowd reluctantly separated enough to let the doctor stumble into the street with his black medical bag at his side. The smallish man forgot about his own dignity as he ran as quickly as he could manage through the dense mud of Second Street to tend to the victim.

No one stepped forward to help him, including Mackey

or Billy. The two lawmen eyed the crowd steadily. The Tent City residents were an unfamiliar bunch and in a damned restless mood. Mackey knew they were unhappy that the sheriff had disrupted their show. And given how badly Mackey and Billy were outnumbered, the best they could do was watch the doctor's back while he tried to save the shotgun victim's life.

Mackey kept an eye on the crowd as Ridley ducked under the collapsed tent and knelt beside his patient. He and the town doctor had never gotten along until recently. Ridley was a pious, religious man who had helped settle Dover Station after the War Between the States. Ridley often objected to Mackey's strict enforcement of the law, claiming his methods were against God's law. Doc Ridley had often told him, "Just because it's legal doesn't mean it's right."

But after Darabont's siege of the town, the two men had attained an unspoken respect for each other. He was the town's acting mayor until a new one could be elected the following month. But Ridley had never been a politician. He was a believer in humanity and in his own skill at easing the suffering of his patients. That was what he was trying to do now as he knelt in the mud, struggling to save the life of a stranger.

Mackey could see by the way the proud doctor's shoulders sagged that the struggle had ended.

Ridley slowly stood, looked over at Mackey and shook his head. "He's gone. The blast took out half of his throat. I'm surprised he managed to hold on for as long as he did. He must have been a very strong man. Young, too."

He glared at the people looking at him from their tents and their spots along the boardwalk. "Like most of you. Young and in a bad way, fighting against the world. It isn't bad enough that you have to live like this, do you have to kill each other, too?" His voice rose to a shrill. "I hope you bastards are happy. You certainly got your show, didn't you?"

Mackey called out to the crowd. "Anybody know the stranger's name?"

A man in the crowd said. "I see three dead men, Sheriff." The man was tall and skinny with a misshapen hat, a scraggily gray beard, and clothes that were little more than rags. "Three hardworking men ground to dust in the machinery of this place. The gears of greed have been oiled today by the blood of the workers."

A murmur went through the crowd, and the man continued. "We must make sure their deaths were not in vain."

Another murmur went through the crowd. It was clear they knew him, but Mackey had never seen him before. "Step forward. I want to talk to you."

But the gaunt man did not step forward. "And what if I don't, Sheriff? Will you shoot me, too? I think you've done enough of the Dover Station Company's bidding for one day, don't you?"

The man stepped back, and the crowd shifted to block Mackey's view of him. The sheriff decided not to push the matter.

The quicker they got out of there, the better. He gestured toward six young men standing near Doc Ridley. "Go fetch a flatbed, load up the bodies, and take them over to Cy Wallach's place for preparation for burial. And make sure you bring the wagon back where it belongs after you're done."

The six men looked at each other and laughed, embarrassed by the sudden attention and unsure of what to do.

But Mackey didn't laugh. He hadn't holstered his Peacemaker yet, either. "You boys just saw what happens when people defy me."

The six men bolted like scared horses. Mackey tucked the pistol back into his holster and shifted the Winchester to his right hand. "Go with them, doc. Make sure they don't forget what they're supposed to be doing."

Ridley looked down at the dead young man, whose worn shoes were sticking out from beneath the ruined tent. "What are any of us supposed to be doing, Aaron?" He looked at the half-built buildings and the tents and shacks of Second Street. "This used to be a fine place to live. Now look at it. Being torn down and rebuilt, only to be made worse than it was before. People living like pigs in the mud and squalor? Workers dropping from exhaustion? Is this what progress is supposed to look like?"

First, a bunch of nonsense from a mouthy stranger, now poor Doc Ridley was getting in on the act. Mackey had no intention of discussing weighty subjects in the middle of Tent City. The longer they stood among the mob, the more likely they were to become targets.

"There'll be plenty of time for questions later, doc. Right now, we have to clear these bodies off the street, and I'd appreciate your help doing it."

As Doc Ridley reluctantly followed the six men, Mackey turned his attention to the Bollard twin he had hit.

Billy had managed to roll the big man onto his back, despite the thickness of the mud. There was a large gash at the man's belly.

"Looks like I was right," Billy said. "Bollard, too. His brother wasn't staggering because he was drunk. He caught a bad one in the belly before he blasted that man."

"Didn't give him the right to scalp anyone," Mackey said, "but at least we know why it happened."

Mackey felt all the eyes of Tent City on him and decided this was no time to leave. It was dangerous to turn away from a mob, especially when it was watching your every move. He had to say something.

"I know none of you wants to be living like this, but it's the best any of us can do until more houses get built. A lot of people want me to break up this place and send you up to the old mining camps and logging camps Darabont burned out when he attacked the town. Since the company hasn't rebuilt them yet, I don't want to do that."

He made a point of looking as many of them in the eye as he could. "But I won't have a choice if things around here get out of hand. You've all got a hard time of it here. I know that. But don't make it worse by stealing and killing each other. Don't make me come back." He looked at the collapsed tent that partially hid the two corpses. He pointed at the dead man in the mud at his feet. "You won't like it if I do."

Mackey stood alone as he watched the grumbling crowd slowly ebb away, ducking back into their tents or shacks or moving elsewhere. He made a point of stepping up onto the boardwalk and walking back toward the jailhouse. When the crowd had thinned out enough, he looked down at the dead man at his feet.

"Big son of a bitch, wasn't he?" Billy observed.

Talking about it would not make him any smaller. "You grab one arm, and I'll grab the other. Drag him over to the others. Might as well let Doc Ridley and his new friends make one trip of it."

With their rifles in one hand and one of Bollard's arms in the other, the men grunted under the weight of the corpse.

Billy said, "Can't believe we lost both Bollard boys in a single morning. The world may never recover."

Mackey struggled to keep hold of his rifle as they dragged Bollard's deadweight through the mud. "I'm sure they've got brothers. Bastards usually do."

When they had finally dropped the corpse next to his brother, Mackey noticed ten or so stragglers scattered around the boardwalks and the alleys along Second Street. He recognized the look in their eyes. They might not have been sporting feathers, but they were vultures just the same.

Billy had noticed them, too. "How long after we leave before they strip these bodies? Tent, too?"

"Fifteen seconds after we turn our backs," Mackey said. "At most."

Mackey and Billy raised their rifles as a group of men came barreling toward him. Mackey thought an angry mob from Tent City had come to avenge the death of the Bollard brothers. The riot was finally starting.

But they quickly lowered their weapons when they recognized the men as some of the ironworkers who were building the Municipal Building.

Mackey called out to them. "What's going on?"

Another man said, "You'd better come quick, Sheriff. Jed Eddows is fixing to hang Foreman Ross right now before God and everyone!"

Billy trailed behind Mackey as they ran. "So much for a quiet morning in Dover Station."

CHAPTER 2

A stiff wind blew up Front Street as Sheriff Mackey gauged the situation.

It was not good.

Three stories above, framed against the gray sky of a coming storm, Mackey saw the wiry Jed Eddows had not only bound and gagged the portly foreman Jay Ross. He was also holding him at the edge of the scaffold by the back of the foreman's pants.

Eddows had cinched a noose around Ross's neck, and the sheriff had no doubt the other end had been secured to one of the many iron beams of the building. Mackey hoped Eddows was stronger than he looked, or Ross would be dead before they had a chance to talk.

The wind took most of what Eddows shouted down at him, but Mackey caught the gist of it. "You stay right where you are, Sheriff. And that buck you have for a deputy best stay on the porch where he belongs. Either of you take one step toward this building, and I swear to God my oppressor will hang!"

Mackey squinted to make sure this was really Jed Eddows talking. He had always considered Eddows to be a quiet, forgettable man who came and went from his job at the Municipal Building construction site without incident or notice. He had never spent time in jail for being drunk or disorderly. In fact, Mackey only knew his name from hearing it called out so often during the summer while Mackey and Billy sat on the jailhouse porch, watching the future of the town rise across the street.

But judging from the amount of blood he could see on the foreman's shirt and the swelling about his head and face, Mackey now knew that a quiet fury had been building inside Eddows for some time. He had given his foreman one hell of a beating before trussing him up and bringing him outside to hang.

There would be plenty of time to find out why this had happened. Right now, he had to find a way to keep a skinny man from allowing a fat man to hang from the biggest construction site in the territory.

From behind him, Mackey heard Billy call out, "I'm not going near you, Eddows. I'm just going to speak to the sheriff about how to keep anyone from getting too close to you. I won't go an inch past him, I promise."

Eddows stammered before saying, "You try anything, black boy, and Ross hangs. Understand?"

Billy stopped a few paces behind the sheriff. "Let me shoot this son of a bitch, Aaron. I can take his head off with the Sharps, even in this wind."

Mackey had to hold on to his hat by the brim to keep it on his head. He had no doubt Billy could hit him, especially with that buffalo gun he carried. Billy Sunday had been the best shot in the outfit when they had served together in the cavalry, and his skills had only improved in the years since.

But there was a time for gunplay and a time for other

things. "Can't shoot him. Look at the way he set it up. If we shoot Eddows, he lets go of the foreman's belt and Ross hangs. He's also got Ross too far out over the edge so we can't try to wing him and knock him back inside."

Mackey looked over the setup again in the hopes that he had missed something, but he had not. "Looks like Eddows is a more complicated man than we thought."

"Then what are we going to do?" Billy asked. "We can't just stand here and watch like everyone else."

Mackey looked out at the crowds beginning to gather on the boardwalks. Whether it was Tent City squatters over on Second Street or old-line Dover Station townsfolk on Front Street, everyone enjoyed a spectacle.

"I think we can talk him down," Mackey said. "If Eddows wanted to kill Ross, he could've shot him or just thrown him off the building. He didn't. He's doing this because he wants an audience. He has something to say. Let's give him the chance. Maybe the more he talks, the longer Ross lives." He grabbed his hat again before it blew off his head. "Besides, there isn't much we can do about it anyway."

Billy held on to his hat, too. "Might not be able to stop him anyway if the wind stays like this. And when Grant finds out what's going on down here, he's liable to turn this into a goddamned circus."

Mackey knew the general manager of the Dover Station Company was not one to shy away from public events. He knew Grant would be here the moment he heard of it. If Eddows hated his foreman, it stood to reason he probably hated Grant even more.

Mackey did not want that to happen. Three men had just died less than a block away. But, then again, Mackey knew he rarely got what he wanted, especially when it came to James Grant.

To Billy, he said, "Hang back by the jailhouse with the Sharps. If we have to, you hit Eddows, and I'll take Ross. In the meantime, watch the crowd, and steer Grant clear of this place until we know what Eddows wants."

Billy slowly took a few steps back toward the porch. "I will. I'm right here if you need me."

The number of spectators cramming the boardwalks around the site had nearly doubled in the short amount of time Mackey had been speaking with Billy. The horror of the townspeople was only rivaled by their curiosity about what would happen next.

The cluster of workers at the base of the building had begun jockeying for position for the best view.

With the storm kicking up and Grant on his way, Mackey decided it was time to get Eddows talking. "All right, Jed. You've got your audience, and you've got my attention. No one's coming near you, and Billy and me are in plain sight. How about you pull Mr. Ross back from the ledge and tell us what's on your mind?"

"No way," Eddows shouted back. "I know what that black bastard of yours can do with that Sharps of his. I swear to God, I see him so much as look in my direction, Ross swings, understand?"

"No one's aiming anything at you and no one's going to, either, as long as you don't do anything stupid. You've obviously got something on your mind, so might as well say it." He motioned to the crowd that now jammed every available space on the boardwalk. "You've got plenty of people here willing to listen."

Eddows looked away. He still held on to the foreman's belt but clearly hadn't expected the chance to say anything.

One of the workers clustered at the base of the building

yelled to Mackey, "Just shoot the son of a bitch and get it over with."

"Yeah," another called out. "Blow his damned head off and let us get back to work. This nonsense is costing us money.

Still another yelled, "There's ten men in Tent City who'd take Jed's place, and the company's got other foremen they can send to run the job."

Mackey ignored them. He didn't think Eddows had heard them because of the wind, but the man had been quiet too long to suit him. "Come on, Jed. Speak up and let's talk this through."

Eddows looked confused, as if he had only just realized what he had done. But his grip on Ross's belt never faltered, and the foreman was still pitched dangerously at the edge of the scaffold.

"It wasn't any one thing that done it, I guess," Eddows yelled. "It was a whole bunch of things balled up into a knot. Him yelling at me, screaming all the time. Threatening to fire me or throw me off the goddamned building because I wasn't working fast enough or because I'd made a mistake. You know how long I've been working here?"

"Not exactly, but it's about four months near as I can figure." He decided it would be a good idea to add, "Billy and I remember sitting in front of the jailhouse seeing you go to work. Saw you here every single day, rain or shine. Heard good things about you."

"That's a lie!" Eddows screamed. "The only time you heard my name was when this cruel son of a bitch screamed at me over something I'd done or hadn't done yet. Nothing I do is ever good enough for him. He's an oppressor. He feeds off my labor and does none of his own. He needs to be stopped."

He pushed Ross closer to the edge of the scaffold. The foreman screamed and so did many of the spectators, as much out of excitement as fear.

Mackey kept his rifle aimed at the ground. The wind was still too strong.

Eddows laughed as he eased Ross back a bit from the edge. "This is the quietest I've heard him since I started working for him. For once, he ain't yelling at me about staying on his goddamned schedule so he can make his goddamned bonus. None of us get any bonuses, Sheriff. Only him. That sound fair to you?"

"No, it doesn't. I didn't know about that. I can talk to Jim Grant about that if you want."

But Eddows had not heard him. "You know how many houses I framed for him? Ten in three weeks. Ten! A lot of us did. He worked us like dogs and whipped us worse, but we got it done, didn't we, boys?"

Some of the workers cheered up to him. Most hurled curses at him.

Eddows went on. "And now he's working us even harder to get this damned building open in a month. This place look like it'll be done in a month to you, Sheriff?"

One of the ironworkers called out, "It would be if you weren't pulling this shit now, you crazy bastard."

Mackey had to yell over the ensuing argument to get Eddows's attention. "I know you're tired, son. A lot of people have been working real hard to change this town, and we appreciate it, even if Ross doesn't. You remember seeing me and Billy on the porch all those mornings, don't you? So you know I'm not just saying that."

The sheriff couldn't be sure, but he thought Eddows pulled Ross a little farther away from the ledge.

Mercifully, the wind had died down, so Mackey didn't

have to yell as loud when he said, "I know you've had a bad time of it. A lot of people have, so how about I make a deal with you? Take that noose off Ross's head and pull him back inside, and I promise I'll talk to Jim Grant about easing up their schedule some. I know my head could stand a little less banging and I'm sure yours could, too. A bump in wages and a slower pace. Sound fair?"

"Sounds like a bunch of bullshit, if you ask me," Eddows yelled. "I know all about you, Mackey. You're just as bad as the cruel bastard I've got strung up right here. I saw you riding around with Mr. Rice after Darabont hit us. His company owns you like it owns everything else in this damned town. There ain't no way I live after what I've done. Hell, even I know that, and I'm an idiot." He pushed Ross to the edge and the foreman screamed again. "Ain't that right, Mr. Ross? Ain't that one of them pet names you've got for me?"

Mackey gripped the Winchester at his side a little tighter. If he let Ross fall, Mackey would have no choice but to shoot Eddows. And he'd have to do it fast before the wind picked up again.

He had to give it one last try. "I don't think you're stupid, Jeb. I just think you're tired and scared and need some rest. And there's no reason to kill you over what you've done so far. Who cares if you hurt Mr. Ross? Hell, I can't think of a soldier or a workingman who hasn't dreamed of hurting his boss at one time or another. I know I have."

Eddows's face grew scarlet as he yelled, "I want him dead! I want my oppressor dead! I want fair pay for fair work and I want to be treated like a human being!"

Despite his rage, Mackey could see Eddows changing

somehow. He could not tell if that was good or bad, but he knew he had been given the chance to end this.

"But you're not a killer," the sheriff continued. "If you were, you would've done it by now. You're doing this because you want to be heard and you want help. I'm offering all of that to you right now. All you've got to do is pull him back inside and end this peacefully."

Eddows surprised him by stepping back and pulling Ross with him. The foreman was now practically standing on the scaffold, though the tips of his feet were still over the side. Ross would still hang if Eddows let go.

But he was safer than he had been since the entire mess began, so Mackey kept pushing. "That's a good start, Jeb."

"It's not going to end too well for me if I end up in jail," Eddows yelled back.

"I'm sure he won't press charges against you," Mackey lied. He didn't know Ross at all, except that he worked on the Municipal Building. But there was a time for the truth and a time to lie, and this was no time for the truth. "You've got everything you want, Eddows. You'll have accomplished something for you and your friends. All you've got to do is pull him back inside and take that noose off his neck."

"That true?" Eddows nudged Ross closer to the edge again. "That true about what he said about you not pressing charges? I want to hear you say it."

"Of course!" Ross screamed. "I-I was wrong to say those horrible things to you, Jeb, and I'm sorry. Things will get better, I promise. Just don't let me hang. Please. I've got a family to feed. Please."

"Family?" Eddows's rage seemed to spill over as he yanked his boss all the way in from the ledge so that they were practically standing next to each other. "You don't think I have a family? What about my wife and my kids? You think I take the strap from you all day every day because I like it? You think I let you treat me like a dog just because I think that's all I am? You talk about *your* family, you miserable . . ."

Mackey saw Eddows shift his weight.

His anger had finally won the battle.

He was going to throw Ross off the scaffold.

Billy had seen it, too, because both lawmen raised their rifles and fired at their chosen targets at exactly the same time.

The impact of the fifty-caliber slug from Billy's Sharps threw young Eddows back into the building.

Mackey's shot struck Ross high in the right shoulder and sent the bound man spinning before he fell back and out of view. The amount of slack on the rope still hanging over the edge of the scaffold told him that the foreman had not been hanged.

Mackey joined the flow of ironworkers and townspeople running into the building. He yelled back to Billy, "You stay here and try to keep everyone back. I'll go check on Ross."

Mackey raced into the building, but found the way clogged with carpenters and ironworkers scrambling to get back into the building. He yelled for them to clear the way, but it was no use.

By the time the sheriff forced his way through the crowd and up to the third floor, he saw the workers cheer as they cut loose the last of the foreman's bindings.

A small group had gathered around the spot where Eddows's body had landed. Billy's fifty-caliber round had made a massive hole in the left side of his chest, probably killing him on impact. They might not have seen what a gun designed to kill buffalo could do to a human body before, but Mackey had. It was never pretty.

Mackey quickly made his way over to Ross and found one of the workers had already rigged a tourniquet for the foreman's right arm from some of the rope that had previously bound him.

The wounded man smiled up at Mackey. His nose had been broken, and a couple of teeth had been chipped, but he looked happy. "That was some damned fine shooting, Sheriff. I owe you and your deputy my life. Which one got me?"

"That was me," Mackey admitted. "I tried to wing you, but . . ."

"No need to apologize. I thought that crazy son of a bitch was going to kill me for sure."

"Just be grateful you're still alive." To the worker who had tied the tourniquet, he asked, "How bad is it?"

"You hit him through and through," the man told him. "Nicked the bone some, but I saw worse on the trail out here. Me and the boys will get him to Doc Ridley right quick, don't you worry."

Mackey stepped aside as six men scrambled forward with a wooden plank to carry Ross down to the street. Eddows had screamed that he hated Ross, but enough of the other workers seemed fond enough of the man to make sure he got medical attention.

That told Mackey something about Ross. But it didn't say much about the man who had threatened to hang him. What had driven Eddows to the edge of murder? And to do it so publicly? And what of his talk about oppressors and fair wages? Eddows had sounded like the mysterious stranger at the shooting at Tent City. Mackey knew there were malcontents in any outfit who enjoyed complaining, but to try to kill a leader was something else.

As he stood aside, waiting for the men carrying Ross to pass, he realized he had never seen Dover Station from such a height, at least, not this close.

From up there, all of the other original buildings looked smaller than he had expected. Even the jailhouse looked tiny by comparison.

It was one of the few stone structures in town, built by a former sheriff who had been a mason. He wanted a building that would stand up well enough to fire, should one start in a town where most of the other buildings were wooden. The walls were over a foot thick, and the heavy ironwood door facing Front Street was the only way inside. There were no windows in the cells, only the barred window from where Mackey and Billy could look out on Front Street.

The jailhouse had long been seen as the only permanent building in town until the Dover Station Company began to build the iron and brick monstrosity where Mackey currently stood across the thoroughfare.

From where he stood, Aaron Mackey could see what Dover Station had been. The town he had known as a boy and as a captain returned from the army. He saw the streets and avenues Billy and he had patrolled and the stores whose locks he checked each night. They were the old Dover Station. They were the past.

The Municipal Building and all of the other new construction symbolized what the town was to become. A town he no longer recognized. A town filled with strangers who didn't know him, only of him. He was Sheriff Aaron Mackey, formerly Captain Mackey, the Hero of Adobe Flats. Lately, and over Mackey's objection, James Grant had taken to calling him the Savior of Dover Station. The

general manager of the Dover Station Company saw it as
some kind of attraction to draw people to town and make
them feel safe, as if news of Frazer Rice's interest in town
was not enough of a draw.

From the third floor of the iron building, Mackey wondered if this new town held any attraction for him. He
wondered if there would be any place for him in this building
after it was finished. He wondered if he even wanted one.

When he heard another commotion down on the street,
he rushed to the edge of the scaffold. "Christ," he muttered
to himself. "What now?"

He was not surprised to see James Grant on the boardwalk in front of the jailhouse, waving at the cheering
crowd. He had Walter Underhill and two other men with
rifles standing by him. Brandishing firearms was illegal in
town, even for employees of James Grant. Underhill, a
former United States Marshal from Texas, had helped repel
Darabont's raid of the town six months before, so Mackey
often let his indiscretions slide.

None of the townspeople seemed to notice this violation
of town law. Everyone cheered Grant like a conquering
hero. Given that he represented the company that had
made many of them wealthy, Mackey could understand the
adulation.

But understanding James Grant proved a much harder
task for the sheriff. Grant was older than Mackey by more
than a few years, which put him in his mid-forties. His
sandy blond hair and full beard had begun to gray in all
the right places, making him look more distinguished than
old. What he lacked in height, he made up for in powerful
build; he was broad shouldered and thick around the chest.
He looked more like a laborer than a man who worked in
an office all day. Mackey imagined this was part of his

appeal for the public. For, Mackey knew, James Grant had not always worked in an office.

He had been a rancher in a neighboring town, and before that had owned a stagecoach station after he had run a telegraph office. Rumors abounded that he had once served as a lawman in some capacity in Nebraska, though the town and the time of his service was a matter of some debate.

But there was no debate that Grant had managed to amass a lot of influence since Mr. Rice's partner, Silas Van Dorn, hired him to manage the operations of the Dover Station Company. The reasons for Grant's hiring were as obscure as his past, and Mackey did not care how he got the job, only that he had it now. Grant had quickly established a reputation for not only setting aggressive construction deadlines, but beating them.

As he watched the ironworkers gently carry Ross down to the street, Mackey began to wonder if Grant's ambition had caused Eddows to snap. He wondered how many other men like Eddows were ready to fall.

In Mackey's experience, ambitious men needed to be watched.

Grant held his hat aloft as he bellowed from the jailhouse boardwalk. "Ladies and gentlemen, I have just learned that Jay Ross is alive and expected to make a full recovery. Let us have three cheers for Jay Ross. Hip-hip. Hooray!"

Underhill and the two riflemen had formed an arc in front of Grant to keep the crowd back as they cheered.

When the echo of the last hurrah died away, Grant pointed up at Mackey on the scaffold. "And three cheers for the brave man who saved that good man's life. The Hero of Adobe Flats! The Savior of Dover Station! Sheriff Aaron Mackey! Hip-hip."

The crowd chanted "hooray" without any prompting from Grant.

Mackey saw Billy taking in the whole scene from the doorway of the jailhouse. The black man smiled up at Mackey, touched the brim of his hat, and went inside to make a fresh pot of coffee.

Grant waited for the crowd to quiet before continuing his speech. "Now, I'm well aware that you good people have been tolerant of all the changes the Dover Station Company has been making here in town. But change isn't easy. It never is. But we're more than halfway through our initial phase of work and that much closer to undoing all of the damage Darabont left in his wake when he attacked this fair town. This morning I received a telegram from Mr. Rice in New York City, wherein he gave me permission to inform you of some wonderful news. Later this week, the Dover Station Mining Company will be reopening the living quarters at the mines, the Dover Station Lumber Company will reopen their living quarters, and the Dover Station Cattle and Land Company will be hiring fifty more cowboys, farmers, and more."

Hats were thrown in the air, and the people clapped and cheered.

Grant spoke over them again, struggling to make his voice heard over the euphoria. "My friends, our work has not finished. Indeed, it is only beginning. But men of vision and generosity like Mr. Rice and his partner, our neighbor Mr. Silas Van Dorn, cannot be relied upon to do everything. We have an election for mayor coming up in a month, and we are distressed over the lack of interest among all of you to run for office. We thank Doctor Ridley for filling in as mayor after Brian Mason resigned the office to join the company, but we need the good people of Dover Station to elect a good, strong leader, lest all of our hard work goes for nothing. Look to yourselves, and I implore you to consider running for this noble office."

Mackey looked over the crowd as one man yelled out, "Grant for Mayor!" A few more people took up the chant and, within seconds, it echoed as if one voice through the narrow streets of town.

Mackey saw a few familiar faces in the sea of people, but most were total strangers. The rapid growth of the town over these past six months had served to change it so much that he hardly recognized it anymore.

Four men had just been killed a block away from each other within twenty or so minutes. But no one he saw seemed to care about that. They were cheering for a man they hardly knew to run for an office no one wanted. Grant waved it off, of course, but he accepted it all the same.

No, Mackey decided, he did not know these people anymore. People he considered outsiders, even though the town did not belong to him.

Mackey ducked back inside and began heading downstairs.

He needed a mug of Billy's coffee more than he needed the adulation of strangers.